Carl Patrick was born in Oxford. He has been writing fiction
since ' ʳas at school and wrote his first novel at the age of
1   ıe rape of a fellow pupil. Whilst at University, he
            write a Science Fiction trilogy, which is yet to be
      ·d. He then moved to London and trained as a
   ·ar·ered Accountant. He continued writing and has written
   ... ıber of erotic short stories with Netherhall Gardens
      his first contemporary gay novel.

      ɔw lives with his partner of 14 years near Brighton.
      ɔth enjoy wild sex, cooking and entertaining friends.
      .its however that, apart from sex, the best fun he has is
      which he is forced to do in his spare time after
      his own small business, going to the gym, reading,
      ; to music and travelling to his favourite destinations
      uch as San Francisco, Provincetown, Amsterdam and
      ·e in Spain.

CARL PATRICK

NETHERHALL GARDENS

Matador
9 De Montfort Mews
Leicester LE1 7FW, UK
Tel: (+44) 116 255 9311 / 9312
Email: books@troubador.co.uk
Web: www.troubador.co.uk/matador

All characterisation   or dead is purely

ISBN 978 1906510 633

A Cataloguing-in-Publication (CIP) catalogue record for this book
is available from the British Library.

Mixed Sources
Product group from well-managed
forests and other controlled sources
www.fsc.org Cert no. TT-COC-2082
© 1996 Forest Stewardship Council
FSC

Typeset in 11pt Stempel Garamond by Troubador Publishing Ltd, Leicester, UK
Printed in the UK by The Cromwell Press Ltd, Trowbridge, Wilts, UK

Matador is an imprint of Troubador Publishing Ltd

ACKNOWLEDGEMENTS

Thank you to the following:

Graham; Sharon and Maggs; Mum, Dad and the family; Guy, Chris and Bo; Sandra, Pip and Willow; Alan and Marlena; Denise; Terry and Mark; Hans and Paul; Aziz and Steve; Don Pluckthun; the Kings; the Johnstons; Michael and Marbellys; Heather McCall; Keith and Andre; Roberta and Irene; Julia and Peter; Lucy and Duncan; Penny Powell; Glenda and the boys; Keith Laker; Andy and Linus; Ron van Hout; Leyton; Jerome and Sheila (ILM) and Fiona; Sheena Mitchell; Lyn McLarin; Helen and Dave; Richard and Leigh; Tony Sinclair; Mike and Brian; David Berry; John Applequist; Geoff Kinch; Derek Reece; Alex Cameron; Les and Jerry; Village Drinks South (formerly the Sussex Gay Professionals) and Mark Rose for his Fanny.

With special thanks to:

Sara Hibbard for her valuable insight and editing skills.
Jeremy Thompson, Terry Compton and Julia Fuller at Troubador Publishing Ltd for their patience.

Appearances by:

Marlena Spieler, Dusty Springfield, Tina Arena, Erasure, Moodswings, Napoleon XIV, Madonna, St.Etienne, Frazier, Stephen Baxter, Jerry Springer, Expectations and Scooby Doo.
Cameo by Matron Jane

Chapter One

IT WAS A PLEASANTLY warm Friday evening in early May as Mark slammed the door to his Bayswater bed-sit, ran down the stairs, flew through the large outer door to his building and hurried off towards the nearest tube station. He was going to dinner with his dearest friend Stella at her comfy flat in Netherhall Gardens, Hampstead, and he was both hungry and impatient to see her again.

As he descended to platform level, his mobile phone lost its signal just moments before a text arrived that would've completely changed his plans that evening, had he received it in time. As a result, his rather staid and predictable life was about to be transformed.

Despite the burgeoning crowds at Baker Street, he crossed quickly from the Circle line to the Jubilee line and jumped smartly onto a train just as the doors were closing. He checked the time and was smiling at his good fortune when the train came to a grinding halt. A jaded monotone voice in the carriage ceiling blamed the delay on signalling problems in the Wembley area. They heard nothing more for nearly an hour.

He was eventually dropped off, flustered and bothered in the rumbling depths of Finchley Road tube station, unbearably late. As he ran up the moving staircase, his mobile picked up a signal and then bleeped to let him know a text had arrived. He clicked appropriately, noting the time it had been sent, and read the following: *sorry sweetheart, hughs got BIG problems. must go to him. c u another night. call me. love stella xx.*

'Shit,' he muttered.

He punched Call Sender. The phone rang several times before a flustered female Scottish accent said, 'Halloo?'

'Hi Stella, it's me.'

'Mark!' she cried. 'Sorry about tonight. You got my message?'

1

'Yes, just now. I've been stuck in a tunnel for ages with no signal and I've just arrived at Finchley Road tube station...'

'Oh, no... I'm so sorry. Wait there, I'll come down... We can go to the Crown & Thistle for a quick drink.'

Mark looked across the road at the Crown & Thistle. It was a pokey, smoke-filled bar with little to interest him.

'But, I've brought a really nice bottle of wine,' he said temptingly. *And an empty stomach*, he thought. 'And I've got some really wicked stuff with me.'

'Oh, Mark. I have to go to Islington tonight,' she said. 'I'm sorry, but Hugh's had some really bad news.'

That bloody Hugh.

There was a moment's pause, then her voice chirruped, 'Oh, come on up then.'

Mark cut the connection, pocketed his mobile and turned left out of the station. As he searched for a safe place to cross the busy Finchley Road, the excitement that had been mounting all day rapidly cooled. Stella was blowing him out for Hugh, her erstwhile boyfriend.

Although Mark had never met him, he understood from Stella that Hugh was a handsome devil, estranged from his wife and daughter, and that she loved him - at least most of the time. It was a rocky ride though that pitched and yawed like a playground seesaw - one moment they were passionate lovers, the next they were hurling abuse at each other and the next it was all over, as it had been this past week. Then another crisis would unite them - like the one this evening it seemed.

So, no dinner either. His stomach rudely gurgled in protest.

Following a steep climb up from the Finchley Road, he reached the vast flaking dark green door to Stella's home at last – the once magnificent Netherhall itself. Netherhall was originally a Manor house and had survived intact up until the early sixties when it had been recklessly converted into thirteen bed-sits and flats. Stella was fortunate in renting a cosy one-bedroomed self-contained flat on the second floor with the added luxury of its own intercom system, quite separate from the main doorbell servicing the rest of the house. He pressed the necessary buzzer and heard, 'Da da dada da,' as the intercom crackled and hummed, like something Alexander Graham Bell had cobbled together in a moment of madness. Then Stella's metallic-tinted voice boomed, 'Halloo?'

'Big Dick Escorts!' Mark shouted back. There was a loud clunk, then silence and a few moments later Stella appeared as the door flew open and a petite blonde human dynamo slammed into him. Mark hugged her. They smacked lips, noisily.

'I'm sorry… Really sorry,' she whispered into his chest, 'but Hugh's having problems at the moment.'

Mark nodded. Stella led him inside the grand hallway, up the echoing wooden staircase to the second landing and then through a dark recess and finally into her small flat. A Monstera cheese plant, the height and breadth of the living room, was crouched in front of the large open window. It was so enormous that it looked ready to step out of its pot and re-house itself. There were a few books, a couple of magazines, bits of computer and pieces of ancient furniture scattered just about everywhere the eye cared to roam. Mark's eyes finally settled on the few dirty pots and pans in the kitchen sink, just off from the lounge. He gazed hungrily at them for a moment too long.

'Sorry,' she apologised. 'Are you hungry?'

'No,' he lied. 'I had a late lunch.' He smiled and hugged her again. 'It's so good to see you. Come on, let's open this bottle - it's still quite cold.'

They sat together on the sofa overhung by the Triffid (as the plant was affectionately known), feet up and facing each other, wine glasses cupped to bosoms.

'Tell me about Hugh,' Mark suggested. 'What's he been up to now?'

'No, no. It's too horrible.' Stella's face pinched up tightly for a second as if she were sucking a lemon. She took another sip of white wine.

Mark placed his glass onto the nearest flat surface, reached into his shirt pocket and retrieved a Café Crème tin. He opened it and withdrew a pre-rolled joint. 'Perhaps this'll loosen your tongue,' he said and lit up.

Stella rose and found an ashtray beneath an old copy of Vogue.

She snuggled back onto the sofa. 'So, how's *your* love life?' she demanded.

Mark smiled at her through the haze, held a breath and then let out a stream of thick blue-grey smoke. 'I tell you everything I do,' he replied, offering her the joint.

Stella accepted the joint and snuggled further into the cushions, making herself comfortable, before taking a dainty little puff. Then a thought struck her and she struggled to sit up. 'Hey, have you been following the news about this gay serial killer…?'

'He's not a gay serial killer, Stella, he's a killer who happens to like men,' Mark corrected her, sipping his wine.

'There's a difference?' asked Stella, passing the joint and snuggling back down.

Mark took a drag, held it and then spoke through the smoke. 'Of course! He's not someone who hates gay men and wants to kill them. He likes gay men, all men I guess, but he gets his kicks by killing them in an unspeakable manner.'

'Ooh, how horrible!' said Stella. 'So, is he a serial gay killer or a gay serial killer or a serial killer of gays?'

Mark peered at her thoughtfully, though his thoughts were far from clear by now.

'I… Er…'

Stella giggled, then said, 'Well, whatever - just you be careful out there, ok?' There was genuine concern in her voice.

Mark took the offered joint and finished it. As he was stubbing it out, he said, 'I'm not really gay anyway. I haven't even had sex with a man yet. Not properly.'

Stella took a long sceptical look at him. 'Yeah, right!'

'No, I mean it, Stella. Listen, ok, so I've played about a bit with a few guys, but I've never done you know… that! Besides, it's who you love that matters, isn't it?' He peered at her earnestly. 'Isn't it about who you most want to be with? Getting your rocks off is just part of it - a great part admittedly - but I can do that with men or women. And as you know… it's you that I love.'

Stella's eyes softened further then hardened an instant later. 'But, you know I love Hugh,' she said. 'I love you too, of course, but…'

Mark nodded gently. 'I know, I know - it's different!' But he looked hurt all the same. After a while, he said, 'Why don't you tell me about Hugh? What's the problem now?'

Stella looked away, then slowly back at him. 'His daughter gave birth to a dead baby today.'

'Oh, Jesus...'

'By his first wife,' Stella added.

'Eh?'

Stella pushed herself into a more upright position, but still virtually horizontal.

'His daughter - by his first wife.'

'Oh,' said Mark solemnly.

'It was perfectly formed,' continued Stella. 'About 28 weeks or so, I think.'

They were silent for a long time.

Eventually Stella said, 'Hey, got another joint?'

Mark removed one from the Café Crème tin. 'Be very careful,' he warned, brandishing the nicely rolled joint, 'this is extremely good stuff.' He inserted it into the corner of his mouth and torched the end with his Zippo, took a drag and passed the joint to Stella. Back and forth it passed between them and like an ice-cube between mouths of hot lovers the joint seemed to melt. Eventually, it was gone.

'It's gone, Stella,' said Mark, crushing out the remains in the ashtray and finishing his glass of wine.

'So am I,' Stella replied dreamily.

Silence.

Mark closed his eyes and small fireflies danced on a rich black backdrop. Minutes later, he felt Stella rise off the sofa.

'Glass of water, please,' he murmured.

After a while his aching thirst roused him. He opened his eyes and blinked to clear his vision. He peered around him with wide eyes. The door to Stella's flat was wide open. Maybe she was putting the empties in the re-cycling bins.

What empties? They hadn't even finished off one bottle yet!

'Stella?'

Nothing.

'Hello? Stella?'

Still nothing.

He lay on the sofa a few minutes more, keeping a wary eye on the doorway. She must be putting the rubbish out.

Still nothing.

Managing to haul himself into a sitting position and then unsteadily onto his feet, he slowly edged towards the open door and cautiously shuffled into the dark recess, finally peering out into the vacant hallway. There were two more doors on this landing, but they were both closed. The hallway itself was large with functional black and white linoleum laid over wooden floorboards, and totally deserted. The sudden, muffled sound of a door banging downstairs made him jump.

He waited in the open recess for a few moments until he felt too uncomfortable, then he retreated. Closing the front door, but leaving it slightly ajar, he entered Stella's tiny bathroom and swished his mouth out with deliciously cold tap water. He felt almost human again and moved back into the lounge where he crossed over to the sofa and sat down once more beneath the monstrous Triffid.

It was then that he noticed the two roaches in the ashtray and was instantly consumed with paranoia. What if Stella had flipped and was outside, running up and down the Finchley Road, trying to grab the attention of a policeman and have Mark arrested for plying her with drugs? What if she'd gone to put the rubbish out and been stabbed like a human pin-cushion by some drugged-up half-crazed Camden Council rehabilitated knife-wielding maniac who was even now approaching the half-open door to her flat? *This* flat! Or, even worse, what if the gay serial killer, or serial gay killer, or killer of serial gays, or whatever, was in the building and creeping up the stairs to get him, right now…?

The telephone rang sharply and Mark rose in a burst of panic. He shot to the front door and slammed it shut with a resounding bang that seemed to shake the entire building.

The telephone continued to ring ring, ring ring, ring ring. Mark just stared, stared, stared, trying hard to control his dilating pupils. The clamouring thing was small and black and very fuzzy around its edges.

Should he answer it?

No, of course not. This wasn't his flat.

It could be Hugh. What would he say?

Hugh would come round there and beat him up or kill him or something even worse...

No, don't be so silly, he told himself, *it's only the phone.*

But he wished it would stop.

Ring ring, ring ring, ring ring...

Damn noise! He made a sudden decision and sprang across the room, snatching it from its cradle and holding it at arm's length. He heard a woman's voice sounding like a few million miles away across the void. He cleared his throat and brought the receiver up to his ear.

'H... Hello?' he said.

'Is that Mark?' It was definitely a woman's voice, but not Stella's. The accent was different, more of a drawl.

'Er, er, yes. Who is this, please?' he asked, his voice almost a squeak.

'My name's Laura. I'm a friend of Stella's. I live in the basement flat.'

'Oh. Well, I'm afraid she's not here. I mean, she was a moment ago, but...'

'She's here,' Laura cut in, 'with me. I think you have some explaining to do...'

Oh my God! thought Mark. *The police are probably already on their way...* 'Is she alright?' he stammered.

'What do you think? She's as stoned as a parrot, can hardly speak, is covered in blood and she says it's all your fault.'

'What? Oh my God. What blood? I haven't touched her. Please don't call the police...' Bile forced its way up from the very pit of his stomach. He started to shake.

'I suggest you get down here - right now!' Laura replied. There was a click and the line purred loudly in his ear.

Mark replaced the receiver with a bang. He was shaking all over. What in God's name was going on? Blood? What blood? Had she fallen over? Maybe she'd been attacked? He ran for the door.

Keys! screamed the solitary sane voice in his head. He raced back into the lounge and finally found a bunch on the small wooden table right next to the phone. He pocketed them and stumbled hurriedly out of the door, slamming it for the second time, and collided with a handsome young man in leather trousers and a green top on the landing. Mumbling his apologies, he fled down the remaining steps three at a time, yanked open the front door and dashed out into the gathering dusk of a warm May evening.

℘ℂ℞

Pierre Morgan was 24 years old, although he often pretended to be younger or older, depending on the circumstances. He was a *mature* student of French and often pretended to be French, speaking with an exaggerated accent sounding as if he cared a lot about what he said, but not how he said it.

Quite the opposite of what one would expect of a native Frenchman.

Camden College was a brisk twenty minute walk from Netherhall and for the past two semesters he'd spent his weekdays asleep in class and the evenings wide awake, sometimes performing the *Full Monty* and sometimes acting as a male escort. His clients comprised the sex mad, the fanciful, the paralytic and the idle rich. And sometimes all four in one. Although not exclusively heterosexual, Pierre much preferred his clients to be female.

It was early evening and Pierre was looking good. Brushing his short, thick blond hair in the full-length oak-rimmed mirror - the only item of furniture in the room that he actually owned - he surveyed his bronzed, naked torso with a loving eye. He squatted down and performed fifty fast press-ups and then stood panting before the mirror, flexing his hardened biceps.

'Hm, pretty good,' he murmured to his reflection, casting a critical eye down the cleave of his chest. He pulled on a soft green Polo shirt, zipped up his black leather jeans and inserted a well-rolled joint between thick, dark-red lips. He lit the end with a Zippo and inhaled the aromatic smoke, took a couple more hits and left the joint smouldering in the ashtray on the corner of the dresser. Picking up his keys, he headed out of the bed-sit and down a flight of stairs where he was knocked aside by a dashing young man in a mad panic.

'Hey!' he shouted. 'Watch where you're fucking going!'

'Sorry,' the guy mumbled.

Muttering curses, he followed the madman down the stairs at a more leisurely pace and then stepped out into a beautiful spring evening, expectant with the onset of summer.

Pierre carefully closed the huge front door to Netherhall, which the madman had left open, and headed down the steps towards the bustling Finchley Road. He ran across between swift moving traffic and entered the tube station, flashing his pass as he passed through the barrier, and hurried down the moving escalator.

He was late.

He did not like to be late - not for a client.

Experience had taught him that it was generally a bad idea to be late. Clients became very demanding when he was late, as if the wait had somehow put their imaginations into overtime. And overtime rates could be both rewarding and costly at the same time. Laura, his downstairs neighbour and occasional pimp, had informed him earlier that day that a lovely lady with a slight German accent, over here on business with a friend, had specifically requested his services - and it was well-known that Germans respected punctuality. Still, being late could make the evening more interesting. On one occasion, he remembered with a grin, a rich middle-aged widow was kept waiting for almost an hour through no fault of his own. On his approach to her exclusive apartment block somewhere in Hampstead Garden Suburbs, the violent twitch of a net curtain was quickly followed by a monosyllabic command from her private intercom ordering him up to the first floor. She literally ripped his clothes from him, screaming that he was a very, very naughty boy. She calmed down, eventually, after over an hour of tortuous but immensely satisfying sex for both of them. She had tipped him handsomely on that occasion but he had carried the marks for over a week.

And now, with the next southbound train still 9 minutes away, he was going to be late again. As his cock stiffened against his tight black leather jeans, it didn't seem to worry him quite so much.

☙❧

It was much darker around the side of Netherhall and Mark's haste was frustrated by dense scrub. Almost blinded as a bramble scathed an eyebrow, he emerged with loud curses and the occasional yelp onto the paved patio area a few metres in front of a dark green door. The door opened and a dumpy silhouetted figure appeared as a bright beam of torchlight sliced through the gloom and riveted him to the spot.

'Don't come any closer.' The heavily loaded accent was straight from CSI New York. 'I have a gun pointing at your head.'

'It's me. Mark. Don't shoot!'

There was a deep, but relieved sigh. 'Why didn't you come down the back stairs like any civilised person?' the figure demanded, switching the torch off and standing back to let him in. Mark could see no evidence of a gun. 'I'm Laura, by the way,' the voice added as he stepped over the threshold into the faintly odorous oblong kitchen with its blackened hob to one side, cupboards, both open and closed on the other and a Yale locked door in the far corner to which Laura was obviously referring. An open archway led through into another room.

'Very pleased to meet you,' Mark said, shaking the small chubby hand held out towards him. Through the archway, he could just make out the crumpled figure of Stella, lying face down on a couch. His breath caught in his throat. Her hair, which had been perfectly coiffeured just minutes earlier, was now in ruins. Her black silky top was ripped from the top of her right shoulder to the bottom left in a jagged edged gash. As blood seeped down her left ear, dripping onto a rouged cheek, she moaned incoherently. Mark ran to her.

'Stella? My God, what's happened?'

Laura closed the back door and locked it firmly. 'You're lucky I didn't call the cops,' she said, following him into the lounge. 'She was in such a state I thought she'd been attacked but then realised she was just pissed or something and it was probably the brambles. Don't know why she didn't use the backstairs either.'

Stella moaned, opened her bleary eyes and, lifting her head like a broken rag doll, blurted out, 'No more doooope for me. Ever!'

Mark grinned sheepishly and looked up at Laura tending to Stella's wounds. 'We've had a few joints,' he explained. 'We call it *dope*. You probably call it *pot*. I know my American friends do.'

Stella moaned again, more loudly.

Laura straightened up. 'Mm,' she said. 'Got any more of this, er, *dope*?'

Chapter Two

IT WAS A GLORIOUS SUNRISE. Mist swirled in a gentle breeze, spreading like a soft pink eiderdown over the entire length and breadth of Hyde Park. Trees poked above the mist like antlers of giant beasts and appeared to Pierre, in his current state, to be roaming the land in search of fresh pasture.

He stood, swaying happily between a handsome Germanic couple, on the seemingly insubstantial balcony of the Park Suite, feeling as if his feet were treading marshmallows. In one corner, a giant aspidistra looked poised to stand erect, its long root tendrils seeking support before hoisting its bulk for a stroll along the Serpentine. The side street pavements directly below were deserted but there were a few motorists making their weary way home along the main Bayswater Road after their regular Friday evening's outing to restaurants, bars, theatres and clubs. Now where was it that Pierre had been? He swallowed painfully and his parched lips begged for something cold, something wet.

'It's late,' the man's voice broke through the thick comforting duvet around his brain. 'You must stay here. We will be back tonight... For some fun,' he added with a grin in his voice.

The woman's voice was light with laughter, almost a chuckle. 'Don't go away,' she said.

With that, they guided him round from the balcony and led him firmly inside, frog-marched him towards the king-sized double bed and then watched as he thankfully collapsed over it. He was soon snoring gently, his thirst momentarily forgotten.

The couple flashed handsome toothy grins at each other and their eyes locked. A moment later, the man nodded slightly and the woman opened her purse, withdrawing from within an ordinary-looking fine-tipped ink pen. She unscrewed the cap and held it up to the early morning light streaming in from the balcony. A slight squeeze and a few small drops of clear liquid spurted towards the ceiling. Bending over Pierre, the man reached under him and unclasped the belt of his tight leather jeans. With a grunt, he forced them down below the cute firmness of Pierre's buttocks. He took the fake pen from the woman and made a quick stab into the hard muscle and then squeezed. It was over in a few seconds. He gave Pierre's bum a resounding smack.

'Uugh,' moaned Pierre, then fell silent. The man leant over and lovingly placed a kiss on both buttocks, then roughly pulled off the leather jeans and tossed them aside. The pen was returned to the purse and without another word the couple left the room, locking it firmly behind them.

෨ଔ

Saturday morning hit Mark with sudden clarity of thought. Something warm and hairy was lying across his forehead. He screamed. Laura rushed into the lounge from the kitchen, her large frame clad in a pink fluffy dressing gown that had been hurriedly tied at the waist whilst her feet made strange clomping noises in matching pink fluffy slippers that came up to her ankles. In stark contrast, her legs were as white as ivory and very, very smooth. She looked to Mark like an animated marshmallow. He sat bolt upright on the couch and the blanket slipped to reveal his nakedness. He hastily covered himself.

'You've met Freud, I see,' Laura said, staring at Mark's torso with a gleam in her eye as her sleek black tomcat slunk under the table. 'Now, what would you like for breakfast? I'm afraid I've only got toast and coffee... Will that do?'

Mark nodded. 'Thank you ... Er, where's Stella?'

'She went back to her own flat around three... Don't you remember? No, I don't suppose you do...' She peered at him closely. 'You look terrible, by the way.'

'Thanks.' A thought struck him. 'She didn't go to Hugh's then, after all?'

Laura walked over to the curtains and pulled them open with a

12

swish. Light flooded the room, making Mark wince. 'No, I don't think so. She was in no fit state to go anywhere.'

Last night flashed back.

'None of us were,' Mark said, reaching for the underpants draped over the nearest chair. He couldn't quite reach. Laura watched him struggle, then inched the chair a little closer.

'Thanks.' He grabbed his whites. 'Did she go back through the brambles in the middle of the night? She could be dead by now!'

'No, she used the civilised route this time. Can't think why she didn't use it last night, the silly girl! Besides, there's a perfectly good path through the brambles - if you know where to look,' she added, having a good peek at Mark's thighs as he struggled to put his pants on and hide his modesty. *Mmm, hairy,* she thought. *Very nice!*

He won the fight eventually and looked up at her accusingly. 'You said you had a gun pointed at my head...'

'Oh, it's just a toy one,' Laura replied, recovering her composure quickly.

'Oh!'

'Neat, huh? Now, get some clothes on and we'll have breakfast.'

ഇൗൠ

They chatted over burnt toast and dark coffee that was far too strong for Mark; the white lumps of dairy crud floating on the top didn't enhance the flavour either. Laura was clearly a little eccentric and Mark found her highly comical, but in a nice way. She was easy to talk to and had an outlook on life that he found strangely romantic. Her family back home in New York were wealthy: Laura, however, was not. She could have been, could have lived an easy life if she'd resigned herself to a career in the family business. Instead, music had inspired her and she'd shrugged off the family's disdain, and its fortune, and pursued a solo career as a flautist. Even now, on the wrong side of forty, she was still planning for the *big break,* supporting herself teaching the flute. Naturally, she made no mention of her other more illicit money-making activities.

'So, do you have any plans for today?' Laura asked, munching on her fifth slice of dry burnt toast. She really should adjust the toaster, but couldn't be bothered.

Mark shook his head slowly as he tried to remember, then gulped down the last few dregs of a second cup of coffee, knowing it was a bad idea. The coffee tasted quite revolting but Mark was enjoying the chat and he'd accepted another cup because it seemed the polite thing to do.

'Then you can help me shop,' she announced. 'I'm having a party this evening. Just a few close friends… I'd love you to come.'

'What, shopping or to the party?'

'Both.'

Mark thanked her. 'That would be great,' he said, putting down his coffee cup.

Laura heaved herself up from the table and started to clear away the dishes.

'Hey, let me do that,' Mark said, getting to his feet.

'Certainly not,' Laura said, adding with a wink, 'You're going to need all your strength.'

Mark thought, *Oh Christ, I think she's got the hots for me.* 'Listen, we'll have to hurry,' he said. 'I've some things I need to do at home.'

'Ready when you are!' she trilled, dumping the dishes in the sink. Mark distinctly heard something break.

ഇരു

Waitrose on the Finchley Road was only five minutes walk, all downhill. Laura singled out a trolley and they pushed it gleefully through the automatic barrier into the salad and vegetable section. It felt very domesticated to Mark, who bought most of his groceries in corner shops. He was suddenly reminded of his own bare cupboard at home.

'I think I need a few things,' he said to Laura, who was busy sorting the firmest ripe tomatoes. 'I'll catch up with you later.'

She nodded, humming to herself as she moved on to the lettuces.

Mark wandered up and down the neighbouring aisles, relieved to be alone for a while. Laura was fun to be with, but exhausting. Searching for the final item on his mental shopping list, he caught sight of a tall, middle-aged woman staring at him. In her late forties, she wore far too much make-up, flat shoes and a chequered gabardine raincoat, despite the clement weather. As their eyes locked, she cried, 'William!' and ran towards him.

Then she stopped, tears welling in her eyes. 'Oh, I'm so sorry. I ... You look *so* much like my son,' she sniffed. 'He ran away to London, you see, about 18 months ago and I'm so worried about him with this serial killer on the loose... I came down to try and find him. Silly, I know - he could be anywhere by now...' She turned away, pulled a delicate lace handkerchief from her purse and dabbed an eye.

Mark was very moved and unsure what to do. Instinctively, he moved closer and she turned towards him at once. 'You look so much like him, you don't know.' She sniffed, and tried to blow her nose. She wrung the handkerchief in her hands, 'I'm staying with a friend ... and I'm not going home until I find him...' Her voice trailed off into a sob.

'There, now,' Mark said gently, 'I'm sure you'll find him. I'll ... I'll keep an eye out for him, if you like?'

She managed to control her crying and said, 'Oh would you? The more people the better. I have a photo of him in the car with my number on the back. I'm parked just outside.' They were coming up to the bank of twenty-four checkouts and she steered her laden trolley towards the one closest to the exit. 'You're so handsome and so kind - just like my Will,' she added. 'What's your name?'

'Mark,' said Mark.

'His proper name's William, but he'll always be my Will.' She didn't volunteer her name. Instead, she started loading her shopping onto the conveyor belt. Mark put his shopping basket on the end and started helping. When the cashier started to put through her groceries, the woman moved smartly forward to pack and he helped with that too. They were almost finished when she suddenly said, 'Oh, I've forgotten the eggs! Mark, would you be a dear and fetch me half a dozen medium? Make sure they're free range.'

He hurried off to the farthest corner of the large store where he'd noticed the eggs earlier. When he eventually returned, the cashier was putting through the last of his groceries: a tin of beans, a small malted brown loaf, a pint of milk and a jar of reduced-fat mayonnaise. He searched for the woman, putting the eggs absently onto the conveyor belt, a queue forming impatiently behind him.

'That'll be £94.73 pence please, love,' exclaimed the cashier, a small Asian woman with an east-end accent.

'Eh? For some beans and a loaf of bread? I think you've made a mistake...'

'No, there's milk, mayonnaise, eggs and the rest of your mother's shopping.'

'M ... Mother's shopping?'

'Yes, your mother. She said to tell you she was taking the shopping to the car. She said you were paying.'

Mark gasped again. 'That wasn't my *mother!* I've never seen her before in my life!'

'Well, she certainly seemed to know you pretty well, *Mark.*' There was a sarcastic edge to her voice that Mark didn't like.

'Seems like everyone does.' Pointing at his groceries, he said, 'Look, I'm only paying for these five items.' He picked up the eggs and added, 'In fact, only these four. The eggs aren't mine either.'

'That's right,' sniffed the cashier. 'They're your mother's.'

'She's not my mother!'

'Is there a problem here?' a bass voice asked. Mark spun round to face a tall dark-haired and blue-chinned man in his early twenties, dressed impeccably in dark blue trousers and a lighter blue short-sleeved shirt, with the word 'Security' embroidered on his left breast and a tattoo clearly visible on his right bicep.

Then a strong New York accent from another checkout down the long line had him spinning round again.

'Yoo hoo. Mark!'

Everyone turned towards the voice as Laura bustled towards him, her trolley stuffed full of plastic carrier bags with French sticks poking out like a forest of pine stumps and her face beetroot with effort.

'Mark, I need another £3.42p; can you lend it to me?' She stopped abruptly as she saw a mixture of both grim and amused faces staring at her.

'Laura, could you please explain to these people that I am not shopping with my mother.' said Mark quietly.

A large crowd was gathering and Mark was beginning to feel rather peculiar. A combination of no dinner, too much wine, way too much dope and very little sleep the previous evening coupled with breakfast that morning that was either burnt, too strong or rancid, suddenly caught up with him. Just before he passed out, he saw extraordinarily large muscular arms envelop him and his head, suddenly heavy and buzzing, weaved around before flopping against a blue-black image on the guard's upper arm. The word *Mother* in jet-black ink swam before his darkening eyes.

ಒಂದೇ

Pierre awoke to the peel of a distant church clock. Was it eight or nine bells? Or perhaps later? He may not have heard the first of the chimes. Remaining daylight framed the thick, expensive velvet curtains that draped the balcony doors. A green softness tinged the frame. In fact, it seemed to tinge everything in the room.

He slowly rolled over, as if physical exertion would help to clear his head. He felt fuggy, if such a word existed. Where the hell was he? Slowly, he slid his legs towards the edge of the bed, the swish of satin sheets sending shivers of pleasure to his loins. The pleasure centres of his brain urged him to do it again, but he resisted. He needed to know where he was and what he was doing there before he could allow himself to enjoy it.

Pierre sat up and his feet reached spongy shag pile. His leather jeans lay in a heap on the floor beneath a delicately framed picture of a robust bowl of ruby black cherries apparently leering at him. He stood and searched unsteadily for the bathroom. It was en suite, for which he was truly thankful.

As he splashed water on his face and gulped large handfuls, he gazed at his reflection. 'Mm, still looking good,' he muttered. Then he sat down too hard on the loo. 'Ow!' he yelped, and leapt up. Turning his head, he tried to locate the source of the pain. There was a small tender spot on his right buttock.

Then his mind flashed back to the previous evening. He'd been late, of course, and met up with a biker guy at some appointed bar who'd taken him to another bar on the back of a large throbbing motorbike and then introduced him to a most charming couple. They had their first drink in a quiet brasserie in a side street on the western edge of Soho. For the rest of the evening, they had plied him with drinks at a number of fringe venues, paying for them with large bills until they suggested, amidst giggles with obvious intentions, a final night-cap at their flat in Bayswater. They had paid him £50 for his escort that evening, with a hint of more to come.

So, where the hell were they now? The man had been called Otto, or something, but he couldn't remember the woman's name or the biker guy's. That was fine by him: some insisted on total anonymity.

Pierre sat down again, rather more cautiously, and managed a torrent of very yellow pee but little else. As he sat there, cradling his throbbing head with the palms of his hands, a vague recollection stirred of a sharp pain and a rough slap. Then it came clear. What the hell had they injected into him? His pulse suddenly raced and he broke into a sweat, almost smelling his own fear. His head buzzed and he felt heat in his bowels. Moments later, he was violently ill at both ends.

Pierre continued retching until he could retch no more. Moaning and shivering from exhaustion, he swilled his mouth out with water and splashed his face and neck. Peeking into the mirror, he screamed and spun around. The handsome couple were standing in the doorway, watching him. Otto was dressed in black from head to toe and the woman in a white evening dress. She was clasping a small black purse in both hands. The man glared at Pierre for a few moments.

Pierre glowered back. 'What the fuck…?'

'Quiet!' said the man in English, adding to the woman in German, 'I've gone off him now. Get me another one. Tonight!'

Haughtily, he turned and walked over to the window, his back to them. Pierre immediately took a step forward and the woman put out a hand to restrain him. Without another word, she bent and picked up his crumpled leather trousers and held them out. Pierre snatched them and climbed into them, zipping and belting them quickly. When he was done and about to complain further, the woman pushed another note into his hands and walked him to the door.

'Go home,' she said, in perfect English, 'and be thankful.'

'Now just you wait a fucking minute,' Pierre began. 'You two fuckers have injected me with something - that's a fucking violation of my basic human fucking rights. I could fucking have you for that.'

The woman pressed another £50 note into his hands. 'It was a harmless muscle relaxant,' she said, waving her hand dismissively and slamming the door in his face.

ഋCആ

Everybody who was anybody was at the party, none of whom, except for Laura, Mark knew. Stella had failed to appear although Laura had assured him she was coming. He was feeling rather foolish. Not just because of the incident that morning, but because at the last minute Laura had informed him that it was a fancy dress party. He'd made a half-assed attempt and had whitened his face with a face pack, preventing him from smiling too much for fear of cracking, and added some dummy fangs that now protruded at an irregular angle from his upper lip - none of which helped him feel at ease: he knew it was a poor effort.

Laura, at one point, had added a musical conundrum to her outfit and using a bold black marker pen had scrawled every item of shopping she could think of onto a long piece of toilet roll and then hung it around her neck. She refused to say who, or what, she represented. That was all part of the *fun*.

A cellist and a flautist, a young couple from East Finchley in red checked ties and kilts, provided live music. During a lull in the entertainment, they both gravitated towards Mark who was devouring French bread and Brie, having conveniently lost the Dracula teeth.

'Hi. Great music,' he said appreciatively. The two gushed with pleasure.

'It's our first public performance really,' announced the taller one. He had cropped blond hair and a whisper of a goatee. 'Isn't it, Gerald?'

Gerald nodded. 'And probably our last!' He was smaller, slightly older and stockier with darker hair and more robust facial hair. He turned to Mark. 'So, how do you know Laura?'

Mark swallowed a mouthful of crusty bread that lodged in his throat, making his eyes water. 'Well, I only met her last night, actually,' he said, choking and coughing. 'I feel like a gate crasher.'

'We'll see if we can find you one,' retorted Gerald playfully as they both collapsed into a fit of giggles. Mark did his best to laugh with them.

'So, why the kilts?' he asked.

'Ah, well. You see, I'm Gerald and he's Patrick.' Gerald nodded towards his fellow musician.

'Yeees?'

'Well, I'm Gerald Fitzpatrick and he's Patrick Fitzgerald. Geddit?'

Mark smiled faintly just as Stella walked in and he saw his chance to escape. 'Excuse me, would you? My friend's just arrived.'

'See you later, handsome,' Patrick said and winked at him.

From behind, Mark thought Stella looked perfect. Apart perhaps from the fact that she was swaying just a little. She hadn't spoken to anyone as yet, had helped herself to the largest glass of wine from the variety on the drinks table and was just standing there, gulping and swaying. Mark stood directly behind her for a moment, then tapped her gently on the shoulder. She spun around and kept on going. Just before she collapsed in a heap, Mark managed to whisk the drink from her and grab her by the waist. She fell into his arms instead of crashing into the drinks table.

'Stella, you're drunk already!' he said accusingly.

'Oh, Mark, Mark,' she slurred. 'More stoned actually. Hugh's upstairs and refuses to come down.'

'Why? Because you didn't go to him last night?' Mark asked. She nodded. 'Did you tell him it was all my fault?'

'No!' she snapped, pulling away from his embrace as her features tightened. 'Mark, you'll never come between me and Hugh.' Her face softened, 'This is my doing, nothing to do with you. OK?'

'Oh, ok.'

She looked about her, at the revellers, then down at her almost empty glass. 'Can we go outside?' she asked, sounding depressed. 'I need some air.'

'Sure. Come on.'

Mark held her tenderly as they moved onto the patio. It was a comfortably mild evening and there were dozens of people thronging the crazy paving.

'Laura seems to know a lot of people,' he commented. The music had started up again, this time from the stereo, and guests were gyrating to Dusty Springfield's *Reputation*. Mark led Stella over to the far corner of the garden and sat her down on a knee-high wall that bordered the patio where a Japanese Flowering Cherry tree made it darker, more secluded. *Cosier*, Mark thought.

'Hugh hates you,' Stella began. 'He's never fucking met you and he hates you.' She hung her head.

'Oh! Then you did tell him about last night?'

Stella sobbed, 'I had to. I couldn't think of anything else.'

'So, he blames me?'

Stella nodded.

'What about you?' he asked.

'What about me…?'

'Do you blame me as well?'

Stella sighed as she lifted her lovely face to meet his gaze, her blonde hair falling across her eyes. She brushed it aside with the back of her hand: a very feminine gesture. Mark could see tears glistening on her ashen skin, ghostly in the moonlight.

'I'm sorry Mark, I've handled this really badly.' she said finally and added quickly, 'Have you got a joint? I could do with it right now.'

'Of course,' he smiled, 'if you're sure…?'

'Of course!' she mimicked, smiling back at him.

Mark produced a well-rolled joint and lit it. It glowed in the twilight as he took a deep drag and passed it surreptitiously. 'Better be careful,' he cautioned. 'Don't let everyone see it.'

A few minutes later, as they sat together in silence, a bouncing ball of fun gushed up to them.

'Well!?' Laura demanded. 'How do you like my outfit?'

Mark stared at her for a moment. 'You've got a piece of bog-roll on your head… You're… er… I know, Elton John?'

'No!' Laura cried. 'Can't you see? A famous composer?'

'Oh! Very good,' said Mark, still puzzled.

'No!' Laura yelled at him. 'I am a *particular* famous composer. Go on, guess which one.'

Mark and Stella shrugged through the haze.

'You two are stoned again!' Laura said flatly. 'Liszt,' she hissed and walked off. Stella and Mark sat and stared at each other, then simultaneously burst into a fit of giggles.

'She's quite crazy, you know,' Stella chuckled.

'You don't have to tell me - she's after my body!'

Stella looked at him coyly. 'That doesn't make her crazy.'

'It will,' he said with a wink.

They had to hold onto each other as the tears of laughter coursed down their faces.

₨⇓

Pierre was angry enough to break down the door that had just been slammed in his face, but he decided against it; it wasn't worth the aggravation. Besides he had three £50 notes in his back pocket. He dug them out and fondled their crisp newness, allowed himself a small smile and followed the exit signs down the landing and eventually onto the street. He looked up at the huge block of flats wondering who owned them. A bicycle was chained to a railing right next to a *No Cycles* sign. A curtain twitched momentarily but there were no other visible signs of life. He turned and walked off in the direction of the Bayswater Road where he joined the general throng of life on a Saturday evening in London.

Feeling flush, he hailed a passing black cab to take him home, jumped in and slumped onto the back seat. The cabbie started chatting as they crossed the Marylebone Road and into Abbey Road. 'You look like shit, mate,' he said. 'I hope you're not gonna puke in my cab.'

'Nah, I'm fine,' Pierre replied. 'No problem.' He sat up and imagined the Beatles immortalising the zebra crossing on their Abbey Road album almost forty years earlier. He looked out for it, but didn't see it.

They eventually emerged from St John's Wood onto the Finchley Road passed through Swiss Cottage and then the cab driver slowed down.

His voice suddenly echoed from a small speaker. 'Whereabouts, mate?'

Pierre sat up straighter. 'Near the tube station... next to Waitrose.'

The cab driver put his foot down and then stopped abruptly as a car screeched past, its horn blaring.

'Bloody maniac,' shouted the cabbie, and then turned to Pierre. 'Just call it twenty quid, mate, ok?'

Pierre handed him a £50 note. The cabbie took it without a murmur and switched on the overhead light. Holding it up with podgy yellowed fingers, he glanced at it. Glowering, he took a firmer hold and leant closer, his eyes squinting.

'This ain't real, mate,' he said. 'It's a dud. I want twenty *real* notes.' He handed it back

Numb, Pierre offered him another, knowing that it too was a dummy. The cabbie inspected it briefly and quickly shook his head. 'By rights, I should report this,' he said ominously. 'Now, let's just have the twenty quid and I'll be on my way.'

Pierre swore under his breath.

'Yer what?' the cabbie asked, his features hardening.

'I said, I'll fucking kill 'em,' said Pierre, gritting his teeth.

'You do that. Now, in the meantime, let's have the twenty quid. It'll be twenty-one quid soon if I have to wait around much longer.'

Pierre pulled out his wallet. He had only two crumpled notes; both tenners. 'Keep the change,' he said, pushing them at the cabbie and swiftly jumping out of the cab. Glancing back, he saw the cab driver check the notes. Satisfied, he switched off the overhead light and pulled out into the road. He sped past Pierre with a curious glance.

So, what was he going to do now? Pierre peered at the three crisp notes, the front of each depicting the Queen smirking in all her finery. On the reverse side, a formidable ogre of a man, Sir John Houblon 1632-1712, frowned out at him. The silvery broken strip that was supposed to run from top to bottom was missing.

'Fucking bastards!' he yelled. 'I'll fucking kill you, you bastards!!'

A dark-haired young man with a large kebab halfway to his mouth looked at him, grinned and then bit into the greasy processed lamb. 'Life's a bitch, man,' he mumbled with his mouth full, adding, 'and then you marry one.' He laughed and ambled off, a whiff of processed meat and onions following in his wake.

Pierre stood waving his fist in a southerly direction. He was livid. He was going to get in the next cab and go straight back down there. Yeah! Confront the bastards; call the cops; anything! But get them, he would.

He hurriedly crossed the road and searched the southbound traffic for another cab. An orange light appeared in the distance. As he raised his arm, a thought struck him: he hadn't any real money! As the cab slowed, he turned to walk away. The cab accelerated aggressively and shot past him, its horn blaring. It was then that Pierre suddenly remembered that he had some money stashed away in his dope tin. He ran the few hundred metres to the steps leading up from Finchley Road into Netherhall Gardens and took them three at a time. As he neared Netherhall itself, music reached him together with muffled squeals of laughter. Of course! Laura's fancy dress party! He remembered receiving the invite weeks back - hand-written on white card, with musical notes issuing from a flute drawn in black marker pen in each corner. Well, maybe he would drop in later, after he'd completed his business. Laura would want her usual cut and he didn't want to disappoint her. He reached the front door as another burst of laughter echoed from around the side, heightening his resolve. He was going to have the last laugh; just let those bastards wait and see.

Once inside his room, he lunged for the dope tin stashed on the bottom shelf inside the wardrobe and held up two ten-pound notes in triumph, hearing the fanfare in his head. Then he noticed the unfinished joint in the ashtray. It had gone out as he knew it would and he lit it with his Zippo and inhaled the smoke again, feeling the instant buzz in his legs before it hit his brain. A few more tokes and he began to mellow. *They should hand this stuff out at football matches*, he thought and smiled.

Another burst of wild laughter wafting up from below, followed by shrieks of delight and loud catcalls, heralded the arrival of yet another partygoer. It was going to be a long night for the residents of Netherhall. Pierre couldn't help but smile. Maybe he'd join them sooner than he thought, but then, on the other hand, maybe he wouldn't. He felt another surge of anger bubbling.

It was almost midnight by Mark's watch. Stella had already left to go upstairs and presumably shag Hugh's brains out. But before she went and after the hysterics had subsided, she had spoken more intimately to Mark than usual about their relationship. She really loved Hugh, it seemed, and Mark had not protested when she'd picked herself up, dusted herself down and pecked him on the cheek.

'I love you too, Mark,' she'd said. 'And no, I don't blame you.'

Mark had watched her leave through the kitchen. Presumably, she'd taken the back stairs that wound its way up from the basement through the centre of Netherhall to the grand hallway. She would've then climbed the stairs excitedly perhaps, or perhaps not, to where Hugh was presumably still waiting to shag her brains out...

He was hugging his fifth can of beer and still musing when Gerald Fitzpatrick and Patrick Fitzgerald came mincing over.

'Hi, handsome,' gushed Gerald with a practised wink. They were both obviously on the wrong side of five cans themselves.

'Patrick here,' continued Gerald, 'insists you're a Virgo. I, however, think you're a Gemini. Now, put us out of our misery, which is it?'

'Does it really fucking matter?'

Patrick and Gerald exchanged knowing glances. 'Butch, or what?' Gerald said, adding, 'He's all yours, darling.'

Patrick watched his friend retreat, then turned awkwardly and just stood, staring at Mark, suddenly tongue-tied.

Mark stared up at him. 'Well, are you going to sit, *or what?*'

Patrick sat, a smile on his lips. 'Er, sorry about Gerald. He can be a bit obvious, sometimes.'

'It hardly matters,' Mark said, looking away. 'I'm not gay, anyway.'

'Oh!'

Mark turned back to face him. 'So, what did Gerald mean by, *He's all yours?*'

Patrick, still recovering from the first admission, cleared his throat, 'Oh! Er, I ...er like masculine men.'

'Aren't they all? By definition I mean?' Mark was teasing him now.

Patrick rolled his eyes. 'If only,' he said.

Mark studied him in the darkness. 'Just how old are you?' he asked.

'Eighteen,' Patrick declared proudly.

'And you're telling me you like to be fucked?'

Patrick nodded eagerly.

'You're too young to know what you want!'

Patrick stuck out a stubborn, firm jaw into the night. 'Are you sure we're still talking about me?' he said thinly.

Mark was quiet for a moment. 'So, how did you meet this Gerald?' he asked, ignoring the question.

'Laura introduced us.'

'And how do you know Laura?'

'She's been teaching me to play the flute since I was nine. Nearly half my life!'

'Well, you play very well, as far as I'm any judge,' Mark said, adding, 'I hope you use a condom.'

'Thank you. And hey, I may be young but I'm not stupid.'

'Glad to hear it.'

Then Mark had a thought. 'From the age of nine, you say? Surely that's *more* than half your life, unless my maths teacher was lying...?'

Patrick went red. 'Ok, I'll be eighteen a week tomorrow.'

'Well, happy birthday for a week tomorrow!'

'Thank you!'

They lapsed into silence for a while, watching the party going on around them. Most of it had moved inside where the music was loudest. Eventually, Mark asked, 'So, are you old enough to smoke a joint?'

Patrick shook his head. 'I'm sure I am, but Gerald wouldn't approve.'

Mark shrugged and removed the thin Café Crème cigar tin from his back pocket, took out a joint, one of several in the tin, inserted it into his mouth and applied the Zippo.

Patrick eyed the tin. 'I like men who smoke cigars though - big fat ones.'

'The men or the cigars?'

'The cigars, silly... I like my men lean and muscular. Not that there's anything wrong with fat guys – just not my type.'

'Well, it hardly matters. But no I don't smoke cigars, just joints. And, like I said, I'm not gay.'

Mark took another drag whilst Patrick lit a Camel. They sat and smoked in silence, watching the last of the party animals move inside.

'It's been a good party, hasn't it?' Patrick said eventually.

'Good enough.'

Another silence, then Mark stubbed out the joint and stood up, dusting off the back of his jeans. 'It's time I made a move.'

Patrick stood expectantly, facing Mark.

'Home,' Mark emphasised, just in case Patrick had misunderstood him.

Patrick stumbled forward and grabbed hold of Mark to steady himself. They stood facing each other, the strains of *Dancing Queen* by Erasure beating the night air.

'Where do you live?' Patrick asked.

'Near Bayswater.'

'On your own?'

'Of course.'

Patrick moved a step closer. 'Take me home with you.'

'Look, I've told you, I'm not gay,' said Mark firmly.

'Oh. Right. Well, can we be friends?'

'Sure.' Mark turned to go. Jesus, what a situation! The last thing he needed right now was a seventeen-year-old boy with a crush on him hanging around. 'Laura's got my number,' he lied and strode off towards the open kitchen door.

'Mark?'

He stopped and cast a quick glance over his shoulder. 'What?'

'I... I think I love you.'

'Don't waste it on me kid! Oh, and be careful out there: there's a killer loose.' He turned and went into the noisy, smoky kitchen filled with the kind of people you found in most kitchens at parties - drunk, stoned, deep in conspiratorial conversations. He pushed through and sought out Laura, thanked her for a lovely evening and headed on home.

Chapter Three

DETECTIVE CHIEF INSPECTOR DICKENS was a heavy sleeper these days. He hadn't always been. In fact, in his younger days he hardly needed sleep at all. Now though, at the ripe old age of 37, his body or brain or whatever it was that required sleep was paying him back with a vengeance. Consequently, his emergency phone rang almost half a dozen times before he finally fumbled for it and pushed the required button. It was light outside, he noticed absently.

'Dickens,' he said. 'What is it?'

'Sir, there's been another murder,' said a familiar, younger, cockier man's voice. 'Same signature: Pretty young man, at least what's left of him would suggest he was pretty, disembowelled, dismembered... It has to be our guy.'

'Shit.' That made four. Dickens glanced at the bedside clock: 6.30am, Sunday morning. His one day of rest. He sighed. He had been anticipating this; they all had. Probably everyone in London had been too. 'Where this time?'

'Bayswater. A car's on its way to pick you up.'

'Fine. I'll be there shortly.' He cut the connection and stared at the other side of the bed for a few moments. It was empty. His wife had left him a while back. *Couldn't bear the early morning calls*, she'd said. *The not knowing when or if he'd be back*, she'd said. He'd said, *You watch far too much bloody television*. But she'd gone anyway. Took her time deciding though. Fifteen years, in fact.

Dickens sighed to himself as he padded through to the bathroom.

⊱⊰

Laura Bowles was in the act of depositing a black bin-liner full of empties into the local bottle bank behind Waitrose on the Finchley Road. She carefully separated the greens from the browns and the clears and then listened gleefully to each cavernous metallic crash deep within the depths of the various colour-coded containers. After hurling the last one, she was completely satiated: it was almost as good as sex, if her memory served her right. Wondering what it would be like to wrap her legs around Mark's cute butt, she crumpled up the plastic bag and dumped it into the appropriate recycler. She turned and froze.

Watching from a safe distance, smoking a cigarette, was the security guard who'd carried Mark to the store's rest room the previous day after his fainting fit. *Now, what was his name? Think Laura, think! Was it Graham? No. Len? No. Stan? No. Think, think. Through the alphabet: Alan, no, Barry, no, Christopher Wren, NO, Darren, no ...no ... GLEN! That was it: Glen.* She let out a deep breath, slowly, slowly. Composing herself and putting on a broad smile, she walked up to six feet of God's special clay and said, 'Hi Glen, how ya doing?' Cool as milk.

Glen nodded and smiled back. 'Fine. You?'

'Yes, wonderful, thank you.'

'Say...' Glen began awkwardly.

'Yes?'

'Say, how's Mark doing, huh? Been wondering if he's alright.'

Laura's smile faded. *Bugger*, she thought. *Another bloody fairy.* London was full of them. All the best looking men too! She smiled again to hide her disappointment.

'Oh, he's fine,' she said. 'I guess I shouldn't have taken him shopping; he'd had a heavy night.'

Glen took a long drag of his cigarette and blew the smoke aside. 'Well, you know, I was just wondering if he was ok. Thought I might look him up?' He took another drag of his cigarette. 'Got his address and that in the records.'

Laura nodded. 'You just do that,' she said.

⁊Œɡ

Detective PC Steve Evans watched the approaching black sedan and moved to open the door. Detective Chief Inspector Dickens got out. 'Any chance of some coffee and a roll?' he asked.

'I'll see to it,' the detective said. 'Meanwhile, you'd better go inside. Lots of activity going on. No reporters yet, thank God, but residents are kicking up and this crowd,' he indicated the growing throng held back by hazard tape alone, 'are getting ugly too, some of them.'

Dickens nodded. 'Don't worry about them - just get me some breakfast.' He was directed under the tape by a policewoman and went into the building. He noted the luxurious style; the serial killer had taste, if nothing else.

A police constable directed him to the third floor and he entered a large room with the thick drapes open to reveal a remarkable view of Hyde Park, a huge pot plant to one side and a picture of a bowl of black cherries on the opposite wall. An en-suite bathroom to the right caught his eye momentarily but what held almost his full attention was the amount of blood on the sheets covering the bed. The body lay underneath another sheet which was also bright red, turning brown. He wanted to pull the sheet aside, but knew what he'd see. He'd seen it three times already in as many weeks.

Just then the forensic team arrived and he pushed past them with hardly a nod in search of his breakfast. He doubted they'd find anything new. At this rate every gay man in London would be dead before they got any closer. They were dealing with a clever bastard alright. Clever and meticulously careful.

 …

Stella was in a state of total chaos. It was 11.30 in the morning and she was running around like an overactive hamster on its exercise wheel. She was due to start work behind the bar at the Hollybush public house at noon and it was a very brisk 15 minutes walk away, at least.

'Hugh, I can't find m'shoe!' she wailed. 'Hugh! Will you get up!'

'Mmm?' Hugh mumbled into the pillow.

The telephone started ringing.

'Jeeesus! Hugh, answer the bloody phone. And get up will you!'

Hugh reached out a hand from beneath the bedclothes and fumbled for the receiver. 'Hm, Hello?' He listened for a moment, nodded and said, 'I'll just get her... Surprise, surprise, it's for you, hen.'

'And will you get some clothes on!' Stella hissed, eyeing Hugh's naked body as he rose from the bed. 'Hello? Who's speaking?'

'It's me,' came the faraway voice of Iris, her elder sister.

Stella sighed. 'Look, I'm in a real hurry...'

'We've got a problem,' Iris cut in.

'What do you mean, *we*?'

'It's Mum. She's coming down.' Iris pronounced it *doon*.

'Oh, for God's sake, no.' Pronounced *noo*. 'When?'

'Next week,' sighed Iris.

'Oh, for God's sake, no. No! NO! She can't come down. I've got a tiny flat, half a job and no husband material to show her.'

'Eyy!!' came Hugh's voice from the bathroom.

'You don't count; you know that,' shouted Stella, 'You're married. Remember?'

'She doesn't know that,' Hugh mumbled through a mouthful of bristles and toothpaste.

'That's not the ...'

'Hey, who's paying for this call?' a far-away, raised and very Scottish voice demanded.

'Oh, sorry Sis. Look, she can't come. That's all there is to it.'

'Well, she's booked her ticket. She's coming.'

Stella's eye suddenly caught the glint of the toecap of her missing shoe. She squealed.

'What's going on?' Iris demanded.

'I've found m'shoe. Look, I'll have to go. I'll be late for work. I'll call you back tonight. She's not coming down. No way. Talk to you later, OK? Bye!' Stella slammed down the phone and grabbed her shoe. She noticed Hugh, still naked, his teeth gleaming.

'Time for a quickie?' he asked.

Stella looked pointedly at his stiffening cock. 'Hugh, I'm late already!'

'Call in sick,' Hugh suggested.

'No, Hugh. Now get dressed. Don't you have to be somewhere?'

'Not really, it's Sunday. Anyway, what's this about your ma?'

'I haven't got time now, Hugh,' Stella pleaded. 'Just get dressed will you? You're going have to let yourself out...'

'*Get dressed Hugh,*' he mimicked. '*Don't you have to be*

somewhere Hugh? Let yourself out Hugh... Don't keep telling me what to do! I am not your pet poodle!'

Stella closed her eyes and sighed. 'Alright, alright, Hugh,' she said quietly. 'Look, I'm sorry about what I said earlier. You do count, to me, but not to my mum.'

'Why not?' Hugh demanded. 'She doesn't know anything about me!'

'She knows everything about you. Iris told her... Hugh, she's a Catholic and you're a married man. You know what that means. She's an old woman and she's not going to change her beliefs now. To her, you simply don't count.'

'And what about to you?' he asked.

Stella busied herself with her shoes. 'What about, *to me?*' she replied.

'Do I count to you Stella?'

Stella stood up and faced Hugh. 'I love you, Hugh,' she said quietly.

'Yes, but do I count?' he asked. Stella couldn't answer him.

'Well?'

Stella remained silent, thinking.

Hugh exploded. 'Jesus Christ! I suppose I only count in bed... Is that it?

Stella turned away. 'Don't, Hugh.'

'Now, what's the score?' Hugh continued, ignoring her. 'Oh, yes. Once, twice last night; once this morning...'

'Stoppit Hugh!' Stella cried, turning to face him, her eyes blazing for a moment and then softening. 'You know I love you. Isn't that enough, for now?'

'For now, huh?' demanded Hugh, still angry. 'And what about tomorrow, next week, next month, next year? Eh? Tell me about then! You want me to hang around, pop over, go home... just whenever you feel like it.' He paused for breath, before adding, 'Well, if I'm not good enough for your mother, then maybe I'm not good enough for her daughter either.'

'Hugh, I'm going to be late for work,' pleaded Stella. 'Please, can we discuss this later?'

'I'm going to meet this mother of yours,' he threatened, 'and see

just how good *she* is. Maybe the old bat's not good enough for me!'
'Don't be childish,' Stella told him, putting on her coat. 'And
don't call my mother names.' She reached up and planted a kiss on
his mouth. His moustache tasted minty. She noticed that his cock
had shrivelled right up. *Poor man*, she thought. *All these women in
his life must be emasculating him. What he needs is some male
bonding.* 'See you later,' she said.

'We'll see,' he replied under his breath as Stella hurriedly opened
the front door and then slammed it shut after her. 'We'll see, alright,'
he added to himself.

❧❧❧

Sunday afternoon seemed intolerably long. Pierre was lying on his
bed in a cold sweat, naked from the waist up, drops of perspiration
beading his tanned pecs and his mind in turmoil.

'Those fuckers,' he said aloud, idly fondling one nipple, then the
other. 'Those fucking fuckers,' he said, more quietly. He felt his cock
stiffen. *Christ almighty*, he thought, *now a stiffy*. Something bad was
happening to him. Real bad. *I need to relax*, he thought, and quickly
swung his legs off the bed. He moved closer to his one and only
cupboard, in the wall next to his bed, and removed his dope tin from
the bottom shelf where he kept it hidden amongst his dirty laundry.
He opened the tin and removed Rizlas, a piece of white card, a
cigarette and what was left of his stash. *Christ, I'll have to see Dave
again soon and get some more of this wonder weed,* he thought. He
sat on the edge of his bed, a glossy magazine on his knees, and set
about his creation. Two minutes later, he lay back on the pillows and
lit the well-rolled spliff with relish.

The dope took hold after the second drag. Pierre idly rolled the
tip of the joint around the inside lip of the ashtray resting on his
chest. He shrugged down until he was horizontal, his head propped
up on two pillows, and took another drag. He let the smoke fall from
his nostrils in two thick, grey plumes.

He went over it again in his mind. Unable to sleep, he had risen
before dawn, dressed to impress in his sexy black trousers and a
white polo shirt that emphasized both his cock and his biceps, and

then caught a black cab to Bayswater. He'd waited opposite the building for a few minutes composing himself then crossed the road and entered the block of flats through the open front door, walking slowly up the wooden staircase to the first floor, and pressed their bell. Eventually, the woman opened the door. She was even more beautiful than he remembered.

'I've come back to finish what we started,' he said. The woman faltered, but Otto appeared behind her and smiled.

'Come in,' he said, the spider to the fly.

A couple of hours later and he was on his way back home.

In his warped mind, he savoured those couple of hours again and again and again. Each time, a little bit differently. Each time, a little bit more erotically. He looked down, noticed his hard cock and took another drag of his joint, smiled, reached down and took a firm grip. This was going to be a rough ride. And afterwards, or maybe sometime tomorrow, he really would get his revenge on those fuckers, rather than just fantasize about it.

ဢၥ

It was late afternoon when Stella unlocked the door to her flat in Netherhall Gardens. She was exhausted. The Sunday lunchtime crowd in the Hollybush had been particularly demanding and she had spent far too long pushing her way through them, collecting their empty glasses and slopping out their half-eaten roasts. By four it had thinned out enough for her to collect her things from behind the bar and get out, far away from the madness. She was officially employed from noon till 3.30pm on Sundays, plus various shifts in the week, but could never get away on time. Or arrive. Which was one of her problems.

She walked through to her bedroom, threw down her handbag, ripped off her coat and flopped onto the bed. She grunted as she pulled off each tight-fitting shoe and flung them aside, pushed her legs out straight in front of her, like a little girl on a swing, and wiggled both sets of toes. Her stockinged feet looked impossibly small, but exquisite. Stella loved her feet and hated herself for abusing them so. *I really must get a desk job*, she thought, *but then they'd*

34

only get puffy from lack of exercise, she consoled herself and grinned. Thrusting out her legs one more time, she squeezed her firm thighs tightly together and found herself thinking about Hugh, and about last night. Twice, he'd taken her, and once more this morning. She heard his lovely deep voice in her mind; his raised voice, demanding to know whether he counted.

'Of course you count, Hugh,' she said aloud. The problem was her mother. God, her mother! She jumped up and ran to the telephone in the lounge and quickly dialled her sister.

෫෬

'Well, she's coming down in two weeks!' Iris shouted. She'd been on the telephone with Stella for over twenty minutes and they were both near to screaming.

'I'm telling you now,' Stella yelled, 'if that bitch comes down here, I'll end up swingin' for her.'

'Me and you both, for sure,' Iris agreed. 'But, she's coming and we'll have to cope as best we can.'

'Why couldn't you stop her?' cried Stella.

'You've asked me that a hundred times,' Iris said. 'You know why.'

'Oh aye, because ye're soft. And daft.'

'Who are you calling daft?' Iris demanded. 'Who was it who went and fell for a married man? After all what Ma drummed into us as bairns?'

And so the conversation moved on. Their mother was coming *doon* and that was that.

'Well, where's she staying then?' Stella asked, eventually returning to the subject in question.

'She's booked herself into the Post House.'

'My, my, she is splashing out,' Stella remarked, pronouncing it *oot*. With her plucked eyebrows raised, she added worriedly, 'Not the one here in Hampstead?'

'Aye, so she says.'

'Oh, for Jesus Christ. Why the fuck…? Why not in Hackney near you?'

35

'There's not that many Post Houses in Hackney, funnily enough,' Iris replied, her voice dripping with sarcasm.

'Well, why not a B & B then? Actually, come to think about it, why not a B & B? Why a Post House? She's really splashin' out? How come?'

Iris's voice dropped from a shriek to a whisper. 'That's what I wanted to tell you this morning.'

'What d'you mean?'

'She's won the bloody lottery!!' Iris screeched. 'Isn't that something?'

Silence.

'You still there, Stella?

More silence.

'Stella, she's not won millions, if that's what ye're thinking.'

'H...how much?' came a small voice.

'She got five numbers plus the bonus ball,' Iris said in an even voice. 'Or so she says.'

'How bloody much!?'

'On a roll-over,' added Iris, cheerfully ignorant of the fact that this would really only affect the size of the jackpot.

'Iris, how much did she win?' Stella demanded through clenched teeth.

'She reckons she only checked her numbers this morning, daft old cow.'

'IRIS, HOW FUCKING MUCH HAS SHE WON?'

'Wash your mouth out, hen,' scolded Iris, adding, 'Ma wouldn't like that sort of language.'

'If you won't tell me, I'll call her myself,' hissed Stella and promptly hung up.

ॐ

Laura had just finished giving a private flute lesson to one of her star pupils and was busying herself boiling the kettle for a cup of tea. It was so traditional, so English, she thought, to have afternoon tea, especially on a Sunday and with such good company.

'You will stop for a cup of tea, won't you Patrick?' she insisted gently. Her star pupil had entered the kitchen having first cleaned out the saliva and then packed his flute away in its blue velvet-lined box. 'Oh, er sure, Miss Bowles, that would be very nice,' he replied. 'There was something I wanted to discuss with you, anyway.'

'If it's about my charges, I'm sorry, but needs must…'

'No, no,' he interrupted her. 'That's not the problem.'

Laura raised an eyebrow as she spooned loose tea into the teapot. 'There's a problem?'

'Not really a problem, no,' Patrick admitted. 'More of a situation, really, and I'm not sure what to do about it.'

'In that case, you'd better go through into the lounge and I'll be right with you,' she said and began loading cups and saucers and spoons onto a small tray. She eased the top off an old festively-decorated cake tin, revealing a half eaten fruitcake, the other half of which she'd eaten herself, and cut two large slices plus a small taster, which she munched happily as she placed the slices on small plates. Adding the teapot, sugar bowl and milk jug onto the tray, she balanced the two plates on top and carefully walked through into the lounge, swallowing hastily.

'So, Patrick,' she said eagerly, as she sat next to him on the sofa and placed the tray on the coffee table, 'you have a *situation*?'

'Well, yes. I suppose I do,' he replied. He hung his head and seemed to stare longingly at the paisley design on the triangle of sofa exposed between his open thighs.

Laura busied herself with the tea strainer and pot. 'Go on,' she urged, teapot poised.

'Well, you've known me for quite some time now, haven't you Miss Bowles… May I call you Laura?'

'Of course, Patrick. Yes, since you were nine, I believe.'

'That's right. Half my life!' Laura nodded to him, encouraging him to go on. 'Well, when I was nine, everything seemed so simple…And now, well, nothing seems to be.'

'That's because you're more responsible now,' Laura explained. 'And not just *for* yourself, either, you're responsible *to* yourself too, and to others. Am I right?'

Patrick paused, confused. 'Do you mind if I smoke?' he asked.

'Go ahead.'

Patrick took out a packet of Camels, lit one and let out a lungful of grey smoke. The room quickly took on a hazy quality and the furniture appeared grubbier.

'You've cleaned up well since last night,' he said, appraising the room. From what he remembered it had been quite a mess.

'Just bottles mainly,' replied Laura, as she handed him a steaming cup of black tea and gestured to the milk and sugar. 'Some people like to put the milk in first,' she rambled. 'But, I think you can make it too milky that way.' Patrick nodded and accepted the cup. Laura left the cake in place until he'd finished his cigarette.

'So,' she said, leaning back with her tea in one hand, staring at his profile. 'Tell me more.'

Patrick turned to look at her. 'Well...' He took another drag of his cigarette; smoke curling upwards from his nostrils as he continued, 'Me and Gerald are, as you know, *together*, an item, and yes I do love him.' Laura smiled and nodded. 'Well, last night, at your party - which was really great by the way,' he added sincerely, 'I er met someone else - one of your guests - and I think I've fallen in love again.' He looked away and then back at Laura. His eyebrows lifted enquiringly. 'Do you think it's possible to love two people at the same time?'

'Of course, Patrick. But there are many different kinds of love, you know, and don't confuse love with lust. That's something else entirely.'

Patrick shook his head. 'Oh, I know, I know. There's sex and then there's love and then there's sex and love together... I think I know the difference.'

Laura nodded, not so sure that he did. 'We all love somebody or something, a pet, whatever. Take Freud, for instance; I love him with all my heart. And I love you too, Patrick. And we can love many things, all at the same time.'

Patrick listened to Laura. What she said made a sort of sense to his young mind. 'But, can you really want to be with more than one person, possess them both entirely and at the same time?' he asked her.

'Well, that is a bit different,' Laura admitted. 'How do you really feel about Gerald? You say you love him and you say you're *in love* with this stranger. There's a huge difference in the two. You can love someone from afar without too much pain. But, to be *in love* means having to have them near you.'

'I can see that,' Patrick agreed. 'Gerald and I love each other, I guess, but I'm afraid it might be like a puppy with its favourite toy. Show him one that's new and interesting enough and he'll go for it and forget all about his favourite one for the moment. But, of course, he soon goes back to his favourite, because it is his favourite. I'm afraid Gerald doesn't seem to understand this too well.'

'You've discussed this with him?' asked Laura.

'Not in so many words, no.'

'Then, perhaps you should,' she suggested.

'Well, that's just it, Laura... I'm nearly eighteen. I'm not a puppy. Maybe I won't go back to Gerald. Maybe he won't have me anyway, especially if I tell him what I've told you.' Patrick stubbed out his cigarette and took a sip of tea. Laura leaned forward and handed him the slice of fruitcake.

Her mouth full, she said, 'Mmm. Yes, I can see how confused you must be. You do seem to have gotten yourself into a *situation* here. But, does this other person know? I mean, is he - I take it, it is a *he*...?' Laura paused whilst Patrick nodded encouragingly. 'Is... Is he aware of this *situation*?'

'He knows I fancy him... I even told him that I think I love him!'

'And?'

'He told me not to waste it on him; said he wasn't gay.'

'So, why are you pursuing...?'

'Oh, he's gay alright,' Patrick cut in. 'He just hasn't admitted it to himself yet.'

'Mmm... He was at my party, you say?'

'Yes.'

'What was his name?'

'Mark... but I don't know his last name. He said to ask you for his phone number.'

'Oh, did he?' Laura said. 'More tea?'

'Hi Hugh, it's me Stella... Are you there? Please pick up if you are. I have something to tell you... Look, I'm sorry about this morning, I really am... Well, if you're not there, you're not there. Call me when you get this message. Please?'

ಬಂಡ

'Hugh, it's nearly 10.30 so I know you'll be watching Frazier. You and that Comedy Channel! Come on, bloody well pick up will you! Please...? Hugh! HUGH!! Look, I have something important to tell you. It's about my mum... Oh, bugger you then.'

Chapter Four

MONDAY MORNING'S ALARM CALL pulled Mark from a crazy dream that he instantly forgot. He hit snooze, then slumped back into the warmth, pulling the duvet tightly around his shoulders, and drifted. Nine minutes later, it happened again. This time he was decidedly groggy. He moaned inwardly, pushed back the duvet and forced himself into a sitting position. Grabbing his towel and toiletries, he left his bed-sit and found the bathroom occupied.

'Won't be a mo,' came a feminine voice from within. Five minutes later, Vivienne emerged, a towel imitating a turban on her head with another, larger towel, squeezing her boobs. She smelled of apples.

'Morning, Mark,' she said sweetly and smiled at him. 'Sorry, I over ran a little.'

'No problem,' mumbled Mark, his tone a little brusque. Now, what was the point in having a rota if nobody stuck to it? He smiled past her and into the apple fog. He cursed silently and went in. The mirror was beaded with condensation. He gave it a wipe with a dry flannel. Condensation immediately returned. It was like trying to dig a hole in a sugar bowl. He sighed and decided to use his electric shaver in his room later. Turning on the shower, he dropped his towel and stepped into the white enamelled bath, pulling the plastic shower curtain around the inside rim. Five minutes later, he was back in his room with five minutes to spare before the next guy was due to ablute.

Breakfast was a meagre bowl of muesli. Someone, and he could not be certain who, had used up most of his milk. The bastards! The sooner he found a better place to live, the better. His intention had only been to stay short-term anyway. He decided to call his landlord that day and give notice. Then he calmed down and told himself that it was quite central and reasonably cheap and that he could put up with it for a while yet. Feeling better, he selected a burgundy and dark blue tie, donned his city suit, picked up his suitcase, left the building and strode briskly towards the tube station. He turned down Porchester Mews and stopped abruptly. A barrier had been erected across the width of the road and a policewoman was dutifully informing all pedestrians and street-users that the area was officially sealed off. No, she did not know for how long and, No, she could not say why. She appeared to be a bit tense. Further down the road, four police cars and a mobile forensics unit were parked in a semi-circle outside a block of well-maintained late Victorian flats. There was a bicycle chained to the railings outside.

The policewoman shuffled her feet. 'Move along, now,' she prompted. 'You can take a quick detour via the next road down on your right... Move along now.'

Mark did so. As he moved along, a voice spoke in his ear, 'Nasty business, eh?'

Mark turned to meet the eager prying face of another *City Gent*. Mark had to hide a smile as he noted the archetypal pinstriped suit, briefcase and tiny rimless glasses perched at the end of his strawberry nose. He was attempting to hold in his paunch using bright red braces almost an inch wide and looked close to forty years old but sounded much younger.

'What's going on?' asked Mark. They turned into the parallel road and headed down it towards the station.

'Police knocked on my door yesterday evening,' the man replied, panting to keep up. 'Told me that a murder enquiry was underway and had I seen or heard anything unusual over the weekend.'

'A murder enquiry?' repeated Mark.

'Yes... Hey, slow down old chap!'

Mark slowed slightly.

The man continued, still panting. 'Apparently a young man was found mutilated early yesterday morning by the cleaning lady, or so I heard. I think it's the work of the gay serial killer.'

'God, how awful!'

Leaning closer, the man continued darkly, 'Funny time for a cleaning lady, if you ask me, especially on a Sunday! Mind you, there're some funny goings-on in that block. Some of the flats are rented out by the hour, no questions asked - know what I mean?' he nudged Mark with his elbow and winked.

'How do you know that?'

'You keep your ear to the ground, you hear things.'

'Did you tell the police?'

'Too bloody right, I did!' the man said righteously. 'I've been waiting for something like this to happen.'

Yes, I bet you have, thought Mark. They arrived at the tube station and parted at the barrier. Mark bought a copy of *The Guardian* at his usual kiosk but there was no mention of the murder yet. He ploughed his way down the escalator towards the Circle line platform. The warm rushing wind heralded the tube's arrival and as soon as the doors parted he surged on with the flow. It was unbearably warm inside and all seats were taken. He clung to a wobbly knob that hung like a stalactite from the roof and tried to read the front page. Wedged between his fellow commuters, all he could think about were the victims of this cold and callous murderer and how disturbed his mind must be.

Mark changed tubes at Baker Street onto the Bakerloo line and exited to street level at Oxford Circus. It was a short brisk walk to the offices of Berkeley Price & Simpson, Chartered Accountants. He entered through the double doors and grunted a reply to the cheery receptionist's morning greeting. He caught the lift to the fifth floor and stepped out into the empty audit room. Grabbing a cup of warm coffee from the dispenser, he stalked over to his desk and opened his briefcase, removed his Parker roller-ball pen and calculator and then felt a little better. Nothing like a bit of tedious routine to relieve a shaken mind.

Fiona, the audit secretary, hurried over to him.

'Morning,' she said brightly and gave him a broad smile. She looked stunning as usual. Tall, bobbed chestnut hair and an aerobic toned figure, Mark often told her she should have been a model. She was holding a stack of grey audit files in her arms.

'Hi Fi,' he said and found himself smiling back.

'Reception said you were in a foul mood.'

'That was quick work.' He looked away, the smile gone.

Through the glass window, the British Telecom tower near Warren Street blinked at him. Once, twice, again. The light was blood red.

'Mark? Come in Mark?' prompted Fiona.

He turned back abruptly. 'Oh, er, sorry Fi. There's been another murder – right near where I live. The police have sealed off the area.'

She screwed up her face and became more beautiful. 'Oh, dear.'

'It looks like it's the work of the gay serial killer.'

'Well, you're safe then!' she said, smiling and looking even more beautiful.

Mark said nothing. His sex life wasn't common knowledge at work. Not that there was much to tell.

'Anyway, there's not much point thinking about it now. You're scheduled for the Inner City Re-Housing Association audit this week.'

Mark sighed. A week with the less desirables! The ICRA offered sheltered housing to society's problem tenants. People who, for one reason or another, found it difficult to integrate into the community – drug addicts, psychiatric patients and ex-petty criminals mostly, who found it difficult to get a job and were often in arrears with their rent. The ICRA didn't seem to find this a problem; only the auditors did. He sighed again.

'Who's coming with me?'

'No one. You're on your own. This will be the first on your own. The partners think you're ready.'

Mark mugged a face. 'Well, fancy that,' he said. 'I take it it's only an interim?'

Fiona shot him her most winning smile. 'Don't put yourself down,' she chided. 'This is the full audit.' She dumped the grey files on the table in front of him. 'Here you are. Now, you'd better start reading - your brief's at ten with Donald.'

Mark feigned a star-struck pose. 'Senior partner stuff, eh?'

'Yes, so you'd better look sharp… Oh, and stop thinking about this murder thing; you don't want to sound distracted in front of Donald.'

'Yes, Ma'am!' Mark saluted as he watched her move back to her office. What a lovely bum, he thought.

ഌ

Mark's meeting with Donald passed without serious incident. The senior partner of Berkeley Price & Simpson was a lofty, upright Surrey man with a most peculiar squint. He smiled continuously and pursed his lips occasionally in a manner suggesting that he was privy to an enormous secret, and you were not. This was not his intention at all and he would have been most alarmed if he knew of the impression he gave. He was a gentleman of the *old school* and more than tolerable.

'So, you do understand,' Donald concluded in his crisp Surrey accent, 'the future of this audit, indeed our future interests in housing associations *per se*, rests in your capable hands... You see, we have to make a profit this year, despite an even tighter budget than last year, and that is why you must go it alone. You are as capable of carrying out this audit as any one of our seniors, but your charge-out rate is substantially lower. You do understand, don't you?'

Mark nodded. Donald closed both eyes, clenched them and, with his inevitable squint over until the next urge took him, held out his hand to Mark who caught a brief insight into the way a novice lion-tamer would feel, given his first time alone in the ring. His hand was clasped firmly and briefly.

'Good man. Right, send Fiona in would you?'

He was dismissed.

৪১উ

Laden down with last year's audit files, his briefcase and the burden of the future of housing association audits *per se*, Mark hailed a cab from Regent Street North, right next to the BBC, and was soon taxiing eastwards along the Euston Road towards Islington.

Twenty minutes later, he paid the cabbie, claimed a receipt for petty cash, and gazed somewhat dismayed at the grubby three-storey townhouse that constituted the nerve centre of the Inner City Re-Housing Association. Judging from the shabby types Mark saw leaving the building, it doubled as a community doss-house. Feeling out of place in his pinstriped city suit, he strode purposefully up to the front door and rang the bell.

The door opened immediately, which took him by surprise. A small frail looking old woman with a shock of dyed blonde hair, the grey roots clearly visible, and bright red lipstick smeared above, on and below her lips, snarled at him. The house must be full of nutters. Mark stepped back in alarm.

The woman then grinned widely and started yelling and singing at the same time, 'So, you've come to take me away, ha ha, he he, ho hum, to the funny farm where...'

'Margaret!!' screamed a man's voice from within. 'Now, you just stop that, do you hear?' The voice became clearer and louder, as if it were coming from a long tunnel and moving rapidly closer, then the door swung wide and an extraordinarily tall man, wearing wire-rim glasses and a green jacket with wide lapels and brown arm patches, extended his hand. 'You must be the auditors,' he said, revealing dark yellow teeth. 'The name's John - John Taylor. I'm the accountant.'

Mark found his voice. 'Auditor,' he corrected. 'Just the one, Mr Taylor.'

'Oh, call me John, please. Come in, dear boy, come in.'

ഇൽ

It was almost one o'clock when Mark leaned back in his chair and surveyed the cramped upstairs room that was the financial nerve centre of the ICRA. On the wall in front of him were open bookshelves stuffed full of Tolley's tax tables, statements of accounting practice, legal books, Microsoft Excel for Windows and numerous other manuals. His desk, shoved up against the corner, gave him a window seat but not much of a view. The back garden was small and overgrown and ended abruptly in a high brick wall that formed the back end of a small factory building. The sound of sheet metal being hammered into shape was constant but not too distracting. Besides, his mind was on the crime scene investigation he'd stumbled upon that morning. A murder had taken place just a few blocks from where he lived. How close was that! Still, it was London and statistically quite likely to happen in front of him sooner or later. His mother had warned him to be careful living in London.

The sudden ringing of the doorbell made him jump, its hollow chimes sounding like a funeral march. Moments later, he heard, 'So you're coming to take me away, ha ha, hee hee ...' followed by

John's scream, 'Margaret!!!' Mark smiled to himself and glanced at his watch. Almost one o'clock - lunchtime at last. He shuffled the few fixed assets papers he'd been auditing and laid them neatly aside, put his calculator and pen into his briefcase and closed and locked it. *One can never be too careful*, he thought, especially in a house full of supposedly reformed criminals and hopelessly incurable nutters.

He lifted his eyes to the ceiling as Margaret started up again... 'To the funny farm, where...' Then he heard a new voice. It was deep and masculine with an accent from the Highlands and it said soothingly, 'Now Margaret, it's only me, Jock.'

Mark opened the door and stepped out onto the dimly lit landing. There were three other doors between him and the top of the stairs. One of them, slightly ajar, was the bathroom.

'We've got the auditors in today, Jock,' came John's voice from below.

Just the one! Mark thought and stifled a giggle. He didn't want to be caught eavesdropping on the first day of the audit. 'Come upstairs; I'll introduce you.'

Mark started forward and reached the end of the landing just as John and Jock started up the stairs. Margaret was nowhere in sight.

'Ah, there you are,' John boomed, coming to an abrupt halt so that Jock almost collided into him from behind. 'You coming down? I want to introduce you to Jock here.'

'Yes, it's lunchtime,' Mark said. 'I thought I'd grab a sandwich.' He started down the staircase and joined John and Jock at the bottom.

'Goodness me, is that the time?' John introduced the two men. 'Jock's ... er... our voluntary gardener and er... legal advisor. Jock, this is Mark. He's er... the auditor.' Singular.

Mark noticed that Jock had large, hairy hands as his own hand was crushed and shaken. Jock's face was rugged and handsome. His eyes were green, his skin tanned and his full lips were guarded by a thick, black moustache, untrimmed. He looked thirty, but was probably closer to forty.

'A sandwich, you say?' said John into the silence. 'Well, look... Jock, let me give you some petty cash and you can take Mark to the *Edward* for a ploughman's. What do you say?'

'Och, are you sure about the *Edward*?'

'Erm, maybe not. How about the *George*?'

'Fine by me… Mark?'

Mark nodded. 'Yeah, sure, that sounds great. Thank you.'

'Good, that's settled then.' John started up the stairs. 'I'll just get you some petty cash.' He returned a few moments later with a crumpled ten-pound note that he smoothed out and handed to Jock. 'Be sure and get receipts,' he said. 'We don't want to upset the auditors by not having receipts, now do we?' He chuckled to himself as he led them to the front door. 'Enjoy yourselves. Don't be too long.'

'We'll be back in time for afternoon tea,' laughed Jock as he turned right onto the pavement and waited for Mark. They walked along Upper Street side-by-side.

'So, what's wrong with the Edward? Mark asked, breaking the silence

'Och, well. It's just a wee bit unusual,' Jock replied.

'How do you mean, *unusual*?'

'Just a wee bit different, that's all. Great food, mind.'

'What, better food than the George?'

'Aye, much.'

'Is it far?'

'What, the Edward or the George?'

'Either; both?'

'The George is a wee bit further on.'

'Right, so the way I see it,' summed up Mark, 'is either we can go to the Edward, which is closer and where the food is much better, or we can go to the George, which is further away and where the food is worse. That's a difficult one, that.'

Jock chuckled. 'Och aye, but the Edward's a wee bit unusual.'

'How? Horrible decor; dirty?'

'Noo, noo, quite the opposite in fact.'

'A bit rough then - the patrons, I mean?'

'Some nights they can be,' Jock admitted with a wry grin.

'And at lunchtimes?' prompted Mark.

They had walked about a hundred metres. Jock stopped and pointed across the road and up a side street, 'Well, it's up there, the Edward,' he said. They paused for a moment.

'Well, come on,' said Mark, 'I don't mind a bit of rough.'

Jock eyed him speculatively and then led Mark across the busy main road and up the side street. 'Well, don't blame me.' 'I won't.' His smile hid his true thoughts. What the hell was he doing? He couldn't understand why he'd so badly wanted to go to the Edward. Perhaps it was because Jock had been so reluctant to take him there. Maybe it was just that he wanted to see what it was that this handsome Jock hadn't wanted him to see; hadn't wanted him to know. It was all very mysterious.

He was still musing when Jock pushed open the door and gestured for him to go in first. As he went in, Mark felt the warmer, smoky air tinged with a pleasant beery odour wash over him. The music, though frenetically up-tempo, was low and tinny. Something by 2 Unlimited or Snap, if his early teenage memory was working right. There was nothing unusual about the place at all, so far.

Jock passed him and headed for the bar. A tall blonde barmaid beamed the moment she saw him and turned to greet him like a long lost lover. A half-finished cigarette with a rim of bright red on its filter was left smouldering in an ashtray.

'Jock, sweetheart, lovely to see you. Ooh, and who is this gorgeous piece of manhood?' she gushed.

Mark knew, instantly, from the gravel in her voice that this was no ordinary barmaid.

'Och, this is Mark,' replied Jock. 'He's an accountant.'

'A city gent, no less?' she enquired, raising one eyebrow. 'I do love a man in a suit.' She held out her hand to Mark. He didn't know whether to shake it or kiss it. He decided to be daring.

'Ooh, how lovely… Marilyn, I'm sure,' she squealed. 'Now lads, what's it to be? Me - or something from the bar?'

Jock turned to Mark. 'Well?'

'Orange juice and lemonade, please,' replied Mark uncertainly and blushed.

'I knew it,' Marilyn moaned. 'It's this hideous dress, isn't it? You don't like my dress!' She pretended to half-faint.

'Och, it's a lovely dress,' said Jock, good-humouredly. 'We're just thirsty, for now. I'll have a pint o' yer best.'

'I'll believe you this time,' said Marilyn, recovering quickly. She laughed and turned to fetch the drinks.

'I see what you mean,' Mark whispered.

'Don't say I didn't warn you,' Jock whispered back. 'Now, let's take a look at the grub.'

Mark followed him over to the cold food display and they both chose a Ploughman's, except Mark asked for mayonnaise instead of pickle. Marilyn produced a red ticket with the number 9 on it. Jock took it and led Mark over to a corner table. Marilyn followed shortly afterwards with their food and drinks and a proper receipt.

'Enjoy it, loves,' she said and winked at Mark.

'I think you're in there, lad,' Jock said as Marilyn retreated, bum wiggling.

Mark laughed.

They settled down comfortably. Jock removed the tray to give them more room on the small, highly polished table and they hunkered over their meal, pulling apart the crusty French bread with bare hands. Jock took a sip of beer, leaving a white foam trail along his moustache. He casually sucked it off.

'Mmm, great pint,' he murmured. 'You do drink? Generally, I mean?'

'Oh yes,' Mark assured him. 'But never when I'm working. If I drink at lunchtime, I'm useless in the afternoon. And I don't think the clients would appreciate that, considering how much I'm costing them.'

Jock nodded, his head bobbing up and down just a few inches from Mark's face. 'You like your job?' he asked.

'Yeah, apart from the studying,' Mark replied candidly. 'I'm expected to work a full day, then go home and study all night *and* at weekends.' He took a sip of his drink. 'It gets a bit much sometimes.'

'Och, well, life's a bitch,' Jock said bluntly.

'Then you marry one,' finished Mark. 'Or not, as the case may be.'

Jock raised an eyebrow. Mark blushed. Something unspoken had passed between them.

It was 4.30pm. Mark sighed as he ticked off yet another cheque stub to its corresponding entry on the bank statement. He put down his pen and stared out of the window to his left. Not much inspiration there, but it was restful and allowed him to think. It had turned out to be quite an interesting day in the life of one young trainee Chartered Accountant. Firstly, that shocking business this morning, so close to home - it made his skin crawl just thinking about it. Then his meeting with Donald, the firm's senior partner. It seemed he was being singled out for possible promotion, if he managed to complete this housing association audit within budget. Next, the housing association itself and the mad woman who *they* were coming to take away. The sooner, the better, in Mark's opinion. And finally, and far more significantly, the welcome appearance of the handsome Jock. Mark pictured him sipping the beery froth from his hairy black moustache and felt a tightening in his lower abdomen. He wondered if he'd ever see him again after today.

In another hour or so he'd be on his way home and Mark felt gloomy at the thought. He was going to have to study all evening, and every other evening and most of the weekends, if he was going to have even a remote chance of passing his fast-looming exams. He sighed and ticked off another entry from the cheque stub to the bank statement.

An unexpected knock on the door made him jump. 'Come in,' he called.

Jock put his head around the door. 'Sorry to disturb you,' he said, not looking at all sorry, 'John's already left for the evening - he said he'd see you tomorrow - and I shall be locking up in about 10 minutes.'

'Oh.'

'Is that OK?'

'Yes, yes fine,' Mark managed. *Bloody great*, he thought. *Fantastic, in fact. They start late and leave early. Perfect!*

'Righto,' said Jock. 'See you downstairs in a few minutes then, ok?'

'Ok.'

Jock withdrew his head and closed the door. Mark opened his briefcase and threw everything inside, locked it, had a quick pee in the men's small loo on the landing, which was surprisingly clean considering the number of times Mark had heard the chain being pulled, threw on his jacket and was downstairs all within the space of two minutes.

Jock was waiting for him in the hall. 'All set then?' he asked.

'Just about.'

'Righto. You getting the tube?'

Mark nodded.

'Good, then I'll show you the way. Follow me.'

Mark already knew the way. He'd seen the tube station from the back of the cab that morning but he said nothing as he followed Jock through the front door. Jock locked the door and then they turned right onto Upper Street.

'I've just got to drop the keys off,' Jock explained as they took a side street. 'John lives up here.'

'No problem.' They strode along, side by side. 'Don't they trust you with the keys then?'

Jock laughed out loud. 'Ha! Fat lot they've got to nick. That ten quid we used for lunch is the most they've ever got in the safe and the computer system's way past its sell-by-date. No, I've got to drop the keys off because I only come in on a Monday... I won't be back again this week.'

'Oh,' Mark said. 'That's a shame. Who am I going to have lunch with tomorrow?'

Jock turned to him coyly. 'Never mind lunch tomorrow,' he replied. 'Who're you having dinner with tonight?'

'Nobody,' Mark said quickly. 'I had planned to do some studying.'

'Plans are made to be broken,' Jock said. He stopped outside a plain black wooden door that opened directly onto the street and stooped to shove the keys through the letter box. Mark noticed that Jock had a very well-defined V shape to his back and a beautiful close-cropped natural neckline. He felt another tightening in his lower abdomen.

'So, what do you fancy?' asked Jock, straightening up and leading him back towards Upper Street.

'P... Pardon?' Mark was confused and a little embarrassed by the question. His cheeks turned a pinker shade of crimson.

'Italian, Indian...Scottish?' Jock gave a wide shrug of his shoulders, his hands open and pointing to the sky. 'Whatever you want.'

'Oh,' said Mark, relieved. 'Scottish?' he queried.

'I do a mean Haggis,' Jock boasted. 'Always keep one in the freezer. They don't take long if you microwave them first.'

Mark pulled a face.

'It's not that bad,' Jock continued, amused at Mark's turned up nose. 'Tastes great with gravy, tatties and neeps.'

'I'm sure.'

'You don't fancy it?' asked Jock. 'Don't worry, I won't be offended.'

'Not really,' said Mark being honest.

They were approaching the Angel tube station. 'Well, I'll see what else I can rustle up. Come on, I live just past this junction.'

They waited for the lights to change, crossed over in front of the tube station and into Goswell Road. Eventually, they arrived outside a terraced house in Spencer Street.

'Here we are,' Jock announced. He led the way down a few steep concrete steps that showed signs of neglect. They were cracked in places and weeds were taking full advantage. A large hydrangea bush grew unchecked, half-blocking their descent. Mark pushed past it and heard the jangle of keys. Moments later he was being ushered inside.

The house was small, clean and smelled of a plug-in air freshener. There was a steep staircase to the right and a dark hallway that ended in a light airy kitchen, whilst off to the left a lounge cum diner ran from front to back with patio doors leading out onto a raised garden. The small patio was crowded with a white plastic table and four chairs. The garden was well-tended, mainly grassed and faced due south. Early evening sunlight struck the far eastern corner.

'It's very nice,' Mark mused. 'Have you lived here long?'

'Just moved in,' Jock replied. 'Here, let me take your briefcase and jacket.' He deposited them in the hallway. 'Now, you wanna drink, first?'

'First?' Mark queried. Jock threw him a mesmerising sideways glance, his moustache quivering thoughtfully. 'Yeah, or a joint first. Which will it be?'

'Both, I think.'

Jock beamed and led Mark through into the kitchen. 'That's that settled then. Beer or wine? Nothing much else.'

'Beer's fine.'

'Good. Go through to the lounge and make yourself at home; I'll be right with you.'

Mark did as he was instructed. The lounge was the front part of the open plan room hidden from prying eyes by white net curtains slung from top to bottom of a bay-fronted window. Mark was gazing out at the steep concrete steps and a clay brick wall that ran parallel to the road as Jock appeared with two open bottles of Becks. He handed one to Mark.

'Care to sit?' he suggested, indicating the large burgundy coloured sofa. Mark sank into it, his knees somewhat higher than his bottom. Jock plonked himself down beside Mark and set his Becks down on the pine coffee table in front of them.

'Voilà!' he said, and produced a nicely rolled joint. 'Got us a little number already rolled,' he smiled and put it to his lips, burying the end in his thick black moustache. He lit it and took a lungful, held it a few moments and then exhaled through his nostrils.

'Aah, that feels good,' he said. He took another toke and passed it to Mark. They passed it back and forth in an easy silence.

Sitting there, with his eyes losing focus, his knees weakening and his mind full of delicious thoughts, Mark cast a glance at Jock. He seemed to be in another world too as his unfocussed eyes locked with Mark's. He leaned a little closer.

'Phew, this is good stuff,' said Mark, breaking the moment. Jock leaned backwards, his head rolling almost onto Mark's shoulder. Mark leaned forward, resting his arms on his knees.

'What's the problem?'

'I… I feel a little dizzy; it's no problem,' Mark replied, resting his head in his hands.

Jock immediately sat up and put his right arm around him. 'Just keep your eyes fixed on something,' he insisted, hugging him reassuringly.

'I would if I could focus,' Mark snorted. His head began to feel a little better and his eyes stopped juddering when he tried to focus. He leaned back and fell into the nook of Jock's arm. It felt very comfortable and satisfying somehow and it gave him an instant erection. Jock didn't seem to notice. He had an instant erection himself holding his attention. They sat with eyes closed, silent except for their subtle breaths, enjoying the close familiarity of each other, neither moving for several minutes.

'Well,' Mark said opening his eyes eventually, 'this wasn't what I expected.'

Jock looked at him. 'You expected dinner?'

Mark shook his head. 'Wasn't what I meant.'

'What then?'

Mark sat up straight. 'Doesn't matter,' he said. After a moment, he added, 'Can I ask you a direct question?'

'If you like,' replied Jock. 'Though you might not get a direct answer.'

'Are you trying to seduce me?'

'Do I have to try?'

'To tell you the truth, I don't really know. I've never been to bed with a man. I've fooled around a bit, but nothing more...'

Jock was clearly surprised. 'How old are you?'

'Twenty-three.'

'And you've not had sex yet?'

'Not with a man, no.'

'But you have with a woman?'

Mark nodded.

'Well, thank god for that. I thought for a moment you were either highly religious or just plain weird!'

Mark laughed. 'It's not weird to save yourself, you know.'

'It is for a gay man. After all, he can't be saving himself till he's married, now can he?'

'Well, that's all about to change.'

'Granted, but that's a new consideration.'

Mark conceded the point. 'Ok, you're right. I guess it just hasn't interested me enough.'

'And now..?'

'Well, like I said, it's not what I expected. I only ever seem to find straight men attractive. The men that've come on to me haven't aroused me one little bit - until now, that is... Are you sure you're not straight?'

Jock laughed and nodded his head towards his crotch. Mark glanced down and saw a fairly hefty bulge pressing against the denim of Jock's jeans. He looked up as Jock leaned closer and he felt Jock's bristly moustache touch his lips. Jock used his arm around Mark's neck to gently force their mouths together. Mark felt the hot probing tongue and opened his mouth wide. He felt Jock's moustache envelop his whole mouth and his stubbly chin rasp against his own day's growth. It was perhaps the most exciting moment of his entire life and he surrendered himself completely. The thrill in this action left him gasping for more.

The telephone rang.

'Ignore it,' mumbled Jock, his breath smelled of musk. Mark wanted to inhale it. The ringing continued as Jock enveloped Mark in his strong, heavily muscled arms, and then the answering machine cut in.

'Hi, can't come to the phone right now, please leave a message after the beep...BEEP.'

'Hugh, for fuck's sake it's me, Stella. Pick up will you!? Please pick up... Look, why aren't you returning my calls? I have some really important news. Didn't want to tell you on the phone, but... well, my mum's won the bloody lottery and she's coming down in the next week or so. Call me back soon... Love you.'

Frozen rigid, Mark was unable to even breathe. All of the numbers suddenly tumbled into place. That was Stella - this was Hugh - he was Mark.

Hugh hadn't reacted, yet.

'Sorry about that,' Jock said finally.

Mark nodded numbly. 'I... I think I'd better go,' he said and got up unsteadily.

'What? Why? She's only a friend, nothing more.' Jock looked puzzled.

'I have to go,' said Mark more firmly and, grabbing his jacket and briefcase from the hall, was out onto the street before Jock or Hugh or whatever his bloody name was could stop him. He hurried to the tube station completely numb and joined the rush hour commuters.

Mark left the tube at Bayswater and walked home deep in thought. *Fuck, what a situation.* He paused at the entrance to Porchester Mews. A makeshift police barrier still sealed off the road from traffic, but pedestrians were allowed through. Evidently, the murder investigation was still going on.

He started to walk up the mews and then noticed a familiar figure approaching from the opposite direction. The figure stared at him momentarily and then quickly looked away. Mark thought he recognised the face. The young man hurried off in the direction of the tube.

Mark continued up the mews, trying hard to place the face. Then he forgot all about it as he reached the building where the murder had taken place. A mobile police investigation unit had been installed between the rows of cars on either side of the road. Small wonder that the avenue was sealed off to traffic. He looked but couldn't see any signs of activity either from the unit or from the house and so he passed by unhindered.

As he continued up Porchester Mews, he suddenly stopped. *Yes,* he thought. That guy - he did know him, or rather knew of him. He was sure he'd seen him on the stairs in Netherhall the other evening wearing leather jeans and a green top. The same evening that Laura had pointed a gun at him. What a small world!

₧

'Shit, shit, shit, shit, shit. Fuck, fuck, fuck, fuck, fuck. Shit, shit, shit, shit, shit.' These were the eloquent words hissing from Pierre's mouth as he hurried towards Bayswater tube station. Had he been recognised by the guy in the suit? The same guy he'd seen running out of Netherhall last Friday evening? The one who looked so much like him? And what the fuck were the police doing outside and, presumably, inside that weird couple's flat? What in God's name was going on?

As he approached the tube station, an Evening Standard headline grabbed his attention: *MURDERED MAN IN FASHIONABLE BAYSWATER MANSION.* Pierre found some coins and grabbed a copy. He read: *Another young man's body was found mutilated beyond recognition, this time in an exclusive residential area of Bayswater, in the early hours of yesterday morning. The murdered man, thought to be in his early twenties, is the fourth victim in as many weeks to be...* Pierre read on, oblivious to the stares from passersby that skirted him warily as he stood muttering, 'Oh my God,' to himself over and over again.

It could have been him!

He read on, then gasped aloud at: *...Unconfirmed reports indicate that a counterfeit £50 note had been found pinned to the man's naked chest...*

'Oh, shit, oh shit, oh shit!!!' He fingered the three fake £50 notes in his pocket and swore again, too loudly, and suddenly became aware of people staring at him. Folding the paper, he darted into the station.

Chapter Five

TUESDAY'S TABLOIDS carried the full story. Mark was standing on the crowded Circle line, his briefcase on the floor between his legs, hanging onto the metal handrail, reading the headlines on the front page of the *Independent* this time. A murder hunt was in progress and more gruesome details were given; though not the full picture by any means, Mark suspected. Still, the details given were enough to make him wish he had a seat. He looked up from his paper and stared unseeing over the various shaped heads of his fellow commuters. It wasn't just the murder or the guy who lived in Stella's house playing on his mind, there was Hugh or Jock (or whatever he called himself today) running through his thoughts. What would have happened if he'd gone to bed with him and then found out it was Stella's boyfriend? How would he have felt then? How would Stella react? If she ever found out, would she laugh or cry or have hysterics? Probably all three in one. And, to top it all, she'd said that her mother had won *the bloody lottery*! Was Stella now heiress to a fortune?

He was snapped abruptly from his musings as the tube train pulled into the Angel station. He fought his way through the commuters who were staying on the train to the City, stumbling over feet and bags. Once on the platform, he shuffled out and up the long escalator. Usually he walked or ran up escalators: today he felt far too drained for enthusiasm of that nature and slowly rode to the top with the rest of the crowd.

Mark walked along Upper Street, past the side street where John lived and was soon outside the Inner City Re-Housing Association. He sighed, squared his shoulders and walked up to the front door, pressed the bell and expected to hear, 'They're coming to take me away ha ha hee hee...' followed by 'Margaret!!' but he was greeted only by silence. He pressed the bell again. He looked at his watch. It was a quarter to nine. He sighed again and resigned himself to wait.

ഇഐ

Mid-morning found Laura in a buoyant mood. She tra la la'ed to herself as the kettle whistled, gently at first and then a merry crescendo as it reached boiling point on the kitchen hob. Sunlight filtered in through the jungle outside the windows of her lounge cum diner cum sitting room, highlighting the flurry of dust motes that she was pounding into the air. *There's nothing like a spot of late spring cleaning to raise the spirits*, she thought, *particularly after a wildly successful party*.

She heard the main doorbell chime at the front of the house and ignored it. *Let some other lazy bugger in the house answer it for once*, she thought. Anyone who knew her well enough would come around to her own private back door, so it probably wasn't for her. Still, she crept into the dark hallway and opened her passageway door - the one that led up to the main hallway and swept majestically on up to the rest of the house. She listened as the bell sounded again, much louder this time.

She sighed and was about to climb the stairs when she heard another door open from higher up the house, followed by light footsteps on the stairs. After a while she heard voices.

'Hello, can I help you?' It was Stella, sounding very sleepy.

There was a man's cough. 'I hope so. Does Mr Carter live here?'

'No idea,' Stella replied. 'So many live here. Sorry.'

'His full name's Mark Carter,' the voice said. It was a very familiar voice.

'You mean *Mark*?'

'Yes, Mark Carter.'

Laura shot out of her door and, despite her ample bulk, was up the stairs in moments. She hurried to the front door and, pushing Stella roughly aside, flung the door wide open.

'Glen!' she bellowed theatrically. 'Hello.'

'Why, Laura, do you live here as well?' he asked, surprised.

'No, just me,' Laura replied, laughing as if he'd just told a hugely funny joke.

'And me,' said Stella, annoyed.

'Yes, and my friend Stella here,' Laura admitted grandly.

Glen looked puzzled. 'And Mark?'

'Mark lives in Bayswater,' Stella cut in.

'Oh,' said Glen. 'This is the address he gave to the supermarket last Saturday.'

'No, I did that,' Laura admitted. 'I didn't know his full address, you see - we'd only just met - and I guess he was too out of it to think straight, so I gave mine.' Glen looked disappointed. 'But, hey, come in, I'm just making some coffee.'

'Erm, w... well I...I have to be back at work soon,' Glen stammered.

'A strong cup of coffee will get you moving twice as fast,' Laura insisted. 'Now, come on in.'

Glen couldn't see a polite way to refuse and, besides, he wanted Mark's address.

'Won't you join us, Stella?' Laura asked. Stella was taken aback. Here was Laura, faced with the chance to be alone with an absolutely gorgeous hunk of masculinity and she was asking Stella to join them? She was so shocked that she agreed, then regretted her hastiness as Laura raised her enormous eyebrows. Only Glen appeared to have missed the squelch of her hormones.

'Well, come on through. Just follow me,' Laura said, leading the way. 'Isn't this cosy?' She headed for the kettle, still boiling its merry way on the hob. Stella and Glen walked through into the lounge, Stella flirting madly although Glen didn't seem to notice. Laura suppressed a smile as she took her cafetière down from the cupboard, hefted three level scoops of coarsely ground coffee into it and poured on the boiling water, expecting any second for it to crack and scald her to death. Oh well, at least Glen was here to save her. What a silly notion! She continued tra la la'ing as she took down the remains of the cake, dividing it into three small slices on top of plates and loading the tray.

Glen rose from his seat beside Stella to assist Laura with the heavy tray.

'No need, no need,' she told him. 'Just clear a space for me on the coffee table, if you would.'

Both Stella and Glen dived for the table, Stella giggling as they bumped shoulders. Laura glared at her, set down the tray and sat next to her, Glen retiring to the easy chair. The chair was absolutely covered in cat hairs, he noticed.

'So,' Laura said, 'we'll just wait a moment for the coffee to draw. Now, Glen, what was it you wanted with our dear friend Mark?'

Stella shot her a glance. 'He's more *my* friend, actually,' she said.

'Oh,' replied Glen uncomfortably, visibly reddening. 'Er, well, you know…just wanted to make sure he's alright after his… er… his fainting fit.'

'Of course,' Laura said. 'You're very kind. He's fine as far as I know. Stella?'

'Ooh, aye, well enough,' Stella confirmed, nodding vigorously.

'I'm glad,' said Glen, adding, 'Do you have his address? I would like to contact him personally. Customer care is taken very seriously at Waitrose, you know.'

'Of course, I'm very pleased to hear that but, unfortunately, I don't have it,' Laura explained. 'Stella?'

'Not off the top of my head, no...'

'Say!' exclaimed Laura. 'I'm having a dinner party a week on Saturday; why don't you come Glen? Mark'll be there; Stella too.'

Glen brightened. 'Well, that would be great, thanks,' he said and beamed. 'If it's no trouble…'

'None at all!' Laura replied enthusiastically, plunging the cafetière. 'It would be a pleasure… Now, how do you like your coffee?'

ഇന്ദ

Hugh had a number of jobs, mostly involving law. He was a qualified barrister, a law lecturer, wrote articles for a number of journals and also helped out in the community. He'd never had a problem concentrating in his life. Until now. He was standing at the back of a classroom full of young offenders, housed within the secure confines of the Islington Detention Centre, his arms folded, casting slow glances from left to right. As he ambled quietly towards the front of the class, he fought to stay focused on the task at hand: invigilating a mock exam, but his thoughts had other ideas. They were doggedly drifting back to the previous evening and to Mark. The backs of these young delinquents' heads were of all shapes, sizes and colours, but almost without exception were shaved or number one crops. None, however, had the masculine attraction of Mark's. Mark had passed that magical point of no return when the young male emerges as an adult male. And in Mark's case, a very horny one.

Hugh suddenly found himself staring at the wall at the front of the class and he looked up in horror at the clock. He spun round and yelled, 'Right you lot, time's up, put your pens down! Make sure your name's on every sheet and pass them to the front.' Papers rustled as they were passed hand over hand. Hugh collected and counted them. 'Right then, lunchtime,' he announced and immediately the room erupted. Above the noise of desks banging, chairs scraping, people talking excitedly, Hugh shouted, 'See you all next time.'

'Fat chance!' they chorused and laughingly jostled and pushed their way out of the room in the manner of eager young males. No bloodshed though, this time.

Hugh, alone in the empty hollow classroom with the rough clamour dwindling down the corridor, sighed and again thought of yesterday evening. He had been so close and then Stella had rung and Mark had suddenly bolted. Why? It didn't make sense. One minute they were going to have sex and the next he was on his own in an empty house. He had to know why. He glanced at the clock and made a quick decision. Grabbing the papers he'd have to grade later and his jacket, he hurried out of the classroom and made his way through three sets of security gates before signing himself out.

 හෙ

Mark had wasted over half an hour waiting for someone to open the ICRA's offices and then spent the rest of the morning auditing the fixed assets register. He had made preliminary arrangements to visit three of the properties owned by the Trust that afternoon and John was busy organising transport and a driver.

They were sitting in the *nerve centre* and John was on the telephone; Mark half listening as he compiled his sample schedules. When the doorbell rang, John hastily finished his call and was striding towards the door as Margaret screamed, 'They're coming to take me away ha ha, hee hee, to the funny farm...'

'And not a moment too bloody soon,' Mark said under his breath.

'Margaret!!' John shouted running down the stairs.

Mark leaned back in his chair and grimaced to himself. Minutes later, John returned, beaming triumphantly.

'Sorted out the driver problem,' he announced, and held the door open wide. Jock walked into the room. Mark's grimace turned into a false smile.

'Jock here knows all the properties and their housekeepers,' John continued, 'You'll have no problem gaining access to any of them.'

'Hello, again,' Jock beamed.

Mark found his voice. 'Oh, hi.'

John looked at him doubtfully. Mark recovered quickly. 'Great,' he said, 'when do we leave?'

'Whenever you're ready.' Turning to John, Jock asked, 'Which properties do you want us to check out?'

'Oh, it's not up to me Jock. The auditors have their own fancy sampling methods.' He peered at Mark. 'Isn't that right?'

Mark nodded. 'I've selected three properties - here they are.' He held out a spreadsheet which John quickly scanned.

'No problem with any of these. I suggest you go to the one in Wood Green first. Mrs Harris, the housekeeper, has a local office-cleaning job and will be out later in the afternoon. Then you can work your way back. You'll miss the rush hour on Green Lanes that way, as well.'

'Good thinking,' Jock agreed, glancing at the list over John's shoulder. 'Is there enough petrol in the van?'

'Should be,' John replied. 'I put some in on Friday and I don't think it's been used all weekend. I'll just get you the keys.'

Left alone, Jock smiled again at Mark. 'Enjoy yourself last night?' he asked.

'I did, for a while,' Mark agreed.

'So, what happened?'

'Oh…things,' Mark replied, busying himself with his papers.

'Things!' Jock exclaimed. Then, more quietly, 'What things?'

Mark looked at him for a moment. 'It doesn't matter,' he said, turning back to his papers.

'Sure it does!' Jock grabbed his shoulder. 'We were getting along real fine and then suddenly you left. Why? Was it the phone call?'

'It… Well, it just broke the moment,' Mark responded, feeling Jock's heavy hand contract.

Jock looked hurt. 'Couldn't have been much of a *moment*, if that's all it took.'

'No, that's not true. It's just that…'

John barged back into the room, keys jangling. Jock's hand vanished from Mark's shoulder in a moment.

'Here you are then,' John said, holding out the keys. 'Wish I was coming with you…'

'No need,' Jock cut in. 'I'll bring both the van and us back in one piece.'

'Right then, have fun. I'll see you both later. Make sure you're back before half past four. I shall be at home after then if you get stuck in traffic.'

'Sure thing, John,' Jock said brightly. 'Right, let's get going - we can grab a sandwich on the way.'

ഇ

'What I don't understand,' Jock said a little while later as he munched on a grated cheese sandwich, 'is… Bugger! Why did I go for *grated* cheese?' He brushed the twists of soft yellow cheddar from between his legs onto the floor of the van. 'Sorry. What I don't understand is why you went so far and then just left so bloody suddenly. I thought we were doing really well.'

Mark was staring straight ahead, absently chewing his chicken and salad baguette. They were coasting along the busy Holloway Road, the University of North London on their right, about to turn onto the Seven Sisters Road. The pavement was littered with students in small groups, smoking, chatting and laughing with assorted bags, folders and books tucked over or under their arms. Numerous second hand furniture shops, their wares spewed out to the curb, were entwined with greasy spoon cafes, their tables and chairs draped with students. Mark took it all in and remained silent for a moment.

'Well?' Jock demanded.

Mark continued to stare out through the windscreen. 'Hugh, it's complicated,' he said.

Hugh raised an eyebrow, his eye on the road ahead, and clicked on the indicator to turn right into Seven Sisters Road. 'It's Hugh now, is it?' he remarked. 'My, my, aren't we being intimate?'

'Don't be sarcastic, Hugh's your real name.'

'So?'

'So, it makes a difference.'

'Don't be daft,' laughed Hugh.

'I'm not. Look, just pull over will you… I have something to tell you.'

'I can't pull over right here: it's a red route - no stopping for any reason.'

'Well, don't then. Just keep driving.'

'So, are you going to tell me, or what?'

Mark paused. 'Hugh, do you like me?'

'Like you?' Hugh snorted. 'Jesus, I'm crazy about you. I couldn't sleep after you ran out last night. I couldn't concentrate at work this morning – I nearly let a bunch of delinquent fucking kids get the better of me. I thought I'd blown it and couldn't think how.'

They passed Finsbury Park station and started along the edge of the park. Traffic was moving well: *No problems to report as* the *Eye in the Sky* on Capital Radio might've put it. *No problems to report*, thought Mark. *Well, here goes one.*

He took a deep breath. 'Then, what about Stella?'

'Stella?' Hugh exclaimed, mystified.

'Yes, Stella. Where does she figure in all this?'

'She's… well, just a friend.'

'She's more than that, Hugh.'

'Well, yes, I guess she is.'

'Hugh, she's in love with you.'

Hugh shook his head in disbelief. 'Mark, how could you tell that from what little you heard?'

'Well, she used those exact words for a start!'

'Oh, that's just Stella!' Hugh laughed.

Mark drew in a deep breath. 'No, it's not.'

'What do you mean? How the hell would you know?' Hugh demanded, the anger rising in his voice.

'Just pull over, will you?' said Mark, angry himself now.

'You're not making any sense!'

'You don't get it, do you?'

'Get what!?'

'Pull over.'

'I can't,' Hugh said, exasperated. 'You'll have to wait till we get onto Green Lanes'

At Turnpike Lane station, Hugh indicated left and they joined the slower moving traffic.

'Look, we're almost at a standstill,' Hugh said, looking at Mark. 'What is it I don't get?'

Mark stared out of the windscreen. The east side of Finsbury Park was on his left, there were two lanes of traffic ahead and a row of kebab houses, an off-licence and a hairdressers on the other side, all of which failed to captivate him. Nothing held his attention. He wished he had never started this conversation.

'Well?' Hugh insisted.

'I… I think it would be best if we forgot all this,' Mark said eventually.

'Like hell!' Hugh barked.

Mark made a snap decision: it was easier to suffer the consequences than keep these things bottled up; just let his tongue run wild and live amongst the ruins. It was easier to pick up the pieces than walk on eggshells.

'I know Stella,' he said quickly. 'Known her over a year. She's a friend of mine.'

It was like watching the coming of dawn as realisation spread from Hugh's wrinkled forehead to his wide-open eyes, to the twitch of his untrimmed moustache to the round O of his mouth as his bottom lip sank slowly into his chin. It was comical, in its way. Mark almost laughed. Then Hugh closed his eyes and gently laid his forehead on the steering wheel, covering it with his arms. Luckily, the van was at a standstill, the traffic not moving.

Eventually, he opened one eye, sat bolt upright and said, 'Funny old world, is it not?'

Stella decided that she was having a day off work. After all, it wasn't every day your mother won the national lottery. Even though she still didn't know how much her mother had won, Stella had her excuse to skive off. Who could concentrate behind a bar knowing you were an heiress? She laughed to herself, then stopped abruptly. Hugh had been a bit funny with her last night when he'd finally deigned to call her back and had refused to come over. What was the problem now, she wondered? Her mother again, most likely.

The doorbell rang. Let somebody else answer it this time. No, maybe it was that hunk Glen again, returning for Mark's telephone number or something. She clambered off the bed and hurried downstairs to open the door just as it rang again.

They look far too young to be policemen, was her first thought. The next was, *Oh my God, what's happened?* Was it Hugh? Her mother? A drugs raid? Her face remained calm but her mind was in turmoil.

'Good afternoon, Miss,' said the shorter, stockier one. He was in full uniform, his cap under his arm. 'We're sorry to disturb you, but we're conducting house to house enquiries. You may have heard about it on the news? A man was found dead in a flat in Bayswater…?'

Laura appeared beside Stella, as suddenly as if she'd been beamed down from an orbiting spaceship. 'What's going on?' she asked.

'Shh, there's been another murder…'

'Where?' Laura demanded, horrified.

'Bayswater!'

'That's where Mark lives!' cried Laura, covering her mouth with her hand.

The stocky policeman coughed loudly. 'As I was saying,' he continued, 'a man was found dead…'

'It's Mark, isn't it!?' Stella screamed. 'Oh, my God!' She screamed again.

The taller policeman stepped forward. 'The victim's name is not Mark,' he said gently. 'Now, who is this Mark?'

'Just a friend of ours,' explained Laura, adding aside, 'Do shut up, Stella, it's not Mark.'

'Thank God,' Stella said, 'I don't know what I'd do if…' the words hung in the air for a moment, then she looked puzzled. 'W…why are they here? We're miles from Bayswater…'

'I don't know,' Laura snapped at her. 'Perhaps if you could control yourself for a moment, we might find out!' She turned back to the patient policemen and smiled with what she considered to be her *winning* smile.

Unperturbed, the stocky policeman smiled back. 'As I said, we're conducting house to house calls.'

'Well, as my hysterical friend here has already pointed out,' Laura said sweetly, 'we're a long way from Bayswater, Officer. Just how many houses have you called at?'

The stocky policeman was a patient man, not so his taller colleague. 'We have reason to believe,' he interrupted, 'that a possible suspect lives in this area.'

'The murderer lives around here?' Stella gasped.

'Oh, my God!' Laura said, her hand to her mouth again. 'I refuse to leave this house after dark until this guy is caught! It is a male, I presume?' she added darkly.

'Yes, but he is only a suspect,' the stockier policeman countered.

'What does he look like?' Laura demanded.

'We have reason to believe that he's in his early twenties and that on Saturday evening he caught a cab from Bayswater Road to Finchley Road tube station - just down the steps there.' He pointed to the end of Netherhall Gardens where the road ended abruptly in a steep flight of steps that led down to the Finchley Road.

'That's just across the road!' Laura gasped.

'Exactly,' the taller policeman agreed. 'So, you can see, we haven't made that many house calls as yet.' His tone was just on the polite side of sarcastic.

'What time on Saturday evening?' Laura asked, ignoring the tone.

'Around 9pm,' the stockier policeman said quickly. His taller colleague was on the verge of blowing this interview, damn him.

'I was having a party, Officer,' Laura admitted. 'There were quite a few young men here.' She smiled and tried to blush, but failed. 'Any one of them could have caught a cab from the Bayswater area, although only Mark actually lives there as far as I know.'

The stocky policeman grunted. 'Mmm,' he managed, thoughtfully. 'I think it would be better if we came in.'

Laura opened the door wide and ushered them in through the hall and down her narrow flight of stairs. Stella followed, closing the door after them. Her flat felt tiny with the policemen's presence. Laura obligingly put the kettle on the hob.

ℬℭ

The traffic on Green Lanes was moving at last. An impatient hoot from the car behind spurred Hugh into action and the van leaped forwards as they sailed through a set of green traffic lights. Both Hugh and Mark had been silent for a few minutes.

Finally, Hugh said, 'It must've come as quite a shock hearing Stella's voice like that, eh?'

Mark smiled ruefully. 'Just a bit.'

'Sorry about that.'

'It's not your fault,' Mark said, thinking the opposite.

'You gonna tell her?'

'Are you?'

'Doubt it… Shall we go and grab a coffee somewhere?'

'Have we got time?' Mark asked, checking his watch.

'Plenty,' Hugh assured him. 'All night, if necessary,' he added, raising his eyebrows suggestively.

'I've got to check out these properties,' Mark protested, tapping his file with a finger. 'I'm working to a very tight budget and …'

'No problem,' Hugh cut in reassuringly. 'Tell you what, let's have a quick coffee, then whiz around all of them and then go back to my place.'

Mark raised his eyes to heaven. Hugh caught the gesture. 'Anything wrong with that?' he demanded.

'You know there is, Hugh. You'll probably roll a joint and we'll be right back where we started, nothing solved.'

Hugh looked thoughtful. 'You've got a point,' he agreed, adding, 'Got one all ready as it happens.'

Mark rolled his eyes heavenward and then changed the subject. 'How much did she win, by the way?' he asked.

'Who?' Hugh asked, then realised. 'Oh, right. No idea. Stella doesn't even know yet.'

'Must be really exciting. What if Stella's a millionaire now?'

'It's her mother who's won, not Stella.'

'Yeh, but, it's still her mother,' Mark argued. 'Stella's bound to get some of it, don't you think?'

'They don't get along very well,' Hugh said. 'And she doesn't like me at all.'

Mark was quiet for a moment. 'What's she like, her mother?'

'No idea, I've never met her.'

'Then how come she doesn't like you?' Mark asked innocently.

'Because I'm still married... Hey, look, there's a greasy spoon. Let's stop for that coffee.'

ℕℛ

The policemen were just leaving.

'Thank you, Mrs Bowles, you've been most helpful.'

'Miss,' Laura corrected him.

'Sorry, er Miss Bowles. Miss Roberts, too.'

The first policeman nodded his thanks. 'If you have no objection, we're going to make a few more calls in this block. How many flats are there?'

'13,' Laura replied, 'But there isn't a number 13 - it's known as 12b.'

'Thank you again, and goodbye.'

Laura watched them approach Mrs Rosenberg's door across the hall, a worried frown on her brow. She turned quickly and closed the door behind her, plunging the policemen into darkness and padded back through to the lounge with a grim look on her face. Stella was just finishing her mug of coffee.

'Shouldn't you be at work?' Laura asked, plumping up the cushions on the sofa where the policemen had been sitting.

'Didn't feel like it today,' Stella said and put the empty mug on the coffee table. Laura raised an eyebrow, but said nothing.

'So, what do you think, eh?' Stella asked. 'One of your guests is the gay serial killer?'

'Don't be silly,' Laura scoffed. 'If he was, he could've had his pick Saturday night. No. Pure coincidence!'

71

'There were a few wearing leather trousers that night, if I remember rightly.'

'Exactly,' said Laura. 'It's common enough.'

'What about the forged fifty quid notes?'

'Well, yes, that would be less common,' Laura admitted. She paled visibly. 'But that doesn't mean he came to my party. Did you see any £50 notes that night?'

'Hardly, but then we're not likely to; at a party, I mean.'

Laura nodded in agreement. 'Well, we'll all just have to be more vigilant from now on, won't we?'

ഇൻ

It was almost 6 o'clock when Hugh eventually drew the van to a halt outside the office in Islington. Mark had verified the existence of all of the properties in his sample and that each had the requisite number of units or beds. Therefore, according to certain theories, he could be statistically certain that the assets register of the ICRA gave a true and fair view of the company's assets. Their valuation, however, could possibly be in question: one of the properties had been in a poor state of repair.

'I just can't get over that poor old lady living on her own in that bed-sit,' Mark grumbled to Hugh. 'It's not right. It stank in there. And did you see how she was heating up her dinner…?'

'I know, I know. But, look, you can't do anything about it, so you may as well forget it.'

'Just because I can't do anything about it doesn't mean I have to pretend it isn't happening,' Mark scolded him.

He started to open the door to the van. Hugh grabbed his arm.

'Look, I know. Alright? I know. By rights, she shouldn't even be a resident of the ICRA. We sort of inherited her. She could be on the streets. Instead, she's got a roof over her head and someone to keep an eye on her. But, yes I know, it is very upsetting. I've been doing this sort of work for quite a while now and, believe me, there are a lot worse things out there than old Mrs Wiggins having to heat up a tin of rice pudding against an electric fire.'

Hugh let go of Mark's shoulder and they sat in silence for a moment, before he went on, 'I used to get really angry to begin with,

72

seeing the way some people live, but you get used to it. You have to. You'll go mad otherwise. Anyway, come on, let's dump this van and go to my place... I promise I'll cook for you this time.'

His stern expression softened into a strikingly handsome grin and after a moment, Mark grinned back.

'As long as it's not Haggis,' he said.

∞∞

Pierre was sitting on his bed, his knees up and clasped in an embrace, rocking back and forth in silence. Sunlight filtering in through gaps in the thin curtains highlighted the dissipating swirls of smoke. A joint butt was smouldering in the ashtray by his side.

He had been questioned. About the murder! How had they managed to trace him all the way to his home so quickly? Or at all? They had given nothing away, of course, only asked him about his whereabouts on Saturday evening, and then only briefly. They had left but he was absolutely one hundred per cent totally positive they'd be back.

'Shit,' he said and shuddered. What was he to do? He had to tell somebody the truth before they came back for him, otherwise they'd assume he was the murderer. He rolled off the bed, put on his shoes and was through the door in moments. There was only one person he could tell.

∞∞

Laura was entertaining for the third time that day. It was a jolly good thing she hadn't any flute classes to teach, although she could have done with the money. Still, never mind; she was enjoying herself immensely. So far. Seated opposite her in Laura's favourite armchair, her only armchair as a matter of fact, was old Fanny Rosenberg from across the hallway. They shared the basement, a flat apiece, but only Laura had use of the garden because her flat was the only one with an outside door. This fact alone was the source of much ill feeling from Fanny Rosenberg, but she rarely let it show. Today, however, was going to be an exception.

Mrs Rosenberg was an apparition in salmon and peach chiffon, which wafted around her as if she was sitting in a constant draught, smelling strongly of mothballs. She held the bone china teacup between the forefinger and thumb of her left hand, her little finger splayed and pointing away and up to the left, with the bone china saucer in her right hand, just below bosom level.

'Call me old fashioned, my dear,' she was saying, 'but in my day, just after the war it would've been, a lady would be chaperoned if a gentleman called.'

'Things have a habit of changing, Mrs Rosenberg,' Laura explained carefully, 'but, in this case they happen to be my students.'

'Students?' exclaimed Mrs Rosenberg. 'Why my dear, whatever is it you teach?'

'Surely you must have heard the music?' Laura asked, surprise and sarcasm intoned in her voice.

Mrs Rosenberg chose not to answer. She shifted position and Laura watched as the chiffon settled a few moments later. Instead, she continued, 'You must think I'm an interfering old woman, my dear, but people do talk.'

Laura was feeling distinctly uncomfortable. 'About what?'

Mrs Rosenberg shifted uncomfortably again in her chair and eventually said, 'We feel we must warn you that...'

'We?' Laura interrupted, her voice raised in question.

'Yes my dear, *we!* The Ladies' Watch. We're all honorary members of the Hampstead Ladies Bridge Club too, of course, and have lived in and around this area for far longer than we care to remember...'

'Probably longer than most of you *can* remember,' Laura cut in.

Mrs Rosenberg's eyes grew smaller and her voice turned icy. 'Possibly, my dear. But we're still able to see and hear well enough.'

'Well enough for what?' demanded Laura. 'Just what is it that you feel you must warn me about?' This had suddenly all turned rather sour.

'You're very quick on the defensive.'

'Wouldn't you be? I invite you in for a nice cup of tea and a friendly chat and then, out of the blue, you start accusing me of... of...'

'Being a *kurve?*' finished the old lady.

'A what...?'

'Prostitute, whore, slut, whatever!'

'You can't be serious! I only have one room!'

The old lady looked about her. 'It has a bed in it.'

Laura looked at the old lady in disbelief. 'It's a sofa at the moment,' she protested.

Fanny Rosenberg smiled smugly. 'Precisely. *At the moment.*'

There was a knock on the door.

Laura got up impatiently. 'Excuse me,' she said. Who on earth could this be now? She went through the kitchen to the door that led up into the house, not the garden. She opened it and her heart sank.

'Not now, Pierre,' she hissed, 'I have a visitor.'

Pierre was obviously agitated and even more clearly stoned. 'I have to see you. I'm really desperate!'

Just then a voice from right behind Laura said, 'Don't worry young man, I'm just leaving.' The apparition in salmon and peach chiffon wafted past her in a cloud of mothball fumes and out into the hallway, then turned to face Pierre. 'Desperate, is it? Well, you've come to the right place, young man.'

Pierre said nothing. Laura closed her eyes slowly and squeezed them tightly shut.

Turning to Laura, Fanny added, 'Mind my words, Miss Bowles. Those nice policemen this morning certainly did. They took plenty of notes.' She opened the door to her own flat, turning again at the last moment to glance disapprovingly at Laura.

Laura pretended to ignore her last comment and turned her attention to Pierre. 'You may as well come in,' she said, adding wearily, 'Tea?'

She slammed the door in the old lady's face.

ഔൽ

'Voilà,' Hugh declared in triumph, setting down a steaming, oval dinner plate in front of Mark who was seated at a small, old oak table. It was still light outside, but two white candles were burning down slowly, the wax forming a hot puddle around the wick and reflecting the flame.

'Let me guess,' Mark said. 'We're having pasta and some salad?'

'Correct. But the pasta is to die for... Just some freshly chopped basil, crushed garlic in olive oil drizzled over pasta twirls with lots of Parmesan. Um mmm. You'll love it.'

'You've lived too long on your own,' Mark laughed.

'Not so long, actually,' Hugh countered, returning to the table with the side salads. He sat down and poured Mark a second glass of White Burgundy, his own was still more than half full. There was a musical clink of glass on glass.

'To us,' said Hugh seriously.

'To us,' repeated Mark.

'And to Stella and all her mother's millions,' Hugh added.

'To her mother then,' Mark said.

'No bloody fear; the old bag hates me,' Hugh growled, putting his glass down.

'Stella said that *you* hated *me*,' Mark said, spooning Parmesan.

'What?' Hugh asked, clearly alarmed.

Mark passed the Parmesan. 'Yes, she told me last Saturday evening at Laura's party. She said you blamed me for getting her stoned and preventing her from seeing you on Friday evening. You were having a bad time, something about your daughter?' He filled his mouth with pasta and realised he'd stumbled onto a touchy subject.

Hugh's face fell. 'I'd rather not talk about that,' he said. 'I love my daughter but her mother and I don't get on. She lost her baby and I got a call at work. She was hysterical. Her mother I mean. My daughter too, naturally. Anyway she vented all her anger and everything out on me - as per usual.' He took a sip of wine, wiped his moustache with his napkin and continued, 'I needed to see Stella right then - and she let me down very badly. When Stella told me why she couldn't come, I blamed you of course. But I never said I hated you, not really, I just saw you as an obstacle. It was Stella really. She knew the state I was in that night and it was you I blamed when it should have been her.' He paused and took another mouthful of pasta. 'You like the pasta?'

'Delicious. My point is though: Stella's mother might not hate you once she's met you... She might be nicely surprised.'

Hugh conceded the point with a smile.

They ate and drank in contented silence for a while.

Then Mark said, 'You live a complicated life, Hugh, don't you think?'

'Ha, tell me about it!' Hugh rolled his eyes heavenward and Mark decided to take the literal meaning.

'Well,' he started, 'you're married…'

Hugh nodded. 'About to divorce my second wife.'

Mark raised his eyebrows. 'Second wife?'

'What can I say? I make mistakes.'

'Ok, so you're about to divorce your second wife. You have at least one grown up child… any more?'

Hugh shook is head.

'Grandchildren?'

Hugh shook his head sadly. 'This would've been my first.'

'I'm sorry, I didn't mean to upset you,' Mark said softly.

Hugh waved it off. 'It's ok… go on.'

Mark hesitated and then continued, 'Stella's obviously your girlfriend… Do you have a boyfriend too?'

Hugh shrugged. 'Not sure yet.'

Mark coloured slightly. 'So, anything else I should know? Any more skeletons in your cupboard?'

Hugh laughed. 'I think that's enough, don't you?'

'Yeah, just a bit,' Mark agreed. 'Anyway, here's to a little complication.'

Hugh responded and they clinked glasses again.

'So, what are we going to do about Stella? Are we going to tell her anything?'

'Is there anything *to* tell her?' asked Hugh, raising his eyebrows and grinning. It was soon wiped off.

'Don't be coy, Hugh.' Mark scowled. 'She's a friend of mine and a lover of yours. I'm a part of this now.' He gestured at the half-finished meal. 'Look, I'm having dinner with you. That in itself is something we would ordinarily tell her about.'

'Yes, ordinarily.'

'Yes, *ordinarily*. But, it isn't ordinary, is it? I mean, this is sort of a date. I feel I'm having an affair behind her back.'

'I wish,' Hugh grinned.

'I wish, too!' Mark blurted out. Hugh's grin widened considerably. 'But, I don't want her to be hurt,' Mark added.

'Well, neither do I,' Hugh replied. 'But, she's going to be if we tell her.'

'So, are you saying we don't tell her?' Mark demanded. He finished the last of his meal, picked up his napkin and wiped his mouth.

Hugh chased the last piece of pasta around his plate, speared it with his fork and munched thoughtfully for a moment.

'Well?' Mark asked.

'I suppose I am, for now,' he said.

'Well, I'm sorry Hugh,' Mark said slowly. 'But, I can't do this behind her back.'

'Why not?' Hugh demanded, 'Who knows where this'll go, if anywhere?'

Mark was not impressed. 'Great,' he said. 'Just great. So, we'll have a little fling and when it's over, you can go on with Stella and she need never know. Is that how it's going to be? Is that your little plan?' Mark picked up his napkin, screwed it up and dropped it on his plate. He stood up. 'Thanks for dinner.' He started to leave the table.

'What do you think you're doing?' Hugh demanded, 'Running out on me again?'

'Walking, actually,' Mark replied and headed for the hallway, took his jacket from the hook, picked up his briefcase and opened the front door. He closed it quietly behind him.

As he walked back to the Angel tube station, his dark mood began to lighten, a spring appeared in his step. By the time he reached the station, quite a few bemused homeward-bound commuters had been treated to the unusual sight of a young city gent swinging his briefcase in outrageous arcs as tears of uncontrollable laughter coursed down his cheeks.

And if they'd asked him why, he couldn't have told them.

ଅଠଃ

'I think you should leave now,' Laura said. 'It's getting late.' She stood and hoped that Pierre would do likewise.

He didn't. He just nodded miserably. 'What am I going to do?' he bleated, raising his troubled face towards Laura.

'We've just been through all that, a dozen times,' Laura replied and sighed. 'Just don't *do* anything. The police can't trace anything back to you.'

'But what about the fingerprints?' Pierre persisted. 'I was there all day. My prints and DNA will be everywhere.'

'We've been over this. You've already told me your details aren't on file anywhere.'

'No, not now, maybe. But they might be one day...'

'They'll have caught the murderer by then,' Laura told him angrily. 'The file'll be closed.'

'And if they don't?' Pierre was almost tearful.

'Ok, ok. So, what's the alternative?' Laura demanded. 'You go to the police and maybe they'll believe your story, maybe not, but you tell them that I made the introduction and I'll be deported quicker than I can poke your eye out with a sharp stick.'

Pierre looked horrified. 'I'll say I met them in a bar, which is true!' he protested. 'I won't involve you at all.'

Laura raised her eyebrows. 'Police were round here today talking about forged £50 notes. And guess who had one in her purse, just a few inches under their long noses?'

'I told you it was a forgery,' said Pierre loudly. Laura shushed him. 'You should have thrown it away,' he added with a hiss.

'Yes, but little slips like that can be fatal,' said Laura. 'I can't afford any more slips like that. If you go to the police, who knows what you might say under duress. And I do mean *duress*.'

'Yes, ok, ok, I get the picture.'

'Do you? I mean, *really*?' Laura asked. 'They're not just going to believe your every word. They're going to cross-examine you over and over, probably without sleep, certainly without dope. You could be held for days without a joint.'

Pierre looked up. He hadn't thought of that. 'That would be a bit difficult,' he admitted. Without a joint or two every day, he knew he would crack eventually.

'So, just keep quiet and hope it all blows over, is that it?' he asked, hopefully.

'I think so, don't you?' said Laura, her voice silky smooth once more. 'It'll work out, you'll see. Now, if you don't mind, I think you'd better leave. I expect that nosy old cow next door's timing you.'

ΣΟΩ

'Hi Stella, it's Mark.'

'Oh, hi. What time is it?' Stella asked sleepily.

Mark glanced at his watch. It was difficult to tell in the gloom. 'About ten thirty, I think.'

'It's late. I must have fallen asleep. Where are you?'

'In a bar somewhere. Compton Street, I think.'

'West End?'

'Yeah.'

'What are you doing there?'

'Getting drunk.'

'Oh, Mark, be careful...'

'Yeah, alright. Don't worry. I'm not going home with anyone. You ok?'

'Yeah, of course, why? Shouldn't I be?'

'Yeah, course you should, sweetheart.'

'You *are* drunk. Get a taxi. Go home.'

'I'm having a good time!' he argued.

'Ok, ok. So, what do you want?'

'Oh um, I wanna see you, and soon.'

'Ok. When?'

'I dunno. When are you free?'

'You should know by now, I may be cheap, but never free,' she laughed. Mark giggled along with the old joke. 'How about Thursday?' she added. 'I'll cook you a meal.'

'What, like last week?' he teased.

'I've said I'm sorry about that... And no, not like last week, I promise.'

'Ok then. Thursday. Same time?'

'About eight?'

'Great. See you then. Night, night.'

'Night, night.'

Mark ended the call and pocketed his phone. Bar noises and smells came crowding back. He peered through swing-glass doors into the bar area. It was filled to capacity with gay men, despite the potential threat of death from every stranger. Most of them were just standing around acting macho, pint glasses or designer beer bottles clutched to their chests. There were signs dotted around the walls warning people to be vigilant and careful and not to go home with strangers. *Yeah, right.* An endless procession moved in single file through the heart of the throng, searching to the left, to the right. Trawling, they called it. Like deep-sea fishermen casting their nets wide, Mark thought a little inaccurately. He hoped they would all be safe tonight. His thoughts were really with Hugh, which made him feel good somehow, despite the complications.

He left his half-full pint on the nearest table, picked up his suitcase and headed up the stairs and out onto Compton Street. He walked at a brisk pace towards Tottenham Court Road and then hailed a cab. Twenty minutes later, he was home.

Chapter Six

THE PIERCING SCREAM of, 'They're coming to take me away, ha ha hee hee,' jerked Mark awake. He yawned and tried to focus on the Housing Association Grant applications, or *HAG* applications, as they were known. *Hag's right*, he thought, as he heard John shouting at Margaret to shut up. With her peroxide blonde hair and make-up that looked as if a labourer had applied it with a shovel, Margaret could have passed for an ugly straight man in very bad drag. Certainly not someone he would like to meet on a dark night.

It was late morning, the sky outside the window was heavy with rain, but it was a mild spring day. Thursday, in fact. And, tonight, Mark was going to have dinner with Stella. Hugh hadn't tried to contact him at all yesterday, which was a little disappointing. Just then, as if the thought of Hugh had conjured him into existence, there came a rap on the door. Not a knock, or a tap, but a *rap*. Not John then. John always tapped, like a mouse.

'Come in,' Mark called.

The door opened and Hugh strode into the room. 'Lunchtime!' he almost shouted. 'Just passing, thought you might like a bite,' he said loudly, adding quietly, through tightly clenched teeth, 'Don't you dare say no.'

Lovely! Mark almost yelled back, but restrained himself. Just. He cleared his throat. 'Lovely,' he said. He got up and put on his jacket, locked his briefcase and logged out of the PC. 'Do I need a brolly?' he asked loudly.

Hugh looked at him. 'Only if you're made of sugar,' he replied. Mark left the umbrella where it was and followed Hugh out onto the narrow landing and down the threadbare staircase.

John appeared in the hallway. 'Lunch again, eh?' he asked. 'You'll have to pay for it yourself this time. I'm afraid ten pounds was all we set aside in the budget for bribing the auditors.' He laughed loudly at his own joke.

'I think we'll manage, John,' Hugh replied grinning. He opened the front door and led Mark outside. It was spitting with rain. 'Come on, let's hurry,' he urged.

'Where to?' Mark asked.

'The Edward?'

'Ok.'

They walked briskly, side-by-side, Mark matching Hugh stride for stride. There were quite a few people on the street intent with their own lives, hurrying here and there, idly chatting, out shopping, waiting for buses, peddling the Big Issue... Mark broke the silence first.

'So, to what do I owe this unexpected pleasure...?'

'You're seeing Stella tonight,' Hugh hissed. His whole demeanour had turned abruptly sour. 'What are you going to say to her?'

Mark was momentarily stunned. 'Um, nothing,' he said. 'Nothing about us, anyway... You're going to do that.'

'Oh, I am, am I?' demanded Hugh. They crossed the road and turned up the side street leading to the Edward public house. 'And why would I do a daft thing like that?'

Mark groaned. 'Because it's not up to me and it has to be done - if you want me and you to get it together, that is.'

'Is that what *you* want?'

'Yes, no... Yes. I don't know. What's the question? I'm confused. Look, I don't want Stella hurt, but I do want...' his voice trailed off.

'What?' Hugh asked. 'What *do* you want?'

'Oh, I don't know. It's a strange situation.'

'You can say that again.'

Mark resisted the childish urge to repeat himself.

They reached the door of the Edward. As they entered, muffled music gave way to a strong, fast high-energy beat and then the familiar smell of cigarette smoke and beer assaulted their nostrils. A few heads turned in their direction and, long before they even reached the bar, Marilyn was standing in place waiting to take their order.

'Boys,' she cried. 'How lovely of you to come visit your sister. Come here...' She leant over the bar and gave Hugh a huge smacker on the cheek.

'Hi, darling' said Hugh, returning the kiss. 'How you doing?'

'Ooh, much better now,' she pouted. 'Now that you and that gorgeous hunk have pitched.' She smiled enormously at Mark and winked outrageously.

Hugh pretended to be hurt. 'You're only interested in my friends,' he pouted back. They all laughed, good-naturedly.

'One of your *friends*, eh?' said Marilyn, raising both eyebrows so high that Mark was sure her blonde wig was going to fall right off the back of her head. Instead, she managed to save herself the disgrace with a practised nudge using both palms, fingers splayed outwards. 'Oops,' was all that was required and, of course, another smile.

'Now, boys,' she continued. 'A pint and an orange juice with lemonade, right?'

'You got it,' Hugh agreed. He turned to Mark. 'Ok?'

Mark nodded.

'Oh, and two ploughmen's - one pickle and one mayo.' He turned to Mark again. 'Ok?' he asked.

Mark nodded a second time.

Hugh handed Marilyn more than enough money and told her to keep the change. Marilyn winked at him. 'Coming right up,' she said, handing him a ticket with the number four on it this time. 'Take a seat, boys, and I'll bring it over.'

They found a quiet corner table. It was still early and there were less than a dozen like-minded punters dotted around, mostly on their own. All of them, however, kept stealing glances in the direction of the two handsome men. Even Marilyn couldn't keep her eyes averted.

'You're quite a hit,' said Hugh, catching some of the glances.

'You're not so bad yourself,' Mark replied, looking around. Marilyn, from behind the cold food bar, gave him another wink as she spooned a large dollop of mayonnaise onto a plate. Mark quickly turned his attention back to Hugh.

'Will she be bringing our drinks over too?' he asked.

'Seems like it,' mused Hugh. 'We are honoured.'

They continued making small talk until a piercing scream made them jump.

'Sixty nine!!!' It was Marilyn holding two plates in the air from behind the bar. 'Oh, it's you two, is it?' She yelled and giggled again. She minced around the bar and over to them. 'I'll just get your drinks,' she added, plonking the plates down in front of them and distributing real cutlery wrapped in pink paper napkins. She wobbled her way back to the bar, returning moments later with their drinks on a tray.

'I don't do this often,' she hissed, 'so take advantage while you can.' She paused for a moment. 'I said, Take advantage while you can… Oh, never mind.' She laughed crudely at her own joke and left them to their meal.

Hugh picked up his pint glass. 'Cheers,' he said. Mark did likewise with his orange juice and lemonade. 'So,' Hugh continued, pulling apart his crusty bread, 'you don't want to see Stella hurt then, is that it?'

'Of course I don't,' Mark replied. 'Surely you don't either?'

'Stella's no angel, you know,' said Hugh, cutting into his farmhouse cheddar.

'What's that supposed to mean?' Mark demanded, a piece of celery halfway to his mouth.

'She's quite capable of looking after herself.'

'So…?'

'So, if the tables were turned, she'd do whatever was in her own best interests. Believe me, I know.'

'That doesn't mean we can just trample all over her. She has feelings too, you know,' said Mark, biting into his celery.

'I know that,' Hugh replied with a sigh, 'but I think we should keep this to ourselves for a bit, until we're sure there is something to tell her. I don't want you storming in there and exploding the bag before we're sure it's worth it.'

Mark was nodding. He replaced a chunk of crusty bread, which he had just smeared with butter, slowly back down onto his plate.

Hugh could read the signs. 'You're not going to walk out on me again, are you?'

Mark looked thoughtful for a moment, picked up the bread again and added a slice of cheddar. 'I don't like it very much,' he said as he took a bite, adding with his mouth full, 'but I'm coming around to your way of thinking.'

Hugh was visibly relieved.

'However,' he continued, 'it can't go any further, Hugh. Not just yet. I can't face Stella knowing I'm up to something behind her back. She's my *friend*…'

'And she's my *lover*,' Hugh cut in. 'I'm the one who should be taking the moral stand, not you…'

'Moral stand, huh?' Mark cut back.

'Look, lovers do it all the time.'

'Yeah, maybe, but friends don't,' Mark replied. 'Look, I'm sorry, Hugh. As much as I would love to take this further, I can't, not like this.' He took a gulp of cold orange juice and lemonade.

Hugh was angry now. 'Then fine,' he said. He took a long draught of his pint, grabbed the chunk of cheese from his plate, and stood up. Waving the chunk of cheese at Mark, he hissed, 'This time, don't expect me to come running.' He sidled out from his corner, threw a curdled glance of thanks to a startled Marilyn and stormed out. The door banged shut after him.

Mark sat immobile for a few moments, then resumed munching. He looked up and noticed Marilyn standing in front of his table.

'Well,' she said, 'was the pickle off or what?'

❧❦❧

It was five o'clock in the evening and Stella didn't know which way was up, down or sideways. One of the barmen at work had hurt his back and Stella, or *muggings here* as she kept referring to herself, was required to finish off his shift, putting her horribly off schedule. She sighed as she pushed open the huge door to Netherhall. At some point in the next couple of hours she needed to clean up, shower and then cook a fantastic meal for two, to make up for last week. She was delighted though that Mark was coming to see her. She could do with a good chat.

She struggled up the wide staircase with three loaded plastic bags of Waitrose groceries, thankfully dropped the load outside her door and then fumbled for her keys. Strange, the deadlock was unlocked.

She cautiously used the Yale key and pushed open the door. The television was blaring and Hugh was sitting wearing just his shorts, beer in hand, watching Jerry Springer. He turned to face her.

'Hi hon,' he said, which was better than *hen* by which he usually referred to her.

'What are you doing here?' she asked, relieved and peeved at the same time. She grabbed up her groceries and hurried into the kitchen.

'Nice to see you too,' he called after her.

Stella shouted to him, 'You can't stay, Hugh. I've got Mark coming to dinner, remember?'

'So, he won't mind me,' Hugh replied, eyes on Jerry Springer.

Stella came over and stood in front of the TV. 'Oh yes he bloody well will. You hate him, remember?'

'Remember, remember?' Hugh mimicked. 'Christ, you sound like a bloody Womble.'

'What's a *Womble* got to do with anything?' asked Stella, completely mystified. She was of a different generation to Hugh.

'Oh never mind. Come and give me a kiss,' he insisted, holding his arms out to her. She faltered a moment, then sat on his lap. She kissed him full on his hairy mouth.

'Ugh,' she said. 'You smell like you've just eaten an ashtray.'

'I've just had a joint. Want me to roll another?'

'No, Hugh. Look I've got to have a shower and start cooking. Mark'll be here for 7.30,' she lied. He was due at 8pm.

'I'll help you,' he said. 'What're we having?'

'*We* are having nothing,' she insisted. 'This evening is going to be just me and Mark.' She struggled out of his embrace and stood up.

'Why?' Hugh demanded. 'Why can't I be there?'

'Because, Hugh,' Stella replied, walking into the kitchen, adding over her shoulder, 'Just because.'

'Great explanation.'

'Look,' she said, putting her head round the door to face him, 'he's *my* friend, not yours. You don't even like him. I'm looking forward to a nice cosy chat with a good friend of mine and I don't want it to turn into an awkward threesome. OK?'

'Oh, so I'm gonna make it awkward, eh? Like I've no social skills, I suppose. I'm incapable of making polite conversation, is that it?'

'Hugh, I don't want an evening of *polite* conversation. I want a friendly chat with a close friend of mine...'

'Oh yeah, right. How *close* are you two? Planning on going to bed with him, eh?'

'Hugh!' exclaimed Stella, shocked. 'How could you say such a thing? Anyway, he's gay and you know it.'

'Yeah, but does he?'

'What do you mean?' asked Stella, confronting Hugh as he stood up to face her. This conversation was rapidly spiralling out of hand. What was Hugh's problem? 'What's got into you?'

'You know what I mean,' Hugh retorted, adding, 'And nothing's got into me.'

'Something certainly has,' she said thoughtfully. 'What is it, what's wrong?'

'Look, nothing's got into me. I guess I'm feeling a little bit left out, that's all.'

'Oh, baby,' said Stella and put her arms out to cuddle him. 'I'm sorry, what with my mum coming down and everything else, I suppose I have been taking you a bit for granted.'

They sat down together on the sofa and cuddled for a few minutes. That turned into a few stolen kisses and then before Stella had a chance to protest, Hugh had flipped her onto her back and slid his right hand up her thigh. Within moments, he had pulled her gossamer thin tights down to her knees and then his rough hand started back up the inside of her thigh until it reached her soft mound. It was bushy and wet, just how he liked it. He slid his thick forefinger easily into her and at the same time kissed her passionately on the lips, his hairy black moustache thrilling her as it always did. She started to moan and, as if on cue, he picked her up from the sofa and carried her through into the bedroom. One of her shoes fell off and she kicked off the other. She felt light headed. He was going to take her and she couldn't wait. Her legs felt weak as he lay her down on her bed, *their* bed. They had bought it together, just recently.

She looked up at him as he smiled and ripped off his shorts. His cock was dark, veined and solidly erect. It caused her to shiver. Hugh noticed this and his smile widened. He pulled off her tights completely and tugged open her blouse. Her bra came off easily, as did her skirt. He kissed her breasts, biting gently at first one nipple, then the other. As he did so, Stella slid both of her hands across his chest, down the front of his firm muscular stomach and into the black pubic hair from which his hard cock sprouted. She caught hold of the glistening end and felt its wet glans, ready to fuck her.

Hugh moved his lips to her throat, then her neck and then gently bit her ear lobes, first one then the other. She had a firm hold of his cock with both hands and slowly guided him towards her. She lifted up both legs as he angled himself between them. He was about to enter her and she threw her arms around his neck and kissed him almost savagely. He responded with a quick thrust and was in her before she could voice her surprise. They wrapped themselves around each other and fell into a rhythm that brought them both to a swift and satisfying climax.

Afterwards, they lay wrapped in the arms of the other. Stella glanced at the clock on her bedside table. It was just gone five-thirty. She looked up at Hugh and noticed he was almost asleep. She nudged him. 'Don't fall asleep, Hugh. Mark'll be here soon and I've got to start cooking.'

'Yeah, okay,' he replied softly. He opened his eyes and looked at her. 'I want you again, tonight,' he whispered roughly and nuzzled her ear.

She squirmed in his embrace and giggled. 'Then you'll have to come back later. Go off to the pub or something and come back when Mark's gone.'

Hugh shook his head. 'Can't be arsed to hang out around here. You'll have to come to me when he's gone.'

'Oh, Hugh, I don't want to have to go out that late at night. Not all on my own.'

'Why not? You've done it before.'

She extricated herself from his arms and propped herself up on his stomach. She spread her long blonde hair down both sides of his chest and looked up at him. 'There's a murderer loose around here, in case you haven't heard.'

'Yeah, of gay men!'

'Well, he might decide he wants a change!'

Hugh looked at her snidely. 'Are you coming or not?'

'No, I can't be arsed either.'

'Well, in that case,' he said, 'I'll have you again now.' He grabbed hold of her torso and deftly flipped her over onto her stomach. His semi-hard cock hardened quickly and whilst she lay there, squirming, telling him she hadn't got time for this, he lifted up her buttocks and entered her roughly from the rear. Just the way he liked it.

෨൝

He was early this time, so Mark decided to pop in and see Laura first. He pushed his way through the brambles, careful not to scratch himself or his black leather jacket, and made his way around the side of Netherhall to Laura's back garden. As he passed by the window to her lounge cum diner cum bedroom, he glanced inside and froze. Standing with her back to him, Laura was holding up what looked like a large bank note to the ceiling light and cursing loudly.

Mark couldn't quite make out what she was saying, but it sounded rude. He moved a little closer, pushing aside more brambles, careful not to make too much noise. Eventually, he was almost up to the window and could see that it was a £50 note that Laura was holding up to the light. She stopped cursing and then opened the lid of a small porcelain Buddha on a shelf near her and popped it inside, closing it carefully afterwards.

Mark watched for a while, puzzled, and then eventually gave up. He was slowly withdrawing from the window, retracing his steps with stealth, when a voice from behind startled him.

'Well, well, well. Now, what's a nice boy like you doing in a nasty place like this?' Mark spun around to face a bemused Patrick, flute case in hand.

'Er, erm, I was … I could ask you the same question,' Mark stammered.

'Well,' said Patrick, spreading his arms around him, 'I'm on the path leading to Laura's back door. You, on the other hand, appear to have strayed well away from the path… What's going on?'

Suddenly, as if in echo, Laura's voice shouted from around the side, 'What's going on? You two having a secret affair or what?'

'Damn, you caught us,' said Mark, recovering well and moving into sight of Laura. She was standing on her patio, the £50 note and foul mouth gone as if they had never existed. 'I was just on the way to Stella's and was early; thought I'd pop in and say hello.'

'How lovely of you,' Laura said, 'but, I'm afraid it's Patrick's lesson time.'

Mark looked at Patrick and smiled broadly. 'What a shame.' Turning back to Laura, he shrugged, 'Oh well, I'm sure Stella won't mind if I'm early.'

Patrick appeared awkward. 'Er, what time will you be leaving Stella's?' he asked.

'Oh, no idea, quite late,' Mark replied. He turned. 'Better be off, then. See you soon.'

He walked as quickly as he could back through the brambles but hadn't got far when Laura called after him 'Oh, Mark, hang on a sec.' He turned as she approached. 'I just wanted to invite you to my dinner party,' she said, lowering her voice.

'That's very nice of you,' he smiled down at her. 'When is it?'

'A week on Saturday. Can you make it?' Her face was completely circular, just like a full moon, he noted, and quivering with anticipation.

'Of course, I'd love to,' he said. 'What time?'

'Seven for seven-thirty,' she beamed. 'See you then.'

෨෬

'Well, I must say, that was delicious,' Mark exclaimed, wiping his mouth with a paper napkin. Stella positively glowed.

'It's one of Marlene Spieler's recipes. She's very good. That was just a basic one using garlic, olive oil, basil, pasta twirls and loads of Parmesan, only I didn't have any Parmesan so I used a strong cheddar instead.'

Mark nodded. Obviously Hugh used the same cookbook.

As if picking up on his thoughts, Stella giggled and said, 'Actually, you nearly didn't get dinner *again* this evening.'

'Oh?' said Mark, frowning.

'Hugh came round,' Stella explained. 'Well, he was here when I came home from work, actually,' she added, slightly peeved.

'And you're not happy about that?' Mark quizzed her.

'I gave him a key, although he hasn't given me one to his new place yet. Anyway, this is the first time, as far as I know, that he's been here without me knowing about it.' She picked up her wine glass and took a sip. She placed it next to her empty plate and shook her head. 'Actually, it's not that that I'm bothered about, or the keys issue. No, he was in a funny mood. He kept insisting on staying to dinner for some reason.'

Mark looked around him. 'So, where is he then?' he asked, smiling.

'Ha ha,' said Stella, without humour. 'I got rid of him.'

'Nicely, I hope.'

'Oh yes,' Stella replied with a glint in her eye. 'Very nicely.'

'Good,' Mark said. 'I am pleased.' He took out his familiar Café Crème tin and showed it to Stella. 'Would Mademoiselle care to partake in a little light-headedness?'

Stella giggled. 'Ooh, why not?' she said, her eyes dancing.

'Try not to go overboard this time, ok?' he said, taking out a neatly rolled joint and inserting it into his mouth.

Stella nodded. 'As long as you don't try and rape me,' she said and giggled. 'Twice in one day could be considered a little careless.'

Mark gave her a puzzled look as he exhaled a plume of blue-grey smoke. She dismissed it with a wave of her hand. 'Only joking,' she said.

'You sure? Twice? When was the first?' Mark exhaled another plume and passed the joint to Stella.

'Let's go and sit on the sofa,' Stella said, taking the joint. They rose from the table and moved over to settle themselves comfortably on the sofa beneath the Monstera cheese plant. It was growing yet another couple of leaves. Stella pulled up her feet and sat facing Mark. She took a drag of the joint and inhaled sharply, then continued, 'No, I was only joking – me and Hugh had a bit of a wild time this afternoon, in the biblical sense, if you know what I mean.'

'But, he didn't rape you, surely?' Mark insisted.

'Well, he was kind of rough,' she said, exhaling and then taking another drag. Her beautiful lips puckered up with the effort. She passed the joint back. 'Phew, that is good,' she said, exhaling. She unfolded her short legs and stood up, walked rather unsteadily to the table and picked up their wine glasses. As she returned, she tripped and spilled expensive white wine all over his trousers. Unperturbed, he stood up and removed them. They were both giggling away merrily.

'Ooh, what lovely legs,' Stella remarked. 'Can I pull the hairs on them?'

'No, you cannot,' laughed Mark. 'Now, where can I hang these to dry?'

'Give them here,' she said, taking them from him. 'I'll put them in the airing cupboard. They should be dry in an hour. I am sorry.'

When she came back into the lounge, Mark was pouring more wine. They sat on the sofa again and Mark re-lit the joint, took a drag and passed it to her.

'Now, where were we?' he asked. 'Oh, yes! Hugh. So, he wanted to stay to dinner, you said no, so he raped you. Is that about it?'

'No, he didn't really rape me, he just likes to pretend he's rough and likes to dominate. I like it and play along.' She seemed pensive and her mood darkened a moment. She took another drag of the joint and then stubbed it out in the ashtray. Mark was quiet himself for a moment as he digested this tantalising morsel of information.

'Anyway, let's not talk about Hugh,' she continued brightly. 'So, who else has Laura invited to her dinner party, did she say?'

'No, and I've no idea. Not that Patrick kid anyway, I hope. She kept her voice low when she invited me so that he couldn't hear.'

'Well, I shall be there,' said Stella. 'And Hugh, of course.'

'Of course,' Mark said, imitating her Scottish accent, just a little. Stella eyed Mark seriously. 'Are you ok with that?' she asked.

'I'm looking forward to it,' he replied, adding, 'Just as long as he doesn't get *rough* with *me*.' They both laughed, a bit too much and soon they couldn't stop.

∞⟡☾

The doorbell rang. Hugh was at a crucial point in Frazier, his favourite programme on the Comedy Channel, and decided to ignore the caller. After all, it was nearly 10.15 on a Thursday evening. *Probably just kids*, he thought.

The doorbell rang again. Frazier paused for a commercial break so Hugh hauled himself reluctantly to his feet and padded into the hallway. He paused in front of the door. What if it was a mugger? Or the serial killer? He'd better be careful.

'Who is it?' he called.

No answer.

'Who's there?'

Still no answer. He shrugged and went back into the lounge, over to the window and peeped out from behind the curtain then shot back into the hallway, yanked open the door and yelled, 'Oi! Come back!'

Mark spun around and walked quickly back down the steps to Hugh's front door. Hugh hugged him and invited him in.

'Didn't think I'd be seeing you again for a while,' he said, closing the door.

Mark walked through into the lounge. 'No?' he said, raising his eyebrows.

'I acted like an ass today, I'm sorry,' Hugh said, picking up the remote and switching off the TV.

'No more than me. Anyway, you're probably wondering why I'm here.'

Hugh shrugged. 'I thought you were having dinner with Stella,' he said.

'I was, or rather I did. She wanted an early night. I left there about twenty minutes ago, caught a cab and, well, here I am. Don't ask me why.'

'I don't need to,' Hugh replied, catching hold of Mark by the shoulders and pulling him gently towards himself. Mark gazed into Hugh's green eyes, noticed his smooth olive skin and thick muscular arms, his short black tousled hair, his hairy black moustache perched above succulent red lips and knew that this was the moment for which he'd waited since first setting eyes on this handsome man.

They kissed, their stubbled chins grinding against one another. Mark could hear and feel the rasp of his cheek against Hugh's. His cock stiffened instantly. He licked Hugh's moustache and Hugh responded by gently biting Mark's tongue. They laughed and parted.

'So, what made you change your mind about all this?' Hugh asked, sitting on the sofa and pulling Mark down with him.

'I just suddenly realised what it was that I wanted and to hell with everything else.'

'From what I know, that doesn't sound like you at all,' said Hugh, adding, 'Has Stella said something?'

'Don't analyse it Hugh, just accept it. I want you, ok?'

'Fine, no problem,' Hugh replied, and kissed him again, passionately. 'Do you want to go upstairs?' he whispered.

'Yes please,' Mark replied. He felt Hugh suddenly squeeze his cock and jumped.

'Bit nervous?' Hugh asked him. Mark pulled away from his kiss and nodded. 'Don't worry, I'll be gentle.' With that, he turned and led Mark along the hallway and up the steep staircase. At the top of the landing he turned and pointed. 'That's the bathroom,' he said. 'D'you need to use it?'

Mark nodded.

'I'll be in the bedroom when you've finished,' he said and kissed Mark again, long and hard. They parted. 'Don't be too long.'

Mark managed a quick wee, despite his semi-hardon, and then washed his foreskin under the cold tap. If Hugh was going to fuck him, then he'd better make sure his arse was clean too. He soaped a finger and gingerly rimmed himself then washed it off in the sink. He was sure he was doing it all wrong. He pulled the chain, left the bathroom light on and walked out onto the landing.

There were two doors, but only one had a light coming from beyond it. He pushed open the door to the back bedroom and walked in. Hugh was sitting up in bed, the duvet up to his waist, exposing his tanned, muscular upper torso. On the bedside table was a tube of lubricant, two condoms and a white towel. He smiled. Mark smiled back, his cock stiffening again.

'You've never done this before?' Hugh asked him.

'Nope,' he replied.

'You sure you want to?'

In reply, Mark unzipped his jeans and pulled them down, along with his pants, exposing his hard cock. 'What do you think?' he asked, grinning. He slowly removed the rest of his clothes as Hugh watched, then he stood before him, naked and hard.

As Hugh reached to touch him, the doorbell rang, once, twice.

'Shit! Who the hell can that be!' Hugh announced, his temper flaring. He jumped up and put on a dressing gown. 'Don't go away,' he urged and kissed Mark hard on the lips. He went into the front bedroom and cautiously peeped out from behind the curtains.

'Oh, shit!' he murmured.

'Who is it?' asked Mark from close behind.

Hugh turned, the whites of his eyes visible in the dark. 'Fucking Stella!' he hissed.

Mark was indignant. 'She told me she was having an early night!' he said, his cock rapidly shrinking.

Hugh peeped through the curtains once more. 'Yeah, well, that's Stella.'

The doorbell rang again, longer, more urgently.

'What are we going to do?' urged Mark. 'Ignore her?'

They heard a whispered shout from below. 'Hugh, it's me, Stella! Let me in!'

Hugh turned to him. 'Look, I can't just *ignore* her. All the lights are still on downstairs. She knows I wouldn't go out and leave them on.'

'Well, you can't let her in with me here. What would she think?'

'I don't bloody know. Look, I'll let her in, you hide in here and then sneak down and let yourself out, quietly, when the coast is clear. Ok?'

Mark nodded in the darkness. Trust this to fucking happen. This relationship between him and Hugh was fated, he realised. 'This isn't meant to be, is it Hugh?' he said sadly.

'Eh, what? What are you talking about?'

'Us,' replied Mark. 'We're just not meant to be. Someone up there is trying to tell us something.'

'Don't be so bloody daft.' Hugh grabbed him and enveloped him in his huge arms, almost crushing the life from him. Mark gasped as Hugh forced his hairy mouth onto his. Hugh grabbed Mark's hand and moved it down to where his cock had begun to stiffen again. 'Hold my cock,' he breathed into Mark's open mouth. Mark took a tentative grip on Hugh's hard cock, feeling the pulsating warmth of a solid column of flesh.

The doorbell rang again and again and again.

'Remember this feeling,' said Hugh, pulling away, adding, 'It gets better. Now, put your clothes back on and hide in here. Get out when the coast is clear and don't make a sound!' Then he was gone. Mark removed his clothes from Hugh's bedroom, wondering what might have been. He could hear Stella's excited voice in the hallway as Hugh opened the front door. He returned to the front bedroom and sat behind the door, trying to make himself as inconspicuous as possible. He strained to hear their voices and then he heard them return to the hallway. He perked up, *Great, she's leaving*, he thought and his heart began to energise again. But then he heard footsteps on the stairs and what sounded like slurping noises. He heard a high moan followed by Stella's breathless voice, 'Oh, Hugh, I want you to fuck me, really hard, like you did earlier.'

Hugh responded with a growl. Mark covered his ears. He didn't want to hear anymore. It should have been him.

He waited a few minutes and uncovered his ears. He could hear lewd noises from Hugh's bedroom; snorts, grunts, squeals, regular banging of the headboard, the occasional sigh of delight. He slowly opened the door and stepped out onto the landing. The sounds were much louder. As he passed Hugh's door he couldn't resist a peak. The door was slightly open, enough for him to cast a furtive glance inside. Stella was kneeling on the bed and Hugh stood naked behind her, his glistening cock pumping in and out. Hugh had hold of both her breasts and was squeezing them hard.

Some sixth sense must have been at work because Hugh chose that exact moment to turn his head aside and look straight at Mark's flushed face. He just smiled his handsome smile and continued thrusting. Mark couldn't be sure, but it didn't look like he was wearing a condom.

Mark let himself out of the front door as quietly as he could. He could picture Hugh thrusting his bare cock in and out of Stella's bare fanny. It was a moment to savour and had given him another erection. He looked back momentarily, then he turned and pushed past the hydrangea bush onto the path, took a right and headed towards the tube station.

Across the other side of the road, a sleek black coupé sports car started its engine and its lights came on. The car was eased gently into first gear and slowly began to follow Mark.

It drew alongside.

Mark had been thinking of Hugh and noticed the car now for the first time. He stopped and the driver's window was lowered.

'Hi Mark, get in,' came a young man's voice from within. It took him a few moments to realise who it was.

'What are you doing here?' Mark asked, bending down to peer into the interior of the car.

'I followed you from Laura's,' said Patrick, adding, 'I could ask you the same question.'

This made Mark angry. 'Yeah, well don't!' he replied. 'And what d'you mean, you *followed* me? *Stalked* me, more like. Now, go home and forget all about me.'

Patrick looked sad. 'Can't do that,' he said. 'I've never met anyone like you before.'

Mark's anger turned to frustration. 'Patrick, you hardly know me! How can you say something like that?'

Patrick looked miserable. 'Please get in,' he pleaded.

Mark sighed deeply, considering his options. Then he skirted the car, opened the passenger door and got in. It smelled of leather and cigarette smoke. He noticed the ashtray half-full of cigarette butts. 'You smoke too much,' he said.

'I'll give up if you want me to,' said Patrick, brightening.

'Look, you do what you want to do,' he replied sternly. 'I have no right to ask you to do anything. However, if you want my opinion then yes, you should stop smoking.'

'Well, you smoke,' said Patrick defensively.

'Only the occasional joint, nothing more. Anyway, forget all this,' Mark waved his hands about. 'What are you doing following me all over London?'

'I wanted to see where you lived,' Patrick replied.

'Well, I don't live around here,' said Mark, snorting loudly.

'No, so I noticed. Strange goings on though, if you ask me! Who was that handsome man with the moustache who hugged you?'

'Never you mind.'

'And that woman who arrived,' continued Patrick. 'I'm sure she's a friend of Laura's.'

'We're all friends of Laura's,' said Mark.

'Wow, a conspiracy. What's she done?' asked Patrick, his eyes wide with curiosity. 'You plotting something against her?'

'What? Look, this is not Scooby Doo!' Mark shook his head in exasperation. 'Now, get this straight - Laura's got absolutely nothing to do with any of this, ok? OK?'

Patrick nodded.

'Right then, are you going to take me home or what?'

'Yes, Sir,' Patrick replied with a wide grin.

Chapter Seven

'IT'S A LONG SHOT, Miss Bowles,' said the young forensic policeman, 'but this whole case has been a series of long shots.' It was Friday morning and he was standing in the entrance to her kitchen, having taken the back stairs down from the main hallway. Just who had let him and his cohorts in through the front door remained a mystery.

'Yes, but fingerprinting and taking DNA samples of my whole flat? Just because I had a party? In my country, what you're doing could be construed as *harassment*.'

'Yes, Miss Bowles, and in this country what you're doing could be construed as *obstructing police enquiries* and carries a heavy penalty. Now, are you going to let us in or do we have to come back later with a search warrant as well?'

Laura had to think furiously for a minute. Eventually she said, 'I've cleaned the place from top to bottom since my party, so you'll not find many prints, except for mine and those of a few friends who have popped in to see me recently. I am extremely busy and it would be a waste of my time and yours. Good day, gentlemen.' With that, she closed the door behind her and gulped for air. She sagged against the door for a moment, getting her breath back, and then launched herself at the cupboard underneath the sink where she kept her cleaning equipment.

With an intensity bordering on manic, she rushed around the flat with her rarely used upright vacuum cleaner whilst at the same time spraying on and wiping off furniture polish wherever a shiny surface presented itself. In her haste, she nearly forgot the Buddha. She ran to it, pulled off its head and grabbed at the £50 note. Then her conscience got the better of her. This was hard evidence. She couldn't destroy it and she certainly couldn't be found in possession of it. What on earth should she do? And what on earth was she doing obstructing police enquiries and now cleaning her flat? She was beginning to behave irrationally. She gazed uneasily at the root of her anxiety, the £50 note. What could she do with it? The police would be back soon with a search warrant and they'd be really thorough now.

ഇൽ

By mid-morning Mark was nearing the end of his audit assignment. He would be sorry to leave, since he'd rather enjoyed his week. He was putting the finishing touches to his audit papers, making a few recommendations for next year's audit, when he heard the doorbell, followed by, 'May God go widgou, Mr McDonald,' from Mary, the Trinidadian lady from the lively Evangelical Baptist Church nearby who Mark had met earlier that morning.

Mary was a large lady, but dressed like a little girl in a daffodil-yellow cotton smock dress that had buttons up the back and appeared at least a couple of sizes too small for her. It was tight around her ample bosom and her impossibly large back stretched the gap between the buttons so that you could see her exposed skin all the way down her spine. To top it all, she wore a large blue hat with a floral band around its brim and white sling-back shoes with large chunky heels that increased her height to an imposing six feet.

'Och, hello Mary,' boomed Hugh's voice. 'And how are we today?'

'We is fine, tank the Lord, and your good self?'

'Never better, thank you Mary. Now, if you'll excuse me, I need to have a word with the auditor.'

'You go right ahead,' said Mary, stepping aside. 'He's upstairs messin' about on dat computer ting. I took him a cup of tea earlier. Would you like me to make one for you too?'

'No, I'm fine, thank you,' Hugh replied, clearly impatient to climb the stairs.

'You is always rushin', innit. You should slow down,' she advised him. 'God will wait for you, you know.'

Hugh gave her an uncertain look. 'Yeah, right, thank you Mary, I'll bear it in mind.'

'See that you do,' she said and turned and headed back along the hallway to the kitchen.

Hugh leapt up the stairs, two at a time. He burst in on Mark who feigned surprise. 'Oh, hi,' he said.

'Look, I'm sorry about last night...' Hugh began, but Mark cut him off.

'Stop! All we seem to do is apologise. I've been giving this a lot of thought. There's nothing I would like more than to get to know you better, but the odds seem stacked against us.'

'But, we can...'

'Let me finish,' Mark urged him. 'From the first moment we met, I have wanted you. I think about it night and day, but every time we get close, something always comes between us. Call it bad karma, bad luck, fate or whatever, something's preventing it. I have a gut feeling about this and I'm sure that...'

Hugh cut him off by striding forward, grabbing him by the scruff of his neck and locking jaws with him. Hugh held him roughly, his kiss hard and passionate. Mark struggled for a few helpless moments, then relaxed and let Hugh do whatever he liked.

'Just shut the fuck up, will ya,' Hugh said into Mark's open mouth.

They kissed for a long time.

ഇറ്റ

This time there were four policemen at her door and Laura wasn't surprised to see them. The tall one at the front cleared his throat.

'I am Detective Sergeant Johnson of the Metropolitan Police and we have a warrant here,' he said, indicating a slip of official looking paper, 'to search your premises. May we come in?'

Laura smiled sweetly. 'But, of course. Please, come in. Would you like a cup of tea?'

'Thank you, but not at the moment.'

The Sergeant waved his hand at his men who mobilised themselves into action and stormed Laura's flat... At least, that's how she described it to Stella, later that afternoon, when her friend popped down for a chat after work bringing with her a cheap bottle of wine.

'And did they find what they were looking for?' Stella asked her. She was sipping a rather tasteless medium dry white that had been bought in haste and she was now repenting at leisure. 'Sorry about the wine, by the way.'

Laura took a sip and just checked herself from pulling her *sucky-lemon* face. 'No problem,' she said. 'To answer your question, I don't honestly know. They dusted some silvery looking powder around all over the place, collected a few samples of cat hairs, took some pictures – they use digital cameras now, you know – but, they were polite enough and only stayed about an hour. Then they left.'

Stella took another sip of the revolting wine. She pulled a face as she said, 'So, what's going to happen if any of the prints match those of the murderer?'

Laura paused in the act of raising her glass to her lips. She thought for a moment and a dark frown crossed her face momentarily. 'I've no idea,' she said. 'I guess they'll want to take fingerprints and DNA samples of everyone who was at my party.' *Thank God Pierre didn't come to it,* she thought, *Thank God I cleaned the house thoroughly.*

'You know,' said Stella after another pause, 'it's clever how they managed to link a murder in Bayswater to your party so quickly. Something to do with a £50 note, wasn't it?'

'You know it was,' said Laura gruffly. 'And it's not all that clever,' she added, 'it was the cab driver. If he hadn't contacted the police, none of this would be happening to us... I could do without this, you know.'

Stella looked at her sympathetically. 'Still not sorted out your Visa?' she asked.

Laura shook her head. 'I've done everything short of marrying someone.'

Just then, a vibrating sound came from Stella's hip.

'Oh, excuse me,' she said to Laura and grabbed her mobile phone. 'Hi,' she said into the mouthpiece. 'Can I call you back...? Look, I'm having a glass of wine with Laura... I said I'd meet you, didn't I...? There's plenty of time... Oh, alright!' she said grumpily and promptly hung up. She looked at Laura. 'Sorry about that,' she said. She looked at her watch. 'I've got to be going, I'm afraid. That was Iris. Did I tell you, my bloody Mum's arriving from Scotland this evening?'

Laura arched an eyebrow. Although she knew little about Stella's mother, she knew about her own and understood Stella's mood perfectly.

❧

Mark arrived home on Friday evening feeling elated. He had completed the audit well within budget and had therefore safeguarded the future of housing association audits *per se*, just as his boss, Donald, had hoped. He'd dropped the audit files back off at the office but hadn't seen Donald. Playing golf, probably. He had also spent a delicious lunchtime with Hugh in the Edward public house and now had a dinner date with the same. It looked like tonight was the night!

He opened the door to his bed-sit, flung his briefcase onto the bed, tore off his clothes and proceeded to do fifty press-ups and a hundred sit-ups in his underwear, both in sets of 25, resting in between.

He was on his way to the bathroom, wearing just a clean white towel around his trim waist, when he met Vivienne coming out, a dark green towel around her head that contrasted nicely with her apple-white bathrobe. There was steam everywhere as usual.

'Oh, hi,' she said. 'You had two lots of visitors earlier; two policemen and then a man on his own. They asked if I knew where you worked. I told them you were an accountant, but that's all I know. You in some sort of trouble?' she asked, raising her eyebrows.

'Don't tell anyone, but I'm a spy,' he said and winked at her.

'Me too,' she whispered, peering all around. 'The weather in the highlands is fitting only for ducks,' she said mysteriously with a rather good French accent and then laughed.

Mark laughed with her then turned serious. 'Did they say what they wanted me for?'

'No, just that they would be back.' At that precise moment, the doorbell rang. She looked at him and pulled a face. 'That's probably one of them now.'

'Damn,' said Mark, 'I need a shower. I'm going to nip in quick –
can you go answer that, I'll only be two minutes?'

'You going to use the fire escape?' she asked eagerly, her eyes
shining. 'Oh, what fun. Can I come with you?'

He gave her a withering look. 'Earth to Vivienne?' he said,
tapping her gently on the head. 'I just want a quick shower,
otherwise I'll be late. If it is for me, just let them in, would you? I'll
be out very shortly.'

She smiled coyly at him. 'Got a hot date?'

'You bet,' he replied and disappeared into the fog, closing the
door and locking it behind him.

He was soaping his hair when there came a loud knock on the
door. He groaned inwardly. 'Shan't be a minute,' he called. *Can't
they let me finish?* he thought.

An authoritarian voice boomed above the sound of the water.
'Open this door. Now!'

Mark jumped and quickly washed the suds out of his hair. Good
thing it was short. He turned off the shower, pulled back the plastic
curtain, grabbed his towel and stepped out of the bath. He unlocked the
door and it swung open. Filling the hallway was a thickset policeman
with a young policewoman at his side, both uniformly dressed. Mark
could see Vivienne hovering near her door, an anxious look on her face.

'What's going on?' he demanded, suddenly angry.

'You are Mark Carter of 103 Bayswater Terrace?' the policeman
with the booming voice asked him.

Mark nodded, his throat suddenly dry. A stab of fear hit his
stomach and his knees almost buckled. 'What's wrong?' he demanded.

'I'm afraid I'm going to have to ask you to accompany us down
to the police station for questioning,' the policeman said firmly.

'Why? What do you mean *for questioning*?' Mark demanded.
'About what? What's happened?' Had somebody *murdered* his
parents? 'Is it my mum and dad?'

The policewoman looked at the policeman. She turned back to
Mark. 'No, Mr Carter,' she said soothingly. 'We're interviewing
people who may have seen or heard something in connection with
the recent murder in Porchester Mews. If you have no objection, we
would like you to accompany us now to aid us in our investigation.'

Mark felt both relieved and peeved. 'But I do,' he said, 'object, I mean. I'm going out soon. I have a dinner date.'

The policeman cut in, less diplomatically. 'Well, I'm afraid you will just have to cancel it. Come on, get some clothes on, we haven't got all day.'

Mark looked closely at the policeman. He was about thirty, over six feet tall, blond crew cut hair, clean-shaven. He had a truncheon sticking down his right leg and a sexy sneer to his mouth. Mark decided not to argue. He looked over at Vivienne and shrugged his shoulders. She smiled back uncertainly.

Ⅴ∓

'Hugh, it's me, Mark.' Mark was using a telephone provided for him by the policewoman. It was on speakerphone and echoed around the small room.

'Where the hell are you?' Hugh exploded. 'You're supposed to be here in ten minutes. I'm running around like a blue-arsed fly trying to get everything ready. I'm really looking forward to tonight,' he added sexily. Hugh had the cordless phone trapped under one ear whilst he mashed an avocado pear and tomato with some virgin olive oil, lemon juice and freshly ground pepper.

The receiver fell from his grasp. Hastily grabbing it up off the floor, he yelled, 'You're where!!? Scotland Yard!? Why?'

'I'm sorry, I've got to go now,' Mark said, noticing the policeman making a winding motion with his finger. 'Sorry about tonight. Again!'

He replaced the receiver. The policeman sneered. 'Sorry to disrupt your plans, but I'm sure your boyfriend will find something to do. Or *someone*,' he added, and laughed contemptuously.

Mark bristled, but said nothing. *Best not to say anything*, he thought.

Ⅴ∓

Hugh was furious, as well as anxious. He dialled 1471 and was told, very nicely, that he had been called today at 19.20 hours, but that the caller withheld their number. Bugger! He grabbed the telephone directory, looked up Scotland Yard, and hurriedly dialled the number. When he was denied access to Mark, he hung up, rushed around the kitchen turning off the stove, shoved a few things back into the fridge and then grabbed his coat and was out of the door in less than two minutes. He hailed a passing cab.

'New Scotland Yard, and step on it!' he yelled at the surprised cabbie. Given a moment to reflect, he began to wonder what Mark could possibly have been up to now.

The journey was short, despite the late rush hour traffic, and twenty minutes later he paid the cabbie and hurried up the famous steps, pausing briefly to admire the silver sign outside. He daydreamed, momentarily, that he was an eminent barrister and that this was where he spent most of his time; then shook his head and rushed through into reception, surprised at how empty it was. He approached a busy-looking policeman behind the desk who was shuffling papers and only looked up when Hugh coughed.

'Yes, Sir,' he said. 'Can I help you?'

'I understand that Mark Carter is being held here for questioning. I would like to see him please.'

'And who might you be?' the policeman asked.

'Hugh McDonald, his solicitor.'

'I see. One moment, please.' The policeman picked up a phone and spoke briefly into it. He then turned back to Hugh. 'Would you care to take a seat, Sir? Detective Chief Inspector Dickens will see you shortly.'

Hugh sat down on a hard grey plastic seat, one of many in a row against the wall. The wall itself was covered in information posters about various crimes, all endorsed with the black and white Metropolitan Police logo. He squinted at a photofit mug shot of a man apparently in his early twenties wanted for everything from arson to murder. He looked like the elder brother of at least a couple of his delinquent law students at the Holloway Detention Centre. No doubt the police were hoping to arrange that particular family reunion sooner rather than later.

Hugh was so absorbed he failed to notice the detective arrive. 'Mr McDonald?'

Hugh stood immediately and held out his hand. 'Yes, I'm Hugh McDonald,'

'Good, I'm Detective Chief Inspector Dickens. Call me Charles.'

Hugh raised an eyebrow.

'Blame my parents - they named me,' the detective said and smiled quickly. He was a tall man, in his late thirties, about the same age and build as Hugh, although he looked about ten years older. He was wearing a plain dark grey suit, white shirt and blue tie. The only indication of his personality was a gaudy gold tiepin, matching cuff links and a ghost of a wedding ring on his left hand. Hugh felt outplayed in his jeans and polo shirt.

The detective frisked him and then led Hugh through security doors, down a brightly lit but bare corridor to a small interview room. He indicated that Hugh should sit in front of a small desk and sat down opposite him, taking out a packet of Benson & Hedges and offering one to Hugh who declined with a shake of his head. The detective put them away without taking one himself.

'Coffee perhaps?' he asked. Again Hugh shook his head.

'Well, let's get right to the point then, shall we?'

'I'd like to see my client.'

'Let's not play games, Mr McDonald. He's your boyfriend. We have already established the fact.'

Hugh coloured visibly. 'So? That's no longer a crime. On what grounds are you holding him?'

The detective grinned. 'On the same grounds as we're holding you,' he said, adding dramatically, 'For murder.'

Hugh jumped up immediately, sending his chair reeling upside down into one corner of the room. The detective jumped reflexively just as the door flew open and two more policemen rushed in, armed and primed to attack. Hugh's arms shot up. He was too shocked to speak. Moments later, he felt a powerful grip on his arms and within seconds his hands were cuffed behind his back. It was a manoeuvre that he'd been planning to use on Mark that very same evening to be followed by forcing him down onto his knees and shoving his cock deep down his throat. The thought gave him a semi-erection, but the situation brought him to his senses before it became noticeable.

'Thought you were being clever, didn't you?' the detective sneered, picking up the chair and making Hugh sit down again. 'Got this all worked out between you, just in case. Plan B was it? Or Plan C?'

Hugh managed to find his voice. 'You're making a big mistake.'

'Very original,' the detective said. 'If I had a pound for the number of suspects who've told me that...' The other two policemen laughed with him but he turned serious before they had finished laughing. 'Porchester Mews,' he said menacingly. 'Ring any bells?'

Hugh had to think. He shook his head.

'The Bayswater murder?' the detective prompted.

A light suddenly dawned in Hugh's memory. 'I read about it,' he admitted.

'Then you'll know very little,' the detective said, leaning further forward so that his face was inches away from Hugh's bristling moustache. Hugh flinched instinctively at the feel of warm breath on his cheek. It didn't smell bad, actually.

'What you won't know,' the detective continued, 'is that from the evidence, we know that at least four people were involved, that at least two of them emptied their balls of cum and that one of them was brutally murdered. We also suspect that one of them went to a party in Netherhall in Hampstead last Saturday evening...'

Hugh gasped.

'Ringing some bells now?' the detective asked.

Hugh remained silent. 'I'm not saying anything,' he said after some thought.

'I suppose *you'll* want a solicitor now, will you?' the detective said, showing his crooked tea-stained teeth in a wide smile.

'I don't know. Where do I come in all this?'

'We happen to believe it was a gay-motivated murder, just like the others. We have evidence that points to your boyfriend and by implication to yourself. So, take your time and tell me *exactly* where you were last Saturday evening through to Sunday evening... Is the recorder still running?' he asked one of the other policemen.

'Yes, Chief.'

Hugh said defiantly, 'You do realise you're breaking all the rules here, don't you?'

The detective sneered. 'Well, if you've nothing to hide, I suggest you let me worry about that,' he said.

Hugh shrugged. 'Can't you just take a DNA sample and a set of fingerprints?'

The detective's eyes narrowed as he considered this. 'Take him to the cells,' he said eventually. Hugh started to protest but the detective cut him short. 'Shut the fuck up,' he said. 'This is a murder enquiry and we have to be thorough.'

His tone was almost apologetic.

⁂

Stella hung up her mobile phone. She'd tried Hugh's home number three times now and the answering machine was off. He never left home without switching it on. She was sitting on a Piccadilly line train heading slowly towards Heathrow and total oblivion with Iris next to her staring glumly out of the windows. The tube had ventured out into the open and was crossing a bridge over a road that lay somewhere between Hounslow East and Hounslow Central. Stella was suffering from a mild headache as a result of drinking the cheap wine earlier.

'Does he not have a mobile?' Iris asked.

'No,' Stella replied calmly.

'Why not?' Iris asked. 'Everyone's got one nowadays.'

'That's why,' Stella replied.

Iris tutted.

'What's that supposed to mean?' Stella demanded. A sharp glance at Iris and her headache cranked up a notch or two on whatever scale it was that measured headaches.

'Oh, never mind,' Iris said, looking away, her nerve failing her.

'Look,' said Stella, 'it's bad enough with Ma not liking him, and she's never even met him, but what have you got against him?'

'I don't trust him,' Iris replied. 'He's got shifty eyes.'

'He has not!' said Stella indignantly. 'You're just jealous cos he's so bloody gorgeous. That wimpy excuse you've got your paws into couldn't turn on a gas stove!'

'You leave Jim out of this,' cried Iris. 'At least he's not married and knocking off another woman half his age.'

'Oh, so that's it. You think he's too old for me.' Stella raised her eyes to heaven.

Iris softened. 'Stella, I just want what's best for you, that's all.'

Stella looked down miserably. 'I know,' she said softly, 'but what I think is best for me and what you think is best for me are… Oh, I dunno. Anyway, right now, we've got more urgent things to worry about.'

'Too bloody right,' Iris agreed. They both stared glumly out of the window as Hounslow Central swept past.

'What time's her plane supposed to land, again?' Stella asked with a sigh.

'Eight-ten.'

'I ask you, who bloody arrives at ten past eight on a Friday night when they could come at any time, day or night?'

'It was a late booking and you know what she's like, she'd only fly if it was with British Airways.'

Stella grunted. 'How long's she staying then?'

The train slowed as it approached Hounslow West and Iris turned to face her impatiently. 'Look Stella, we've been through all this. Read my lips, *I don't know*, OK?'

'Well, how long do you *think* she'll stay?'

Iris gave up. 'About 6 months, I should think.'

'WHAT!!?' Stella screamed, jumping up from her seat. The other passengers turned to look at her briefly before quickly turning away again. As far as they were concerned, there was yet another mad person on the tube and they were going to ignore it, just as they had yesterday and the day before that and the day before that.

'Well, how the bloody hell should I know?' Iris yelled back. 'For the love of Christ, sit down will you and shut up!'

Stella sat down and brooded in silence, her headache throbbing now. The train sped up and continued on its journey, taking her closer and closer with each passing second to the moment when she would see her mother again. She wondered if she'd changed very much in the last few years.

☙❧

Glen, the security guard from Waitrose, had been busy. Unable to wait another week or so to see Mark at Laura's dinner party, he had taken matters into his own hands. After Mark had recovered from his faint on Saturday, he had paid for the food, but only his own, using a debit card. Glen had managed to obtain the details, and then had found out Mark's address through an ex-lover of his who worked for the Metropolitan Police. He smiled at the thought of the handsome Mark fainting into his arms and wondered what it would be like to embrace him properly and kiss those luscious lips. He felt his cock stir.

He called at Mark's Bayswater address just before six o'clock and a very attractive young lady informed him that Mark wasn't home from work yet. Fifteen minutes later, he glimpsed Mark through the rear view mirror of his old Ford Escort parked a few metres past Mark's front door, but on the opposite side of the street. Mark was hurrying homewards from the direction of the tube station, swinging his briefcase. He looked a proper city gent. Again, Glen felt his cock stirring to life as he imagined Mark wearing Calvin Klein underwear beneath a pinstriped Armani suit. What he could do with his cock and Mark's mouth was best not thought of right now. He slunk down in the seat as Mark approached. He didn't want to be seen just yet. He felt it better to wait a while to give Mark time to relax.

Glen watched in his side mirror as Mark opened the front door and disappeared inside. *Right*, he thought, *I'll just give him another fifteen minutes to get organised.* He lit a cigarette and opened the side window to let out the smoke. It was a little chilly, he noticed.

A few minutes passed idly and then Glen noticed a police car enter the street. He flicked his cigarette out of the window just as the police car came to an abrupt halt and double-parked outside Mark's front door. A large policeman and a petite policewoman both jumped out and marched determinedly up the steps. They pressed the bell, several times, and were eventually allowed in.

A few minutes passed and then Glen was astonished to see Mark appear at the door with a police escort and marched straight towards the waiting car. His hair looked wet. Within moments they moved off, passing Glen. He started up his car and followed.

He kept a reasonable distance behind, but it soon became clear to Glen that they were heading for New Scotland Yard. True enough, the police car drew to a halt outside and Mark and the police couple got out. Mark was looking a bit sorry for himself and Glen was wondering what on earth was going on as they disappeared inside the building.

He decided to sit around and wait, found a parking space where he could observe the main entrance, turned up the radio and lit another cigarette. Surprisingly, there was little activity. He was expecting to see people coming and going in a constant stream and, after a few more cigarettes, he was about to give up when a cab arrived and a very handsome dark-haired man with a bushy black moustache jumped out.

Wouldn't mind swinging on his dick, Glen thought, noticing the firm thighs and solid buttocks as the handsome man dressed in jeans and a polo shirt ascended the steps of the main entrance, paused for a moment as if he had caught Glen's wish, and then disappeared inside the building.

Hoping to see the man again, he decided to hang around for a while longer and then, if nothing happened, he would go inside and say he was a friend of Mark's and had heard that he had been brought here and could he help in any way. He waited half an hour, extinguished yet another cigarette and then made his move.

ഇരു

Detective Chief Inspector Charles Dickens couldn't believe his luck. Their third suspect had just arrived in reception. He scanned his notes: Glen Cooper, aged 22, currently a security guard with Waitrose on the Finchley Road, named as the instigator of an illegal enquiry on the Metropolitan Police computer earlier today concerning Mark Carter. Suspected homosexual. No further information available.

Dickens was beginning to doubt his good luck: this was becoming all too easy. He sighed to himself and went to meet his third suspect. It looked like another long evening ahead.

ഇരു

The airport was crowded, as usual, and Stella and Iris battled their way through hordes of tourists flocking to their respective flight desks. They checked that their mum's flight was arriving on time and found that it had already landed.

'Bugger,' Iris said, gritting her teeth. 'If she thinks we're late, we'll never hear the last of this, you know that don't you?'

Stella nodded. 'Hopefully we've missed her and someone's kidnapped her so we won't ever have to hear of it,' she muttered under her breath. Her head was still pounding.

They fought their way to the arrivals lounge and merged into the waiting crowd of hopefuls waving pieces of card with names scribbled on them. Stella and Iris emerged at the front of the barrier just in time to see their quarry appear, clasping the arm of a young male baggage handler pushing a trolley. They could see that she had brought just one large suitcase and one smaller bag with her. Stella breathed a sigh of relief.

Morag Roberts was dressed in a tartan edged black coat with black stockings and what appeared to be hob-nailed boots. A long black skirt, like a nun's habit, peeked out from below the hem of the coat and a black headscarf was tied beneath her chin, hiding her iron-grey hair. 'She looks like a bloody penguin with a tartan trim,' whispered Stella as she and Iris rushed to meet her, their arms wide open. The baggage handler stopped the trolley and handed their mother into their care.

Iris offered her arm and her mother grabbed hold of it, saying gruffly, 'You got here then.' Iris nodded and kissed her on the cheek. Stella, standing to one side, grabbed hold of the trolley and trailed in their wake, poking her tongue out and pulling faces at her mother's back as they headed for the exit to the underground.

'And you can stop that right now,' her mother said loudly without pausing. Stella turned red, just as she used to as a child, and stopped pulling faces.

ഇ෬

It was nearly one o'clock in the morning when Mark, Hugh and Glen found themselves descending the steps of New Scotland Yard. After extensive interrogation, followed by the negative results of their fingerprint typing, they had been provisionally released pending results of their DNA testing. However, as Detective Chief Inspector Dickens well knew, he had no evidence at all on which to keep them locked up for the evening.

Glen was the first to speak. 'Well,' he said, 'I've got my car over there.' He pointed across the road. 'Can I give you both a lift anywhere?'

Hugh looked at Mark who shrugged. He turned back to Glen. 'Let's go back to my place. I could do with a cup of strong coffee and a coupla joints to start off with.'

Glen grinned. 'Now you're talking,' he said. The three men walked down the famous steps and crossed the road to Glen's car, got in and wrinkled their noses at the stench of stale smoke.

Mark sat in the back feeling anxious. As Glen started up the car and pulled away, the feeling grew stronger. Hugh and Glen were chatting each other up and he didn't know whether he felt jealous or excited. What if they were all going to end up in bed? Was this the way he was going to lose his virginity, with two hunky men who he hardly knew? Would they be gentle or rough? He was musing, when he realised that Hugh was talking to him.

'Er, sorry?'

'I said, You're very quiet back there.' Hugh was staring backwards at him, his twisted face glowing and fading with passing orange neon from the street lamps. They were cruising along the still congested Marylebone Road and had just cleared the lights at Baker Street.

'Oh, just thinking.'

'About what?' Hugh coaxed.

'About what happened tonight, obviously,' Mark lied. More like what *would* happen tonight. 'We've all three been arrested for murder,' he said. 'Murder! For god's sake, what would my mum say?'

Hugh laughed. 'But we're innocent,' he said.

'Yes, but how did we ever get mixed up in it? And you,' he said, turning on Glen. 'Where on earth did they dig you up from?'

Glen reddened, deepening the orange neon glow that bathed him. He considered how long and complicated his story was, and then gave up.

'Search me,' he said and shrugged.

They were approaching the underpass at Warren Street and he turned his attention to manoeuvring into the correct lane. Mark cast a doubtful glance at his eyes in the rear-view mirror. Glen looked away, signalling to move into the right hand lane. Mark made a mental note to pursue that particular line of questioning another time.

It was only a few minutes later that they were standing outside Hugh's house. Hugh opened the door and Mark and Glen followed him in.

Glen cast a complimentary eye on the interior. 'Mm, nice place,' he said, 'and a garden, wow... I wish I had a garden.'

'You like gardening?' Hugh asked him, moving to stand beside him as he looked out through the patio doors.

Mark interrupted them. 'Can I use your loo?' he asked, feeling a bit like a lone gooseberry in a fruit salad.

'Sure,' said Hugh, as he continued to stare into the garden. 'You know where it is.'

Mark hesitated, turned, went up the stairs, had a quick pee and then came back down, quietly. He walked in on them in a passionate embrace, sucking at each other's faces and groping each other's crotch with an intensity that frightened Mark. They separated abruptly.

'Time for a number, me thinks,' said Hugh. 'Mark, would you put the kettle on?'

'Um, well, actually, I think I'd better be going,' Mark said. 'Can I call a cab?'

'Certainly not,' said Hugh instantly. He crossed over to where Mark stood in the lounge doorway and put a friendly arm around him.

Mark shrugged him off. 'Then I'll walk,' he said and was out of the front door before Hugh could stop him. Hugh ran after him.

'Look, I'm sorry, I didn't mean to... It just happened... Please come back...' He reached out to grab Mark but Mark was striding away too fast and too angry to stop now. Hugh let him go. He didn't look back as he turned the corner.

Mark was about to try and hail a cab when a familiar sleek black sports coupé drew to a halt beside him. The window wound down smoothly and Patrick's voice came from within, 'My, my, you do lead an interesting life, don't you?'

Mark was enraged. He stuck his head in through the window and shouted menacingly, 'STOP FUCKING STALKING ME!!! NOW, PISS OFF!!!'

He withdrew his head just in time. The window whirred upwards and the car shot off with a screech but not before he had noted, with some satisfaction, the look of absolute horror on Patrick's face.

'Teach the little fucker a lesson,' he said aloud.

Two minutes later, he was cooling off in the back of a London black cab. For the first time that evening, he felt safe and able to relax.

Chapter Eight

SATURDAY WAS A SCORCHER, despite the gloomy weather forecast. It was a cloudless day with top temperatures in the mid-twenties and Laura had thrown caution to the wind along with most of her bedding, which was now draped across the small clothes line and spilling across the various shrubs growing in her secluded garden. It wasn't an effect that Mrs Rosenberg cared for and she was standing in the middle of Laura's kitchen telling her so when Detective Sergeant Johnson and company appeared at the door. Again, someone had obviously let them in through the main front door, although Laura had not heard the doorbell.

'Got your own key?' she asked them sarcastically.

The detective smiled pleasantly. 'The door was wide open.'

'Well, it shouldn't have been,' replied Laura, angrily. She turned to Mrs Rosenberg. 'Shouldn't you be keeping an eye on things like that, rather than where I put my washing to dry?' she demanded.

Mrs Rosenberg gave her a haughty look, shifted it to the policemen and then back to Laura. 'Why bother,' she retorted, 'when the police are always at the door? More trouble I presume, Miss Bowles?'

The detective could see this flaring up into a nasty squabble and cut her off quickly. 'May we come in, Miss Bowles?' he asked.

Laura sighed and opened the door wide. Detective Sergeant Johnson crossed her threshold accompanied by two constables, one of each sex. He introduced them as they entered Laura's kitchen. Laura hurried Mrs Rosenberg out through the same door and closed it with a pronounced bang.

'Tea?' she asked them, although she was clearly not in the mood to make any. They all declined.

'We'll get straight to the point,' said Detective Sergeant Johnson following Laura through into the lounge cum diner cum bedroom.

'We made several arrests yesterday evening in connection with the Bayswater murder...'

Laura gasped. 'Anyone I know?' she asked, her legs suddenly weak as she more or less fell onto the sofa. She indicated for them all to sit down.

'Well, yes, as a matter of fact,' the detective said, 'which is why we are here.'

'Before you go any further,' she interrupted him, feeling the walls closing in, 'I have something for you.'

She stood up, rather uncertainly, and went over to her precious Buddha and lifted off the lid, reluctantly removed the £50 note from its bowels and handed it to the detective. He took it carefully by its edge, held it up to the window and then blinked several times.

'How did you get hold of this?'

'I found it clearing up after my party,' she lied.

'Why didn't you say something to us earlier?'

Laura summoned all of her skills as a thespian and replied, 'I thought it was a real £50 note. I couldn't believe my luck. I hid it and waited to see if anyone claimed it.'

'I take it that they haven't then,' the detective chipped in, handing it to WPC Grimes who sealed it carefully in a plastic folder.

Laura shook her head

'Pity,' said the detective. 'Anyway,' he continued, 'we arrested three men last night and we...'

'Three!!' exclaimed Laura.

'Yes,' said the detective. 'You sound surprised.'

'Well, I er... I am,' Laura stammered, annoyed with herself. What was going on? She had expected to be told that Pierre had been arrested, that it was all some horrible mistake and would she mind terribly being deported? Instead, there were three people involved.

'You said that it was someone I knew. All three of them?' she asked.

'Possibly, although only one claims to have been at your party on the evening in question... a certain Mr Mark Carter. Do you happen to know at what time he arrived and left your party?'

Laura suddenly had to sit down again. She slowly shook her head. 'Not really. Around eight-thirty until sometime after midnight I think. What about the other two? Who are they?'

'I'm sorry, Miss Bowles, but we cannot divulge that information.'

'Why not? You've just told me about Mark...'

The detective interrupted her. 'That was to corroborate his alibi. The other two insist they were elsewhere at the time.'

Laura nodded. 'So, does that mean Mark's alibi lets him off the hook?'

'He has been released, yes, along with the other two. The evidence that we have does not point to them. However, we must now turn to you.'

Laura's eyes widened again. 'Why?' she gasped. 'Surely you don't think I did it?'

'Miss Bowles,' said the detective smoothly, 'we know that you were having a party that evening. But,' he added and held up the £50 note, 'you've just produced what might well be vital evidence.' Laura cursed herself silently. 'So, what we need from you is a list of everyone at your party. Can you do that for us, together with addresses and telephone numbers?'

Laura pulled a face. 'Well, I'll try,' she said. 'But, some of them were friends of friends, you know. It could take me days!'

The detective smiled.

The policewoman said gently, 'That's all we can ask of you.'

Laura stood and followed the three of them out through the kitchen, up the stairs into the vast hallway and then out through the front door. She closed it thankfully behind her and walked slowly back to her flat, cursing her own stupidity at handing over the forged banknote.

⊗⊙⊗

Stella awoke with a sudden clarity of thought and a sinking feeling of dread. Her mother was in town. She moaned and pulled the duvet over her head and tried to immerse herself in a cocoon of cotton and happy thoughts, but to no avail. Her mother was here and she had to take her to see the sights and maybe do some shopping. She brightened a little; perhaps the old bag would buy her something nice, for once, now that she had some money.

As childhoods go, hers hadn't been all that bad, but the fact that she had escaped to London soon after leaving school, as street-wise as any young girl from a small village in Scotland could be without satellite TV or access to the internet, was some indication of the frustration she'd felt as a child. Growing up in Iris's shadow and hand-me-downs hadn't helped. Her mother had wanted a boy; her sister had wanted a puppy and her father had wanted another woman. In the end, none of them got what they wanted which generated a lot of bitterness, a lot of shouting and a lot of unhappiness. Stella put aside these thoughts, kicked off the duvet and stood, stretching and yawning.

And then suddenly remembered Hugh.

She rushed to the phone and grabbed at it, punched in Hugh's number and waited impatiently as it rang. On the sixth ring, the answering machine should've cut in, but it didn't, just like the previous evening. Which meant that Hugh had not been home all night. She was about to slam the phone down when a sleepy, deeply male voice said, 'Hello?'

'Hugh, is that you? It's me. Where the hell have you been? I've been trying to get you since yesterday evening!'

Hugh coughed. 'Och, sorry hen, I've been a bit tied up.'

Stella distinctly heard a man snigger in the background. 'Who's that there with you?' she demanded.

'Och, just a mate I haven't seen for ages. I bumped into him yesterday and we went out on the piss. What's up?'

'Eh?'

'You said you'd been trying to get hold of me since yesterday.'

Stella shook her head. 'Oh, yeah, my mum's down. She's staying at the Post House in Hampstead. I'm off out shopping with her now. When do you want to meet her?'

'Is *never* ok?' asked Hugh.

'Don't be funny, Hugh,' chided Stella. 'You said you wanted to meet her. Well, now's your chance.'

'Look hen, I've had a rough night...' Another snigger. 'I'll call you later, ok?'

'Suit yourself,' Stella said and hung up. *That bloody Hugh*, she thought. He's always bumping into people and going on the piss. Well, he was going to have to stop that, if she was going to marry him. *Oops*, she thought and went quite red. That was the first time that she'd ever thought about marrying Hugh. Perhaps it was getting serious.

ഓരു

Hugh put the phone down and turned to face Glen. He noticed with a violent surge in his loins the musculature of his broad back, the nape of his neck where his close-cropped black hair ended in a whisper of bristles and the bulging bicep with the inky-black word *Mother* in bold contrast to his winter-white skin. Glen was lying face down on Hugh's bed with one huge arm tucked under a pillow, on which he was resting his stubble-covered jaw, whilst his other equally impressive arm was tucked ~~down by his~~ side. The duvet just covered his butt, leaving a mound that drew Hugh as a moth to a flame. He reached forward and gently pulled the duvet down to reveal a rounded pair of butt cheeks covered in soft black fur that centred on a darker, tantalisingly puckered hollow that Hugh already knew the texture and smell and taste of. Hugh threw the duvet onto the floor and knelt between Glen's hairy legs, pushing them wider apart with his knees. He reached forward and opened the bedside cabinet and withdrew lube and a condom.

'You ready for this?' he said, slapping his cock against Glen's hole.

A grunt came from deep inside Glen and a grin formed on his lips. 'You bet,' he said, adding, 'Don't be gentle.'

'Wouldn't fucking dream of it, mate,' Hugh replied, rolling the condom onto his stiff cock. He squeezed out some lube and slapped it in place, squirming his finger inside, then two fingers. He squeezed some more lube onto his cock and rubbed it all over, loving the feel. His hard cock jutted outwards and upwards from his groin. He was ready. Positioning himself, he started to apply pressure, felt a little resistance, but then felt himself slide in right up to the hilt. Glen grunted and winced, but then his face resumed smiling.

Hugh bent down and kissed him behind the ear, just where the stubble was thickest. 'Hang on,' he whispered. 'This is going to be a rough ride.' Then he grabbed hold of Glen's neck with one hand, slapped his buttocks with the other and started to thrust long and hard, gathering more and more momentum with each slap and thrust.

കരു

Pierre was propped up in bed watching Saturday morning TV and drinking strong black coffee from a cracked mug with a Far Side caricature imprint. He enjoyed living alone in the small bed-sit on the top floor of Netherhall, sharing a small bathroom with the occupants of two other small bed-sits.

On one side was a young girl who frequently had her boyfriend staying, usually moaning all night and then screaming at each other during the day. On the other side was a tall, dark-haired interesting-looking young man who only ever wore black, including eyeliner. Pierre had spoken to him only once, and then only briefly. He didn't know the names of either of his neighbours. He wouldn't mind getting to know them. At least there would be someone else to talk to around here other than Laura.

He took a gulp of very strong, very black and very sweet coffee. He had just completed the rolling of a masterpiece of a joint and was ridiculously pleased with the result. 'Looks almost too good to smoke,' he said aloud.

Just then there came a loud knock on his door. He jumped, quickly hid the ashtray and its contents under the bed, grabbed a tee shirt over his head and went to the door.

'Who is it?' he yelled.

'It's me,' Laura said. 'We need to talk.'

'I'm still in bed,' he called back. 'I'll come down to you in ten minutes or so, ok?'

Laura grunted and stomped off.

Pierre jumped back into bed and pulled the ashtray from under his bed.

'Now, where were we, my beauty?' he said and inserted the joint into his mouth, lit it and relished the thick swirl of smoke as it hit the back of his throat and plunged into his waiting lungs.

കരു

Half an hour later, Pierre was ushered into Laura's lounge. He was pleasantly stoned, dressed in a tee shirt, a scruffy old pair of jeans and had obviously not bothered with a comb. He still looked good though, he pointed out to himself, as he passed a mirror on the wall of Laura's lounge.

'Ten minutes, you said,' Laura ticked him off like a child.

'Sorreee,' Pierre sang.

Laura peered at him closely. 'You're stoned. Honestly, it's ten o'clock in the morning!'

Pierre shrugged. 'It's what I do, when I do it.'

'Yes, well if you're not careful, you won't be doing it for much longer.'

'What do you mean?'

'Sit down,' Laura ordered, 'and listen… The police have just been round here, again.'

Pierre's eyes widened and the blood drained from his face.

Satisfied, she went on, 'They've arrested three people in connection with the murder…'

'Really?' Pierre jumped up, the colour returning to his cheeks.

'Sit down! I haven't finished!'

Pierre slowly sank back onto the sofa and she added, 'They've let them go. They were the wrong people, apparently.'

'Oh… Shit,' Pierre said, putting his head into his hands.

'Precisely,' Laura agreed. 'On top of that, I've now given them the £50 note.'

'What?' yelled Pierre, jumping up again. 'What d'you go and do a stupid thing like that for?'

Laura sucked in her lower lip for a moment. 'In case you're unaware, this is a murder investigation, and that £50 note is vital evidence. And withholding evidence is a serious crime.'

'And so is murder!' cried Pierre.

'Only if you commit it.'

'But, I didn't!'

Laura's voice softened. 'Then you have nothing to worry about. I suggest you go to the police and tell them what happened. Those people who replied to my escort agency ad could well be the murderers and only you can give a description.' ·

'How do you know it wasn't one of them who *was* murdered?' Pierre demanded.

Laura picked up Friday's copy of the Evening Standard and thrust it at Pierre. 'Look. There's a photo and a description. The boy's very young.'

Pierre looked. The young man was only nineteen and had been a male escort for only a few months. He was exceptionally good looking and the photograph showed off his brilliant white teeth, long blond hair and blemish-free skin.

'Looks a bit like me,' was all that Pierre could say.

'Don't kid yourself,' Laura muttered under her breath.

'What?'

'I said, *It must be like looking at yourself*. Now, the point is, *you* know who the murderers are. You know their names and what they look like. You have no option but to go to the police.'

'That's not what you said the other day,' Pierre protested.

'I know. I was wrong, ok?' Laura bit her lower lip: a metallic taste told her she'd drawn blood. 'Just try and keep me out of this, if you can.'

Pierre was sober enough now to realise the likelihood of that. 'It's bound to come out, Laura. It says here that the deceased was introduced by an escort agency. It's not illegal to run an escort agency, is it?'

Laura looked at him. 'That depends,' she said, 'but whether it is or not, just me being here is illegal. My Visa's run out and I haven't been able to renew it. If they get suspicious, they might pry.'

'Well, the worst they can do is send you home, isn't that right?'

'You make it sound so simple,' she sighed and patted his knee as he sat down beside her. 'Anyway, this is more important. You must go to the police right away.'

Pierre thought for a minute or so. 'Yeah, I guess you're right.'

₾₿

Mark had been unable to sleep for most of the night, even after two wanks. He couldn't help but imagine all kinds of wild scenarios that would have taken place if he'd stayed at Hugh's and, in the cold light of morning, he cursed himself for leaving the pair of them alone together. He should have stayed and either joined in with whatever games they decided to play, or made sure that Hugh and Glen were kept well apart. He realised, suddenly, that whilst he lusted after Hugh, he wasn't about to fall in love with him.

Still, what should he do now? Study? Boring! The day was too warm and sunny to stay indoors, so he decided to make the most of it. He put on his swimming trunks, shorts and a white tee shirt, rolled a few joints and set off on the short walk to Hyde Park.

At the north gate, a crowd of well-dressed Japanese tourists were standing around taking photographs of each other in various poses, giggling a lot and enjoying themselves. Mark smiled as he passed and took a narrow path that wound between the trees, crossed a small footbridge over a tributary of the Serpentine, and was soon far enough away from crowds and prying eyes to smoke a joint. He sat down on a small tree stump and lit it, inhaled, held it and then exhaled noisily.

'Enjoying that?' came a masculine voice from behind.

Mark spun around as a tall, blond-haired man appeared from the bushes. Around thirty years old, he was well built, tanned with a carefully trimmed blond moustache and goatee. The man reached into the pocket of his jeans and took out his id card. 'Detective PC Evans,' he said.

Mark stayed calm, the joint still smouldering in his hand. The policeman came up to him and held out his hand. Mark gave him the joint. To his enormous surprise, PC Evans took a drag and handed it back.

'Mm, not bad,' he said, surprising Mark even more. 'Though I know where you can get a lot better.'

Mark hesitated, and when the policeman smiled, showing his even white teeth, he took another drag and sat back down on the tree stump. PC Evans sought out another stump and perched on it. They faced each other and Mark was pleased to see that not only was PC Evans a good looker, he also had a large cock. The bulge was becoming more and more obvious.

'So,' said Mark, eventually, dragging his gaze from the policeman's groin, 'what are you doing around these bushes? Watching out for someone?'

'Could be,' said PC Evans, shifting his position to ease his cramped cock. Mark passed him the joint. PC Evans took another drag and passed it back. 'Better not have any more of that,' he said. 'We get tested now and then.'

Mark nodded. Dope testing was routinely carried out at some of the companies he'd audited, especially stockbrokers for some reason although it was a practice that was dying out: they were losing too many of their best staff.

'So,' he said, 'who're you watching out for?'

The policeman just tapped his nose and smiled secretively. After a few moments, he said, 'Care for a blow-job?' and grabbed his hard cock through the denim of his jeans.

Mark could see its bulk extending halfway down the policeman's leg. He took a last drag of the joint and stubbed it out with his foot. He got up, moved closer to the policeman and kissed him full on the lips, licking around the edge of his moustache. He pulled away. 'I'm sorry, Officer,' he said, 'but I can't.'

'Why not? I'm as horny as fuck! You've got to... Please?' The policeman was actually pleading with him.

Mark thought for a few moments and then smiled. 'Ok,' he said, 'but not here. I'm not the outdoor type.'

The policeman laughed out loud. He had a deep, sexy laugh and a nice smile to complement it. His white teeth, framed as they were in dark blond bristles, lit up his clear blue eyes. Mark's eyes always went slightly red when he smoked dope.

'You're very handsome,' the policeman said and pulled Mark to him. He kissed him gently on the mouth, probing the softness inside with a strong tongue. The goatee bristles rubbed Mark's upper lip and chin deliciously. Mark grabbed hold of PC Evans's head with both hands and forced him to rub harder. His ran his right hand through the policeman's short blond hair whilst pushing on the back of his head with the other. PC Evans let out a rush of air.

'Whoa,' he said. 'You really want it, don't you?'

Mark had been 'really wanting it' ever since his first meeting with Hugh. In fact, he had thought of little else since. He looked PC Evans in the eyes and nodded.

'Just be gentle,' he said.

Stella was sitting facing her mother who was next to Iris. They were riding in a black cab on their way to Knightsbridge with her mother wittering on in a broad Scottish accent that was frankly grating on Stella's nerves. She hadn't realised just how much of her own accent she had lost. She loved her homeland with all her heart and was tirelessly proud of her heritage but, staring out of the window, she wished more than anything that her mother was back on the other side of the border. Suddenly, she screamed.

She pulled down the window feverishly as the cabbie swung around the east side of Hyde Park just in front of the Dorchester Hotel.

'Mark!!' she yelled through the window. Her mother grabbed her forcefully and pulled her roughly inside.

'Behave yourself, child,' she said sternly.

Stella was indignant. 'But, it was a friend of mine,' she protested. 'He was crossing the road with er... with another friend.'

'Showing yourself up like that!' continued her mother, ignoring her. 'Is this what living in London has done to you? Is it? You've no standards, my girl, just like that no good father of yours.' Stella was about to make a comment but Iris shut her up with a fierce look. Her mother continued unabated. 'I don't like your accent, by the way. You sound English,' she said and sniffed, as if that was enough of an insult.

'Now, Ma,' said Iris gently, 'you promised to be nice.'

They saw the tension in their mother's shoulders shift as Mrs Roberts settled back again in her seat. 'Where are we now?' she asked, peering out through the windows.

'We're at Hyde Park Corner,' Iris informed her. 'We should be at Harrods in a few minutes... See that,' she added, pointing at Admiralty Arch in the distance, 'that's the er... er monument thingy.'

Stella rolled her eyes heavenward. 'It's Admiral's Archway,' she said.

The cabbie shifted in his seat, biting his tongue.

Her mother peered at it. 'Hmm,' she said.

The rest of the journey was short but spent in silence until they reached Harrods where the cabbie dropped them off right outside the main doors. Iris paid him and tipped him 50p. 'Thank you, kindly,' he said and gladly drove off in a cloud of black smoke, leaving them coughing on the pavement.

'Och, this filthy air'll kill me,' their mother wheezed.

Stella said nothing, but Iris could read her thoughts. She wagged a finger at her.

Stella mouthed at her, 'Why did you pay for the cab?'

Iris mouthed back, 'Mum gave me £50 for expenses.'

'Eh, what're you two up to?' demanded their mother. 'Whispering away, like that. Up to no good, I expect.'

'Now, mum, don't be silly. Stella was just telling me who her friend was she saw,' Iris explained, holding onto her arm and leading her towards the entrance to Harrods.

'Who was it then?' the old lady demanded.

'Her friend, Mark. You'll probably meet him at Laura's dinner party next week.'

'What dinner party?' demanded their mother. 'I haven't been invited to a dinner party, have I?'

Stella was standing back aghast and frantically shaking her head. Iris looked at her helplessly.

'I shall enjoy that,' said Mrs Roberts cheerily. 'I've never been to a dinner party. How posh!'

Stella slumped against the outside wall of Harrods, her hand to her forehead, staring at the sky with wide unseeing eyes. Iris ignored her as she led her mother through the gleaming doors.

℘℃ℜ

Mark stopped dead. His new policeman friend, Steve, had to grab him and pull him roughly out of the way of a speeding black BMW. They had just left the park and were heading towards Oxford Street. Steve lived in a house whose freehold was owned by the Duke of Westminster near Old Bond Street. Mark was scanning the road and the passing cars.

'What's up?' Steve asked him cautiously.

'Um, I'm not sure,' Mark replied. 'I just heard my name being shouted. It sounded like someone I know. How strange!'

Steve shrugged his shoulders. 'Maybe they were passing or

129

maybe it was the wind or maybe you're just going mad. Who cares? Come on, I'm feeling horny.'

Mark started moving again. It had been Stella's voice. Just when he's about to have sex with a man, Stella intervenes. She did it with Hugh, twice, and now with this policeman. Well, kismet or no kismet, he was going to have sex with this man whether she liked it or not! And now he was being irrational. How could she possibly have known? Unless she was being guided by a higher being. Maybe he had a fairy godmother, or a spirit guide like those mediums claim we all have. Maybe, they were trying to tell him something. Maybe both Hugh and this policeman were dangerous in some way.

'Hope you don't mind me asking,' Mark began, 'but have you had an AIDS test?'

'You mean, HIV? Yes, I have. We get tested regularly for that too! Have you been tested?'

'Er, no. I've only ever had sex with women.'

They had crossed over into Oxford Street, Marble Arch end, and proceeded to fight their way through the crowds of shoppers and tourists.

'And your point would be?' Steve asked him.

Mark went red.

'If you always practise safe sex,' Steve continued, 'you will always be safe.' He hissed in Mark's ear, 'I presume you always use a condom, right?'

Mark felt a momentary brush of stubble against his cheek. He nodded as he looked around at the crowds pressing in on all sides. No one seemed to have noticed.

'Of course,' he replied confidently, sounding like a seasoned stud. In truth, he could count the number of women he'd been to bed with on one finger.

'Then you're an extremely low risk. Anyway, we'll be having safe sex, you can bet on that.'

Mark wasn't sure that the conversation had gone according to plan. 'I take it you're negative, then?' he asked.

'I was, the last time I was tested, about three weeks ago. And, before you ask, I've had plenty of sex in the last three months. All safe.' They came to a side street. 'Come on,' he added, pulling Mark by the arm, 'it's better this way. Less people.'

Mark followed behind him, and then soon they were able to walk side by side and talk more easily.

'You have a lot of sex, then?' Mark asked in a casual tone.

The policeman looked at him sideways and smiled handsomely. 'If you must know,' he said, 'it was mainly with the same guy. We split up quite recently.'

'Had you been together long?'

The policeman nodded. 'Yeah, but a bit too long, if you know what I mean. The sex was keeping us together. It was totally wild.'

They came to another junction and crossed over into a side-street full of restaurants. The pavement was buzzing with people out enjoying the sun, sipping cold drinks and nibbling on green salads, chatting and laughing or just sitting reading newspapers.

'So, you've never had sex with a man?' he added.

Mark shook his head slowly. 'Almost, but not quite,' he said, then grinned. 'This'll be my first time.'

Steve grinned back and squeezed his shoulder. 'I am honoured,' he said.

They turned another corner and Steve stopped abruptly. 'This is it,' he said, peering up at a shiny black door with grey marble steps. 'Looks a bit grander than it is.'

He produced a bunch of keys and led the way up the steps, opened the door and was greeted by a high-pitched buzzer. Steve punched in a code and silenced it, then led Mark through into a cool, darkened interior that smelled very faintly musty. Otherwise, it was perfect. The floor was a mosaic of small black and white tiles and Steve's boots clicked attractively on them as he walked through into the long, narrow kitchen. Mark followed.

'You want a cold drink?' he asked. Mark nodded. 'Orange juice, beer or water, I'm afraid. That's all I've got. Or maybe some wine?'

'What are you having?'

'Orange juice. I'm on duty, remember.'

'Oh, yes, of course,' said Mark, adding, 'Well, Officer, I'll join you, if I may.'

Steve poured two orange juices and handed Mark a full glass, then he led the way through into a lounge overlooking a small patio area. The patio was surrounded by mature shrubs, with one wall of what looked like a passionflower. It was hard for Mark, with his limited horticultural knowledge, to tell so early in the season. The room itself was tastefully decorated in a light peach and terracotta, with wall lights and a large white sofa and two armchairs. A few peach coloured cushions were scattered around.

'Very nice,' said Mark approvingly. 'The police force obviously pays well.'

'I inherited it from my grandmother, but it's only got another few years left on the lease, then the Duke of Westminster gets it back.'

'Well, it's very nice,' Mark repeated.

Steve walked over to the patio doors and opened them to let in the air. A sweet, unidentifiable smell wafted into the room. Some sort of flowering shrub, no doubt. He returned and sat next to Mark on the large sofa. They clinked glasses.

'Bottoms up,' said Steve and grinned.

Mark grinned back and raised his eyebrows suggestively. He was nervous, if truth be told.

'Er, do you mind if we smoke another joint?' he asked, aware that he was in the home of a policeman.

'Be my guest.' Steve got up to retrieve an ashtray from the mantelpiece and sat back down even closer to Mark than before, placing the ashtray on a glass-topped coffee table in front of them. Mark reached into his shorts and took out his familiar tin, selected a nice fat one, lit it and took a few drags.

'You want some,' he said, offering the joint.

'I shouldn't,' Steve replied, 'but well, what the hell, may as well be hung for a sheep as for a lamb, or something like that.'

He accepted the joint, took a drag and exhaled slowly through his nose, repeated this and handed it back to Mark who did the same and offered it once more.

Steve shook his head. 'I want a clear head when I fuck you,' he said.

Mark felt his insides tighten and his cock muscles twitch. He took another drag of the joint and also felt his leg muscles weaken. He stubbed out the joint and took a large gulp of orange juice.

Steve put his hand on Mark's knee. 'Are you sure you want to go through with this?'

Mark turned to him and grabbed his head, forcing their lips together causing Steve's goatee to rub against his chin, sending delicious erotic impulses to his brain. His cock hardened and he slid his hand down Steve's hard chest, feeling every sinewy contour down to his groin. Mark felt the long hardness of Steve's cock through his jeans and started to undo the zip.

'Mm, not here,' mumbled Steve. 'Let's do this properly.'

He stood up, his cock clearly straining at the denim of his jeans, and hauled Mark to his feet, kissed him and led him through into the hall and then up a short flight of stairs to the first landing.

'I have a games room, with a sling,' he said. 'Uniforms, the lot. But, next time eh? This time, we'll use my bed... You ever used a douche?'

Mark shook his head.

'You had a shit today?'

Mark nodded.

'Good, then you should only need a quick douche.' He guided Mark into the bathroom, which was huge and well lit with a few potted ferns and a washing machine plumbed in. There was a large oval white bath and next to that a small sink and then next to that the toilet and shower cubicle. The large opaque window overlooked the patio. Steve took a small orange rubber douche from behind one of the ferns and showed Mark how to use it. 'Just don't blow any air up your arse or you'll be farting for a fortnight,' he said crudely, closing the door.

Steve grabbed a couple of towels from a cupboard on the landing and went into his bedroom where he stripped, took two condoms from the bedside drawer together with a pot of condom-friendly lubricant and lay down on his bed. He stroked his cock slowly whilst he waited.

⅏

'Would you just look at the price of that?' gasped Mrs Roberts, holding up an ornate cardboard telephone cover. 'A hundred and fifty pounds!? Am I seeing right?' She thrust it under Iris's nose.

133

'Yes, Ma, and keep your voice down; you'll have us thrown out. Besides, you can afford it now, if you want it.'

Stella was standing to one side watching this drama unfold and her patience was at an all time low. 'How much *did* you win, by the way?' she asked.

'Enough!' barked her mother.

'Good, then bloody well buy it and let's get out of here,' Stella retorted. 'We've been here almost three hours and you haven't bought a thing. I've had enough. I want a cup of tea and something to eat.'

Her mother looked at her and then at Iris. 'Are you going to let her talk to me like that?' she demanded.

Iris flashed her eyes defiantly. 'Yes, mother, I am,' she said, adding forcefully, 'Come on, put that down. We're leaving. Right now.'

'But, I've only seen half the shop,' their mother protested, 'and I promised your Aunty Edna something from Harrods.'

Iris caught hold of her mother's arm. 'We'll come back next week,' she said gently. 'Right now, Stella and I want a nice cup of tea and a nice little chat with you.'

Their mother looked up sharply. 'What about?'

'Wait and see. Now, where shall we go for a nice cuppa?'

⁊

Mark was sitting on the loo, not knowing whether he wanted to crap or not. His arse was tender, but nicely so. He dabbed at it gently with tissue, stood up, pulled the chain and walked back into the bedroom where Steve was propped up in bed, his naked torso still glistening with sweat and cum.

'Finished in there?' he asked.

Mark nodded.

Steve jumped out of bed and went to clean up. Mark got back under the warm duvet and lay thinking about what had just happened. It was certainly the most painful sex he'd ever had, but also the most exciting. He would never forget the moment when Steve had gently entered his body, of that he was sure. His cock was growing hard again just thinking about it.

Steve came back into the room and smiled.

'You ok?' he asked, jumping onto the bed and snuggling up to Mark. He put his arm around him and kissed him on the cheek.

Mark lay back in his arms and breathed deeply. 'Sure am,' he replied, exhaling slowly. Then a thought struck him. 'Aren't you supposed to be on duty? You know, at work?'

'I was earlier. I'm a plain clothes policeman. I get paid to wander around and keep my ears and eyes open. I shouldn't tell you, but I'm working on a high profile case at the moment. We arrested three people last night, but had to let them go. Fingerprints didn't match.'

Mark was thinking this through as Steve spoke. 'Anything to do with the recent spate of murders?' he asked.

'Might be.'

Mark began to laugh.

'What's so funny?' Steve asked, propping himself up on one elbow.

'I was one of those arrested.'

Steve immediately sat upright. 'What?' he demanded. 'You're kidding me!'

Mark sat upright too. 'Afraid not,' he replied. 'I guess that means we're finished?'

Steve looked puzzled. 'Why? They let you go; you haven't murdered anyone.'

'Well, technically, I'm one of your suspects,' Mark replied.

Steve laughed. 'Very briefly. And anyway, I wasn't on duty last night. Who arrested you?'

Mark thought for a moment. 'Don't remember his name, but he was blond, short hair, about thirty, over six foot.'

Steve was shaking his head. 'Could be one of a dozen,' he said. 'Who interviewed you?'

'Um, someone called Charles Dickens. Now that name I can remember!'

Steve nodded his head. 'He's my boss.'

'Yeah, well he wasn't so bad. I can't say I've had worse, since I've never been drilled by a policeman before.'

Steve grinned. 'Well, you've been *drilled* by two now.'

Mark raised his eyebrows. 'I certainly have,' he agreed. They kissed for a few moments.

'So, who were the other two arrested? Friends of yours?' Steve asked, idly fondling Mark's balls.

'Sort of. A friend of a friend called Hugh. He's a Scottish guy who's been after my body for the past few weeks. He's been going out with a friend of mine called Stella whose mum's just won the lottery.'

Steve was now playing with Mark's cock. 'I expect he'll go back to her then if she's going to be rich,' he said, squeezing it.

'Well, he hasn't actually finished with her,' Mark explained, wincing as Steve tugged at the hairs surrounding his balls. 'He wanted us both, separately, at the same time!'

'He's bi-sexual then?'

'I guess so.'

'And greedy.'

'Mmm. Yes, I guess so,' Mark growled. Steve had pulled his foreskin right back and was about to lick it.

'Is he horny looking?'

'You fucking bet.'

'How horny?' Steve asked, teasing the end of Mark's pulsing cock with the tip of his tongue.

'Very! Muscular, short black hair, black moustache...'

'But, you've dumped him, huh?' Steve darted his tongue around the head of Mark's cock.

'Yes. Anyway, I think he got off with the other guy. The one arrested with us.'

Steve looked up from Mark's engorged groin, his glistening goatee just tickling the end of Mark's cock. 'Is he horny as well?'

Mark nodded.

'Describe him,' Steve demanded, slowly licking the length of Mark's shaft.

'Uh, mmm that's good... Um, he's tall, dark haired too, more muscular than Hugh, unshaven, handsome smile. He's a security guard at Waitrose on the Finchley Road.'

Steve jerked upright. 'What's his name?' he demanded

Mark looked surprised. 'Um, Glen something or other... Why? Steve, what's the matter?'

Steve was white. 'Oh, shit,' he said.

Mark was worried now. 'What's the matter? Have I said something wrong? Tell me!'

Steve pulled himself together. 'I'm sorry,' he said. 'It's just that I know this Glen. He's my ex - the guy I just split up with!'

Mark lay there open-mouthed. 'You're kidding! Bloody hell. Isn't the world a small place? I only met him last week. It's a long story, but I was in Waitrose with a friend and we had some bother with a shoplifter. Glen came to sort things out and I suddenly felt sick and then fainted. He caught me in those huge arms of his.'

Steve suddenly looked grim. 'And you would be Mark Carter and, of course, you live in Bayswater...'

Mark looked at him, his eyes wide.

Steve waved a hand. 'Glen asked me to do a search on your debit card only yesterday. He said he'd fallen madly in love and needed to trace where you live. I wasn't going to do it, but he pleaded and pleaded so I eventually agreed just to get rid of him. I used the Met's computer... If he was arrested, it must be because I used his real name for the search. Damn! How was I to know you'd turn out to be a murder suspect?'

'He said he was madly in love with me? I hardly spoke to him.'

'He means lust, don't worry.'

Mark nodded thoughtfully, smiling to himself. *So, that's why he couldn't look me in the eye last night*, he thought. Mark was watching as Steve returned his attention to his pubic region. 'Why use his real name for the search, anyway?' he asked.

'No reason not to. Anyway, the computer checks names against addresses and if they don't match, the enquiry can't continue. The results are then posted to that address. The public can get any information they want, up to a point, but not discreetly.'

Mark sighed. 'Oh, well. No real harm done then.'

'I suppose not,' Steve agreed, 'though I bet Detective Chief Inspector Charles Dickens will have a few words to say to me about doing favours for friends.'

'Talking of which,' said Mark looking down at his own erect cock.

Steve licked his lips and took the hint.

Charles Dickens was in his office enjoying an afternoon cup of tea and an ice-cold Kit Kat, which was his favourite chocolate bar in the whole world. He had recently discovered orange Kit Kats and was presently in seventh heaven, stuffing two delicious chocolate fingers into his mouth all at once. Consequently, when his telephone shrilled next to him, he was unable to answer it immediately. Swallowing as quickly as he could, he picked up the receiver.

'Dickens?' he barked.

'Sir, a gentleman calling himself Peter Morgan is in reception in connection with the Bayswater murder. He says he may be able to help in our enquiries.'

'Thank you Sergeant, I'll be out shortly.'

Dickens lingered lovingly over his last piece of Kit Kat before finishing it off with a gulp of tea. He sighed. He hated hurrying his afternoon break. Still, yet another lead just dropping into his lap? He stood and walked out of his office, down the long corridor and out through the security doors into reception and paused: the similarity in appearance of the young men involved in this case was hard to ignore.

'Mr Morgan?' he said.

The young man stood and offered a nervous hand to shake. He smelled of cigarettes and something else. Detective Chief Inspector Charles Dickens knew that smell well. The boy was obviously stoned!

'Please, call me Pierre. My real name's Peter, but everybody calls me Pierre.'

'Well then Pierre,' said Dickens, smiling grimly. 'What can we do for you?'

'Is there somewhere we can talk in private? It's about the Bayswater murders.'

'That's murder, singular,' corrected Dickens. He looked sharply at the Sergeant on the desk. 'Got a room free?'

'Room 3's free for an hour, maybe an hour and a half.'

'Come on then lad; let's hear what you have to say.'

Within a few minutes, Detective Chief Inspector Dickens was on the internal phone to the desk Sergeant demanding a *Category A* room with full recording and interrogation equipment plus the recall of all team members assigned to this case. At last, a real breakthrough!

ℰℭ

Mark was bundled out of the policeman's front door a lot faster than he went in. Steve had received an emergency call and had to return to HQ, on the double. Steve gave Mark his phone number and insisted that he call. Mark agreed to do so. Steve hailed a cab and Mark was soon left alone on the pavement with the memory (and pain) of a thoroughly enjoyable and interesting afternoon. It had been quite different to the afternoon he had anticipated of lounging in a deck chair, enjoying the sunshine, in Hyde Park.

His arse felt as if it still had Steve's hard cock lodged inside. It wasn't uncomfortable, but it did make him wonder if he had done any permanent damage. Steve had a large cock and he knew how to use it. The thought brought a smile to his face and a warm feeling inside.

He set off home and was just outside the Marble Arch tube station, when he heard a shrill scream and turned in time to see a black cab whiz past with a familiar head sticking out of the side window. It was promptly withdrawn and the window banged shut. The cab came to an emergency stop and a small bundle of energy leapt out, ran at Mark and hugged him.

'Oh, am I glad to see you!' squealed Stella. 'I saw you a few hours ago, but we were on our way to Harrods! Harrods! Can you believe it? Anyway, then we...'

'Hey, hold on a minute,' Mark said. 'Slow down, slow down. Do you fancy a cuppa? I know I do.'

Stella wrinkled up her nose. 'Not really, I've just had some. Could do with something cold and alcoholic though.'

'That sounds like an aunt of mine,' Mark joked. 'Ok, let's find a café or bar somewhere. Any ideas?' They looked about but nowhere looked very appealing. Then Mark had a thought: 'There's a gay bar around here somewhere with a garden, I think. Are you ok with that?'

'Sure, why wouldn't I be? Let's hurry; I've got lots to tell you!'

They hurried, despite the heat. It had become an unseasonably warm, late spring afternoon and they were perspiring by the time they reached The Tin Man up a side street off of the Edgware Road. They walked in and carried on through into a small sunlit courtyard. Luckily, there was one table free and they thankfully sat down.

'So, what are you having?'

'Him, over there,' Stella replied, eyeing up a man in his early thirties with long dark hair and long sideburns. He looked like a biker with his leather trousers and boots.

'You like a bit of rough then?' Mark teased.

Stella smiled and blinked coquettishly. 'That's for me to know. Anyway, I think he's more interested in you.'

'Well, it is a gay bar. Anyway, what do you want to drink?'

Stella thought for a moment. 'Um, I think I'll have... um, what have they got?'

Mark raised his hands in an open expression. 'Stella, it's a bar. Whatever you want.'

'Do they do cocktails? If so, I'll have a long comfortable screw, preferably with him over there.'

'You'll get what you're given,' Mark said, leaving Stella to sit and wait and see.

The bar man was very friendly and did not, in any way, resemble Marilyn at the Edward. He was broad and masculine and smiled continuously. 'You from around here?' he asked Mark.

Mark was happy to chat. 'Yeah, I live in Bayswater. You?'

'I live above the pub here. I'm the Landlord.' He poured Mark an orange juice and asked, 'Anything else?'

'Well, don't take this the wrong way, but I'd like a long comfortable screw,' said Mark, hiding a smile.

The landlord smiled even wider. 'You mean a *slow* comfortable screw?'

'Well, both actually,' said Mark, flirting outrageously.

'Well, I'm sorry,' the landlord replied, 'but we don't do cocktails.'

'Who's talking about cocktails?' Mark asked. They both laughed. 'Better make it a vodka and tonic, in a tall glass, with lots of ice and tonic.'

'Coming right up.'

Just then something curious happened. A couple in their mid-to-late twenties came into the bar and stared intently at Mark, looked strangely at each other, turned round and went straight out again. Mark thought nothing more about it.

The landlord was back with the drink. Mark handed him a fiver and waited for the change.

He returned and handed over a few coins. 'Bayswater, you said?' Mark nodded.

'You take care, now,' he warned him. 'There's a murderer about around here. The Police have been in and out like buck rabbits on Viagra. Pretty boy like you… Well, you just be careful. Oh, and don't be a stranger; the name's Douggie.' He held out his hand and Mark shook it.

'Mark,' said Mark.

The landlord smiled and winked. Mark picked up the drinks and walked back outside, sipping his orange juice and smiling to himself, to where Stella was enjoying the view.

'All these men are gorgeous,' she said accepting her drink. She looked at it questioningly.

'Vodka and tonic,' Mark explained with a shrug.

'Fair enough,' she said taking a sip. She sat back in her chair and relaxed. The sun shone on her face when she did this and she revelled in it for a few moments. Then she abruptly sat upright and faced Mark.

'Right then,' she said, 'you know my mother's arrived?'

'No,' Mark exclaimed. 'When did this happen?'

'Oh, she arrived last night. It was all last minute. Didn't I tell you she was coming down? Anyway, she's here and I've just spent three bloody hours traipsing around Harrods with her and Iris.'

'That's a bit much,' Mark laughed. 'Did she spend any of her lottery winnings?'

'Not a bloody penny,' said Stella, about to take a sip of her drink. The drink paused half way to her lips. 'How do you know about that?' she demanded. 'I was just about to tell you!'

Mark blushed. 'Y… You did tell me,' he stammered. *Oh shit*, he thought, *now look what you've said*. He would have to be more on guard from now on. That's what he didn't like about all this business with Hugh.

'I'm sure I didn't,' Stella replied, adding, 'Why have you gone red?'

'Have I?' asked Mark. 'I'm just hot.'

'Mm,' said Stella. 'I don't remember telling you. The only other person I've told is Hugh.'

'Well, they do say I'm psychic,' Mark explained. *And an idiot*, he thought.

'Well, anyway, maybe I did tell you. You get me so stoned.' She started to giggle. 'Have you got any with you?'

Mark shook his head. He'd smoked them all at Steve's. 'I did have this morning, but I've had rather an *interesting* afternoon.'

'Really? Anything rude?'

'Very,' Mark replied, sipping his juice. 'But I want to hear about your mum first.'

'Oh, right. Well, she's won all this money, but won't tell us how much. She says it will be a surprise for everyone in her will. Huh, she'll outlive us all, that one. They say that the good die young, don't they?'

Mark had to agree.

'Well, in that case, she'll live to be a hundred, the old bag.'

'Stella!' said Mark shocked. He couldn't even think of saying such a thing about his own mum.

'Oh, you don't know her,' said Stella defensively, taking a large swig of vodka and tonic. 'She hasn't stopped having a dig at me since she arrived, not to mention the last twenty odd years. Whereas Iris, of course, can do no wrong.'

'Why's that? Is she her favourite or something?' Mark asked, gulping his orange juice.

'Oh, it's a long story… You don't want to hear it now. Iris and I have different fathers. Her father died when she was a baby and mum never really got over it. Later, she met my father and he turned out, according to her, to be a real bastard who nearly drank himself to death… Trying to get away from her probably,' she added nastily.

Mark was unaccustomed to hearing Stella speak with such animosity and he wasn't sure he liked it. Then her face changed and she laughed. 'And now she's won the bloody lottery and I've suddenly got to be nice to her. Well, I don't care about the money. From now on, I'm going to tell her exactly what I think. That should cause a few laughs. Yeah,' she said picking up her glass. 'Here's to the old bag.'

She clinked glasses with Mark and they downed the remainder of their drinks.

'Want another?' Stella asked.

'Why not,' Mark replied. Stella handed him a ten-pound note. 'Same again?' he asked. She nodded.

As he approached the bar, he noticed the couple who had come in earlier and gone straight out again. They were looking at him so he nodded and smiled. The man quickly nodded and smiled back, but the woman gave him an icy look. Probably a jealous fag-hag, he thought uncharitably, having only heard the expression recently.

The landlord was waiting for him. He was average height with large tattooed arms and a solid-looking beer-belly that Mark could find attractive given enough alcohol. He had ears that stuck out a bit, a full beard and short, black hair.

He beamed at Mark. 'Same again, is it?'

'Yes, please,' Mark replied, beaming back. The landlord presented a vodka and tonic on the bar and started on the orange juice.

'Got yourself a boyfriend?' he asked Mark.

Mark thought about Hugh and then Steve. He hesitated for a moment, which the landlord probably misread, then he nodded. 'Afraid so.'

'Pity,' said the landlord, putting the orange juice beside the vodka and tonic in front of him.

Mark paid him, picked up his drinks and turned to go, very nearly drenching the man he had nodded and smiled to a few minutes earlier. The lady companion had obviously left. He smiled at Mark and held out a card. Mark read it. It appeared that the man's name was Otto Meyer and that he was a photographer. There was a mobile telephone number embossed in black ink. Mark looked up into the man's pale grey eyes, shiny blond hair, clear white skin and capped white teeth.

'Call me,' the man said, his accent faintly German.

'What for?' Mark asked innocently.

The man smiled and tiny crow's feet appeared at the corners of his eyes. 'Call me and find out,' he said mysteriously, turned and strode off towards the exit.

The landlord was staring after him. Mark turned to him and showed him the card. The landlord read it and shrugged.

'Obviously wants to take a few pictures of you, probably nude, probably having sex. If you need an extra hand, give me a call.'

They both laughed.

Mark put the card in his back pocket, picked up the drinks for a second time and headed off back to Stella. When he got there, he noticed their table was empty. He put their drinks down with a puzzled expression and looked around him. Stella was sitting at another table and waved him over. He picked up the drinks again and went over to join her.

'Mark,' she said, 'meet Ed. Ed, this is my friend Mark.' Ed extended a hand which Mark shook firmly, noticing the feel of hardened skin on the palms around the base of the fingers.

'Ed's a biker,' revealed Stella. 'He's got a Moto Guzzi eight-fifty.'

Mark raised an eyebrow in feigned awe. He hadn't got a clue about motorbikes. He used to have a Suzuki 100 a few years ago and a moped when he turned sixteen, but all he knew about those was where to put the petrol and oil and how to change a spark plug.

Ed looked him over. 'You two an item?' he asked, indicating Stella with a dismissive nod of his head that Stella evidently missed.

Stella laughed shrilly. 'Och, no,' she exclaimed, 'we're just good friends.'

Ed pondered this, but said no more.

'So, what brings you in here?' Mark asked him, taking a gulp of his orange juice.

Ed shrugged. 'It's my local.'

Mark noted the leather boots, leather trousers with the padded knees, the leather jacket (also padded) and the helmet. 'Yeah, right,' he said. 'You always drive to your local?' he asked sceptically. Bearing in mind that in London everyone lives within a few minutes walk of a bar.

Ed smiled. 'I'm working,' he replied. 'I'm a courier.' He picked up his courier bag from under the table. 'Believe me now?' he asked. He smiled again but Mark could see he wasn't enjoying being cross-questioned. Stella noticed too.

'Well, it was nice meeting you Ed,' she said and got up, adding, 'Mark and I haven't seen each other for ages. Would you excuse us?' She glanced at Mark as she walked back to their table. Luckily it was still unoccupied. Mark shrugged at Ed and followed her.

When he'd sat back down, Stella hissed. 'You were so rude to him. Why?'

'Was I?' asked Mark, puzzled.

'Yes. You'd only just met him and you were cross-questioning him,' Stella replied, still hissing.

Mark shrugged. 'Look, I just didn't like him, I guess. Can we forget about him? Tell me more about your mother. How long's she staying?'

Stella let it go. 'According to Iris, about six months,' she said and sighed.

'What? Where's she going to live? At Iris's?' Mark asked. He cast a glance at Ed and noticed him rolling a cigarette. The guy was scowling as he did so.

'I've no idea,' Stella replied. 'She's staying at the Post House in Hampstead at the moment, though how long they'll put up with her, I don't know.'

'As long as she keeps paying, I suppose,' Mark suggested. 'She must have won quite a bit to be staying there.'

'That's what I told Iris, but the old bag won't say,' Stella said, sipping her drink and scowling too. 'Can you imagine winning the bloody lottery and not telling your own daughters how much you've won?'

'Maybe she's worried you'll bump her off or something.'

'Well, I'll tell you, it wouldn't need to be much,' said Stella seriously. 'Anyway, me and Iris had a talk...'

'Iris and I,' Mark corrected her.

'Oh shut up. We had a talk, right, and it seems it was a fairly large sum of money. Iris is taking her to see some financial advisors next week which Camelot has put her in contact with.'

Mark raised an eyebrow. 'Must've been quite a bit, then.'

Stella shrugged. 'Well, be that as it may, I doubt if my life will change as a result… I'll probably still be tending bars in twenty years from now,' she added, looking glum.

Mark looked at her and now it was his turn to scowl. 'Oh shut up,' he told her. 'Thank your lucky stars you'll still be alive then. Anyway, how's Hugh?' he asked, changing the subject.

'Suffering from a hangover! I rang him this morning - after trying to get hold of him all last night, I might add - only to find he'd met up with a mate and they'd got pissed together. The guy was still there when I rang - I could hear him giggling in the background.'

Mark took this news on the chin. It was just as he had feared. He finished off his drink in one last gulp. He eyed Stella's almost empty glass. She picked it up and drained it.

'Shall we go?' he said.

'Where next?' Stella asked.

'Well,' said Mark looking at his watch and deciding not to tell her about his afternoon delight, 'I should be getting along home. I've some studying to do…'

'But, you haven't told me about this afternoon yet!' Stella pouted, sounding disappointed.

'It'll keep,' Mark replied getting to his feet. 'Anyway, I may have more to tell you next time I see you.' He raised an eyebrow at her.

Stella raised one back. 'Ooh, and don't forget dinner at Laura's next weekend,' she reminded him. 'Thanks to Iris and her big mouth, my mother's going to be there to make sure we behave ourselves… As if!' she added, rising.

He let Stella move first, then followed, casting a glance at Ed the Biker. Ed was talking quietly on his mobile and immediately looked up and then straight back down again. The landlord, however, gave him a hearty farewell and an open invitation to return soon, both inside and outside of opening hours. Mark promised that he would, one way or the other.

&)(3

Hugh had thoroughly enjoyed his morning fuck. Glen seemed to have liked it too. They ate breakfast together on the patio in the sunshine; just some orange juice, cereals and brown toast. Glen had to be at work by noon, so they exchanged telephone numbers, enjoyed a long and passionate farewell kiss and he was gone by eleven.

Hugh's cock felt nicely tender as he soaped it lovingly under the shower a little later. By noon, he was clean, freshly dressed and out of the door on his way to Mark's. He caught the tube at the Angel Islington and spent a good twenty minutes eyeing up a horny man in his thirties who was struggling to keep his two young sons under control. The man smiled at Hugh as he exited at Baker Street. Hugh was tempted to follow him but knew there was little mileage in it. Besides, he wanted to see Mark.

At Bayswater, he felt a surge of excitement as he exited the tube and proceeded towards the street where Mark lived. According to the map inside the station, it was just a few minutes walk. The houses around here were grand, much grander than the area in which he lived. These were Victorian town houses and he noticed that many of them had been converted into three and four star hotels giving eye-catching views of expensive-looking tree-lined avenues as well as Hyde Park.

As he approached Mark's house, Hugh could see Mark standing on the pavement outside the building, squinting up, his hand shielding his eyes from the bright sunshine. He called and waved and then realised his mistake. The young man standing outside was younger, trendier, less well defined but almost as pretty.

Hugh walked up to him. 'Hi,' he said. 'Are you Mark's younger brother?'

The young man laughed. 'I wish!' he replied. 'Think of the fun we could have had!'

Hugh nodded thoughtfully, then asked, 'So, what are you then, just a friend?'

The young man smiled at Hugh. 'That's right.'

'I take it he's not in then.'

'Doesn't look like it. I was just about to write him a note. Have you got a pen handy?'

Hugh shook his head.

'It's ok; I've got one in the car. You want to leave a note too?'

Hugh nodded and the young man led him over to a black Toyota Celica 2.2 with alloy wheels, spoiler, and every other conceivable customisation that could be added without making it look like a dinky toy. He deactivated the alarm and grabbed a pen and notebook from within, leant on the roof of the car and wrote his note, then passed the pen and paper over to Hugh, who did the same. Together, they walked up to the front door and posted their respective notes through the letterbox.

They turned and started walking back towards the young man's car. 'Can I give you a lift?' he asked Hugh, smiling as he added, 'You live in Islington, right?'

Hugh slowly smiled back. 'Yes, as a matter of fact, I do,' he replied, frowning slightly as he did so. 'But, how the hell do you know that?'

'Ah ha,' the young man replied. 'A little birdy told me.'

Hugh was puzzled. 'But, you don't even know who I am, so how do you know where I live?' They arrived at the car.

The young man held out his hand. 'My name's Patrick,' he said.

Hugh shook the hand and introduced himself. 'Jock,' he said, adding, 'I still don't understand how you know where I live…'

'Just get in,' Patrick ordered, 'and I'll explain on the way.'

Hugh raised an eyebrow and did as he was told.

ಬಂಡಿ

On arriving home, Mark was amazed to find three messages waiting for him. All three had been shoved under his inner private door, probably by one of the other tenants, so that he trod on them as he entered his bed-sit. All three looked as though they had been hastily written and all three contained a person's name and telephone number and the words, *Call me*, or words to that effect. Two of them were on identical notepaper, which was curious.

The first message was from Patrick. He decided to ignore that one. The second was from Hugh and he put that aside for the moment. The third was from PC Steve Evans. Mark smiled to himself. 'Can't keep away, huh?' he said aloud and his heart raced a little. He liked this man; a lot it seemed. He was still smiling as he keyed the number on his pay-as-you-go mobile phone.

'New Scotland Yard,' said a pleasant woman's voice. 'How may I help you?'

Mark had been expecting to hear Steve answer the phone at home. 'Er, PC Evans, please,' he mumbled.

'I'm not sure if he's available,' she replied. 'Who's calling?'

'Mark Carter,' he replied.

'I'll put you straight through,' she said quickly. There was a click, a silence, then some awful chamber music and finally Steve's sexy voice. At least Mark thought it sexy.

'Mark, it's Steve. Did you have a nice afternoon?'

'Certainly did,' Mark chuckled. 'What about you?'

'The best,' Steve replied seriously. 'Listen, we've had a breakthrough in the case I was talking to you about and now we need your help.'

'No problem. But what can I do?'

'A car's on its way round to you now. We need you here at the station. I'm afraid you'll have to come quietly,' he said light-heartedly, adding, 'Unlike earlier.'

'You're not going to use the cuffs on me, are you?' Mark asked.

'Maybe later,' Steve replied, hinting of things to come. 'Anyway, these calls may be monitored, so hold up for now. I'll see you when you get here. Ok?'

'Ok,' said Mark. The line went dead. He quickly changed into jeans, clean pants and a clean black tee shirt. He could still feel where Steve's cock had been earlier and wondered if he could or should take any more. It was a curious feeling, not unpleasant, but at the same time a little sore. He hadn't been able to have a crap afterwards at Steve's and he wondered if he should try now.

Suddenly, the doorbell rang. 'Too late,' he said to himself.

He heard the door being opened followed by Vivienne's voice. She was soon at his door with a very peculiar expression on her face as if to say, 'You are a spy!' A policeman stood beside her and asked Mark if he was who he was supposed to be. Mark nodded.

'Your presence is requested at the Yard, Sir,' he said formally. Vivienne's eyes widened even further.

'I'll be with you in a moment, Officer,' Mark replied and watched as the young uniformed man turned and retraced his steps.

'Darling, should I come with you?' Vivienne whispered in her most seductive voice.

'It's too dangerous,' he whispered, grabbing her and planting a last farewell kiss on her puckered red lips. Then he turned and, grabbing his wallet, keys and leather jacket, stalked off after the policeman leaving a bemused and rather tragic-like figure propped up against the landing wall. Vivienne tenderly touched her hand to her lips and a puzzled expression appeared fleetingly on her brow. She breathed deeply twice and then, with a shrug, returned to the solitude of her own room.

ഇരുത

'Am I under arrest?' demanded Pierre. He was sitting across a table from Detective Chief Inspector Dickens. He had finished two cups of strong coffee and inhaled half a packet of Benson & Hedges. The stale air in the small room was eye-watering and the Chief made a mental note not to offer Pierre any more cigarettes.

'No,' the Chief said.

Pierre looked at him suspiciously. 'Then I'm free to go?' he challenged.

'Again, no,' the Chief replied. 'Not just yet. You're in for questioning and will be free to go when we have all the facts. This is a *murder* enquiry.'

Detective Chief Inspector Dickens sighed inwardly. When would these people realise just how serious a murder enquiry was? Someone's life had been taken, for God's sake. In a horribly gruesome manner to boot. You'd think that anyone would co-operate, but no, they all just seem too intent on their own miniscule lives to bother. Only when it actually touched people in some way, maybe a friend, relative, whatever, would they suddenly change. And then, of course, not enough was being done. Not by the emergency services, not by the social services and particularly not by the police. Dickens put it down to guilty consciences, every time. Because, whatever the circumstances, they always had a guilty conscience about some aspect of it. If only they had done this or said that or... His mind was roaming. He quickly re-focused.

Pierre whined on. 'Look, I've told you everything I know. Please let me go.' He was more desperate for a joint than his freedom, but he couldn't have one without the other. The Chief simply stared at Pierre, ignoring his pleas.

Just then, there was a knock on the door and one of the duty officers stuck her head into the room. 'Sir,' she said, 'Detective PC Evans is ready when you are. He's in the next room.'

'Thank you, Williams,' the Chief replied, as he continued to stare at Pierre.

Pierre felt uncomfortable under such scrutiny. He squirmed in his seat. Eventually it got to him. 'What?' he demanded, suddenly angry. Maybe now was the time to call his father?

The Chief continued to stare. Then he got up and left the room without another word. Pierre felt the impulse to ask for a phone, but the moment passed as another policeman entered the room to keep him company.

୧ଠଷ

'We meet again,' smiled Detective Chief Inspector Charles Dickens as he strode into the room, extending his hand and shaking Mark's warmly. 'Please, sit down.'

He indicated one of the plastic chairs across the desk from where he parked himself. 'I see PC Evans has already introduced himself,' he continued. 'He has a habit of doing that with the good looking ones.'

Mark glanced quickly at Steve who smiled and winked.

'Let me get straight to the point,' the Chief went on. 'We've had a breakthrough in our investigation into the Bayswater murder. We know that a particular type of man is being targeted, specifically young, blond, muscular and pretty. We also have a description of the murderer, or possibly murderers.'

Mark interrupted him. 'There's more than one?' he asked.

'It seems most likely,' the Chief conceded.

Mark chewed this over, wondering where it was leading.

'What we intend to do is set a trap for them, which is where you come in. We're putting an ad in a contact magazine which we know has been used before, but we need someone to go along with any responses we do get until they show themselves.'

Mark slowly nodded his understanding. 'And you want me to do this?' The Chief nodded quickly. 'So,' Mark continued, 'how will you know it's them for sure? When they've murdered me?'

The Chief allowed himself a rueful smile. 'We have a full description and a witness to hand. The moment they show up, we'll grab them.'

'So, why do you need me?' Mark asked. 'Why not arrange to meet in a public place and then grab them?'

'Because they're clever and use a third person to make first contact. Once made and casually vetted, the victim is then taken to another venue to meet our couple.'

Mark nodded. 'That makes some kind of sense, I suppose. But, what's the motive?'

'Bizarre sex,' the Chief replied unhesitatingly. 'And it has to be stopped, right now. Believe me, there's no room on this Earth for this particular brand of bizarre sex... And you do not want to hear the details,' he added firmly.

Mark glanced again at Steve who had been quiet throughout. He spoke up, 'Believe him, you really don't,' he said with a shudder.

Mark swallowed hard.

'So, you're going to set a trap,' said Mark after a few moments of silence. 'And I'm to be the bait. Why not someone with training? A policeman, maybe? Why me?'

The Chief was quick to reassure him. 'You're not going to be in any danger. As soon as they show themselves, we'll have them. We've enough forensic evidence to make a conviction. But, to answer your question, I would have thought it obvious: You're their type. They won't be able to resist you. And we don't have anyone on the force young enough and pretty enough. Not even PC Evans here... Sorry Evans.'

PC Evans shrugged. 'I get by, Sir,' he said.

Mark looked from Steve back to the Chief and shrugged. 'Ok, then...'

'Good man,' cut in the Chief, jumping up and shaking Mark's hand. 'I thank you on behalf of her Majesty's Metropolitan Police Force. You will, of course, be compensated for any lost time at work.

Oh, we will need to inform your employers of the situation; we may need you at any time. We'll provide them with whatever is required in terms of paperwork for that. Also, you'll be reimbursed for any out of pocket expenses and we will, of course, provide you with a small reward at the end of it all. Finally, from this moment on, you are officially working for the Metropolitan Police and are entitled to Life Insurance cover. Speak to PC Evans later – we need a few details to complete the relevant forms… Right, any questions?'

Mark could think of at least a hundred. 'When do we start?' was all he asked.

'We've got people working on the advertisement right now. It could be a few days or a few weeks. We'll just keep advertising until they bite.'

Mark had a horrible thought. 'You're not going to use a photo of me, right?'

The Chief shook his head. 'That shouldn't be necessary. Now, PC Evans here will look after you from now on. He's going to have to teach you a few things about being an escort, so listen up and learn. Now, if that's all, I shall leave you in Evans's capable hands.' He shook Mark's hand once more and quickly left the room. Mark and Steve followed at a more sedate pace.

ഇൡ

'Hi Mum.'

'Hello love, what's it like there?'

'Lovely, been sunny all day,'

'It has here. Your Aunty Pauline and I went into Oxford today.'

'Did you buy anything?'

'No, just some food in Marks and Spencer's. I saw a lovely two-piece outfit I might buy for my birthday. I'll be fifty this year, you know dear?'

'Yes Mum, I do know… Mum…?'

'Yes, dear?'

Mark paused for breath. 'Mum,' he said seriously, 'I've been asked by the Metropolitan Police to take part in a sort of re-construction of a murder.'

'Oh,' said his mum. 'Will you be on the telly?'

'No, it's more like they're using me as a decoy to catch the murderer.'

There was a silence on the other end. 'Are you sure you know what you're doing? It sounds dangerous to me, Mark.'

'Oh yes, don't worry. *They* know what they're doing, but just in case, I'm giving them your name as next of kin. They're insuring me well, it seems.'

'What? Oh my Christ! You'd better talk to your father - right now!' There was a loud clunk and then silence.

Mark put his hand over the mouthpiece and whispered to Steve. 'She's gone to get my dad. Maybe I shouldn't have told her that last bit?'

'Too late now,' Steve whispered, leaning forward and kissing Mark on the nape of his neck. His goatee rasped and tickled Mark so that moments later Mark was giggling when his father came on line.

'Hello son, what's this your mother's going on about?'

'Hi Dad. Oh nothing really, it's just that I match the profile of someone who's been murdered and the police have asked me to act as a sort of decoy. Nothing dangerous.'

'So, why have they insured you then?' his father asked.

'They have to. Standard procedure. Look, I have a policeman right here if you want to check it out...'

'Put him on,' his father replied.

Mark offered the phone to Steve. They were sitting in Steve's lounge and it was about 8.30pm. Steve took the phone and introduced himself. Whilst he was explaining the *standard procedure* to Mark's dad, Mark carefully unzipped PC Evans's flies and took out a hefty handful of cock, which was rapidly getting heavier. With a wink, he bent down and started to lick the full length, pausing only to moisten his tongue before enveloping the bulging glans that had erupted from its long foreskin. It smelled like a whole day's worth of musk and man, though in reality, Mark knew that Steve had showered that afternoon after their lovemaking. Still, it turned him on and whilst Steve continued to chat with his father, Mark grew more and more aroused as he continued to suck Steve's cock.

To his credit, PC Evans retained his cool composure throughout, thanks more to his expert training and self-discipline than Mark's ineptitude as a cocksucker.

Steve eventually replaced the receiver and hauled Mark up to kiss him on the lips. 'Your dad's fine about it,' he said. 'I had a nice chat with your mum as well. She sounds really nice.'

'She is,' Mark replied, cupping Steve's testicles in his right hand. He rolled them around, enjoying the feel of a heavy scrotum. He leaned down and sniffed them before taking first one and then the other in his mouth. Steve put his head back and let Mark's tongue roam for a good few minutes.

Eventually, he sat up and grabbed Mark by the scruff of his neck. 'It's no good,' he said, 'I'm going to have to fuck you again. Reckon you can handle it?'

Mark nodded vigorously. 'I'm a tiny bit sore, that's all.'

'Fancy being fucked in a sling with me in leathers?' Steve asked him, grinning.

Mark nodded enthusiastically. 'Try anything once.'

'Oh, I think you might want to try this more than once,' Steve said knowingly, jumping to his feet and stuffing his erect cock back into his trousers. He went into the hallway and removed a small metal box from the cupboard under the stairs, unlocked it and handed it to Mark. 'Here,' he said, 'make us a joint whilst I go and get ready.' He kissed Mark roughly on the mouth and then left the room.

Mark examined the box. It was a small blue petty cash tin and when he opened the lid he found inside a fresh pack of ten Silk Cut ultra low, some red Rizla papers, a few thin strips of white glossy cardboard, a pair of tiny scissors and a small re-sealable plastic bag containing some wicked smelling grass. Mark sniffed the familiar heady aroma with pure delight. He quickly set about rolling them a strong joint.

'You ready up there or what?' came Steve's authoritative voice a few minutes later from somewhere under the stairs. Mark jumped up and headed for the sound. Another door under the stairs led downwards to the cellar.

'Just gotta use your loo. Won't be long,' Mark called back down the stairs.

He hurried upstairs to the loo, quickly douched, felt the tenderness of his arse with gentle prods of his fingers, and was back down again within a couple of minutes. As he passed by the open door to the cellar, his nostrils suddenly flared as he caught the unmistakeable aroma of what he imagined to be an expensive Cuban cigar. Curiously, he felt his cock jerk in response.

He hurried to where the well-rolled joint lay in the ashtray, picked it up and hurried back to the entrance to Steve's cellar where the rich smell of cigar smoke was strongest. He peered into the gloom and then boldly descended the creaking wooden stairs, the smell of cigar growing ever stronger, until he reached the concrete bottom.

The cellar itself was the full length and width of the house, about fifteen metres long and about seven metres wide. The ceiling was surprisingly high, about three metres, with dark wooden beams crossing in both directions. In various places, thick concrete columns painted black held up the ceiling and, presumably, the rest of the house. The light was provided by a single low wattage bulb hanging naked from the centre of the ceiling towards the far end of the cellar. In addition, various candles were strategically placed to lend an air of rough sleaze as their light danced off various full length mirrors that hung from the blackened brick walls.

Reflected in the mirrors was the main focus of attention in the room. Hanging from four thick shiny metal chains, each about two metres in length, was a thick lattice-work sling of leather straps and silver metal studs, itself about a metre long and about two thirds of a metre wide. The body of the sling was connected to the chains at groin height by large silver rings.

PC Steve Evans stood motionless to one side of the sling. He seemed taller in a pair of well-polished black jackboots and a pair of black leather chaps that hugged his muscular legs, bulged around his bare arse and framed a silver studded codpiece. The chaps were studded at the waist and drawn tightly in front with a silver buckle. On his head perched a military style Commandant's leather cap with a plain silver strap around its brim and a shiny black peek. His thick muscular arms were tied tightly with leather armbands and his well-defined smooth chest, with its light dusting of blond hairs, was crossed with a silver studded black leather harness, the centrepiece of which was another large cockring.

A well-proportioned black Cuban cigar was smoking between his goateed lips, its tip glowing like a small ember in the gloom. He moved and took a deep pull on the cigar, its tip glowing intensely bright, then inhaled the pungent white smoke. He exhaled a thick plume of smoke made vivid by the candle light behind and indicated that Mark should approach and stand before him.

Mark was transfixed. He tried to move and his legs almost buckled. Steve indicated again with a slight nod of his head. Finally, as he moved forward, Mark stuck the joint in his mouth and lit it, inhaling the powerful and flavourful weed.

'You'll enjoy that, it's Skunk,' said Steve, inhaling Cuban white smoke. 'A mate brings it in from Amsterdam,' he added, exhaling another plume in Mark's direction.

Mark approached and offered Steve a drag of the joint, which Steve took, offering Mark his cigar in return. The cigar felt heavy and finely textured and surprisingly warm in Mark's hand. Mark took the wet tip in his mouth and drew on it. He gingerly inhaled and then exhaled without coughing. It was surprisingly mild.

He took another drag and, as he exhaled, Steve grabbed his stubbled mouth and sucked on it hungrily. Thrust up against the leather harness on Steve's chest, Mark felt the weed kick in, his legs grow even weaker, and his resistance crumble. Within moments, Steve had him lying naked in the sling with the ankle restraints secure, allowing unhindered access to his tight hairy arsehole.

Mark took a few more drags of the joint and dropped it into an empty ashtray by the side of the sling, where it continued to give off its aromatic animal scent that had given it its acutely apt name. He felt weightless as he watched Steve strut around, adjusting the ankle straps, giving Mark's rock hard cock an occasional quick pull and rubbing his groin against his thighs. Mark could feel the studs on the leather codpiece grinding into his flesh.

Moments later, he felt the codpiece against his mouth and he opened his eyes to see Steve standing to his left and towering over him. He reached up and grabbed hold of Steve's muscular arse. Steve pivoted and Mark caught a glimpse of his V-shaped back defined in the leather of the waistcoat. Steve thrust his hairy arse into Mark's face, exposing his puckered hole. Mark was fascinated by it, but Steve moved out of reach as he felt around the back to undo the strips of leather that held the codpiece in place. Steve pivoted again and, with a hard tug, the knot came loose and Steve's large heavy uncut cock fell onto Mark's eagerly upturned face. It was quickly buried into Mark's mouth and then whipped straight out again as Mark gagged. Tears stung Mark's eyes as Steve offered him a pull on the cigar. He took a deep pull, watching through the haze of smoke as Steve moved around to stand at the end of the sling, his stiff cock resting between Mark's splayed legs. He smiled at Mark as he returned the cigar to his own mouth and reached around his side for the lubricant and a foil-wrapped condom.

'You wanna be fucked by a Leatherman?' he growled, rolling the condom onto his cock.

Mark whispered back, 'Yes, please.'

'Yes please, what?' Steve demanded, motionless now and gazing into Mark's eager face.

'Yes please, Sir!' Mark replied instantly.

Steve took an extra long pull on his cigar and blew the thick white smoke directly into Mark's upturned face. 'That's better,' he said.

With the cigar clenched between his teeth, Steve squirted a dollop of Liquid Silk on to his hand and slapped it onto Mark's eager arse, quickly sliding his middle finger in and out. Then it was two fingers and soon three.

'You ready?' he asked.

'Yes, Sir!' Mark gasped, and moments later found himself impaled on a man's cock for the second time in his life and for the second time that day.

∞∞∞

Patrick was finally over his infatuation with Mark, although he didn't know it yet. The reason being that Mark was far from his mind right now. He was concentrating hard on keeping in rhythm with Jock's thrusts, having his nipples tweaked mercilessly (he'd begged Jock for that) and concentrating even harder on holding off from coming. He was on all fours on Jock's bed, his face forced into a large white pillow and his arse high in the air. Jock was kneeling behind him, a smile etched on his face as he brought himself to a swift orgasm. He told Patrick he was coming and felt Patrick's sphincter muscle contract and convulse rapidly as Patrick's own cum squirted out of him in great wads onto a strategically placed towel. Moments later, Jock withdrew, yanked off the condom and grunted as he spurted half a dozen times over Patrick's bare back.

As their muscles complained, Jock reached for the tissues and ceremoniously wiped up his cum, smearing much of it in, feeling his own thigh muscles tighten and knot. He wiped his glistening cock and then collapsed on top of Patrick. Patrick wriggled himself around so that his mouth was touching Jock's thick black moustache. He licked at it like a puppy. Jock kissed him back, his eyes closed.

A few minutes later, Jock/Hugh opened his eyes. He looked down at the sleeping form of Patrick and groaned inwardly. What had he done now? Things were snowballing out of control. He wondered just where all this was going to end and how many tears would be shed in the process.

Chapter Nine

SUNDAY WAS ANOTHER BRIGHT and sunny day and Stella was having family problems. Her mother was casting a sceptical eye around her flat, wiping her hand over parts of exposed surfaces here and there and then dusting her fingers from one hand against the other immediately afterwards. She was having a good root around in Stella's bedroom and then, horror upon horrors, found a pair of Hugh's underwear lying unobtrusively in one corner of the room. Stella realised he must have gone home without them the other evening after he'd *raped* her. The thought brought a warm blush to her face. Her mother, of course, thought this was her guilty conscience. Iris thought it was pure embarrassment and had gone red herself.

Stella's mother prodded them with her foot. 'I see his name's Jockey,' she said, sniffing. 'At least he's Scots,' she added.

Stella stifled a grin. 'That's the make,' she explained, picking them up and putting them in the linen basket in the corner.

'He'd better not be married like that Hugh fella Iris told me about. You've better things to do with your time than waste it like that.' She huffed and puffed and then strode out of the room to Stella's lounge where the huge Monstera cheese-plant still lurked. Her mother took a look at it and sniffed again. 'Why don't you just live in a bloody greenhouse?' she said.

Iris just managed to grab Stella by the scruff of her neck and stop her from bludgeoning their mother to death with a glass vase. She skilfully replaced it without their mother noticing. Their mother walked across the room and sank down onto the sofa.

'Oh, my bloody back,' she moaned.

'You're lucky it isn't your head,' Stella muttered under her breath.

'Eh? What?' said Mrs Roberts, straining her left ear towards Stella.

Iris intervened quickly. 'Stella asked if you wanted to lie down on her bed.'

Mrs Roberts stared up at her daughters and slowly shook her head. 'D'you think I'm daft, or barmy or just plain deaf, or what? I know what she said. All these snide comments.' She fixed her eyes on Stella. 'Why don't you come right out and say what's on your mind, girl? You always were a bit of a mouse.'

Stella felt the years of frustration, disappointment, hurt and hatred welling up from within. The number of times her mother had dashed her hopes, made her feel miserable, ruined her day, week, year, all with a nasty comment here, or an ill-tempered or just plain bloody-minded command there. Well, she wasn't going to ruin her whole life!

Iris could sense that matters were now beyond her control. Rather than try mediating yet again, she backed off. She was tired of trying to smooth things over between them.

Mrs Roberts's eyes were burning bright as she sat on the sofa staring up at her little girl. She'd had Stella late in life and much against her wishes. Stella's father hadn't been that bad really; in fact, Morag had loved him dearly for a while, but he was a selfish and arrogant sexist pig, just like most men she'd known. Unlike her first husband of course, who had left her too soon, but left her with Iris as a reminder. But Iris wasn't any more responsible for having a good father than Stella was for having a bad one. Was she?

As Stella drew in a deep breath to begin shouting, she saw her mother's defiance crumble, like an unstable brick wall given one good kick. Mrs Roberts's head suddenly drooped and a great sob rent the air. More sobs followed and a handkerchief appeared miraculously out of thin air. It was from Iris, offering it to Stella to give to her mother. Stella took it and gently knelt in front of her, taking her hands in hers and pressing the flimsy piece of cloth into the knobbly hands that were once her mother's most remarkable features.

Morag's first husband had refused to let her take her gloves off in public. He'd said her hands were too beautiful to let just anyone see them. Her second husband however, had never let her wear gloves at all. He'd said they were far too beautiful to hide away. A lifetime spent digging the garden, washing the dishes and wringing out clothes had done this to them.

Morag took the handkerchief that Stella had pressed into her hands and gently dabbed her tears. 'Thank you, my dear,' she said and suddenly flung her arms tightly around Stella. Instantly shocked, Stella took a moment to respond, but when she did, she responded with all the love that had been suppressed these long years. She suddenly let out a great sob herself and before long Iris joined her. All three found themselves in some sort of sobbing, clasping, much-wailing bear of a hug that lasted for quite some time.

℘℃℞

Laura threw open her lounge cum dining room cum bedroom windows forcefully, smiling and tra la la'ing to Classic FM. A fragrant breeze swirled in, rich with the youth and freshness of spring, urging her to burst spontaneously into a higher contralto, much like a forest fire leaps from tree to tree. Then she suddenly stopped, a quizzical expression playing on her tremulous lips and listened with one ear cocked. It was a trick she'd learnt from Freud or was it the other way around? Funnily enough, she could hear a cat wailing; no, now it was two, or was it three? She moved towards the hi-fi, turned the music down and continued to listen.

The noise was muffled and most peculiar. She moved to the window and stuck her head out to listen. She rotated it through ninety degrees in one direction and then ninety degrees in the other and then just as she was about to cock her head once more, a lancing pain shot up through her left ear. She pulled her head carefully back.

'Oh, bugger,' she hissed through clenched teeth. Holding her head in agony and whimpering like a mouse, she crossed to her medicine cupboard and took out two dispersible aspirin, walked through the archway into the kitchen, poured herself a small glass of cold water from the fridge and then popped the aspirin in to dissolve, or *disperse* as they were now supposed to do. Quite what the difference was, Laura was unsure, but she suspected it had something to do with legal technicalities and most likely influenced from her own country of origin.

Her beloved cat, Freud, who had been quite happy listening to Classic FM, not quite so happy with the tra la la'ing, not happy at all

162

with the annoying sobbing and wailing of three female humans coming from upstairs, and simply outraged with Laura's squeaky food impressions, stretched and yawned luxuriously on the sofa where he had been trying to doze. He then leapt easily onto the window ledge and quickly disappeared through the open window whilst Laura was still in the kitchen. He was back within five minutes with a large juicy grey mouse still twitching between his fangs.

By this time, Laura was lying uncomfortably on the sofa with an empty glass by her side and the beginnings of a nasty headache that would hopefully be suppressed by the aspirin. When Freud dropped the dazed mouse onto her lap, she leapt about three feet in the air and came down screaming, jarring her neck even further.

There's no pleasing some, Freud thought and settled down to keep an eye on the mouse, which had sensed, fleetingly, that it might live to see another day.

A knock sounded at the back door. She was expecting Patrick for his flute lesson but was now in no condition to even hold a flute properly, let alone give a lesson.

'Come in,' she yelled, wincing with the effort, 'it's open.'

She heard the door open and close and then Patrick's familiar smiling face appeared. Instantly, a worried look came over him. 'What's wrong?' he asked, striding towards her.

'I've hurt my neck. I'm afraid I won't be able to teach you very much today. I won't charge you, of course,' she added.

'Oh, I'm not worried about that; you just send my dad the bill. I'm more worried about you... You've gone white.'

'You're such a dear,' she said, touching his arm as he crouched down beside her.

'Anyway,' he continued, 'I'd prefer to have a bit of a chat, if you're feeling up to it?'

Laura raised an eyebrow. 'More *situations*?' she enquired.

Patrick nodded.

'Oh, before I forget,' said Laura, easing herself up into a sitting position and attempting to stand. Patrick helped her slowly to her feet. Once standing, she walked unaided over to a cupboard in the corner of the room. She opened it and took out a small brightly coloured elongated carrier bag with string handles and presented it to Patrick.

'Happy Birthday,' she said, smiling despite the pain.

Patrick's face lit up with joy. 'Oh, Laura, thank you. You never forget, do you!'

'How could I forget my star pupil?' she replied, delighted with his response.

Patrick hugged her and kissed her on the cheek and then opened the bag. Inside was a beautiful blood red synthetic silk tie dotted with tiny black musical notes making up a subtle check pattern.

'It's beautiful!' Patrick cried, hugging Laura again. 'Thank you, thank you.'

Laura beamed with delight. 'I'm so glad you like it. I didn't know what to get you to commemorate such an auspicious day… There's a card as well,' she added.

Patrick removed the card from the bag and quickly opened it. The card was rather formal, but there was a badge attached with *I am 18* painted on it in big black lettering. Patrick read the card, smiled at the weak joke and then pinned the badge to the front of his polo shirt.

'I shan't try the tie on,' he said, 'not with this shirt, but I do love it, thank you very much.'

'You're welcome,' said Laura, bustling her way into the kitchen. 'Now, I have a special cake for you. Would you prefer tea or coffee with it?'

'Coffee, please,' Patrick replied, putting the card and tie down on the oblong coffee table in front of the sofa.

Minutes later, Laura was decanting coffee from the cafetière. She slowly plunged it and began to pour. Meanwhile, Patrick lit a cigarette and was blowing smoke rings towards Freud who, of course, considered this to be totally intolerable behaviour. He hopped up onto the window ledge and stepped outside again for some more fresh air and another hunt. The mouse, for now, had escaped.

'So,' said Laura, offering Patrick a cup of strong black coffee. 'What does it feel like to be eighteen?'

'Pretty sore, actually,' he replied.

Laura looked puzzled. She gestured with her open hand. 'Sore? As in pain or anger?'

Patrick grinned. 'As in pain. I celebrated my birthday in bed.'

'Oh,' said Laura, nodding sagely and then wishing she hadn't, the sudden jolt of pain in her neck making her wince. 'With Gerald?' she asked, rubbing her neck.

Patrick shook his head and smiled.

Laura started thinking back to her last similar conversation with Patrick. 'Not with... Mark?'

'No, a gorgeous muscular Scottish man called Jock... But, I won't bore you with the details...'

'You won't bore me, I can assure you,' said Laura, eager to hear more.

'It's a long story...'

'Patrick,' said Laura, firmly, 'it's Sunday. I've got all day. Now, how about me cutting you a nice big piece of special birthday cake and you telling me all about it?'

Patrick nodded, blowing the last of the smoke rings as he stubbed out his Camel cigarette. 'It's a deal,' he agreed, knowing full well that this was one long story that could not be told in its entirety.

⁊♃

Steve may have gone a little too far, Mark thought, as he hobbled around his tiny bed-sit that sunny Sunday afternoon. His arse felt as though it had a traffic cone embedded in it, not to mention the soreness of the sphincter. And his throat looked and felt as raw as a peeled tomato. Next time, Steve promised to introduce him to *poppers*, whatever they might be. They sounded like something your grandmother would wear in bed to keep her feet warm.

Mark was beginning to think that his initiation into gay sex might have been a bit extreme, though he had to admit that it felt good. He doubted if it was the type of sex that all gay men enjoyed or had even tried and he naively wondered how much more Steve could dream up, if any. The danger of a willingness to try anything once is that once tried, expectations rise. Now that he'd had full sex with a man, he knew that he liked it very much and that sex with a woman, at least, would never be the same again. He wasn't sure if that should worry him or not.

There was a gentle knock on the door. Mark stopped packing his suitcase and went to answer it.

'Oh, hi Vi,' he said, opening the door wide. 'Come in, come in.'

Vivienne smiled broadly as she entered. She was wearing a beautiful hand-crafted figure-hugging beige dress that swirled around her knees as she walked and her shiny blonde hair was moulded around her face just like Jennifer Anniston from *Friends*. She wasn't wearing any make-up, Mark noticed, and the skin on her face was the colour of a field of ripe golden corn with red poppies dotted about, giving her a healthy hue. And her eyes! They were the palest blue.

Her smile vanished suddenly when she noticed the packed suitcase on the bed that Mark had been trying to close.

'Are you going away?' she asked in a disappointed tone.

'Yes, but not far,' he replied cheerfully. 'I'm going under cover for a while.'

'Oh,' she responded breathlessly. 'F… For how long?'

'Couple of weeks, maybe,' he replied. 'Why, are you going to miss me?'

'Well, yes, I might,' she said, their eyes locking.

Mark began to suspect that Vivienne might be developing a crush on him. He had to nip this one in the bud.

'Vi,' he said, 'I think there's something you should know.'

Vivienne's eyes sparkled even more. 'You're MI5, aren't you?'

'No,' he replied. 'I'm a trainee accountant, honestly. No, what you should know is that I'm moving in with my boyfriend for a while. He's a policeman and I'm going to be working under cover with him.'

Vivienne faltered. 'O… Oh, your boyfriend? Oh…I… I had no idea.'

'Well, he's not really my boyfriend,' Mark confessed. 'Not yet, anyway. But I'm working on it, you know?'

Vivienne nodded. She was suddenly awkward.

Mark returned his attention to the suitcase. 'Would you sit on this for me?' he asked, adding, 'As the bishop said to the actress.'

They both laughed and Vivienne complied. Within moments Mark managed to secure both fasteners.

'I had no idea you were gay,' Vivienne said, still sitting on the suitcase.

'Neither did I,' Mark admitted, 'but I've had quite a week.'

Vivienne raised her eyebrows. 'You sure that's what you want?'

Mark nodded. 'I think so,' he replied, adding with a shrug, 'But who knows?'

Vivienne stood up. 'Well, I'd better leave you to finish your packing. Be careful, won't you, with this under cover thing?'

Mark smiled. 'I'll try my best,' he promised, showing her to the door.

'Let me know how it all turns out,' she said.

'I will,' he agreed, not knowing whether she meant the *under cover thing* or his moving in with Steve or his being gay. He closed the door behind her and resumed his packing.

Chapter Ten

MARK HAD NEVER been fucked by a man just prior to setting off for work before. Steve took one look at him dressed in his city suit and literally ripped it off him, forced him onto his back and entered him roughly.

As he re-dressed, noting the small rip in his jacket under the right arm, Mark realised he was going to be late. Steve was lying on his back, fondling his cock as he watched Mark dressing.

'Hey, don't forget the Chief will be contacting your boss today.'

Mark nodded, pulling on his jacket and exposing the rip under one arm. 'Any good with a needle and thread?' he asked hopefully.

Steve just laughed. 'Hey, that's the price of passion, mate,' he said. 'I might have to rip the other one tonight if you come home looking that sexy.' He rose from the bed and grabbed Mark round the back of the head. He kissed him, not hard this time, but lovingly. 'You are a sexy man,' he breathed and they embraced for a while.

Mark left for work, glowing from the inside out.

His journey was a lot shorter now that he was staying with Steve. It took him just over ten minutes to walk down Oxford Street to his office near Langham Place, right behind the BBC building. He was greeted by a jolly receptionist and happily returned her cheery greeting. Next stop, the audit room on the fifth floor was full and he returned all the greetings cheerfully and accepted an offer of coffee.

'Where's Fi?' he asked Anne, a qualified accountant with whom he had developed a special friendship. She was engaged to one of the Senior Managers and had taken Mark under her wing and was encouraging him to pass his exams.

'No idea,' she replied. 'Have you done that chapter on *Costing* yet,' she asked him.

'Um, no, not yet,' Mark admitted. 'You?'

Anne glared at him through her thick lenses. 'I'm *already*

qualified,' she told him, 'and you'll *never* be if you don't get and do some studying!'

'I know, I know, I'm sorry. I've been a bit busy lately...'

'Well, I suppose you could always write a little note to the examiner and pin it to your exam papers,' said Anne sarcastically. 'Like, *Sorry, been a bit busy lately. Please take this into account when marking.* Yeah, that should do it.'

Mark took a sip of his coffee as Anne tore a strip off him. They were walking slowly back to her desk when a voice boomed out and the audit room fell silent.

'Mark, can I see you for a moment?'

Anne turned and looked at him. 'It seems Donald wants you. But, listen to me. You can't learn by osmosis. You have to study. Ok?'

Mark nodded his head and turned to go.

'By the way,' she said, 'why are you walking funny?'

Mark went red and said he'd pulled a muscle at the gym. He hurried to Donald's office, exaggerating his limp.

He knocked twice and entered upon command - and was surprised to see Fiona sitting enjoying a cup of coffee with Donald. She smiled at him and her face glowed.

'Sit down, please,' said Donald, indicating a comfortable swivel chair next to Fiona. 'Now,' he said, rustling papers on his desk. 'I understand you finished the Inner City Re-Housing Association audit well within budget. Any problems?'

'I have highlighted one or two things in my report that need to be looked at more thoroughly next time, but otherwise no.'

'Good man,' said Donald and squinted outrageously. It was all Mark could do to keep a straight face. Fiona, on the other hand, who had known Donald for many years, scowled at him to behave. Donald continued, 'Now, onto something completely different. I've had a call this morning from a...' he paused, put on his glasses and peered at a sheet of paper in front of him, 'a Detective Chief Inspector Charles Dickens of New Scotland Yard.' He removed his glasses, leaned back in his chair and looked at Mark. 'I presume you know about all this?'

Mark nodded.

'Have you thought of the effect this might have on your exams?'

Mark shrugged. 'I didn't really have much of a choice, did I? I could hardly refuse to help the Metropolitan Police catch a murderer!'

Donald stuck out his lower lip and stared at Mark, then at Fiona. Eventually he said, 'These exams, they're in June, correct?'

Both Mark and Fiona nodded. 'Right then, from now until this is over you're on special leave. I'll get our training manager, Mr Hughes, to set you a program that you must follow. You'll need to report into him once a week to hand in your work and to go over any areas giving you any problems. You'll be on full pay, of course. Right, that'll be all. Fiona, have Mr Hughes report to me please.' With the end of his speaking came the inevitable squint and Fiona ushered Mark out of the room quickly, just to be on the safe side.

'You're bloody lucky,' Fiona said, escorting Mark back to the audit room. 'Just make sure you pass those exams!'

'Hey, what about staying alive?' asked Mark. 'I'm the bait and the bait usually gets eaten, you know?'

'Don't say that,' said Fiona, 'you're worrying me now.' Her big eyes looked up at him.

'Don't you worry about me,' said Mark, softening. 'I'll be fine. Anyway, what should I do now? Go home?'

'Well, there's no point in you hanging around here,' Fiona agreed.

Mark stopped suddenly. 'Oh, I've just thought,' he said, facing her, 'I've had to move to a secure location. I can't give out the address, but you can always call me on my mobile if you need to… or want to.'

'Keep it switched on and make sure you've got some credit on it, ok?' He nodded. 'Right then, you take care.' She hugged him quickly.

Anne, suddenly sensing something was up, came hurrying over. 'What's going on? You off on another audit already?'

'Would you explain it?' Mark asked Fiona.

Fiona nodded.

'Explain what?' Anne demanded. By this time, everybody in the audit room was starting to crowd round.

'You haven't been fired, have you?' someone asked.

'No, he has not,' Fiona answered quickly. 'Donald's put him on a special assignment, which I'll explain later. Now, Mark, off you go. And you lot, get back to your desks!'

Mark picked up his briefcase and walked over to the lift. Luckily, the lift was there waiting. He stepped in, pressed for ground floor and gave a little wave as the doors closed on a sea of curious faces.

ⅎℛ

When Laura awoke that Monday morning, it was with great difficulty that she managed to wash, dress, cook and eat a full English breakfast and feed Freud. Her neck had stiffened up overnight and she could hardly look to the right without wincing. The aspirin that she had been taking was obviously not strong enough, so she decided to raid her piggy bank and visit the local chemist shop on the nearby Finchley Road.

It was another lovely day and she felt like tra la la'ing even though she was in agony, although in truth it only hurt if she tried to turn suddenly, laugh out loud or sneeze. She hummed a little ditty instead as she crossed the Finchley Road in front of Waitrose and went into the chemist further down. The pharmacist was always friendly and very helpful and Laura was sure he would be able to recommend something that wouldn't break the piggy's back.

Although a small bell chimed as she pushed open the door, nobody took much notice and she proceeded to the back of the shop to the dispensary. Like all small chemist shops, it was starkly white with very useful things on display like foot deodorants, nail clippers, baby food, multivitamins, contact lens solutions and rows upon rows of hair care products. She froze as she recognised the figure talking with the pharmacist: tall, the back of his head shaved and masculine, the V shape of his back clearly defined against the soft black tee shirt he was wearing, his buttocks like chiselled granite through his denims jutting out prominently from the tree-trunks that were his legs. He seemed agitated and kept scratching his genital region.

Laura unfroze and moved quickly to the next aisle, hovering out of sight behind a carousel display of cheap sunglasses, but still within hearing distance.

In a confidentially low voice, the pharmacist was saying, '... must shampoo the affected area and leave it on for five minutes, then wash it off thoroughly.'

Glen was nodding his handsome head as he listened intently.

'Repeat the procedure in two weeks time to make sure you kill any young that may have hatched... Is this your first infestation?'

Glen nodded.

'When did you last have sex?'

'Friday evening... No, Saturday morning.'

'One nighter?' the pharmacist asked. Glen nodded. 'Then it's highly likely you've passed the crabs on. If you're still in contact, I suggest that you tell this person to treat themselves in a similar fashion.'

Glen looked aghast. 'I... I thought maybe that was who'd given me them?'

'Unlikely. They can sometimes take over a week to show up, depending on where they are in their life cycle when you come into contact with them. It's likely you caught them over a week ago, perhaps even longer.'

Laura was agog, her little round eyes darting here and there looking at, but not really seeing, the different sorts of sunglasses on display whilst her ears strained to hear every word.

'You'll need to wash your underwear and bedclothes immediately, on a hot cycle too, otherwise you could re-infect yourself,' the pharmacist continued.

Laura watched as Glen raised his eyebrows and sighed audibly. She giggled to herself. Serve him right for being such a sexpot! Still, she envied whoever it was that had rubbed genitals with that hunk of manhood, crabs or no crabs. She stayed well hidden as Glen paid for the shampoo and quickly left the shop. She was looking forward to teasing him at her dinner party. Things were looking up.

After Glen had left, she quickly approached the pharmacist and started to explain her problem.

 ❧❦❧

Mark had not responded to the message that Hugh had written leaning on the bonnet of Patrick's car and pushed through his letterbox on Saturday evening, and Hugh was now really annoyed with himself for letting his hormones get the better of him - twice! Glen was fun in bed, but he didn't want a relationship with him. They'd exchanged telephone numbers, although neither was likely to call. However, he felt sure that they would meet again and probably soon. Anyway, Hugh knew where to find him if he needed milking.

And as for Patrick, well... He was a wily young man who knew what he wanted and liked what he got and Hugh had seduced him in a moment of weakness. Or had it been the other way round? With a wry smile on his face and a pang in his heart, Hugh left his house and hurried to the Inner City Re-Housing Association where he was due at one o'clock. He hoped to see Mark there.

Margaret met him at the door with her screaming rendition of being taken off to the funny farm which, more than likely, is what would happen to her eventually, if there was a God.

'Good to see you, Jock,' John said, shaking his hand, pleased to see him as usual. 'The auditors have gone now, so we may live again for another year. Hoorah!'

Hugh grinned, but his heart sank at the news. 'We won't be seeing Mark again then?' he asked, cautiously.

John laughed. 'No, nice lad, but a bit quiet. I bet his eyes nearly fell out of his head when you took him to meet Marilyn at the Edward, eh?'

Hugh grinned at the memory. 'Oh, yeah, right. A real riot. I think Marilyn took a real shine to him, though.'

'Not the only one, eh lad?' said John, a twinkle in his eye.

Hugh just smiled.

'You can always call him at work, you know. He works for Berkeley Price & Simpson. The number's on our database.'

'Thanks, I might just do that,' Hugh replied. 'Now, what do you need me to do this afternoon?'

'Actually, Jock, very little,' said John. 'The van's in for its MOT and won't be back until tomorrow. It needs some welding done or something. We've had a few calls from some of the housekeepers to say that their lawns need mowing, but I've told them they'll have to wait another week. And we're not being sued at the moment so if I were you, I'd have the rest of the day off.'

'Right oh,' Hugh said, pleased to have some free time. He

enjoyed his voluntary work, but it was tough sometimes. He found that people demanded more because they knew they didn't have to pay for it, as if it was his duty and their right. Or maybe it was just because they liked getting something for free. Still, he enjoyed it and it gave him a rest from law.

'I'll just go and get that number,' he said and quickly ran upstairs, looked up the details on the computer and returned to John.

'I'll be off now then,' he said.

'Mind how you go. See you next Monday?'

'Sure thing. Have a good week,' Hugh said and quickly left the building. Margaret, thankfully, was nowhere in sight.

He walked down towards the Angel tube station. It was a lovely sunny afternoon and people were out and about, shopping and having lunch, but Hugh was oblivious to them all as he pushed on, intent on getting home to call Mark at his office.

Once home, he dialled quickly and spoke to a charming young lady who sounded gorgeous and sexy and well bred. Her name was Fiona and Hugh had a pleasant conversation with her. Unfortunately, Mark was out of the office and Fiona was explaining that he was uncontactable.

'But, it's very important that I contact him,' Hugh explained. 'I'm his solicitor, you understand?'

Fiona thought that this must have something to do with this morning. 'Well,' she said, 'I may be able to get a message to him. You do realise that he's *under cover*, don't you?'

Unsure what she meant, Hugh lied, 'Of course.'

'Well, if you give me your name and number, then I'll ensure that he gets the message.'

Hugh gave it to her. 'Are you likely to be speaking to him soon?' he asked.

'Probably not until tomorrow,' Fiona replied, adding, 'Is there a problem with that?'

'No, thank you, you've been most helpful.'

'You're welcome,' Fiona said.

Hugh put down the phone and cursed out loud.

Dinner that evening was a gastronomic delight, proving that Steve could cook as well as pick a good wine, among other things.

'That was delicious,' Mark remarked, wiping his mouth on a paper napkin. They were sitting at the dining table in front of the patio windows, the room lit only by candlelight and a faint glow from outside.

'Yes, it wasn't bad, I have to admit,' Steve replied, taking Mark's empty plate and stacking it on top of his own. He stood up and took them through into the kitchen, returned with the wine bottle and re-filled Mark's glass, then his own.

'Let me know when you want pudding,' said Steve.

'Er, not for a long while; I'm stuffed,' Mark replied, rubbing his belly.

'You will be later,' Steve promised with a smirk.

'I am now,' laughed Mark, delighted at the prospect of being fucked by this man, despite his still sore arse.

'Grab your glass. Let's sit in more comfy chairs. You want some more music on?'

Mark nodded and followed Steve through into the front lounge, stopping in front of his CD collection to select another. Moments later, they were serenaded by the strains of Madonna's new album. Mark continued to peruse the rows upon rows of neatly catalogued and labelled CDs.

'Quite a collection,' he murmured.

As he stood there, Steve slipped his arm around his shoulder and drew him in gently for a quick snog. 'Did you enjoy it Saturday night, with me in my leathers?' he asked.

'You fucking bet,' Mark replied, nuzzling Steve's goatee.

'Good, cos I've got another surprise for you tonight,' Steve told him. 'And you're gonna fucking love it.'

The words sent a shiver deep into Mark's belly, making his legs tremble. 'I'd better roll a few joints then,' he said.

'You do that whilst I use the loo,' said Steve and with a last suck on Mark's face, he was gone.

He was back moments later with his tin of stash and put it on the table. Mark sat down and started rolling a couple of joints. To make the roaches, he needed some white card so he took out his wallet and searched through it for an old business card, but found nothing suitable. He stood up and checked his pockets and found a fresh-looking piece of white card in a back one. He realised it was the business card given to him by the man in the pub on Saturday afternoon; the man who probably wanted him to pose naked. He was still looking at it, wondering whether to use it for making roaches or to keep it when Steve returned.

'What's that?'

'Oh, just some nutter who wants me to pose for him,' Mark replied, dismissively. 'He and his girlfriend kept staring at me in The Tin Man last Saturday afternoon after I left your place; then he came up to me and gave me this...'

Steve took it and held it by the edges. 'What did they look like?' he demanded.

'Um, tallish, both blond, in their late twenties, slight accent - maybe German? Why?'

Steve was excited. 'I think we're on to something here. It all fits. Bayswater/Marble Arch area, a blond German couple, you... Yes, it all fits. Have you rung this number yet?'

Mark shook his head. 'No, I forgot all about it. He was a bit scary, to be honest, and the landlord of the pub told me it was probably a sex thing and that if I wanted any help, I was to call him.'

Steve laughed. 'That sounds like Douggie.'

'You know them all!'

'Part of the job,' Steve told him. 'Anyway, I'd better get this card to forensic. I'll call the Chief and see what he suggests we do now.'

'What if he isn't the killer?'

'And what if he is...?'

'That would mean he intends to kill me!' said Mark abruptly. 'Why would anyone want to do that?'

'Don't take it personally. For him, it's a compulsion. You just happen to press his button for him.'

Mark shuddered. Steve handed him some card and he quickly completed the task and lit one of the joints.

Steve turned serious. 'Better not have too much of that. The Chief may want us to do something tonight... I'll call him now.'

Mark continued to smoke whilst Steve got straight through to the

Chief. About twenty minutes later, he put the phone down and turned to Mark. He was smiling. 'The good news is the Chief thinks this is a real breakthrough. He had the mobile phone checked out whilst we were talking and it appears to have no registered owner. He's sending a car round to pick up the evidence. The even better news is that we don't have to do anything tonight. So, as soon as I've handed this over, the sooner you can fire up that second joint and we'll get started on that little surprise I promised.' His smile turned into a wicked leer and Mark felt his heart quicken. He added coarsely, 'You'd better go and clean your arse out while we wait.'

Whilst Mark was on the loo, he heard the doorbell and voices, then silence. He hurried downstairs to where Steve was waiting in the dining room.

Mark sat down and lit the joint and inhaled twice in quick succession, then passed it to Steve. Steve did likewise and passed it back.

'That's all I need for now,' he said. 'Strip naked and come on down in about five minutes. Got that?'

Mark nodded. 'Whatever you say, Sir!'

Steve smiled appreciatively. 'You and me are going to get along just fine,' he said. He grabbed Mark by the throat and kissed him, then turned and headed for the cellar stairs.

Mark watched him go and wondered just how far Steve could push him before he said no. He smiled to himself. He doubted if Steve had it in him, but he was enjoying finding out. He took a long, last drag on the joint and stubbed it out. He jumped up and left a trail of smoke as he headed for the upstairs loo where he swished out his mouth with some Listerine.

He was poised, naked, at the entrance to Steve's cellar, exactly five minutes later as Steve had instructed. There was silence down below and no smell of cigar smoke. Mark could feel his heart pounding as he descended the wooden steps, the anticipation of what was to come forcing blood into his hardening cock. As his head descended below the level of the ground floor, he saw the light bulb swinging at one end of the dark cellar and the sling, also swinging, surrounded by lit candles of all shapes and sizes, all black. He was expecting to see Steve standing beside the sling, spurred on by the memory of his last descent into the cellar, but the cellar appeared empty.

He reached the hard, cold concrete bottom and cast a swift look around him. More than half of the cellar was in darkness and his eyes, still adjusting from the bright light in the hall, could not penetrate the corners. He moved towards the swinging light and caught his naked reflection in one of the wall mirrors. Just as he was admiring his hardened cock he heard a sound behind him.

A leather-gloved hand smothered his jaw whilst another forced his right arm backwards and up against his shoulder blade. He was pushed harshly against one wall, his cheek scraping the cool black brickwork. There was a metallic click and a heavy set of handcuffs were hanging from his right wrist. His left arm was then twisted similarly and his left wrist was cuffed to his right. He was dragged out into the open to be admired in front of the mirrors.

Steve wasn't wearing any leather, except for his gloves, boots and thick leather belt. Instead, he sported an authentic San Francisco Cop's uniform, complete with holster, firearm and baton. On his head, he wore a cap with the SFPD logo stitched to the front in gold braid whilst similar yet larger logos adorned both sleeves of the black cotton shirt, taut against his muscular chest. The short sleeves exaggerated the bulges of his biceps and triceps. The trousers were black cotton too, but of a rougher material than the shirt. Mark could feel the coarseness rubbing his thighs as he struggled for a better look.

'You have the right to remain silent,' Steve growled in his right ear, 'but if you do speak, what you say may be taken down and used in evidence against you. Is that clear?'

'Yes,' whispered Mark, his cock fully engorged.

'I said: Is that clear?'

'Yes, Sir!' shouted Mark. Steve clamped his hand on Mark's chin and yanked it to the side, scraping his goatee and stubble across Mark's yielding lips. Their eyes locked for a moment.

'This is what you want, isn't it?' Steve whispered.

'Yes, Sir,' said Mark. Steve let Mark's head drop forwards in submission, then pushed him roughly to his knees.

Chapter Eleven

When he finally awoke the following morning, Mark was alone in Steve's comfortable bed. He snuggled deeper into the duvet and relished its warmth and softness. He moved his leg and a small pain shot up his buttocks, like an electric current through his balls. It reminded him of last night and once again he wondered if this was doing him any physical damage. It wasn't just the battering he received from Steve's huge cock, but also the intensity of orgasms that punched out his cum in short sharp spurts. The very thought gave him an erection as he continued to snuggle down under the duvet.

He could hear Steve in the bathroom, taking a pee. The sound of it hitting the water continued for ages, then the flush, then the turning on of the shower. He imagined Steve soaping himself down and leapt out of bed, rubbed the sleep from his eyes, and entered the bathroom. Steve grinned at him through the steamed glass door. He pushed it open and helped Mark step through.

'You're insatiable,' Steve told him, nuzzling his ear.

'I never imagined sex like this existed,' Mark whispered. 'Is it normal on the gay scene?'

Steve laughed out loud. 'I doubt it,' he said, rubbing his goatee around Mark's mouth, watching the water run down the side of his handsome face. He noticed that both pairs of nipples were hard. 'Leather and uniforms are a big part of it for me, but everyone's different. Hey, you are enjoying it, aren't you?' he asked, seriously. 'Because we can...'

'I'm loving it,' Mark interrupted him and covered his mouth with his own. They kissed for some time.

The telephone rang. Steve turned off the shower and stepped out. He grabbed the phone and stood dripping on the bathroom mat as Mark followed. He was nodding his head and grunting his agreement.

Minutes later, he put the phone down and turned to Mark. 'We're being picked up in an hour. We've just got time for a quickie *and* breakfast,' he said with a broad grin. 'Come here,' he added, pulling Mark to him.

ΩϾᏰ

Hugh was having a tough time of it. The Berkeley Price & Simpson road was going nowhere very fast. Even if the Lady Fiona did pass on his message, it was unlikely that Mark would ring him back. And what did she mean by *under cover*? Had it something to do with their arrest the other night? Perhaps it was time for Mark's solicitor to put in another appearance.

Twenty minutes later, Hugh was climbing the now familiar steps of New Scotland Yard. Once again, he felt that brief sensation of importance, eminence and power as he stared at the revolving silver sign, then he was pushing through the doors and walking up to reception.

'Can I help you, Sir?' asked the duty officer. He was an old chap, grey hair, weather beaten face. Obviously walked the beat for far too long and now, as a reward for his years of devoted service, he had a nice cosy desk job.

'I was wondering if I might have a word with Detective Chief Inspector Dickens?'

'Oh, I see. Well, he's extremely busy right now. Can I help you at all?'

'No, I really need to speak to the Chief,' Hugh insisted. 'Is he in the building?'

'Now look Mr ...?'

'McDonald. Hugh McDonald.'

'Now look Mr McDonald,' said the officer patiently, 'Detective Chief Inspector Dickens is unavailable right now. Perhaps if you told me what it was concerning, I might be able to help?'

The duty officer was gently digging in his heels and Hugh knew he had precious little time to get any help from him at all. He was about to say something clever when the interior door opened and Dickens himself walked through, quickly followed by a goateed blond muscular guy dressed casually in faded denims and a black tee shirt, and Mark, who was similarly dressed. Hugh blinked in surprise and shouted out Mark's name. All three men turned sharply to look his way. Mark's face lit up for a moment, then quickly clouded over. They were obviously in a hurry. Hugh rushed over to meet them.

'Ah, Mr McDonald,' said Detective Chief Inspector Dickens, 'what brings you here again?'

Hugh glanced at Mark.

'Ah, I see,' said Dickens, nodding his head. 'You want a word with your *client*. Well, make it quick, we're just leaving.'

Mark led Hugh off to one side. Steve eyed up Hugh and looked distinctly uncomfortable, then he followed the Chief out through the doors.

'So, what's going on?' Hugh asked. 'Fiona said you'd gone *under cover*. Are you still involved in this murder case?'

'Fiona who?' Mark asked.

'Your secretary, or whatever. She said…'

'You phoned my office?' Mark demanded. 'Why?'

Hugh looked down at his feet. 'Um, well, if you must know, I'm in love with you.'

Now it was Mark's turn to look uncomfortable. 'Oh,' he said. 'Well, you've got a funny way of showing it. Stella told me that Glen stayed the other night.'

'What?' Hugh gasped. 'Stella doesn't know anything about Glen. What do you mean?'

'Well, she didn't actually say his name, but she said that you'd met up with an *old friend* and that he was still there on Saturday morning when she rang you. I just put two and two together.'

Hugh was visibly relieved.

'I presume you had sex,' Mark continued.

'Well, he is rather hot…' Hugh grinned. His hairy black moustache quivered and Mark had the sudden urge to try and suck it off his face, but he resisted the temptation. 'You should have stayed,' Hugh continued. 'You would have enjoyed it.'

'Hugh,' said Mark sighing, 'why can't you make do with just one person in your life? You're ruining any chances of a long-term relationship with anyone, even Stella, even though she loves you. You're going to get caught out sooner or later…'

'I'll drop them all for you. Right here, right now.'

'Yeah, right.'

Hugh grabbed him by both arms and gazed into Mark's face. 'I mean it,' he said.

Steve came back through the doors and took one look at Hugh holding Mark by the arms and hurried over. 'What's going on here, then?' he demanded.

'Back off will ya, *I'm* talking here,' said Hugh nastily.

'Is this man annoying you?' Steve asked Mark. Mark shook his head.

Hugh turned to Steve. 'I said, *Back off, I'm talking here.*'

'Well, I'm sorry, but your time is up. Mark has some important business to attend to. Right now!'

Mark looked from one man to the other. They were staring at each other as if they were about to start fighting. He stepped between them. 'Right, that's enough. Hugh, meet Steve. Steve, meet Hugh.' He turned to Hugh. 'Hugh, I've got to go now. I'll call you later in the week when this is over. Ok?'

Hugh wasn't happy, but he let it go. 'Ok. Have you got my number?'

Mark nodded.

'Make sure you call me. Oh, and be careful.'

'Thank you, I will,' Mark replied, not knowing for sure what he was referring to. Steve led him quickly though the doors and out to an awaiting car.

'Took your bloody time, didn't you?' the Chief said jovially from the back seat.

'Sorry, Chief,' Mark replied. 'It won't happen again.'

Steve brooded in silence.

ଈୠ

Stella was having a wonderful Tuesday - so far. Her mother had taken her shopping in the West End and treated her to a new frock for Laura's dinner party. Earlier, her mother had called the pub where Stella was due to be pulling pints at midday and told them that Stella was very ill and wouldn't be in for the rest of the week. Stella had wanted to ring them herself and tell them where they could stuff their lousy job, but her mother had warned her of the pitfalls of that course of action, particularly if she ever needed a reference.

'We may have money now,' she told her daughter, 'but nothing ever lasts, believe me, and you never know when you might be glad of another bar job.'

'But I can go to college now and learn something more useful,' Stella had protested.

'That may be so, but there's never any excuse to be that rude.'

Stella thought this a bit rich coming from her mother, considering the way she'd treated Stella most of her life. However, that was all behind them now. She had another quick peek at her new frock and smiled inwardly. Her mother caught her looking.

'Let's have another peek as well,' she urged and Stella opened the bag again.

'That's a lovely piece of material and no mistake,' her mother said admiringly. 'And so it should be at that price,' she added.

Stella pulled a face and they both started to laugh. Stella closed the bag and her mother suddenly screamed. 'Shoes! Have you got shoes to match?'

Stella had to admit that she hadn't. 'Well then, shoes it must be,' her mother said.

They were outside Selfridges and it was lunchtime and Stella was starving. 'Let's have something to eat first,' she suggested. 'Aren't you hungry?'

Her mother nodded her agreement. 'Where shall we go?'

'I know this little pub around the corner. I think they do food. Want to try it?'

'Lead on,' her mother said and Stella took her arm and led her through the crowds. They turned up a side street and her mother was thankful for the relative calm.

'That Oxford Street's a nightmare,' she grumbled as they walked along, arm in arm, 'but this is lovely.'

The sun shone down and the sound of traffic and bustle receded. They turned left and suddenly the pub was in front of them.

'The Tin Man?' said her mother. 'What sort of a name for a pub is that?'

Stella shrugged. 'Any friend of Dorothy's...' she said as she pushed open the door and led the way inside.

The place was unusually busy with a lunchtime crowd tucking in to various dishes, hot and cold, and Stella's mother nodded her head approvingly.

'Yes, this will do,' she said. 'Find us a seat whilst I get the drinks.' She marched up to the bar.

Stella looked around, but all the tables seemed occupied. Suddenly, she saw Mark sitting at a table in the corner. Ed the biker was talking earnestly at him, still dressed in his leathers, and Mark was nodding in agreement. This continued for a few minutes until they both stood up and headed for the door. Stella shrank into the background. If this was what Mark wanted, then good for him. She didn't want to embarrass him.

Another table became free as two more men rose and quickly followed them out of the door. 'How strange,' Stella murmured to herself quietly, noticing that neither of the two men had touched their drinks. She felt goose bumps suddenly and had a horrible feeling that Mark was in trouble. What should she do?

Her mother arrived with two orange juices and a couple of menus. 'Can't we sit in the garden, dear?'

Stella, distracted, said, 'Er, yeah, sure.'

'Stella, are you alright? Stella?'

Stella glanced at her mother and her features softened. 'Yeah, sorry. I... I just had a weird feeling... Can you look after my bag for a minute?' She handed over the shopping bag with her new frock inside and left her mother standing by the empty table as she rushed over to the door. She peeked through the glass in time to see Mark put on a crash helmet and swing his leg over the pillion of a Moto Guzzi 850. Ed the biker was impatiently revving the bike and as soon as Mark was safely on the back, he raced off. Stella saw Mark rock back and forwards before gaining a better hold. The other two men were nowhere in sight. She shrugged and was just about to return to her mother, when a black sedan screeched away from the curb further down. The two men were now wearing dark sunglasses and she felt a sudden chill of fear for Mark. They were following him and meant him harm.

She wrenched open the door and ran straight out into the road. The car swerved with a loud screech and ran up onto the curb, hit a large red post-box on the corner with a sickening crunch and came to an abrupt halt. The post-box, relatively unscathed, was embedded into the crumpled bonnet of the sedan. Steam suddenly hissed from underneath.

There was a moment's silence as Stella stood mortified in the middle of the road. Then noise erupted as the two front doors shot open and the two men jumped out. The younger one turned on her and started yelling but the older one grabbed him by the shoulder and spun him around.

'Get back-up. Now!!' he barked and then turned to Stella.

He put his hand inside his jacket and whipped out a leather wallet. He flashed it at Stella. 'We're police,' he said. Stella nervously read the id.

'Detective Chief Inspector...' she read, before it was snapped closed.

The Chief composed himself before saying, 'What the hell do you think you were doing, running in front of us like that? You could have been killed!'

A small jittery crowd started to gather and people were streaming out of the pub and nearby houses to see what had happened. Her mother appeared and Stella wrapped her arms around her and sobbed.

'What's going on?' she demanded of the Chief who raised his eyes heavenward, threw his hands up in the air and turned on PC Evans.

'Got back-up yet?' he yelled. Steve shook his head.

'OH, CHRIST ALL FUCKING MIGHTY!!!' the Chief screamed, banging his fist down hard on what remained of the sedan's bonnet. Steve just stood there helplessly, his handsome face contorted with a growing look of fear and dread. 'We're gonna lose our fucking heads over this, not to mention your boyfriend's!' he added, his face a mask of anger.

The gathering crowd looked even more stunned and started to murmur amongst themselves.

⍥⍣

Mark almost fell off the back of the Moto Guzzi as Ed slammed it into first gear and shot off. He managed to gain a firmer grip by putting his arms around Ed's waist. Ed responded by rubbing his arse against Mark's crotch.

It had been a surprise to see Ed again. Mark had called and spoken to Otto Meyer. Otto had instructed him to go to the same pub where he had been given the business card and wait to be contacted. When Ed approached, he was dismissive at first, but at the mention of Otto's name Mark invited him to sit down. Ed said he'd been paid highly to pick Mark up and deliver him to an address in Mayfair, not too far from the pub. It wasn't his usual kind of delivery but he was happy to do anything for a few banknotes.

Mark was nervous as Ed led him from the pub. He didn't even glance in Steve's direction, as instructed. Instead, he'd climbed onto the back of the motorbike, and now, here he was, wind whistling in his ears, his eyes streaming from the lack of a visor, being taken at high speed straight to the lion's den. The microphone and tracking device were well concealed in the hem of his tee shirt, but he still felt vulnerable. He knew that Steve and the Chief would be listening in and tracking him right now, but this was all so very new to him and he'd seen films where so many things could and always did go wrong. But that was the movies. This was real life. He crossed his fingers surreptitiously against the tough leather jacket that Ed was wearing and hoped that nothing would go wrong.

A few minutes later, just as Mark was beginning to enjoy the throb of the 850cc engine between his thighs, Ed turned down a small mews in the heart of Mayfair and came to an abrupt halt about half way down. Without warning, the doors of the nearest garage swung openly almost silently and Ed revved his bike until they were inside. The doors started to close and the interior grew darker as the outside world was shut out. Only a low wattage bulb suspended from a flex in the ceiling kept the monsters at bay.

Ed took off his helmet and Mark followed. He stopped the bike in the middle of the deserted garage, cut the engine and then dismounted, urging Mark to do the same.

'I thought you were just dropping me off?' Mark said.

'Yeah, well, I help Otto out on occasion; do a bit of modelling for him. Sometimes he likes a couple of guys to wrestle a bit, you know?'

Mark raised his eyebrows. Thinking that Steve was listening in through the microphone he asked, 'So, who is this Otto? How do you know him?'

'Don't ask so many questions,' Ed replied. 'Now, take my advice and just do as he says; he can be a bit unpleasant if he doesn't get his own way.'

Ed opened a door that led from the garage into the basement of the building. Mark followed him through into a dimly lit hallway, up some stairs and then into another hallway. There were no windows, but the hallway was brightly lit and furnished in buttermilk flock wallpaper and maroon carpeting. It reminded Mark of rhubarb and custard. Ed came to the end of the hallway where there was a small lift, pulled open the double doors and led Mark inside.

Ed was silent as the lift rose creakingly to the fourth floor. Mark caught Ed studying him.

'You're an extraordinarily handsome man,' Ed told him. 'I can see why Otto wants you to pose for him.'

'Thank you,' Mark said. 'You're not so bad yourself.'

The lift jerked to a sudden noisy stop and Ed opened the doors. They walked out into a large open room that was mainly white with a few items of modern furniture dotted about. In one corner a photo-shoot had been set up with a large white screen, several white open umbrellas and three free-standing halogen lights on tripods with flanges attached to direct the beam.

A door off to the right opened unexpectedly and Otto Meyer and his blonde companion entered the room.

'We meet again,' beamed Otto, his white teeth gleaming. Apart from a slight Germanic accent, his English was flawless. 'This is my assistant, Katrin.' Katrin inclined her head gently to the side and smiled wanly. She looked a little drained, as if she had been up all night, or screaming for too long - or maybe both. 'You've met Ed, of course,' he continued, nodding his head towards Mark's ride.

'Pleased to meet you too,' Mark replied.

'Now, refreshments,' said Otto and snapped his fingers. Katrin immediately disappeared through the door. Otto led Mark and Ed over to a small rest area where he indicated that they should sit down.

Katrin reappeared moments later with small china cups and green tea already poured. She carefully handed Mark the cup furthest from her and handed similar cups to Otto and Ed. She held the tray at her side as Otto made a toast.

'In my country,' he said, 'it is traditional to drink this tea down in one.' With that, he presented the toast and they all drank, including Mark. The tea had a slightly bitter taste, but was not unpleasant.

'Right then,' Otto began, baring his pearly-white teeth, 'tell us a bit about yourself, Mark. What made you call me?'

The Chief of Police, Mark thought and had to stifle a giggle. 'I want to earn some extra money,' he answered, as rehearsed.

'Is that all?' Otto asked, laughing lightly. 'And I thought you might have been a little attracted to me, no?'

Mark looked at Ed who stared right back at him, licking his lips. *Mm, Ed's quite a hunk*, Mark mused, *despite his long hair.*

'Maybe just a little?' Otto was saying.

Mark moved his gaze to Otto and noticed for the first time how red his lips were. Quite succulent, in fact. His gaze crossed the room to the far corner where a large bed stood. It was moulded from black metal with the header and footer an art form in sculpted metal. It was surrounded by more lights, with three white umbrellas and two cameras on tripods positioned strategically on either side.

Mark felt a firm hold taken on his chin as his face was turned towards Otto.

'I'd really like you to look at me when I'm talking to you,' Otto said, smiling and nodding his head hypnotically.

Mark felt himself smiling back.

'Now, you do find me attractive, don't you?'

Mark continued to smile and then nodded his head in unison with Otto.

'Well, I'm pleased about that because I've got a little surprise for you, and believe me you'll enjoy it so much more if you find me, and my friends, attractive.' He turned to Ed. 'I think he's ready now, don't you?'

'Yes, Sir,' Ed replied, standing to attention. He took hold of Mark by the upper arms, massaging the muscles there for a few moments, before lifting him to his feet. Mark made no effort to resist. He felt buoyant but heavy all at the same time, as if wading through water up to his neck. His body, carried on by momentum, flopped over. Ed had to struggle to keep him upright. Mark seemed to find this entertaining and started to giggle again.

An instant slap to the face brought him to his senses. 'Stop that,' Otto hissed at him. 'I want you conscious for now. You can pass out when I slit you open and my cock's inside you. Is that understood?' Mark was silent.

'I said: Is that understood?' He slapped Mark again, hard.

Mark briefly came to his senses. He stared at Otto and then at Ed, who was smiling and licking his lips. Ed bared his teeth at Mark and then snapped them shut with a loud clunk. Somewhere in the back of his mind he screamed silently for Steve to come to his rescue. Outwardly, he was calm. Steve was just waiting for the right moment.

Otto and Ed carried Mark between them over to the bed where they sat him down and Otto began to remove Mark's tee shirt. Ed untied his laces and pulled off his boots. Otto slowly and suggestively started to lower the flies on Mark's jeans, his intense grey eyes focused on Mark's. His hand slid inside the denim and he mouthed an outrageous show of surprise and wonder. 'Ooh, isn't that lovely,' he said. 'Such a prize! Katrin, come here and feel this - now!'

Meekly, Katrin did as she was told. Mark watched her put her hand out tentatively, then with increasing confidence. Her eyes went wide with mirth as Mark felt her hard cold fingers touch him. She withdrew her hand instantly and started to giggle.

Otto spoke to her as a child. 'You liked that, didn't you?' he said. She nodded, happily. 'Would Ed like a feel?' he asked, turning to Ed.

'Ed wants a taste,' said Ed sullenly.

'He wants to bite it off, like the last one!' Katrin warned, in a very grown up voice, adding in a very girlish voice, 'Don't let him, please. Oh, please don't let him. Not yet anyway. Make him wait this time...'

'There, there,' said Otto, as if comforting his little sister after a big disappointment. 'Don't you worry. You can have your fun too.'

Then, with a sudden downward movement, Mark's trousers and pants fell around his ankles. Otto pushed him down on the bed and lifted his legs in the air. Ed pulled the clothes from him, then gathered them all up and took them out of the room, returning moments later.

Next, Mark experienced the peculiar sensation of being dragged across white satin sheets and then of his hands and legs being tied to the corner posts of the bed with lengths of soft strong silk. The lights went dim and he saw through narrowed eyes the flickering of a thousand stars.

He felt something hard and wet and bristly graze his solid chest and nipples but didn't have the strength to look. He guessed it might be Ed's goateed mouth and chin.

Then he felt something warm and wet and gentle tickle the sensitive end of his penis and he imagined this might be Katrin's tongue.

Then he felt something cold and hard and sharp touch him in the tender area between his bellybutton and groin. He didn't like to think what that might be. It started to dig in slowly. Strangely enough, he didn't feel any pain.

☙❧

Stella was a little girl again, crying in her mother's arms. 'Here, drink some of this,' her mother urged gently. Stella sipped and then knocked it back in one. She loved brandy.

The landlord, a great brute of a man with sticky-out ears and a kindly face, was standing with them, watching as another black sedan screeched to a halt in front of the two policemen.

'Sort this mess out,' the Chief barked at the plain-clothes policeman in the passenger seat.

The man jumped out, quickly surveyed the scene and nodded to the Chief. 'No problem, Sir.'

The Chief got into the warm passenger seat just vacated and Steve jumped in behind. The Chief shouted something at the driver and they were gone.

The policeman now in charge urged the growing crowd to disperse. He called on his mobile for assistance and again urged them all to go home. Douggie, the landlord, led Stella and her mother back inside the pub and over to a vacant table in the corner of the bar. The show was over and he was pleased to note that his customers were returning to their tables and ordering more drinks. Things were smoothing out again, getting back to normal. Douggie looked at Stella and her mother, Stella dabbing her eyes with a small white hanky.

'Wh… what have I done?' Stella burst out and started sobbing again.

'There, there, love,' crooned her mother, giving her a squeeze. 'You weren't to know. They'll find him, don't you worry.'

'B… But that policeman said the transmitter only had a limited range. What if …?'

'Shh,' said her mother, firmly. 'They'll find him.' She smiled grimly over Stella's shoulder at Douggie who returned her grim smile.

ℴℴℴ

The driver parked the black sedan on double yellow lines in the heart of Mayfair. Steve was studying the tracking device in the back seat whilst the Chief sat impatiently staring up through the windscreen at block after block of well-maintained expensive town houses. Most were converted into flats, of course, but the occasional one was still in its original state. The only clue to this, in most cases, was the uniformity of décor and net curtaining.

'Here, let me have a look,' said the Chief, exasperated. Steve handed over the tracker.

'It could be any one of these buildings,' Steve said, shaking his head.

'Anything on the microphone?' the Chief asked, fiddling with the controls on the tracker.

'Nothing for a while now, not since the man said to the woman with the funny voice that she could have her fun too. Maybe Mark's removed his tee shirt, or something.'

The Chief glanced at his watch and then growled at the driver, 'How long 'til reinforcements get here?'

'Any minute now, Sir.'

'Well, we can't just wait here. Steve, you take that side of the street, and I'll take this side.'

'And do what, Chief?' Steve asked.

'Just knock and see. Look for anything suspicious, anything out of the ordinary. And get a move on, we might not have much time!'

∞∞

Otto Meyer, a man with many aliases, discovered his fascination for dismemberment at a very early age when he'd pulled off the legs of a very large and very hairy spider that had claimed its territory in the woodshed at the bottom of his garden in the Black Forest, near the Swiss border of West Germany, as it was then known.

Having removed all its legs, he put it into a jam jar, sealed the lid with perforated paper and an elastic band and observed it over the next few days, waiting to see how long the spider took to die. Since it could no longer move, it was very difficult for Otto to tell whether it was still alive or not and he soon grew bored. A few days later, he graduated onto a frog, but this had proved very messy and he had thrown it into the lake. He returned to experimenting with insects because they tended not to bleed and lived for quite some time without their limbs.

It was only as he approached adolescence that he remembered the frog and his interest was spiked afresh. This time though, he had recruited his little sister, Katrin, to the game to which she had taken like a duck to water. She was always upset though, when the insect or animal died and always got mad at him if he did anything to accelerate the dying process.

The thrill he got when the second frog split up the middle was more than his thirteen years of life had prepared him for. He'd known that he'd had an erection, of course, but he was not sure why. When he shook and shuddered for almost a minute afterwards and felt his pants turn sodden, he knew. It didn't take much encouragement to do it again and again and again. Pretty soon, every kind of woodland creature in that part of the world had fallen prey to the little monsters.

Right now, he had the hardest erection that he could ever remember. He watched mesmerised as the most handsome, the most beautiful, and the most perfect looking man Otto had ever laid eyes on offered himself up to him. The young man's legs were raised high in the air, held in place now by ropes suspended from the ceiling, and the puckered hairy hole of his anus was absolutely ripe for the taking. Ed was literally chewing on his nipples whilst Katrin's blonde hair bobbed up and down, noisily suckling on the man's hairy balls and flaccid cock. Katrin much preferred them soft. They posed no threat to her in that state and she found she could bite them harder without damaging them quite so much.

In his right hand, Otto held an ancient hunting knife that his grandfather had bestowed on him. It had saved his grandfather's life many times during the Second World War, or so his grandfather had told him on numerous occasions. The old man had died a few years ago, but the knife lived on and was about to take yet another Englishman's life, the fourth in as many weeks.

Otto carefully lowered the blade of the knife so that it rested against the soft flesh between this beautiful man's downy covered bellybutton and his blond pubic area, where Katrin, still suckling like a baby pig, eyed it gleefully. Gently, he lowered it more, creating a small dent in the thin flesh that covered the stomach muscles. Otto was pleased to see no sign whatsoever of any subcutaneous fat. He hated fat and would slice it off like a butcher carving a carcass if he found any on his victims. He particularly hated *love handles*, as the English called them, and had removed them with very messy but very satisfactory results on more than one occasion in the past.

With the knife, he traced a prominent blue vein that ran down the left side of this beautiful young man's hard belly until it disappeared into the depths of his groin just below the waist. Otto's eyes suddenly turned hard and he felt the urge building in him to make that stab, to follow that vein deep down inside this man who had lived simply to die today for Otto's pleasure.

He looked up, from Katrin to Ed and saw their gleaming approving eyes widen in glorious anticipation. Then they both began nodding their heads in unison for him to do it, just do it, do it, do it, do it, DO IT…

With a snarl of triumph, he lifted the knife high into the air, poised to plunge it down and in and from side to side and so create an opening for his rampant cock to enter the body of this perfect being. Savouring the moment just a fraction too long, he was startled by the piercing ring of his mobile phone. He tried hard to ignore it and to focus his concentration on the task at hand, but the moment had passed.

With a roar of disgust, he twisted and plunged the gleaming hunting knife into the silky mattress of the bed. Katrin jerked up her head and a look of abject fear screwed up her flushed face. This was the moment she always hated, when her brother got mad. He tended to do things that she didn't like.

Otto turned and stalked over to the coffee table where his mobile phone was still shrilling. His cock had started to soften and with it his resolve. Soon would come remorse, though that would only last till his next erection. He picked up the phone and, with one sideways look at the beautiful young man lying almost unconscious on the bed, whipped back his arm and threw the mobile phone as hard as he could at the opposite wall.

It missed.

∞⚭⚭

Steve started knocking on doors and ringing bells on one side of the street; the Chief did the same on the opposite. They soon realised however that it would take them too long, since the occupants were either very guarded or extremely forthcoming and curious to know what was going on. Inevitably, a small crowd had gathered on both sides of the street when Steve suddenly had a brainwave.

'Hey Chief, have you still got that unlisted mobile number?'

The Chief spun around and nodded, took out his own mobile and brought the number up on screen.

'Right here,' he said.

Steve ran over to him. 'Right then, you ring it and I'll get this lot to be quiet for a moment.'

He called for hush as the Chief punched the send button. It started to ring. They craned their ears for any sound, but heard nothing.

'Oh, well,' said the Chief, 'it was worth a try. These old properties were built solidly in their day.'

At that moment, they heard the crash of broken glass from above. They looked up and saw a silvery black object sailing out of a window from the top floor of a property further up the street. Glass shards fell clattering to the ground and amid the noise they could hear the shrilling of the mobile phone. It hit the house opposite, just below the window of the next floor down, and then fell like a stone. It stopped ringing when it hit the ground and exploded into numerous pieces.

A moment later, Steve and the Chief were outside banging on the door and ringing the bell. The Chief shouted upwards as loud as he could, 'Open up! This is the police! You are completely surrounded!'

As if to push home their advantage, their back-up squad car appeared at the end of the street and screeched to a nearby halt. Within seconds, the door was smashed in and the police stormed the building.

&)(&

By the time they reappeared, a large crowd had gathered and were standing behind the black and yellow tape strung across both sides of the road. There was an ambulance, three squad cars with their blue lights turning and a large red fire engine for good measure.

The crowd cheered as the Chief finally emerged, although they were unsure why. It seemed the right thing to do. Two men and a woman were led away in handcuffs to the three waiting squad cars. The tall blond man held his head high as he was forced into the back seat of one of the squad cars, whilst the woman and the other man had their heads bowed and climbed into their respective squad cars unaided.

Moments later, they cheered again as Steve and the paramedics brought Mark out unconscious on a stretcher and placed him carefully into the back of the waiting ambulance. Steve sat with him, holding his hand all the way to hospital.

&)(&

Mark finally became aware of his surroundings later that evening. He was lying in a clean bed wearing a thin white cotton shirt that appeared to be on backwards and was hooked up to a monitor that beeped monotonously. He was alone with his thoughts. He knew he was in a hospital, and he knew up to a point that he had been in danger and completely helpless to do anything about it. They had drugged him with the tea, of course, but his memory from that point on was vague. How far had it gone? What else had they done to him? Who had saved him? Had he been saved or was this still some part of the nightmare? Maybe this wasn't even a hospital? Was he dead?

A woman in a matron's uniform appeared reassuringly. She was tall, big-boned, with short dark hair, perky breasts and a lovely smile.

'Sure, you're awake, at last,' she said in a broad and deep Northern Ireland accent. 'How're you feeling?'

She took his wrist and stared at her upturned watch for a few moments. She felt his brow and nodded her head once or twice, picked up a chart from the end of his bed and made a few short notes.

'Where am I?' he asked her. 'I mean, which hospital?'

'The Princess Royal, to be sure,' she replied. 'Now, are you feeling up to receiving a few visitors?'

'Who?'

'Well, first of all there's the police. Then the TV and press, then there're a few friends who've stopped by; also somebody from your office and I think maybe even your mum and dad are on their way. You're quite a hero, don't you know?' She smiled down at him again and felt his brow once more. 'Doctor will want to see you an' all to discharge you, but in my opinion you can go home.'

'No permanent damage, then?'

She shook her head. 'And from what I've been overhearing, I think you've been very lucky. And very, very brave,' she added firmly.

He smiled modestly. 'Anyone would've done the same,' he said.

'Save it for the press.'

He did as instructed.

As Steve tried to clear a path through to the waiting black sedan, they swarmed over him, cameras clicking furiously like a plague of crickets, automatic chargers screeching like a horde of fruit bats, flash bulbs popping like firecrackers. Mark froze, totally disorientated. Steve literally picked him up and carried him to the car, jumped in beside him and squeezed his thigh supportively. They sped off into the night.

His parents weren't coming after all. Once Mark had spoken to them and assured them that he was fine, they were happy to stay in Oxford and watch the story unfold on the news. He promised them he would be home to see them as soon as possible.

Stella and Hugh had appeared separately at the hospital earlier that evening and then left together. No doubt they were somewhere between orgasms right now. The thought brought a smile to Mark's face and a tightening in his crotch.

He turned his attention to the streets of London as they passed, their lights casting stripey grey and orange glows onto him and Steve. He gazed at Steve for a moment as he chatted with the driver. Steve glanced back at him and gave his thigh another surreptitious squeeze, although it was more sexually charged this time, away from the prying cameras.

Minutes later, Steve was opening the door to his home and to Mark's temporary residence. 'I suppose I won't be living here much longer now this is over,' Mark said.

Steve closed the door and turned to face him. He put his arms around Mark's shoulders and pulled him close, kissing him on the neck, then cheek, then lips. They kissed for a while.

There were tears in Steve's eyes as they parted. 'Well, that depends,' he said. 'We need to talk.'

He led Mark through the hallway and into the kitchen where he uncorked a bottle of chilled Sauvignon Blanc.

Chapter Twelve

The following morning Mark awoke once again in Steve's bed, but this time feeling vaguely groggy. The room had been cleared of the debris of their passionate all-night lovemaking. His clothes were now neatly folded on the chair, the floor had been cleared of tissues and the ashtray emptied of used condoms. He could hear Steve preparing breakfast downstairs, if he listened hard enough.

He stretched cautiously and yawned, pushed back the duvet and walked across the soft-piled carpet to draw open the curtains, let in some morning sunshine and then continued into the bathroom where he luxuriated in the power of the shower. He finally stepped out and towelled himself dry in front of the mirror. Steve had stopped him shaving and he gazed at his new face for a moment. It was bristly and quite rugged-looking, he thought, but a bit untidy. He'd have to shave it off soon if he was going to go back to work. Anyway, for now, he could do whatever he liked, and that was a lovely thought.

Downstairs, Steve had laid the breakfast bar in the kitchen with orange juice and a variety of cereals to start with and what looked like scrambled eggs on toast to follow. As Mark entered the kitchen, Steve greeted him with a hug and a kiss.

'Did you sleep alright? No nightmares?' he asked.

'I slept great. No nightmares.'

'I got the newspapers, by the way - over there,' Steve said, pointing at a pile.

Mark picked up the Independent first. He read it and inwardly groaned. They'd made him out to be the people's hero. 'I'm not going to hear the last of this, am I?' he asked.

Steve shook his head. 'Not for a while, at least... And I think you'd better take a look at the Sun,' he added ominously.

Mark rummaged amongst the pile and was horrified with the headline, 'SERIAL GAY SEX KILLERS CAUGHT WITH THEIR

PANTS DOWN.' He read the article, groaning every few words. 'Where did they get my name? How did they find out where I worked? Oh, my god, what will my mum and dad say? What will Donald say?'

'Donald?' asked Steve stiffly.

'My boss,' Mark replied. He covered his face with his hands. 'Oh, no. This is just awful.'

Steve offered Mark some orange juice. Mark shook his head. 'Coffee?'

Mark shook his head again. 'What am I going to say to them all?'

'Nobody knows you're gay, I take it?' asked Steve, sitting down on a white stool and pouring skimmed milk onto his cereal.

'I didn't really know myself until just recently.'

'Well, it doesn't actually say that you're gay...'

'No, it just says *gay sex*, that's all. Anyone who reads it will just assume. You know what people are like! They've made out that these perverts were serial killers of gay men. That's not true. They didn't care if their victims were gay or not.'

Steve munched his cereals. 'Eat your breakfast,' he said. 'Afterwards you can call your parents and then we'll go and fetch the rest of your things. After that, we're going shopping. I want to see what you look like in full leathers.'

Mark could hardly believe his ears. 'Just like that?' he asked. 'My whole world's crumbling around me and you want us to go *shopping?*'

'It's not crumbling around you - it's being built,' Steve replied sternly. 'Believe me, you go into hiding over your sexuality and your whole life will be built on egg-shells. Take it on the chin and move on. If you have to change your job over this, so what? It only means you're working for the wrong people. Take me for instance, everyone at the Met knows I'm gay, and there are plenty more like me. If the Met can handle it, so can Donald. And if he can't, then he can stuff it up his arse,' he paused and took a swig of orange juice. 'You'll find that the majority of straights can handle it, no problem. In fact, anyone comfortable with their sexuality is usually fine with it, so I wouldn't worry too much if I were you.'

Mark nodded. 'It's a bit frightening, though, you must admit,' he said quietly.

Steve reached over and put an arm around him. 'I'm here for you, bud, whatever you decide to do.'

Mark looked him in the eyes, noticed the strong goateed jaw, the masculine shape of the neck, the strength in his shoulders and he thought of their recent coupling. He knew they still had a lot more to explore sexually, particularly after their frank talk last night. Much more to the point though, he was aware that he was falling in love with this man.

∽◌∾

Laura was reclining on her couch after a hearty breakfast of just about everything she could find in the fridge and the larder. She loved the word *larder*. It conjured up some wonderful old-fashioned images of fat-filled food; none of this fat-free nonsense you heard about nowadays.

Freud benefited from her food frenzy too and was stretched out across the piano stool in the corner, purring contentedly. The piano stool was undoubtedly his favourite place in the flat, perhaps in the whole world, and it smelled wonderful to him. Not that he particularly liked the smell of Laura's bottom, of course, but it did lend it a certain air of familiarity that he found particularly comforting. The fact that five years worth of his moult was embedded in the fabric, almost down to the molecular level, helped too, naturally.

Laura was drawing up a seating plan for the dinner party that was almost upon her and which nothing had been organised as yet. She couldn't quite remember how many people she'd invited and was beginning to think along the lines of a buffet, when someone hammered rudely on the inner door to her flat. The loud banging stopped as suddenly as it had begun and then started again. She pushed herself into a sitting position and stared at Freud who hissed angrily. With his back arched, he sprang for the window ledge and was through the window in moments.

'I'm coming,' Laura shouted, pushing herself upright. She shuffled to the door in her pink slippers, pulling her robe around her. She really should have got dressed earlier, when she'd had the chance. Still, she wasn't to know that she was going to receive an unexpected visitor at this time in the morning.

'Who is it?' she asked, before opening the door. One couldn't be too careful, she thought, thinking back to how easily the police had gained entry to Netherhall.

'It's me, Pierre!' came an excited voice. 'Let me in!'

Raising her eyes to the ceiling and dropping them again, she put on a smile and opened the door. Pierre rushed in waving a newspaper in her face. Laura followed him through into the lounge. He was very excited.

'Have you heard the news?' he asked, his eyes shining. 'They've caught the murderer, or murderers or whatever.'

'Really?' said Laura. 'Let's have a look.'

She took the tabloid and read the headline out loud, '*SERIAL GAY SEX KILLERS CAUGHT WITH THEIR PANTS DOWN...* This calls for a celebratory cup of Irish coffee, don't you think?'

Pierre nodded his head vigorously as Laura stormed the kitchen, leaving him to continue reading aloud. 'It says here that there were three of them altogether and that two of them were brother and sister - can you believe that?'

'Horrible,' shouted Laura from the kitchen as she filled the kettle and started to put out cups and saucers.

'It says,' Pierre continued, 'that they used someone as bait. Some pretty boy who almost got killed. Hold on, where was it now, oh yes, some guy named Mark Carter, a trainee Chartered...'

A loud crash from the kitchen interrupted Pierre. He flung the newspaper aside and raced to see what had happened. Laura had dropped a full kettle of cold water into the sink, right on top of the dirty breakfast dishes. Most of the crockery was in pieces.

'Oh, my god. Are you alright Laura?'

'Never mind me,' said Laura gallantly. 'What about bloody Mark?'

She rushed into the lounge and picked up the newspaper, quickly scanning the article. Pierre followed, looking puzzled.

'You know him?'

'He's supposed to be coming to my bloody party!' she muttered, reading down the columns. 'Damn, it doesn't bloody say! How am I going to find out if he's ok?'

'Call the cops?' suggested Pierre, trying to be helpful.

Laura threw the paper down in disgust. 'I think we've had enough of them nosing about lately, although I guess we've heard the last of them for now, thank god.'

Pierre shook his head. 'Doubt it,' he said. 'I'm a witness, remember? I'll probably have to testify in court.'

'Well, we'll cross that bridge when we come to it. Right now, I've got a dinner party to organise and a hero to track down. Where do you suggest I start?'

'I don't know… Why not try the Sun headquarters? They might know.'

'Doubt it. This isn't an interview,' Laura replied, pointing at the paper, 'just a crime reporter on the scene.' She paused for a moment, then her face lit up. 'I know, I'll ask Stella,' she said.

℡л

Stella and Hugh were shagging on the sofa when the phone rang, Stella straddling Hugh as he encouraged her to impale herself with more vigour onto his erect cock. He was smiling; she was grunting. *She never looked prettier*, he thought to himself. Stella stopped gyrating and picked up the phone instinctively. Hugh scowled at her.

'Halloo?' she said.

'Hi Stella, it's Laura. Am I interrupting anything?'

Stella looked down at Hugh's naked muscular chest, followed the contours down his hairy belly to his groin where she could just see the root of his glistening cock surrounded in dense curly black pubic hair mixed with blonde.

'Yes, you are,' she said, 'but go on.'

Hugh's scowl deepened.

Laura paused uncertainly. 'Have you heard the news about Mark?' she asked.

'Yes, I was there when it all happened,' Stella replied. 'In fact, it was due to me that he nearly died!'

'What? Is he ok?'

'Yes, he's fine now, I guess. I haven't heard from him, but the police said he was going to be fine.'

'Is he going to be ok for my party this Saturday, do you think?' Laura asked. 'I'm sorry to be blunt, but I need to know numbers.'

'I'm sure he will be... Ouchooooh!'

'Sorry, what?'

'Ow! Look... I've gotta go. Catch you later... Oooohhh'

She dropped the phone and gave Hugh her full attention.

ഇരു

'So, what did your mum and dad say?' Steve asked, as he drove along the Marylebone Road towards the City of London where they were going shopping for leathers.

'I'm going to go and see them on Saturday and explain it to them properly, but I think they got the gist,' Mark replied, gazing out of the passenger window of Steve's Rover Coupé at the London Planetarium attached to Madame Tussauds.

'Want me to drive you up there?' Steve offered, indicating right and moving into the fast lane. Suddenly, he shouted, 'Out the fucking way, you dithering old git!' as he overtook an elderly gentleman driving an ancient Volvo Estate.

'You'll be a dithering old git too, one day,' Mark told him, as they swung back into the middle lane. 'If you make it that far, that is.'

'Never!' Steve replied. 'I'd rather go out in a hail of bullets than turn out like that. Anyway, you didn't reply to my offer.'

'Won't you be working?'

'No, I don't think so, not this weekend. I haven't been reassigned yet, so technically I'm still working on this murder case. We're just getting all the paperwork sorted and next week there'll be reports to write. Then, of course, there's the court case, which will be months getting organised. So, getting any time off shouldn't be a problem... But only if you want me to.'

Mark watched as Steve put his foot down and just scraped between two converging articulated lorries. The thought of Steve driving him up the busy M40 motorway needed some getting used to.

'Can I think about it?' he asked.

'Sure. I'll book the time off anyway.'

They passed Kings Cross station and about ten minutes later Steve turned off into a side street near Old Street tube station, turned twice more and stopped the car near a junction. He placed an emergency parking permit in the window with a grin and got out.

'Another perk of the job?' Mark observed as he followed Steve from the side street towards the junction.

Steve just winked.

They turned left on to a very busy one-way street. The buildings were very tall and mostly business premises. They came to some stone steps painted grey, at the top of which Steve pressed a buzzer to a grey door. Another buzzer sounded and they entered the building.

It was dark at first and the smell of leather hit Mark the moment he entered. Steve led him down a metal staircase that resounded to the thumping of their boots. At the bottom, it opened up into a subterranean sea of leather and chrome and pulsing hi-energy music. In the centre, a round cash desk was the focal point and a tall, goateed man in blue jeans and a black tee shirt with the word *Expectations* emblazoned across the front in grey and silver stood in greeting with a wide grin on his face.

'Steve,' he yelled above the sound of St. Etienne's, *He's on the Phone*.

Steve led Mark over and shook the guy's hand. 'Nate, I'd like you to meet my partner, Mark.'

Steve extended his hand, 'Partner *in* crime or *against* crime?' he asked, grinning widely.

'Oh, this one's definitely *in* crime,' Steve replied.

Mark shook Nate's hand. 'Pleased to meet you,' he said.

'Likewise, I'm sure,' Nate replied. 'So,' he continued, 'what are you after today?'

'Come to kit Mark out in full leathers,' Steve told him with a grin. 'You got anyone who can do any alterations if needed?

'Sure, no problem. Susie's out back. Don't think she's too busy at the moment - I'll let her know.' Turning to Mark he said, 'You just take your time and don't let Steve rush you. Oh, and the fitting room's through there and at the end of the corridor. Steve knows where.'

Nate left them to serve another customer who was buying camouflage trousers and a large tub of Elbow Grease. Mark noticed the warning: *Not to be used with condoms.*

Steve let Mark have a good look around first. Mark was like a child in a sweet shop, pointing out things and oohing and aahing appropriately. Steve was pleased to show off his experience in such matters, although he had to admit that even he didn't know what some of the small leather and metal-studded items were really for.

Mark tried on his first pair of chaps and stood in front of a mirror. He thought he looked ok in them. Steve couldn't keep his eyes off Mark's exposed crotch, and when Nate came over to take a peek, all he said was, 'Fab.'

He tried on a leather waistcoat next, but without the chaps. Steve didn't want to see Mark fully decked out in leather until later, so Mark had to try each item on separately. A peaked cap, armbands, a harness, and a studded leather codpiece soon followed. For each item that Mark tried on, Steve would walk around him smiling and nodding, occasionally grabbing him and kissing him and rubbing his crotch up against him like a randy pup. Lastly, they picked up some interesting-looking metal cockrings.

Nate happily removed the security tags and price labels.

'Better have some more lube and condoms,' Steve said, bending down and selecting some condoms and compatible lube from the shelves on show below the counter.

'I'll throw those in for free,' Nate announced. Steve thanked him and handed over his credit card. Mark looked away, embarrassed. He felt like a gold digger being treated by his sugardaddy. Nate swiped the card, Steve added his signature and moments later they were walking back up the metal staircase, laden with black shiny plastic bags bearing the company logo - an image of a butch-looking muscular skinhead in boots and chaps. Steve stopped to pick up some freebie magazines as they left.

Once outside, Steve put an arm around Mark as they walked towards the car.

'I can't wait to get you home,' he whispered, his hot breath and goatee tickling Mark's ear. Mark's cock began to stiffen. 'But first,' he continued, 'let's have some lunch. It's gone twelve already! I know a small pub not too far from here that does great food.'

Now, where had Mark heard that before?

಼ಞ

Hugh showered and dressed after shagging Stella and then left Netherhall. Stella wanted him to meet her mother but he had to be lecturing at the Holloway Detention Centre in Islington at 2 o'clock, and he was starving. Besides, he was looking forward to a ploughman's in the Edward and a chat with Marilyn. He needed to talk to someone about his feelings for Mark and he certainly couldn't talk to Stella or her mother!

Hearing about recent events had caused certain feelings to overwhelm him. Feelings that were suspiciously like paternal ones mixed with intense desire and lust. He wanted to protect Mark as well as totally defile him; keep him from harm and yet sodomise him until he cried out in pain. It was this dichotomy of emotion that was so confusing to him and he needed to talk about it.

Imagine his surprise when he walked into the Edward and Marilyn pulled him quickly aside and pointed to the far corner. Mark was hunched over *their* table with *him*! That bloody policeman again. He felt his hackles rise.

Calmly, he said to Marilyn. 'I'll have a pint of my usual, if I may.'

Marilyn eyed him uncertainly. 'You don't fool me, you know,' she said, in that husky voice of hers. 'And, I don't want no trouble. It was you who walked out on him last time you were in here together. Am I right?'

Keeping an eye on Mark, Hugh nodded. 'There'll be no trouble,' he assured her. 'That other guy's a cop.'

Marilyn's eyes bulged visibly. 'Oh shit,' she burst out. 'He's been in here quite a few times. And, right now,' she added, lowering her voice, 'one of our lads is out in the back smoking a fucking joint!'

'Shouldn't worry about it, love,' Hugh replied, turning his back on the pair. 'Knowing Mark, either that cop smokes dope or he's got a massive cock, or both.'

Marilyn swiped at him with the back of her hand. 'You bitch,' she said. 'He looks like such a nice boy.'

Hugh immediately regretted his words. 'I'm sorry. I didn't mean it. I guess, I'm just…Well, you know.'

'In love?' Marilyn suggested, finally placing Hugh's pint in front of him. 'You having anything to eat?'

'Have one for yourself, darling,' he said handing over a £10 note, adding, 'Nah, I'm not hungry anymore.'

'Could do you a nice ham sandwich?' said Marilyn temptingly.

Hugh shook his head and then changed his mind. 'Oh, go on then, but no mustard, thanks - can't bear the stuff.'

Marilyn gave him a little smile and set about making Hugh his sandwich. Just then, Mark rose and walked over to the bar. His eyes suddenly met Hugh's and they widened in surprise. Hugh just stood and looked at him from his side of the bar. Mark immediately walked around to join him.

'Hi,' Mark said. 'You want to join us?' He indicated over his shoulder to where Steve was sitting. Hugh looked and saw Steve scowling back.

'Nah, don't think so. Your boyfriend looks like he's just swallowed a bee.'

Mark glanced in Steve's direction. The scowl deepened. 'He probably thinks we're talking about him.'

'He is your boyfriend, then?'

'Seems like it, yes.'

Marilyn returned with the ham sandwich and some change. 'I've taken for a small diet coke,' she said and then raised her small glass and mouthed, 'Cheers, love.' Hugh gave her a wink.

Hugh took a sip of his beer and leant on the bar. 'You slept with him yet?' he asked. He saw Marilyn frown as she moved out of earshot.

'That's none of your business,' Mark replied.

'So you have, then,' said Hugh, nodding gravely.

'I've moved in with him; what do you think?'

Hugh took this last piece of news like a kick to the stomach. He felt winded, unable to speak. He stood upright, hands on the bar. 'W… When did this happen?' he managed to say.

'A few days ago.'

'Is it what you want?'

'Yes, it is,' Mark replied immediately. 'For now.'

'For now? So, you're not sure long-term?'

Just then, Steve appeared beside them. 'Thought you were getting us more drinks!' he said to Mark. He didn't acknowledge Hugh at all.

'Um, right... Marilyn?'

'Don't bother,' said Steve. 'It's time we left. I'll be outside in the car.'

Marilyn came trotting over as Steve pushed roughly through the double doors. They banged shut loudly after him. It made Marilyn jump. 'Ooh,' she said, 'what's upset him?' Then she realised. 'Oops,' she said, by way of apology. She put on a smile. 'What can I get you, love?' she asked Mark.

'Er, nothing now, thanks.' Turning to Hugh, he said, 'I'd better go. See you around, eh?'

Hugh grabbed him by the shoulders. 'I meant what I said in the police station the other day. I'd give it all up for you, you know.'

Mark looked away towards the door. 'I have to go Hugh. I'm sorry. Look, I'll see you around, ok?'

He shrugged out of Hugh's embrace and headed for the door.

'Don't forget Laura's dinner party,' Hugh shouted after him.

Mark froze and slowly turned around. 'I'd completely forgotten about that,' he admitted. 'I'll call her later.'

Hugh moved towards him. 'You are still going?'

'I... I don't know. I was going to see my parents,'

'Well, you'd better not let Laura down,' said Hugh emphatically. 'After all, it's in your honour! You're a hero, remember?'

There was a loud tooting of a horn and the revving of a powerful engine from just outside. Mark made a snap decision. 'I'll see you there,' he said and swiftly opened the doors and disappeared.

Hugh turned back to Marilyn with a smile on his face. 'Now, those sandwiches look divine,' he said, picking one up. 'Won't you join me? There's something I need to talk to you about.'

Marilyn smiled back, faintly. 'If it's about him, then take my advice: Let him go. A pretty young man like that will cause you nothing but heartache. He's got a life to live. Think what you were like at his age.'

Hugh was married with a kid before he was 20 years old and didn't need reminding. 'I think I'll go and eat my sandwiches elsewhere,' he said. He grabbed his pint and sandwiches and moved over to an empty table near the door. Marilyn watched him go, shaking her head sadly.

₧₧₧

Steve drove faster than usual. He was furious. He couldn't understand why, but for some reason he didn't want that man near Mark again. Ever. Call it jealousy, if you like, although he couldn't remember feeling jealousy quite like this. Whatever it was, it was an all-consuming rage and he didn't trust himself to speak in case he took it out on Mark.

Mark was sitting staring straight ahead, trying not to flinch as Steve hurled the car around corners, across on-coming traffic and between converging vehicles that were far larger than the coupé. He guessed that Steve was angry with him for having spoken too long with Hugh at the bar, but wasn't sure if he should apologise and risk forever being unable to talk to friends, or ignore it and hope that Steve accepted it for what it was. Mind you, Hugh had been coming on strong. It was a good thing that Steve was unaware of this or there might have been fur flying.

'Um, I need to get some Silk Cut and some Rizlas,' Mark said. 'Can we stop somewhere?'

Steve immediately slowed down. 'There's a tobacconist I know just off Baker Street. I want to get a couple of cigars for tonight, anyway, if you get my drift.'

He turned towards Mark and smiled, showing off his even white teeth. His goatee was thick and shiny and he had a day's stubble on his strong jaw. Mark felt a shiver in his loins and his balls tightened involuntarily. He thought of the leather gear in the boot and how he would look and feel fully dressed.

'Can't wait,' he said sincerely.

'You like the scenes so far?'

Mark nodded. 'You bet.'

'Wait 'til tonight. This one's going to blow your mind.'

Steve indicated and turned the car up a small side street. Mark followed him into the tobacconist shop. It was small, smelled strongly of rich tobacco and contained a small walk-in area that was air-conditioned and displayed a wide variety of expensive hand-rolled cigars from around the world. The man who greeted Steve was an upright, silver-haired army captain type with a yellowing grey moustache and round glinting eyes. 'Can I help you gentlemen?' he said, almost standing to attention.

'Just a couple of your Corona Maduros, if we may,' Steve said. 'Oh, and some Silk Cut Ultra and some Rizlas.'

'Certainly,' said the ex-army captain. He walked through into the air-conditioned section and selected two from a tray half-filled with black weighty-looking cigars. 'Would you like them clipped?' he asked, returning to his counter.

Steve shook his head. The ex-army captain put them into a slim cardboard folder and rang up the sale on his cash till.

Mark was shocked at the cost and his eyes widened. As they walked back to the car he said, 'That's money up in smoke, if you forgive the pun.'

'I know, but what can a poor, sex-starved boy do?'

'Well, since you're none of those, who knows?'

Steve laughed. 'Well, we've got leathers, cigars, stuff to roll a few joints, lube and condoms. Do we need anything else to make a perfect evening of it?'

'Nice bottle of dry white wine and some pasta?'

'Got that already.'

'Then what are we waiting for?'

'It's only just gone one o'clock in the afternoon!' Steve protested. 'Still, we could start with a massage or something. Let's do it!'

He jumped into the car, clicked home his seatbelt and within moments they were back dodging the traffic.

'Oh, by the way,' said Mark. 'I forgot. I've been invited to a dinner party at a friend's house on Saturday evening. I've got to ring her this afternoon to confirm. Do you want to come?'

'I thought you were going to see your parents?' Steve protested, slipping the car into third gear and roaring past another slower driver.

'I know. I was. I've just remembered it. What's tomorrow? Thursday?'

Steve nodded.

'If I go home tomorrow, I'll be back mid afternoon on Saturday.'

Steve considered this. 'Who else will be at this dinner?'

'Hugh'll be there, I believe,' Mark replied carefully.

'Who, that fucker in the pub just now?' Steve demanded with a scowl.

'The very one,' Mark replied. 'Look, if you'd rather not...?'

'I'd love to,' Steve replied quickly.

'That's settled then.'

He'd have to break it to Laura gently.

∾◌◞

Laura, sitting next to Stella on the sofa, was listening intently to Stella's account of recent events.

'So, he nearly died because of me,' Stella finished, dabbing at a tear in the corner of her eye with a tissue.

Laura put her arm around her. 'But, he didn't. And anyway, you thought you were protecting him from those men. You weren't to know they were policemen.'

'One of them shouted at me as if I *had* just killed him! He was so rude! It was horrible!'

Stella blew her nose noisily as the telephone rang.

Laura extracted her arm from around Stella and pushed herself upright, grabbing the telephone on its fourth ring.

'Laura's residence. Who's calling?' Stella watched as Laura's face lit up. 'Oh, we were just talking about you!' She put her hand over the mouthpiece and whispered, 'It's Mark.' She removed her hand. 'Have you recovered from your ordeal...? How awful! You must tell us all about it on Saturday. You are still coming right?' She held up a hand to Stella with fingers crossed, her smile giving way to a wide grin as she gave the thumbs up sign. 'Um... er... Yes, of course. Male or female? Really, oh... Well, I can't wait to meet him... Whichever... Red or white, doesn't matter... Oh, around seven for seven-thirty... Great. See you then. Take care.' Laura replaced the

211

receiver and returned her bulk to the sofa. 'He's coming, thank god, but he's bringing a friend with him.'

Stella raised an eyebrow. 'That was quick work. Did he say who?'

'No, I didn't ask… Oh, bugger! I've invited Glen just so he can meet up with Mark again. Oh, well, I'm not going to cancel him, he's too cute.'

'Is it someone he met recently, do you think? Or someone he's known for a while?'

'Stella,' said Laura, gritting her teeth, 'I don't bloody know! I didn't bloody ask, ok?'

'Keep your hair on! I was only wondering.'

Laura snorted. 'Now that's one more I've got to fit around that bloody table,' she pointed to the old farmhouse table in the corner. 'What do you think; could I fit eight around it reasonably comfortably?'

'Yeah, it'll be a bit of a squeeze, but no problem,' she said. 'What about chairs and crockery?'

'No problem,' Laura replied, still looking troubled.

'So, what *is* the problem?' Stella asked, puzzled.

'There'll be *ten* of us,' Laura said sighing. 'I think it'll have to be a buffet.'

☙❦❧

Mark put down the phone in Steve's lounge and accepted a glass of chilled white wine, even though it was only just after four o'clock in the afternoon. He was on holiday, so what the hell? Steve sank into the armchair opposite him and raised his glass. He was smiling like a Cheshire cat and was obviously looking forward to the next few hours. As, of course, was Mark.

Mark's initiation into gay sex had so far been a baptism of fire. Tonight, by the look on Steve's face and the odd dropped hint, Mark was going into the inferno. And he couldn't wait.

They started earlier with a shower and a douche, followed by a sensual massage. Steve proved himself to be a master of muscle manipulation and Mark was luxuriating in the after-glow effect. His hands and feet were radiating warmth from the flow of overstimulated blood. He needed the cool glass of wine to keep him from boiling over.

Both were wearing white towels around their waists, nothing else, as they sat and surveyed each other. Steve's cropped drying hair was sticking straight up. Mark resisted the urge to flatten it with the palm of his hand. His hairy legs stuck out from below the towel and the soft mound of his cock was clearly outlined. The strains of Moodfood by Moodswings, or maybe it was Moodswings by Moodfood, could be heard filling the air with its beautiful harmonies. They were both entirely relaxed.

'So,' said Mark eventually. 'What's next?'

Steve grinned mercilessly. 'All in good time,' he said. 'Enjoy your wine.'

Mark glanced at his glass. 'It's excellent,' he demurred. 'A joint would go well with it, don't you think?'

Steve pulled a face. 'Nah,' he said. 'We're relaxed enough. We'll finish our drinks and then we'll get started, before we fall asleep.'

Mark took another sip. Whatever it was they were to start on, he was ready. He took another sip and then another. Steve watched him and grinned. 'Can't wait, eh?'

Mark looked straight at him. 'Nope.'

Steve gulped his drink down and stood up. 'Ok,' he said. Mark stood and faced him. 'I want you to do exactly as I say, is that clear?' Mark nodded and felt his legs weaken. 'You are to go down to the cellar and light all the candles. Once you have done that, you are to put on every item of leather that I've laid out for you. Take your time; watch yourself in the mirror as you put it on. Understood?' Mark nodded. 'The cigars and an ashtray are next to the sling. The ends have been clipped. I want you to light one up and wait for me to appear. After that you may do as you wish. Ok?' Mark was a little puzzled, but he nodded his head. Steve continued, 'As soon as I smell that horny Honduran aroma, I shall join you. Now, go!'

Mark was soon entering the exciting dark underground world that had so recently captured his sexual imagination. By the light of the single forty-watt bulb hanging on a flex from the ceiling at the far end of the chamber, he crossed the cold well-swept concrete floor and picked up the lighter next to the ashtray. The sight of the two dark Corona Maduros lying side by side, together with the array of leather set out in the shape of a human torso lying on the bench, caused his heart to race with anticipation. He lit every candle that he could find, giving a gothic cheer to the gloom, then stood in front of one of the large wall mirrors and began to dress himself.

He stripped off the towel and started with a metal cockring, the codpiece and a pair of thick grey socks. The chaps posed the first problem, but Steve had adjusted them in the shop to fit perfectly: all he had to remember to do was unzip the legs first. He eventually managed to fasten the chaps and then eyed himself in the mirror. Next he struggled with the harness, which caused him the most difficulty, followed by the armbands, waistcoat and cap. Lastly, he pulled on a pair of Steve's shiny black leather service boots, which fit him perfectly.

He stood and looked at himself in the full-length mirror and had to admit that he looked pretty hot. The armbands and cap gave him an air of authority, so he pulled himself up to his full height and imagined giving the orders instead of receiving them. The thought made his engorged cock jump.

Finally ready, he strode over to the ashtray and picked up one of the cigars, inserted the clipped end into his mouth and sucked life into it. When it was properly lit, he drew hard, inhaling and then exhaling the rich white smoke towards the bottom of the cellar steps. He stood beside the sling and waited.

Moments later, a booted foot appeared on the top steps and started to descend. Mark drew on his cigar again and watched as Steve's lower torso appeared, swathed in leather chaps. His upper torso followed and it was naked. Strapped around his neck was a black leather dog's collar, studded with centimetre-long metal spikes. Dangling from his left wrist Mark caught the gleam of metal and as Steve reached the bottom of the stairs and came closer, Mark saw that it was the heavy duty handcuffs that Steve had used on him.

Mark stood still as Steve approached, the cigar smouldering between clenched teeth. Steve stopped about a metre in front of him and turned around. He then put his arms behind him and offered Mark both wrists. Mark clasped the cuffs and deftly locked the open end onto Steve's right wrist. He had no idea where the keys were.

Mark waited. Steve remained motionless. Mark's cock suddenly jumped as he realised what he must do. He turned Steve around and, taking a deep draw on the cigar, he forced Steve to his knees. In the flickering candlelight, Steve's blond goatee looked thicker and darker as it framed his open mouth. Mark blew cigar smoke directly into it as Steve moaned with pleasure. Then, grasping the back of Steve's head, Mark forced his begging mouth hard into his own groin.

Removing the cigar, he bent down towards Steve's open mouth. 'You wanna be fucked, boy?' he hissed.

'Yes, please, Sir!' Steve shouted, military style.

'Boy,' said Mark, 'are we gonna have some fun.'

Steve grinned to himself in the darkness.

ଚ୨ଓ

Hugh had only been home a few minutes when the telephone rang. He'd had an easy lecture with the young offenders; more of a discussion really with a few case studies thrown in, and he'd arrived home in good humour. Meeting Mark at lunchtime had raised his hopes a little. All Mark needed to do was tire of that policeman, which Hugh was sure wouldn't take too long, and then he'd come running.

'Hello?' he said into the receiver.

'Hugh?' came a questioning voice, straight from the Highlands.

'That's me,' he replied, his heart suddenly racing.

'Morag Roberts - Stella's mother.'

'Och, well, hello. This is a surprise. What can I do for you?'

'I think we should meet before Saturday, don't you? We won't get much time to ourselves then, I shouldn't expect. So, are you available later this evening?'

Hugh tried to think of an excuse. From Stella's various descriptions of her mother over the years, she probably wasn't safe to be alone with.

'Well?'

'Yes, I'd like that,' he found himself saying. 'Where and when?'

'I'm staying at the Post House in Hampstead. We could have dinner in their restaurant, say around 7.00pm? I don't like to eat late – indigestion - I'm sure you know how it is.'

The old bitch, thought Hugh. 'Och, I'll be there,' he replied. Indigestion indeed! He wasn't quite that old.

છુભ્

At 6.45 pm, Hugh emerged from Belsize Park tube station, the closest tube station to the Post House Hotel. It was one of the oldest and deepest tube stations in London and he had been crammed into one of the lifts and brought jerkily to the surface with about twenty other poor sods. He was thankful not to have to do that every day.

He crossed over the road and approached the hotel, an impressive, yet unobtrusive, red brick building with a wide sweeping entrance for picking up and dropping off guests and a wide glass-fronted foyer with revolving doors.

Hugh was dressed casually, but smartly, in beige chinos, yellow polo shirt and a dark navy blazer with black shoes, yet he felt slightly uneasy as he asked directions to the restaurant at the front desk. A camp young man in a maroon and gold two-piece almost drooled over him in his eagerness to escort him the twenty or so metres to the entrance of the restaurant. The young man left him with a pout in the capable hands of the Maitre D', who was a much more severe personage and, whether he was gay or not, would never let his façade down or even attempt a smile.

Hugh was shown to a window table booked in Mrs Roberts's name and was relieved to see that the table was currently unoccupied. He ordered a mineral water and sat gazing out at the varied passers-by on Haverstock Hill. The sun was still shining and people were dressed for a glorious early summer's evening. It was his favourite time of the year, apart from New Year's Eve, of course. Despite a racing heart at the thought of meeting *The Old Bag*, as Stella had so often described her mother, he was full of the joys of spring,

A movement in the corner of his eye shifted his attention from outside the window to the inside. A smartly dressed woman in her late fifties, make-up expertly applied, was approaching his table on the arm of the Maitre D', who looked as if he was about to die of insufferable effrontery.

'Thank you, young man,' said the woman in a broad Scottish

accent as she pressed a ten pence piece into his hand as tip. The eyes of the Maitre D' bulged but he said nothing, not even a *thank you*, as he turned smartly on his heels and left the room.

Hugh was finally alone in an empty restaurant with *The Old Bag*. He stood in greeting and helped her to her seat, pushing it gently in as she sat down. She smiled at him as he returned to his seat opposite her.

'I'm pleased we finally get to meet,' The Old Bag started, only to be interrupted by the arrival of menus and a wine list. 'Just water for me,' she said to the young waitress at her side. Hugh's hopes of getting to drink an expensive bottle of wine were dashed right then and he didn't even dare take a second glance at the waitress, ugly or not, for fear of giving The Old Bag ammunition against his fidelity. If only she knew! 'As I was saying,' she continued, 'I'm glad to meet you at last. I've heard a lot about you, and not just from Stella.'

'Likewise,' said Hugh.

'Yes, I've heard a great deal,' The Old Bag went on, unfolding her napkin carefully. Hugh noticed how tough and roughened her hands were, as if they had been immersed in hot water for too long, the knuckles pinkish with the onset of premature arthritis, though she wasn't all that old. 'I can't say I approve of it all, but I can see what Stella sees in you. At least on the surface.' She lowered her eyes to the menu, almost demurely.

Hugh took the compliment at its face value.

'However,' she began again, 'let us not talk about such things for now. Let us enjoy our meal. Have you seen anything you fancy?'

No, thought Hugh, *thank God.*

Chapter Thirteen

Mark awoke to the sound of Steve singing in the shower. He snuggled down and drew the comfort of the duvet around his neck. Today was Thursday and his second to last official day off from work. On Monday he would return to the demanding financial world that had previously held so much fascination for him; now that his eyes had been opened to the everyday world that went on around him, it seemed to have lost some of its appeal. Could he just return to that world as if nothing had happened this past fortnight? Could he really? Could he juggle the mundane with the profane? People did.

The shower and the singing stopped and then he heard Steve towelling himself dry. He walked back into the room naked with his hair all tousled and smiled at Mark.

'You're awake then,' he said, sitting on the edge of the bed and pulling the duvet down, exposing Mark's smooth chest. He tweaked a nipple and laughed as Mark made a grab at him. They wrestled playfully for a few minutes before Steve pulled away.

'Come on,' he said, 'you've got to get a move on if you want to catch that train.'

'Are you going to miss me?' Mark asked.

'What do you think?' Steve replied, pouncing on him, forcing his arms back against the mattress and kissing him gently on the mouth. 'Just make sure you're back in time on Saturday for some *adult entertainment* before we go to this dinner party. Alright?'

'You bet,' Mark whispered into Steve's open mouth.

୨୦୦ଷ

The train from Paddington to Oxford was more or less uneventful. Now that Mark's eyes had been opened to the world around him, he

218

began to notice the occasional glance he received from other people, both female and male. He'd never really noticed this before. In his carriage, a group of four young men in army uniform were playing cards and drinking beer, even at that time in the morning. They would get up separately, go into the corridor to smoke a cigarette, and then return to the game. Nobody dared challenge them, despite the *no smoking* signs.

One of them, a squat flat-top with Mediterranean colouring and hairy muscular arms stared at Mark the whole time he was smoking his cigarette. Mark found it embarrassing at first, but soon found it flattering and faintly arousing. The guy smoked five cigarettes in just under an hour.

Eventually, the train pulled into Oxford station and Mark joined the hordes as they descended onto the platform. He gave the army guy a last lingering stare, just to be a tease, and was rewarded with a cursory nod. Once on the platform, he joined the rush as they moved through the tunnel under the track and out the other end. As soon as he exited through the main doors, he heard the screams and howls and barks of his dog coming from the back seat of his mother's old Rover car. He ran to the car, threw his bag in the boot and jumped in beside her. The dog went berserk.

Chapter Fourteen

IT WAS EARLY FRIDAY EVENING and Steve was relaxing at home, drinking a glass of full-bodied Merlot and listening to the wondrous voice of Tina Arena.

He was missing Mark, he realised, much more than he would have believed possible. Mark phoned yesterday evening and again earlier that evening and his voice remained clear in his memory as he savoured the conversations. Mark's coming out to his parents seemed to have gone reasonably well at home. He was seeing the rest of his extended family later that evening, which Mark wasn't really looking forward to. His Mum and Dad, apparently, were looking forward to meeting Steve, especially having already spoken to him on the phone earlier in the week. They seemed to think that because Steve was a policeman, Mark couldn't be getting involved in any sordid mischief. They'd both had a laugh about that.

His musings were suddenly interrupted as the doorbell rang. Wondering who on earth it could be at eight o'clock on a Friday evening, he hurried to the door, peeped through the spy-hole and very nearly refused to open it.

'You'd better come in,' he said, turning on his heel and leaving his visitor to close the door after him. Steve walked back into the lounge and sat back down on the sofa.

'I've come to give you something that belongs to you,' the tall, dark-haired man said, his muscles rippling through his white tee shirt. He stood before Steve and took something out of his pocket, which he tossed at Steve. Steve caught it and held it up to the light. It was a sealed clear plastic bottle, of the type usually used for contact lenses or the like. He peered inside.

'What is it?'

'Not it! Them!' his visitor sneered.

'Oh, I see…'

'They're pubic lice, Steve - as if you didn't know.'

'Big deal,' said Steve, taking a sip of red wine. 'I hear you got a shag last Friday night anyway. Some Scottish chap called Hugh. Right?' He tossed the plastic bottle back. 'Better tell him about these little buggers before he passes them on to that girlfriend of his.'

Glen was taken aback. 'What? H… How do you know about him?'

'He was arrested, Glen. I read his file,' Steve explained patiently. 'Now, if you don't mind, I'd like you to leave.'

Glen knew there was an important point here that he was missing, but he gave up, tossed the crabs back at Steve and told him to shove them up his arse where, he said, they probably came from in the first place, and stormed out, slamming the front door behind him.

Steve picked up the small plastic bottle and peered at the pubic lice. They were quite dead, of course, but his eyes and imagination were playing tricks on him and he thought he could see them moving. He thought of the cute guy at the sauna who he suspected had passed them onto him just a few weeks ago, shortly before his break up with Glen. He obviously passed them onto Glen during their last wild sex romp. C'est la vie.

He rose and walked through to the kitchen, threw the crabs in the bin, returned with the bottle of Merlot, refilled his glass and returned the bottle to the kitchen. On his way back, he stopped at the entrance to the cellar and thought long and hard about last night. Mm, this new man of his was definitely the one. Fearless, eager to try anything at least once, completely non-judgemental, open-minded, handsome, warm-hearted, versatile, intelligent, witty, you name it. He stuck his head into the cellar and sniffed. The aroma of stale cigar smoke and heaving bodies still lingered. He couldn't wait to have his man back; they had a whole weekend of endless possibilities to look forward to. He closed the cellar door with a wry smile and returned to his wine and music.

ഉറ

It was a short ride from Mayfair to Bayswater and, after leaving Steve's house, Glen got back into his old Ford Escort, lit a cigarette and set off to see if Mark was at home. The Friday evening traffic was heavy and it took him nearly half an hour to travel the two miles. He almost lost his nerve at one point. After all, what was he going to say to Mark? *Well done on catching those killers?* It seemed a poor excuse. He was going to be seeing him tomorrow at Laura's dinner party, anyway.

He was forced to park his car two blocks away due to the acute absence of any available parking spaces. This resulted in even more lost nerve but, having come so far, he was determined to follow it through.

He knocked on Mark's front door and a few moments later the same tall, slim, beautiful girl with blond hair and the palest blue eyes appeared. She was obviously preparing herself for an evening on the town. Glen stood before her in his white tee shirt and jeans and quite forgot his reason for being there.

She smiled and asked him what he wanted.

Glen found his voice. 'I've come to see Mark. Is he in?'

'Ah,' said the young lady, 'I'm afraid he's not. You see he's not staying here at the moment. Are you a friend of his?'

Glen was disappointed to hear this. 'Yes,' he replied, adding, 'Do you know where I can find him?'

'Afraid not. Do you read the newspapers?'

Glen nodded. 'Yes, that's why I'm here.'

'Well, I think he's still in a *safe* house, somewhere, if that's what they call it. You know, under police protection?'

'Oh, I see. Right. Well, thank you. I'm sorry to have troubled you.'

'No trouble at all,' the young lady said, smiling widely.

Glen retreated up the road. Vivienne watched him go. *Damn, these gay men are beautiful.* It just wasn't fair. She turned with a sigh and went back inside.

⊗⊘⊗

Steve was watching the Nine O'clock News when the doorbell rang again - this time more persistently. He peered through the spy-hole as usual and flung the door open.

'Want your crabs back or what?' he asked rudely.

'I want to know where Mark's hiding out,' Glen replied, breathing deeply.

'Mark who?' Steve asked, feigning ignorance.

'You know who I mean. The one whose address I asked you to get for me from the police computer, and the same one who was used as bait to catch those serial killers...'

Steve grabbed him and pulled him into the hallway, slamming the door afterwards. 'Do you mind?' he said angrily. 'That's police business you're shouting about on my doorstep!'

Glen quietened for a moment. 'Well? Where is he hiding?'

'How the hell should I know?'

'Because you're a policeman?' Glen suggested sarcastically.

Steve paused a moment. 'Why do you want to know?'

Glen didn't reply.

'Well?'

Glen looked away and then said quietly. 'I... I think I'm in love with him.'

'That's crazy!' Steve exploded. 'You hardly know him! Anyway, I don't know where he is. As far as I know, he's gone to visit his parents out of town somewhere.'

Glen looked deflated. 'Do you believe in love at first sight?'

'No. Now fuck off. I want an early night.' Steve pushed Glen towards the door. Glen resisted.

'I loved *you* at first sight, you know?'

'Yes, and look how that ended. Now, please, just get out.'

Glen allowed himself to be pushed towards the front door. Steve opened it for him and pushed him through it. 'See ya around, Glen,' he said as he closed the door with a resounding bang.

Steve returned to the lounge and his glass of wine. He turned the TV off – it was nothing but bad news anyway - and re-started the new Tina Arena album from the beginning, hoping for no more interruptions that evening.

Hugh was watching the new series of Frazier. It was, after all, his favourite programme in the cosmos and he'd missed it last week on account of being in a police cell at the time. This week, he was determined to watch it and had even set his video to record it just in case. The little red light was on and the digits ticking over nicely.

He was distracted. His groin was itching, which at first he thought was nothing unusual. He was susceptible to the occasional rash from residual detergent in his underwear and so, for now, he was trying to ignore it. But, when a particularly painful bout of itching occurred, he began to feel a little uneasy.

The doorbell rang and Hugh raised his eyes to the ceiling and mimed a curse to the Almighty. He rose and walked through to the hallway. Pausing, with his hand on the lock, he called, 'Who is it?'

'It's me, Glen.'

Hugh opened the door, beaming. 'Come back for some more?' he grinned, ushering Glen inside.

Glen wasn't smiling. 'I doubt if you'd *want* me back for more,' he answered gloomily. 'Not after what I've got to say.'

'Why, what's up?' Hugh led him through into the lounge, picked up the remote and switched Frazier on standby, noting that the video continued to record. 'Wanna drink? Glass of wine or some coffee?'

'I can't stay. I have something to tell you.'

Hugh pulled a face. 'Sounds ominous.'

Glen took a deep breath. 'I may have given you crabs. I only just found out myself,' he lied.

'Shit! So that's why I've been itching.' Hugh immediately thought of Stella, then Patrick. He sank down onto the sofa. 'Fuckinghell!' he said. 'What a fucking mess.' How was he going to tell Stella? As for Patrick, well he doubted he'd ever see him again.

Glen stood before him, awkwardly. 'Look, I'm sorry. I didn't know.'

Hugh felt a stab and had to scratch himself quickly. 'Jesus, the little fuckers are biting. You didn't bring anything with you, I suppose, to kill them?'

Glen shook his head.

'Then I'd better get down to an all-night chemist. Damn!' He pushed Glen out into the hallway, grabbed his wallet, keys and jacket and then pushed Glen out through the front door, closing it behind them.

'Look, I'm really sorry about this,' Glen told him as Hugh locked the door.

Hugh looked at him in the orange light from the sodium street lamps. 'If you weren't so damn hot, I'd slug you,' he hissed, grabbing hold of him by the scruff of his firm muscular neck and kissing him quickly, feeling the heat rise.

Glen smiled for the first time that evening.

A sudden itch caused Hugh to curse loudly as he pulled away. Now that he knew what the cause was, he could literally feel them crawling all over his hairy genitals and up the hairy crack of his arse, biting through the soft flesh and sucking greedily on his warm blood.

'Look, I'm out of action for tonight, but see you soon, eh?'

He hurried off in the direction of the all-night chemist next to the tube station.

'Sure thing,' Glen called after him.

He could have offered Hugh a lift, but it was probably quicker on foot. He returned to his car, lit a cigarette, started the engine and headed off to The Hoist, just south of the river. *He* wasn't out of action, and action, right now, was just what he needed.

Chapter Fifteen

SATURDAY MORNING, the day of Laura's dinner party, began grey and overcast, although still warm. It was one of those rare occasions when Laura was up early, much to Freud's delight since he got fed early and then could be outside catching the early bird for dessert. Laura was pottering about in her fluffy pink marshmallow outfit, occasionally cleaning, occasionally re-arranging furniture, but mainly sitting at her table eating toast, drinking coffee and making lists. In addition to eating and drinking, she also loved making lists. Spread out on the table in front of her was a shopping list, a guest list and a list of *Things To Do*.

The guest list was as yet incomplete. She hadn't seen or heard anything from the hunky Glen in over a week, but she hoped to see him today when she went shopping at Waitrose. Stella and her mother were definitely coming, but Stella's sister Iris had yet to confirm. Laura found it irritating that a grown woman couldn't decide if she was available or not to attend a dinner party less than twelve hours beforehand. She'd had two weeks to organise herself, after all! Faithful Hugh, of course, would do whatever Stella told him to do and so he'd be coming. Then there was thoughtful young Patrick, who had rung her yesterday just to check that everything was still on; Pot-head Pierre, who really didn't know which planet he was on and could show up at any time, or not at all, depending on what he was smoking at the time; and finally Mark, the people's hero together with his mysterious date, who nobody knew anything about.

'What an interesting group of people,' Laura mused aloud. 'I do hope they all get on.'

☙❧

The train back from Oxford took longer than expected - surprise, surprise - although it hadn't yet been derailed, for which Mark was truly thankful. He was sitting facing the direction of travel, alternating between listening to his old Walkman, reading a science fiction novel by Stephen Baxter, or just watching the fresh green countryside flash past the window. The grey morning in London had turned into a gloriously sunny afternoon throughout the whole of the South East region and it was quite warm outside the air-conditioned carriage.

Mark glanced at his watch and decided to call Steve yet again to let him know when the train was due in. His thoughts were running wild as to what Steve had planned for their *adult entertainment* that afternoon. Whatever it was, his imagination alone had sustained an erection on and off since the train had left the station at Oxford over an hour earlier. He was finding it impossible to concentrate on his book, his music or the view outside the window. He picked up his mobile phone flush with credit and keyed the speed dial for Steve who answered on the first ring.

'Lover,' Steve said, 'where are you now?'

Mark grinned at the sound of Steve's voice. 'Still on the train, about half an hour from Paddington, I guess.'

'I'll set off now...'

'No, I told you, there's no need. The traffic will be awful and it'll be quicker by tube...'

Steve was insistent. 'I'll use my blue light, no problem. I'll be waiting next to the taxi rank.'

'Ok, lover,' Mark agreed, liking the sound of the word.

'Hey, did you miss me last night?'

'What do you think?'

Steve laughed. 'My turn to fuck you this afternoon, loverboy. You'd better be ready for it... Hey, this meal tonight - it's not a sit-down affair is it?'

'I think so, why?'

'You're gonna wish it weren't by the time I've finished with you!'

'Ha, very funny. Now, get off the phone. You'd better start moving if you're going to meet me - I think the train's on the outskirts of London already.'

'Right. See you in a while.'

The line went dead.

Mark cut the connection and settled back in his seat, his mind on his erection.

෨෬

If Laura wasn't much of a shopper, she wasn't much of a cook either - as her guests were likely to find out later. She was, however, a very good party-thrower and was renowned for having some of the more memorable social gatherings. They were always attended by a mix of varied and interesting people, with plenty of food and drink and usually a reasonable selection of dance music and recreational drugs.

'My mother won't eat that,' Stella said, as Laura loaded her Waitrose trolley with tins of gazpacho soup.

Laura eyed her speculatively. 'Next you're going to tell me Iris is a vegetarian.'

Stella nodded. 'Didn't I tell you...?'

They both burst out laughing. Other shoppers gave them cursory glances but mainly ignored them.

'Stella,' Laura managed to say between giggles, 'you don't honestly think I'm giving my guests *tinned* soup, do you?'

Stella stopped her giggles and looked contrite. 'I'm sorry,' she said, 'I wasn't thinking. So, what are we having?'

'Wait and see,' was all Laura would say, wondering what the hell to give her guests as a starter now. She wished she hadn't brought Stella along with her, but she needed someone to help her carry the bags up the long steep climb to Netherhall.

Nearly an hour later, Stella and Laura were seeking the shortest checkout queue when a hand grabbed Laura's shoulder and she spun around to be confronted with the solid muscular upper torso of a male clothed in a dark blue uniform, white shirt and company tie. She shivered in delight.

'I should arrest you, ma'am,' said Glen seriously, 'but I can see you're busy planning a party.' He beamed at her and both Laura and Stella beamed back.

'Hiya Glen. How's it going?' Laura said, regaining her composure.

Glen was in a buoyant mood. He'd watched a really hot scene at The Hoist last night and was eager to see Mark tonight. 'Great. You?' he replied.

'Getting ready for this evening. You are still coming, I hope?'

'Wouldn't miss it for the world. What time?'

'Seven for seven-thirty?'

'That'll be great. Do I have to wear anything special?' Glen asked, suddenly serious again.

'Anything that makes you look even sexier than you already are,' Laura replied and immediately regretted it. She noticed Stella briefly raise her eyes heavenward.

Glen just laughed. 'I'll see what I can do. Well, I'd better get back to work, so I'll see you tonight.'

Like two lovesick teenagers, both Laura and Stella watched him walk away with a sexy swagger. He was well aware that they were watching him.

'Isn't he gorgeous?' Stella whispered.

'Too bloody right. I envy all those gay men out there with him on the loose. He may be a bit *too* loose, though,' she continued darkly.

Stella shot her a puzzled look. 'What do you mean?'

Laura bit her lip. 'Promise not to say anything to him?'

'Scout's honour.'

'I thought that was only for boys?'

'Is it? Oh, well, I promise, anyway. Come on, dish the dirt.'

'Well…' Laura conspiratorially lowered her voice. 'I saw him in the chemist's last Monday and… guess what he was buying?'

'I don't know… A gross of condoms?' shrugged Stella.

Laura shook her head. 'Shampoo for pubic crabs!'

'Och, nooo!' Stella cried, then hastily covered her mouth as other shoppers turned and stared. 'How revolting,' she continued in a whisper. 'Ooh, how disgusting. Imagine having parasites crawling all over your body, biting and sucking your blood and laying eggs in your pubes. Ooh, how horrible.' She shuddered uncontrollably. 'I've gone right off him now.'

Laura was laughing at Stella's outburst.

'Please don't make me sit next to him this evening,' she begged

Laura. 'I'd be fidgeting all the time… Can you catch them from sitting too close to someone who's got them?'

Laura laughed so much she thought she was going to have a seizure and had to lean on the shopping trolley to catch her breath.

'Don't let him use your loo, whatever you do, otherwise I'll have to go upstairs when I want a pee,' Stella said seriously.

'Well, what do you expect him to do?' gasped Laura. 'Pee out of the window?'

'No, but he can jolly well go outside for a pee.'

Laura stopped laughing. 'Oh, don't be so daft. Anyway, you can't catch them that way; you've got to have sexual intercourse.'

'How come you're such an expert on them all of a sudden?' Stella asked, pushing the trolley into the shortest checkout queue she could see. 'Have we got everything, by the way?'

Laura looked at her list and nodded. 'I think so… I'm not an expert, but I read it in a magazine somewhere. Anyway, he would have got rid of them by now.'

Stella shivered. 'I guess so. But all the same…'

⃝⁕⃞

Sunlight filtered in through chinks in the hurriedly drawn curtains, shedding its light across the two entwined sleeping forms. On the floor, a selection of rubber dildos of varying sizes glistened with a mixture of sweat, grease and cum. On the other side of the bed was an ashtray containing two used condoms.

Steve woke first. He reached out and pulled Mark's sleeping form closer to him so that he could feel Mark's breath on his cheek as he exhaled. It had been a full week since they had met in the park and Steve was totally in love for the first time in his life. It wasn't just the sex, although that was unbelievable. He'd never met anyone so uninhibited and so inexperienced and so innocent before, and who enjoyed doing everything that Steve enjoyed too – so far, at least.

His cock was hard again, but Steve thought better of it. Mark's arse must be so sore now, not just from the dildos, but from the rough way that he'd mounted him and fucked him twice for over an hour in total, taking him in all positions, making him beg for more, finally hearing him pleading for Steve to stop, almost crying with the pain. He didn't ever want to hurt him, but Mark brought out certain emotions in Steve that compelled him to be rough with him. Perhaps it was his innocence, his vulnerability, his youth? He didn't know. Maybe a combination of all three.

Mark stirred as Steve gently brushed his goatee against his furry chin. Mark stopped shaving nearly a week ago and the stubble had grown into a neat beard. Steve was hoping to shave it for him later and leave Mark with a goatee for work on Monday morning.

As soon as Mark realised that it was Steve nuzzling him, he grinned widely and opened his mouth to receive Steve's probing tongue. They kissed for a while, both fumbling between the sheets to hold the other's cock as they did so. As Mark's breathing became shorter and deeper, Steve pushed the bedclothes back, pushed Mark harder into the pillow with his mouth and wanked Mark's cock faster and faster until he grunted loudly and Steve felt the warm sticky cum pump out over his knuckles and onto Mark's flat stomach.

After a while, Steve reached for the box of tissues and wiped away the mess. 'How's your bum?' he asked.

'Sore. But you did warn me.'

'Sorry about that, but you bring out the animal in me.' Steve grabbed him by the chin and growled into his open mouth. His unspent cock was still hard and throbbing in Mark's clenched fist.

'You wanna come again?' Mark asked him.

Steve shook his head. 'Nah, it'll keep. Anyway,' he added, glancing at his alarm clock, 'we'd better start getting ready for this dinner party.' He rubbed the back of his knuckles along Mark's jaw. 'And I want to shave you - see what you look like with a goatee.'

Mark reluctantly let go of Steve's engorged cock and watched as Steve jumped up and headed for the bathroom, his cock swaying heavily in front of him as he did so. Mark slowly rolled out of bed and followed. His arse felt as if it had been through a mincer.

He just hoped it wouldn't make him walk like one.

Laura was enjoying a cup of tea and taking a few minutes off to relax between bouts of frantic food preparation, when she heard a knock on her inner door. She sighed, lifted her swollen ankles off of the sofa and padded through to the kitchen and opened the door. What she saw made her heart sink right down to the soles of her pink puffy feet.

Stella was wearing a light blue cotton dressing gown, her hair soaking wet and she was crying hard, close to hysteria. Laura wrapped her arms around her and helped her into the lounge where she sat down and started to cry even harder.

Laura couldn't understand a word Stella was saying - what on earth *krerbs* were was beyond her understanding - but Laura kept her arms wrapped around her friend and squeezed her soothingly all the same. Eventually she got the gist, if not the detail.

It was something to do with Hugh.

As usual.

Laura's sinking heart was more concerned with her party that evening than with Stella's plight and she wasn't about to let this upset it. After all, Stella was always breaking up and making up with Hugh. It was a key component of their relationship and it kept the fire stoked. She fetched a warm towel from the airing cupboard under the stairs and wrapped Stella's hair in it. Stella thanked her between sobs and finally regained sufficient control to accept a cup of tea which rattled in its saucer as she held it.

She put it down shakily, drew a deep shuddering breath and wailed, 'I don't know what to do! He's gone too far, this time!'

Laura looked at her clock, wondering if she had time for this, and asked warily, 'What's he done that's so bad this time?'

Stella shot her a nasty look, then softened. '*This time,*' she said, 'he's been unfaithful.'

Laura was shocked. 'How can you be so sure?'

'He's given me bloody krerbs!' She starting screaming hysterically again.

There was that peculiar word again. It still made absolutely no sense whatsoever. 'He's given you what?' Laura asked, screwing her face up.

'Bloody krerbs... What Glen had!!'

Laura's jaw dropped open and she tried to distance herself from Stella without being obvious. She stood up. 'Crabs?' she whispered.

'Yes, *krerbs*. What d'you think I bloody meant?'

Laura didn't answer. After a while, she asked, 'Do they itch?'

'I don't know. I've just killed them with some shampoo, which Hugh so thoughtfully brought round. Wasn't that considerate of him?!'

Laura lowered herself gingerly onto the sofa next to Stella and reached for her cup of tea. 'Did he say who the other woman was?'

Stella dismissed the notion with a wave of her hand. 'No,' she said dramatically.

'Did you ask him?'

'Of course, but he says it was just a one-nighter and didn't mean anything. Why do men always say that? Is it supposed to make us feel any better that they would risk a meaningful relationship on someone that means nothing? Are they fucking stupid or what?'

'No, they think we're fucking stupid enough to believe that bullshit,' Laura replied. 'But I guess they can't help it. As the saying goes, *When their cocks are hard, their minds are lard.*'

Stella managed a small smile and then burst into more sobs. 'He's just the limit,' she cried. 'He's so gorgeous; I know he gets the come on from women all the time. And not just the women. I've seen the way the men look at him too.'

Laura giggled. 'Hey, you don't think Glen gave him them, do you?' They both laughed for a good while.

'There's one thing I do know,' said Stella, more cheerfully, 'Hugh is not gay. Not even bi-sexual. He's a real man.'

Laura took a last sip of her tea. 'There's no such thing,' she said. 'It all depends on your definition. Anyway, do you want some more tea?'

Stella nodded. 'Ooh, yes please,' she said, feeling much, much better.

ΩΠΩ

Upstairs, in Stella's flat, Hugh was preparing himself for the worst. He was sitting in the lounge beneath the monstrous cheese-plant not knowing quite what to do next, but positive that he'd done the right thing in telling Stella about the lice. What he hadn't told her, of course, was who had given them to him and who else he'd probably passed them on to as well. They were two major hurdles in one, and he wasn't sure that he could ever face up to that. He thought it best that he should just end it right now with Stella, let nature take its course, and deal with whatever consequences arose all on his own. Contrary to his sexual inclinations, he was a passive guy and the thought of more hysteria made him want to curl up in a ball and roll into a dark place. His trouble, it seemed, was that the older he got, the more problems he caused and the less able he became at handling them. Perhaps he was entering his second childhood?

He jumped as the front door opened and Stella appeared in the lounge doorway, her hair dry and looking lovely, cascading around her face in blonde waves. She was smiling thinly at him.

'Where have you been?' he asked. 'I was worried.'

'Really?' she said, walking through to the kitchen. 'If you must know, I've been to see Laura.'

Hugh nodded. 'And I suppose you've told her everything?'

Stella turned on him angrily. 'No, I just went down there crying my eyes out, near to hysteria, and told her I'd broken a nail!'

'Well, there's no need to be sarcastic,' said Hugh quietly.

Stella looked fit to explode. 'What? There's a need to be whatever I fucking like!' She suddenly quietened down, shocked at her own vulgarity. 'I… I had to talk to someone, Hugh. You've really hurt me...' She stopped, put her hand to her mouth and burst into tears.

Hugh leapt up, ran over and put his arm around her. 'I'm sorry, hen,' he said, gently brushing her hair with his fingers. 'Honestly, I am. I promise it'll never happen again.' The words tumbled out of his mouth before he had even time to think.

Stella let him run his fingers through her hair a while longer before pulling away. She'd like to believe him, of course, but as the old Highland saying goes: *Once the wee beastie has tasted blood...*

She moved away from him and headed for the bathroom. It was getting late and her mother and Iris were due at six-thirty.

'People are on their way,' Laura told Freud, 'so you'd better clear off out or stay and help me entertain - it's up to you.' She was putting the finishing touches to the table on which she'd managed to squeeze place settings for ten people. *Cosier than a buffet,* she thought, nodding to herself.

She cast a last critical eye over her handiwork, at the cutlery which, she had to admit, didn't exactly match, but then it was comprised of a number of different original sets that she'd managed to lose pieces of along the way. Similarly, the glassware that adorned the table was of various different shapes and sizes, and even colours. It all looked very festive though, despite the season.

Laura went through to the kitchen and poured herself a dry white wine from the fridge. She'd set up a carton of Moselle, which tasted fine to her. She took a quick look in the oven where the roasted peppers, garlic and onions were cooking slowly in drizzled olive oil on the bottom shelf, whilst the tarragon chicken in garlic and white wine was just starting to bubble at the top. She added a handful of sunflower seeds to the herb salad, took another large gulp of wine, stirred the layered fruit salad vigorously before she realised her mistake, popped a few whole black seedless grapes on the top and covered it with a paper napkin, took another gulp of wine and then headed back to the lounge where Freud took one carefully considered look at her and decided that she was oiled sufficiently enough to entertain without his help. Besides, he hated being handled by strangers. He leapt onto the windowsill and, with his tail high in the air, slinked through the open window and disappeared off to his own party somewhere in the scrubs.

Laura cast a sly glance at the clock high up on the wall as she returned to the kitchen to re-fill her glass. It was nearly seven o'clock. She went back into the lounge and put on a CD of her favourite female singer – Dusty Springfield. As the strains of 'Wishin' and Hopin'' filled the air, she heard a knock on the inner door and felt the sudden rush of excitement, wondering which of her guests were first to arrive. She hoped it was the hunky Glen.

Mrs Rosenberg was standing in the hallway, surrounded in a mauve chiffon haze, clutching a piece of paper that she waved in front of Laura's nose.

'Thank you for the warning,' she said sarcastically. 'That's two parties in as many weeks. Now, I have a *warning* for you: If you don't keep the noise down, I'm calling the police. Is that clear?'

'Oh, bugger off and get a life, you interfering old cow,' Laura slurred, shooing her away and was about to slam the door when she noticed Stella descending the stairs followed by Iris and two others. She held the door open and hugged Stella, who squealed with delight, and then the vacillating Iris. Stella turned and introduced her indomitable mother and then finally the not-so-faithful Hugh, who gave a sheepish greeting and a quick peck on the cheek, as Stella had instructed.

'Come in, come in,' she beckoned to them, and once Hugh was inside she took great satisfaction in slamming the door in Mrs Rosenberg's face. She graciously accepted a few bottles of wine from her guests and a six-pack of beer from Hugh.

'Now, what would you all like to drink…? Mrs Roberts, what can I get you?'

'Oh, anything that's open,' she replied, casting a critical eye around the kitchen and noting the litter tray in one corner. 'You have a cat?' she asked. Stella and Iris stared at each other aghast, suddenly remembering their mother's old allergy to fur.

'Yes,' Laura said enthusiastically. 'His name's Freud, but he's out for the evening. Gone to a party of his own,' she added conspiratorially.

Mrs Roberts immediately opened her handbag and took out a small white handkerchief, using it to dab her nose and sniffing loudly as she did so.

Laura seemed not to notice as she poured white wine for the ladies and a glass of beer for Hugh and then led them through to the lounge.

'Please, take a seat,' she said, gesticulating widely.

Mrs Roberts took a seat next to the piano; Stella on the piano stool and Iris on the sofa below the open window.

'It's lovely to meet you at last, Mrs Roberts,' Laura said. 'I've heard so much about you.'

'Likewise,' said Mrs Roberts, nodding and smiling and sniffing, all at the same time.

There was an awkward silence.

'Dips, anyone?' Laura suddenly asked, jumping up and offering Stella a dish of sliced raw carrot and celery sticks. She raced through to the kitchen and reappeared with a chilled bowl of avocado dip. The top had turned brown, but she stirred it with a fork from the table and handed the bowl to Stella.

In the absence of a coffee table at this end of the room, Stella balanced the bowl of dip on her knees whilst Iris hungrily scooped it up with the largest piece of celery she could find. Stella joined her using a piece of carrot, whilst Hugh declined with a wave of his hand when Stella eventually offered him some. He had remained standing and was feigning interest in the books on Laura's bookshelf behind the dining table, sipping at his beer and wondering what the hell he was doing there.

Laura spied a movement outside the window and announced loudly, 'Ah, Patrick's here.' She disappeared into the kitchen and flung open the backdoor.

'Patrick,' she called, opening her arms wide. 'How lovely to see you. Come in, come in.'

Patrick kissed her and gave her a hug and handed her a bottle of red wine. 'I nicked this from my dad's cellar, just for you,' he said. 'I hope you like it.'

Laura read the label. 'How thoughtful of you - I'm sure it'll be lovely,' she said, putting it with the rest of the bottles next to the sink. 'Now, what would you like to drink?'

'Just mineral water, for now,' Patrick replied, adding, 'I'm driving.'

Laura nodded, poured him some sparkling water and then led him into the lounge where Stella was hurriedly scraping up avocado dip from the rug, her mother looking on disapprovingly with Iris ignoring it and Hugh trying to hide a grin.

As he looked up, Hugh's grin froze.

Laura led Patrick into the centre of the room. 'This is Patrick,' she announced. 'Patrick's my star pupil. He's been coming to me since he was nine years old, bless him.' She pinched his cheek with her chubby fingers at which Patrick grinned sheepishly. 'And now look at him,' she added proudly. 'A handsome young man who can bend a flute with the best of them. Now, you already know Stella,' she went on with a nod of her head in Stella's direction.

Stella sat back on her haunches and wiped her long blonde hair from her face. 'Hi,' she said 'I've seen you coming in and out.'

I could say the same, thought Hugh for one hysterical moment, fighting to regain control of himself.

'And this is Stella's mother, Mrs Roberts; this is her sister, Iris; and this is her boyfriend, Hugh.'

Patrick held out his hand and shook with Hugh, his eyes never leaving Hugh's face as he smiled and said, 'Pleased to meet you all.'

Hugh pulled his hand away and sat down heavily on the piano stool, a cloud of dust and cat hairs billowing out on all sides causing Mrs Roberts to cover her nose with her hanky.

Laura moved to the corner unit and turned down the sound of Dusty Springfield telling the world that she only wanted to be with them.

'Is your boyfriend, Gerald, or whatever his name is, not with you?' Stella asked Patrick.

Mrs Roberts's eyes bulged dangerously. 'Are you one of those brown owls?' she blurted out, in her broad Scottish accent.

Stella turned abruptly. 'Mother!' she cried indignantly. 'This is the 21st Century!'

Patrick just smiled, casting a furtive glance at Hugh. 'Er, we split up,' he replied.

'Oh, I'm sorry to hear that.'

'Don't worry, he's already found another,' Laura interjected cheerfully, taking Patrick by the arm. 'Funnily enough, a big strapping Scotsman called Jock, but they only met last weekend. You are still seeing him, I presume?'

'Er, um, yes, I certainly hope so,' Patrick replied, casting another furtive glance in Hugh's direction. Hugh was stroking his moustache nervously and staring at the floor. Any minute now the floor was going to open up and swallow him; at least that was what he was hoping.

Laura jumped up. 'I'm sure that was the front doorbell,' she said. 'Excuse me a moment.'

The room fell silent as Laura disappeared through the kitchen and up her own back passage. A trick that Hugh was hoping to achieve himself, very shortly, should the floor not open. They heard

Laura's squeals of delight and then two men's voices. Moments later, she reappeared with a triumphal air.

'Thought I heard the bell,' she said. 'Come in and meet everyone. Everyone, this is the people's hero, Mark, and his boyfriend, Steve.'

Hugh's smile turned to a grimace the moment he saw Steve. He noted their tight matching jeans and polo shirts and thought bitterly that they looked ridiculous with their neatly tucked in shirts, leather belts, black boots and Levi jeans.

They did, however, look fabulously horny.

Mark sported a short blonde goatee that glistened seductively, as did Steve's, although his was thicker and darker. He imagined the two of them locked in a head to head and it caused an instant tightening in his jeans.

Stella was hugging Mark and being introduced to Steve who was smiling and chatting back and being charming.

'You shouted at me,' Hugh heard Stella accusing Steve of something.

He listened in.

'It was a tense moment, I'm sorry,' Steve replied defensively. 'I thought we were going to lose him.'

'Well, I'll let you off,' Stella said and they both laughed. 'Anyway, this is Iris, my sister. Mark, you two already know each other, of course. And this,' she said, indicating her mother, 'is my mother.'

Mrs Roberts stared up at them, her lower lip tight. 'Are you brown owls as well?'

'Mother!' screamed Stella, turning on her. 'Please don't say such things. These guys are heroes and my friends. What they do in their private lives is entirely up to them.'

Her mother looked up defiantly. 'I didn't say it wasn't. I merely asked a question.'

Laura jumped in and pulled Patrick into the group. 'And this is Patrick, but of course you two have already met,' she said to Mark.

Mark smiled and nodded. 'Yes, hello again. How are you?'

'Good, thanks,' Patrick replied. 'Dying for a cigarette though.'

Mark looked at him gravely. 'What did I tell you?'

Patrick grinned as he took out his Camels. 'Do you mind Laura?'

'Of course not; you go ahead,' Laura replied. 'There are ashtrays all around the place,' she added, indicating a cut glass one on top of the piano, stolen in a drunken moment from a local public house a few summers back.

Patrick lit up and exhaled towards the ceiling as he stood in the small group holding his fizzy mineral water.

'Well, let's get you boys something to drink,' Laura smiled, grabbing Mark and Steve by the arms. 'What'll it be?'

'White wine for me,' Mark said.

'Beer for me,' Steve said.

Hugh's ears pricked up. 'Better've brought your own,' he muttered under his breath.

Laura called from the kitchen. 'I've only got this that Hugh brought. Do you drink... er- Grosse?'

'That's Grolsch,' Hugh corrected her.

'Well, Grolsch or Grosse, whatever, will be fine,' Steve said.

She brought him one in a glass and then handed Mark a glass of Moselle. Hugh stood in the background fuming.

'Are we all here?' asked Stella.

'No, two more to come.'

Stella shot Laura a quizzical look. 'Who would that be?'

'Pierre from upstairs and Glen, of course.'

'Oh, yes - Glen. I nearly forgot.' She turned to Mark, 'He's a security guard at Waitrose...'

A sudden crash from behind made her spin round to find Hugh already in a crouch position, picking up pieces of broken glass.

'I'm so sorry...'

Laura rushed to the kitchen for a cloth and the dustpan. Fortunately, Hugh's glass had been almost empty but, unfortunately, it had hit the edge of the piano leg and detonated like a small nuclear device. Everyone stopped to stare at Hugh who watched helplessly as Laura bustled around mopping and sweeping. In moments, it was as if the incident had never happened, except for the shattered nerves of those guests in the room with a nervous disposition. Which now included Hugh.

'What the hell did you think you were doing?' Stella asked him privately, a few minutes later. 'Learning to juggle?'

Hugh was still in shock. First Patrick, then Mark and Steve, and now Glen. This was a conspiracy designed to expose him, to force him to confess his sins, to point the finger of responsibility at him and accuse him of infidelity. His flesh was weak, his mind even more so. He would pay the price...

'Well?' Stella insisted.

Hugh fell back to earth with a bump and re-focussed his mind. 'Eh, sorry, hen? What d'you say?'

Laura jumped up as her bionic hearing detected the chime of the front doorbell again. 'This could be Glen,' she trilled and rushed from the room.

Stella shook her head and moved towards the circle where Iris was giving forth on the topic of forensic social work to the apparent rapt attentions of both Steve and Mark. To the side, Patrick was chatting to her mother, despite having been called a brown owl. She scowled at the thought of her mother's small-minded comment for a moment, but they seemed to be getting on ok. She joined the circle and held up her hand, exposing her fingerprints to Iris.

'So, am I a psychopathic serial killer?' she asked, thinking this wildly funny.

'Stella thinks my work is amusing,' Iris told her audience.

Steve nodded. 'Well, the word forensic does conjure up images of fingerprinting to most people,' he said, just to show he'd got the joke.

Amid the weak laughter for Iris's sake, a solitary male figure appeared in the doorway between the lounge and the kitchen.

'Hi,' he said casually. 'I'm Pierre. From upstairs?'

His eyes were half closed. Or half open, depending on the point of view. Not that he cared.

'Come in, Pierre,' Stella called over to him. 'Laura's gone to answer the front door. You must've just missed her on the stairs.'

Mrs Roberts looked him over and said loudly. 'You're not a brown owl as well, are you?'

Stella had given up with her mother by this stage. Pierre looked at Mrs Roberts dubiously, then at Stella who drained her glass with a single gulp.

'She means: Are you gay?'

Pierre smiled down at Mrs Roberts still perched on her seat next to the piano and shook his head. 'Only if they pay me a lot. And I do mean: Only-if-they-pay-me-a-lot,' he told her, slowly and carefully.

He was as stoned as a parrot and was quite literally talking like one.

Mrs Roberts's eyes bulged so much she reminded Pierre of Betty Blue. It made him giggle.

Laura came bouncing in with the hunky Glen on her arm. She was smiling from ear to ear, as was he until he looked up. He was expecting to see Mark, but not with his arms around another man! And certainly not Glen's own ex-boyfriend! As if that wasn't enough, lurking in the corner near the piano was an even bigger surprise. Glen was so shocked, he almost blurted out Hugh's name, but the stern look on Hugh's face stopped him just in time.

What the fuck...? He felt dazed and lost for words.

'Now, Glen, don't be shy,' Laura told him, sensing that the poor boy was overwhelmed with so many new faces staring at him, quite literally, open-mouthed.

She noticed Pierre.

'Oh, good,' she said to him, 'you made it. You can help me with the drinks. Now, everyone! Who hasn't got a drink...? Glen, what would you like...? Stella, that glass looks empty to me... Mrs Roberts...?

෯෬

'Et, voilà!' Laura announced triumphantly as she placed a bowl of stirred layered fruit salad topped with full fat crème fraîche and brown sugar onto the doyley in the centre of the candle-lit table.

Nine flickering faces, already stuffed with over-roasted peppers and over-dry tarragon chicken stared at her aghast as she took a firm hold on what looked like an industrial blowtorch, turned it full on and then lit it with a hollow *pop*. Her guests sat well back as Laura directed the flame onto the top of the delicious-looking dessert and then watched, fascinated, as the brown sugar began to run and then to crystallize. She added a handful of walnuts amidst the flowing tributaries of molten caramel and then used the flame-thrower once more.

'Never use a plastic bowl for this,' she said with a laugh, her eyes bulging wildly.

Stella, her eyes focussed thoughtfully on the blue flame, nodded slowly. She'd been present when Laura had learnt that lesson - the hard way.

There was a loud crack and the glass bowl parted down the middle, held still for a moment and then fell open with a soft squidgy sigh, the mixed fruit and dark juices slithering out like the entrails of a freshly slit calf's belly.

'Or, indeed, a non-Pyrex one,' Laura murmured, as her surprised guests scrambled away from the table to avoid the rolling mess of blackcurrant coloured sap as it surfed towards them. She turned off the blowtorch and rushed to the kitchen for a large cloth and the dustpan. The others watched in stunned silence as she deftly scooped up pieces of carefully prepared fruit amidst shards of broken glass and ran to the kitchen where she flung the panful into the swing-top bin and then returned to do it all over again. By the third dump, all that remained in the centre of the tablecloth was a large, wet, purple stain.

'More wine anybody?' she offered brightly, as she rushed back from the kitchen. Everyone nodded dumbly; most of them were too astonished to even think.

'I've seen it all before, of course,' said Stella quietly. 'The last time, the bowl caught fire and if it hadn't been for the blackcurrant juice we might've all been toast.'

'Does this sort of thing happen very often around here?' Steve asked, regaining his voice.

Stella nodded.

'Then we must make sure we get invited more often.'

They all burst out laughing. Laura looked a bit hurt, then joined in. Even Hugh managed a smile.

'Well, if there's no dessert, I'll have a cigarette, if I may,' Patrick said.

'Good idea,' Glen agreed.

Stella gazed across the table at Mark. 'Got a spliff rolled?' she asked.

Mark shook his head violently, pointing at Steve who sat across from him. 'Policeman,' he hissed at her.

Stella's hand shot to her mouth in horror and then doubly so realising her mother was glaring at her from across the table.

Mark smiled teasingly, producing his familiar tin. Mrs Roberts was on his right; Hugh on his left. He didn't notice the disapproving looks from his right side as he lit up, took a few drags and offered it across the table to Stella.

Stella declined, singing, 'Pass the duchie on the left hand side.'

Nodding his head and holding his breath, he passed it to Hugh who took a couple of drags and then passed it to Laura who did the same and passed it to Pierre. Pierre hogged it till it was dead, lit another and passed it to Steve who always refused such things in public but was happy to pass it on to Stella. Looking at her mother, Stella took a dainty puff and passed it to Glen. Iris declined, so did Patrick, and so did Mrs Roberts, so it was back to Mark.

'Well, I'm sorry about the dessert,' Laura said, feeling a little light-headed. 'But we do have some spare fruit, coffee and a big box of chocolates to come. More drinks anybody?'

'Yes, please,' they chorused.

'Let's just clear all this mess away and then we can play a few games as well.'

'Like what?' groaned Stella.

'That sounds like fun,' Iris said over Stella's groan. 'What about, *True, dare, double-dare, torture, kiss or promise*?'

'Sounds complicated,' remarked Pierre. 'I know, what about, *I'm boring because…*'

'…You're always stoned?' quipped Laura, finishing off his sentence.

The others laughed.

'Ha, ha. No, you say, *I'm boring because…* and then you name something you haven't done in your life that you think everyone else probably has done. If they have, they lose a life. Everyone starts with ten lives, cos there's ten of us – it's really cool!'

Everyone started talking at once and nodding their heads, except possibly Hugh, who thought it sounded puerile and dangerous. Laura beamed at them all as she collected the unused dessert dishes and took them through into the kitchen, to return with decanted Moselle and the last can of Grolsch. Hugh eyed it jealously and was relieved when it was deposited in front of him. Laura smiled at him and he smiled back. They both looked across the table to where Steve was engrossed in conversation with Stella and Glen. His smile faltered a little, wondering what the hell they were giggling about. Still, at least they were giggling. If they had been talking about a certain something else, Stella would certainly not have that pathetic smile etched on her face.

Laura pulled him from his thoughts. 'Hugh, would you come and help me open a bottle in the kitchen?'

'Certainly,' he agreed warily.

He left Pierre rolling another joint and followed her dumpy form out into the kitchen.

'Here,' she said, offering Hugh the bottle of red that Patrick had brought.

Hugh's eyes nearly popped out of his head as he read the label. 'My god,' he exclaimed, 'this wine's expensive! This would normally cost about a hundred quid, if you could get it at all. Did you buy this?'

'No, Patrick did,' Laura replied. 'Or rather, his dad did. Patrick nicked it from his Dad's cellar.'

'That figures!' Hugh said, inserting the corkscrew.

Laura turned on him. 'What do you mean by that?'

Hugh turned a little red. 'Er, he appears a bit spoiled, that's all.'

'Over-indulged he may be, but spoiled he is not,' said Laura defensively. She suddenly felt enraged that a virtual stranger should be judging her star pupil, someone she had seen double in age and size and goodness knows how much in maturity and ability in the last nine years. How could he judge Patrick so by his behaviour this evening? It was a mystery to her.

Patrick appeared just as Hugh popped the cork and seized the opened bottle. 'Thanks, Jock,' he said and returned to the lounge.

Laura stared at Hugh; Hugh stared back. Laura's hand went to her mouth as if she was about to be sick. Hugh was cornered, like a rat. He didn't know whether to strike or run. One thing was certain; he had to do something. He was just formulating a daring plan when Stella appeared.

'What are you two up to?' she asked, clearly drunk and stoned.

'Now, we're about to start that game, so come along.' She grabbed them both by the arms and marched them into the lounge where everyone had swapped seats so that Mark and Steve now sat at the far end of the table, their arms entwined.

Stella's mum was at right angles to Steve's left, next to Iris, and kept stealing sideways glances at the two canoodling men. Obviously, that sort of behaviour was not consistent with her limited view of the world, although she did find it rather fascinating.

Patrick sat between Glen and Mark, whilst Pierre was perched on the end of the table opposite Mark, rolling yet another joint. It was lucky he'd managed to catch up with his supplier earlier, he was thinking, with all these dope fiends around.

Stella made Hugh sit down next to Iris, Laura next to Pierre and she sat down opposite Hugh but next to Glen. She grabbed hold of Glen's right arm and stroked his bicep with the tattoo of *Mother* peeking out from below the short sleeve of his tee shirt.

'Oooh,' she said, screwing up her face. 'What big muscles you've got, grandma.'

Glen just laughed. 'All the better to squeeze you with when you're naughty,' he growled suggestively.

Stella giggled girlishly. The rest laughed politely.

'Um, Patrick?' Laura said, as the polite laughter faded away. 'Could you give me a helping hand in the kitchen, please?'

'Sure.'

Hugh watched nervously as Patrick followed Laura through into the kitchen. He had another sinking feeling.

'Couldn't you just eat him?' continued Stella, stroking Glen's bicep. 'Hugh, couldn't you just eat him?'

Steve laughed out loud. 'Maybe he already has…?'

Out in the kitchen, Laura lowered her voice as she spoke to Patrick. 'You called Hugh by another name just now,' she accused him.

'Did I?' Patrick replied innocently.

'Yes, you did. You called him *Jock*.'

'Well, he is Scottish…'

'Don't get flippant with me, young man. Now, tell me truthfully, is Hugh the guy you were telling me about - the one you slept with on your birthday?'

Patrick looked through to the lounge where he could hear voices being raised. He looked back at Laura.

'Yes,' he said.

Laura's considerable bulk seemed to sag lower under this added burden, shortening her already stumpy legs. 'Who else knows?' she demanded.

'No one else,' Patrick replied quickly. 'At least, *I* haven't told anybody.'

'Ok, well make sure you don't. In the meantime, you'd better get some special shampoo from the chemist, right away. You might have crabs...'

∞∞∞

Stella had missed the point of Steve's comment, though not so Hugh. He glared at Steve. Steve glared back. Stella, feeling the tension, frowned.

Mrs Roberts had turned her attention from watching Mark and Steve canoodling to watching Steve and Hugh. For some reason, their hackles were rising and it made her nervous. It might, she felt, be a good time to leave. She stood up.

'It's well past my bedtime,' she announced.

'Nonsense Ma,' Stella said. 'Besides, we haven't played the game yet.'

Laura returned to the table, followed meekly by Patrick. She glanced icily towards Hugh who felt a huge pit open up in his stomach.

'Laura, are we going to play this game of Pierre's?' Stella asked. 'Please, it sounds like such fun.'

'Er, hmm,' Laura faltered. 'Well, why not?'

Ignored by the dinner party guests, Mrs Roberts sank back down in her chair, casting a wary look at Hugh and then Steve.

'Has everybody got a drink?' Laura asked. 'Right then, we'll use matches for lives and this,' she said grabbing another, stolen, cut glass ashtray from the windowsill, 'we'll use to throw them into when we lose a life. Now, all we need are the matches...' She ran to the kitchen, returned with a large box of household matches and emptied them onto the table. 'Right, everyone take five each to begin with,' she instructed.

247

Stella made a mad grab for her five, as did Glen and Patrick; the rest took theirs more reluctantly.

'Ok,' Laura said, counting the remainder. 'That leaves another couple of lives each, so we each have seven lives instead of ten.' She distributed the remaining matches and sorted her seven into a neat row in front of her. 'Who's going to start?'

There were no volunteers.

'In that case,' she said, 'since Pierre suggested the game, he can start.'

Pierre was half way through rolling another joint. 'Ok,' he said, his eyes glassy between half-drooped lids. He looked around the table and smiled. 'Right then, I'm boring because... I've never been to Scotland.'

'Well, I have,' shouted Stella gleefully. 'I was born there,' she added, clearly showing her grasp on the game was tenuous at best.

'You lose a life then,' said Iris, dropping a match into the glass ashtray, as did her mother and Hugh. Laura also lost a life, having been to the Edinburgh festival as part of a wind quartet many years previously.

'That's not fair,' Stella protested as Pierre removed one of her matches. 'You're discriminating against the Scots.'

'I'm not Scottish,' Laura pointed out, taking a sip of her wine. 'Anyway, it's your turn.'

'Me? Oh, ok.' Stella thought for a moment. 'Right, well I'm not boring because...'

'It's, *I'm* boring *because...* Not, *I'm* not *boring because...*' Pierre pointed out.

'Oh, right. Well,' she declared triumphantly, 'I'm boring because I've never had sex with a woman.'

Mrs Roberts and Iris looked at her; neither moved another muscle. Mark and Hugh both threw their matches into the ashtray at the same moment, followed by Pierre and Steve.

Stella stared at Glen. 'Never?' she asked sadly. 'You've never had sex with a woman?' Glen shook his head as Stella continued, 'Obviously just not met the right woman yet... Any more takers? What about you mum?'

Mrs Roberts went white, then crumbled. 'Well, it was only the once,' she said, picking up a match and placing it in the ashtray. 'And we had been drinking... And it was the seventies...'

Iris and Stella looked at each other open mouthed in shock. Glen and Steve roared with laughter whilst Hugh gawped incredulously at the woman who up until very recently might well have become his mother-in-law. He'd given up on that idea now. As the laughter died down, Laura added to the shock as she too picked up a match and calmly dropped it into the ashtray. All eyes turned to her.

'Well,' she shrugged, 'it *was* the eighties.'

'But you weren't drunk and it wasn't only the once?' goaded Glen.

The others laughed.

'Mmm, this game's getting interesting,' said Pierre, his eyes screwing up as he lit the finished joint and passed it around. 'Now it's your turn,' he said, pointing at Glen.

'Ok,' said Glen slowly. 'I'm boring because... I've never been on a rollercoaster.'

'Duh, boring!!' said Stella, dropping a match into the ashtray. 'Can't you think of something raunchy?'

Glen looked hurt, but Stella was too ensconced with the fairies to notice minor details. Glen watched as everyone else, except Mark and Stella's mother, lost another life.

Steve turned to Mark and squeezed his shoulder. 'Have you never been on a rollercoaster?' he asked.

'Nope, but I've always wanted to,' Mark replied, shaking his head sadly. He accepted the joint from Glen when Patrick refused it.

'Well, I'll take you to Alton Towers for the day,' Steve promised. 'You'll love it!'

'Can we come too?' squealed Stella. 'I've never been there.'

Steve nodded. 'We'll make a day trip – it'll be fun. What do you say, Hugh?'

Hugh raised his eyebrows and grunted.

'Just the four of us, eh?' Steve taunted him.

'Hey, what about the rest of us?' Laura burst out. 'We might want to come too.'

'Ok, we'll all go,' Steve agreed. 'We'll hire a minibus for the day – what d'you say?'

'Yes,' they all cheered.

Patrick spoke up, 'It's my turn now,' he said. 'So, I'm boring because…' He gave Hugh a nasty look as he finished, 'Because I've never had crabs.'

There was silence as Glen shot Steve a nasty look, picked up his first match and tossed it casually into the ashtray. 'Thanks to Steve,' he muttered.

'You two've been to bed together?' Laura asked in disbelief.

'We were lovers for a few months,' Glen admitted, taking a large gulp of wine. He was staring intently at the ashtray of matches as he spoke. Laura expected them to explode into flame.

She tutted. 'You boys: you certainly get around.' She stared directly at Hugh as she said this.

Steve picked up a match and tossed it into the ashtray.

Stella was sitting motionless, also staring at Hugh. She felt paralysed with an overwhelming desire to scream. Nobody else moved.

Patrick looked around him. 'Anyone else?' he asked, staring at Hugh.

Hugh shrugged and picked up his fourth match and dropped it into the ashtray. Stella watched him do so.

'So, come on then,' she challenged him, 'thanks to who?'

'Hey, Hugh,' interrupted Steve gleefully. 'Do you think they're related to mine and Glen's?'

'I wouldn't be at all surprised,' Hugh replied calmly.

Stella was watching Hugh and waiting for an answer. Iris caught her eye. She had a smirk on her face that Stella took an instant dislike to.

'Anyone else?' Patrick asked into the silence. 'Stella?'

Stella picked up a match and threw it at the ashtray. It missed, ending up with Hugh's remaining three matches. He slowly picked it up and dropped it into the ashtray.

'Thanks to Hugh,' she said nastily.

Iris stifled a giggle.

'What's so bloody funny?' Stella demanded, turning on her sister.

Iris shook her head. 'Nothing.'

Laura was watching this exchange but was more interested in the crossfire between Hugh and Steve. Twice now she had seen Mark dig into Steve with his elbow after a barbed comment and each time the comment had been directed at Hugh. She was beginning to suspect that Hugh was a much more complex character than she had previously imagined. He was certainly a handsome brute and she could see what Patrick found so attractive about him. Hugh was a gentle giant, but he had a dark, passionate, dominant side that many women, and presumably passive men, found extremely arousing. As for Laura, she liked her men a bit more outgoing, and if Stella continued to cling to Glen's bicep for much longer, she was going to start screaming herself.

Pierre threw his third match onto the growing pile, but nobody made a comment.

'I'm still waiting, Hugh,' Stella said.

'Me too,' Laura said. If they weren't from Patrick or Stella, there must be at least one other person that Hugh had been shagging, and probably loads more besides.

Hugh remained silent. As far as he was concerned, it was his right as a condemned man to do so.

Mrs Roberts was eyeing her daughters speculatively. 'So, when did this happen?' she asked Stella.

'When did what happen?' Stella said defiantly. 'When did I find out I had crabs or when did Hugh give them to me?'

'Is there a difference?' Mrs Roberts asked icily.

'Oh, yes,' Glen cut in. 'It depends on what stage of their reproductive cycle they're at.'

Everyone turned to face him. 'I er … I asked the pharmacist,' he mumbled.

'Can you catch them from toilet seats?' asked Pierre, enjoying himself, despite nobody commenting when he'd thrown his match in.

Glen shrugged. 'I'm not sure. I think they die if they don't keep warm.'

'So, how long ago was this?' Mrs Roberts persisted.

Stella looked at her watch. 'About six hours ago,' she said.

'What?' Mrs Roberts went pale. 'He…' she said angrily, pointing a shaking finger at Hugh. 'He gave them to you *recently*?'

'Yes, *recently*, Mrs Roberts,' shouted Hugh. 'I gave them to your daughter, *recently*. Happy now?'

Laura stood up. 'Right, I think we're all getting a bit overheated here,' she said. 'Let's cool down a bit, shall we? Now Patrick, I think that round was a little unfair, don't you? Especially as you probably *do* have crabs, as we speak.'

Everyone gasped and stared at Patrick. 'Thanks to who?' they all chorused.

'Three guesses,' Patrick replied.

'Glen?' Stella suggested.

'A toilet seat?' Pierre shouted.

Laura held up her hands. 'We don't want to know. Ok Patrick?'

'Ohhh,' said Stella, obviously disappointed. Leaning across Glen, she whispered to Patrick, 'You can tell me later.'

'Right.' Laura clapped her hands together like a schoolmistress in front of an unruly class. 'Mark's next.' She sat down again and picked up her empty glass. 'More wine anybody?'

She refilled a few glasses as Mark spoke up. 'Ok then. Here goes, I'm boring because... I don't have an mp3 player.'

Stella screwed up her nose. 'Boring,' she said, watching Steve, Iris and finally Patrick - naturally - lose their matches.

'I've got a little one, but don't have any songs on it cos I don't have a pc to put them on with,' Pierre mused. 'Does that count?'

'You lose a life,' Laura snapped.

Pierre reluctantly dropped a match into the ashtray. He had three left. He looked around the table and saw that Glen and Mark were in the lead having each lost only one life. Clearly, they were the most boring people at the table.

'Anyone want more wine or would you like coffee now?' Laura asked brightly.

'Coffee would be lovely,' Iris said. 'Just black for me, no sugar.'

Laura got to her feet, shuffled out into the kitchen and put the large kettle onto the hob, removed the cafetière from under the sink and put in four heaped scoops of rough-ground Columbian coffee. She took the box of Waitrose Belgian chocolates from the fridge and then searched for ten cups that weren't too badly chipped, piling everything onto a tray.

Her enthused guests were delighted to see her shuffle back through the arch with a huge tray laden with goodies and quickly made room for it on the table. Pierre had rolled yet another joint, which Patrick was now eager to try - much to Laura's annoyance, for she felt very protective towards him. She saw herself, perhaps, as some eccentric middle-aged aunt. Or maybe that's how she thought Patrick saw her. Whatever, she felt responsible for him.

The chocolates, distributed with much *oohs* and *aahs*, were quickly followed by cups and mugs of steaming black coffee. Again, much of the mismatched crockery was chipped and cracked and Mark found much amusement in pointing out to Steve that his cup was leaking from about midway.

The joint was duly passed to Patrick who, under the scrutiny of people older and wiser, took his first puff down the road to ruin. That one puff made his head spin and he quickly passed it to Mark who grinned and rubbed the back of Patrick's neck affectionately.

'Laura, is there any more hot water?' Mrs Roberts asked. 'This coffee's a wee bit strong for me – I'll be awake all night.'

Laura headed for the kitchen and returned with a Pyrex jug full of hot water, topped up Mrs Roberts's coffee and set the jug down on the table.

'Help yourselves,' she told her guests.

They were distracted for a while with coffee and chocolates until Laura suggested they resume their game. 'It's Steve's turn, is it not?' she asked.

'Yeah, come on Steve,' Hugh prompted him, munching a chocolate, 'tell us why *you're* so boring.'

Steve glared at Hugh. 'Right, I will,' he replied. 'I'm boring because I've never been kissed by a great hairy Scotsman called Hugh.'

Hugh swallowed hard and stood up angrily. 'Is that what you really want then? Eh?' He took a step towards Steve, but Iris and Mrs Roberts were in his way.

'Hugh, sit down!' Stella shouted at him. 'What's got into you? Just accept that he's gay. I thought you were more tolerant! What would you say if I told you I'd been sleeping with Laura, for God's sake? Shoot me?'

Hugh held up his hands and sat down. It was all over, he knew. *Just go with the flow*, he told himself, *Just go with the flow*.

Stella's face was flushed as she picked up one of her four remaining matches and dropped it into the ashtray.

Iris's hand hovered above her four remaining matches. 'What sort of kiss?' she asked.

'Any sort,' Steve replied. 'A big sloppy *give it to me baby* type of kiss or,' he added, watching with amusement the resigned look on Hugh's face, 'just a peck on the cheek.'

Mrs Roberts and Iris dropped their matches into the ashtray simultaneously, having both received a peck or two.

'Well, I got one tonight,' Laura said, also dropping a match onto the pile.

'Right then,' Stella said, 'any more before we continue…? Mum, it's your turn now, so for…'

Steve cut her off. 'I think there might be one or two more lives yet to lose here,' he said. 'After all, we wouldn't want someone to be cheating, now would we?'

Stella looked puzzled. She looked at Steve and then at Hugh. Hugh looked away. Her gaze locked onto Pierre.

'Hey, don't look at me,' Pierre said, holding up his hands. 'Handsome he may be, but I'm not into cock unless I'm paid, and I mean…'

'Ok, Pierre,' Laura cut in. 'We get the picture… Right, I think it's time we ended this game…'

'No, hold on a minute,' said Stella. She looked to her left where Glen, Patrick, Mark and Steve were staring back. 'Well?'

Glen picked up a match from his pile of six and idly toyed with it in his large hands. Stella looked at him in horror as he threw the match into the ashtray. With her eyes wide with disbelief, she looked at Hugh.

He met her gaze as he said quietly, 'That's where your crabs came from.'

Patrick chose this moment to pick up a match and Stella watched numbly as he too threw it into the ashtray. 'And if I've caught them, they came from Hugh,' he said. 'Or Jock, as he's known to his bum chums.'

Stella was unable to absorb this at all.

Her mother was staring at Hugh. 'So, you're a brown owl as well?'

This time, Stella didn't even think to issue a reprimand. She couldn't think. She felt her extremities closing down.

Steve was smirking as he said, 'Oh, and just one more, from this table at least.'

And he picked up one of Mark's matches and threw it onto the heap.

Stella stared at the match. Then at Mark. And then at Hugh. For a moment, she was outwardly calm. Then her face crumpled and she ran from the room.

The table erupted as Iris rushed after Stella, Mrs Roberts rushed after Iris, Glen and Patrick started shouting at Steve, and Hugh suddenly lunged at the man he hated most in the whole world at that moment. Within seconds, the relatively calm and orderly after-dinner party had turned into complete chaos. To Laura's horror, she suddenly had two fully grown men brawling in her tiny lounge and she heard screaming. Which, to her surprise, she realised was herself. Pierre just sat amidst the bedlam, too stoned to move or care.

'Do something,' Laura screamed at him, then at Glen, then at Patrick and then at Mark.

Steve, fully trained in self-defence, kick-boxing and a number of other martial arts, quickly gained the advantage and flipped Hugh onto his stomach over the side of the sofa. Hugh yelled with surprise and then pain as Steve pinned his arm behind his back in what appeared to be a very unnatural position.

'Don't hurt him!' Mark yelled at Steve.

Patrick yelled too. Seeing Hugh so helpless and at the mercy of another man drained him of the masculinity that Patrick found so arousing. The agony on Hugh's face as he bent over the sofa with Steve's crotch tight up against his ass could have been ecstasy. Patrick turned away.

'Oyyyy gevalt!!' screamed a ghostly pale figure in lemon chiffon from the doorway between the lounge and the kitchen, its face pure white with two round, dark holes where the eyes should have been. Patrick screamed too.

Laura's head swivelled fast, causing her to wince in pain. The look on her face was satisfaction enough for Mrs Rosenberg, standing in her nightgown and wearing a white face pack.

'Meshugeners, all of you! And you, you khazer,' she said pointing an accusing finger at Laura, 'you've gone way too far this time. The police are on their way...'

Laura's eyes bulged as she surged towards her meddling neighbour. Mrs Rosenberg's confidence faltered at the sight of a very large and very round and visibly irate woman bearing down on her. She turned hastily.

'Not so fast, old woman,' Laura shouted, grabbing her by the arm. 'It might interest you to know that those two guys happen to be a policeman and a solicitor; and that one,' she said pointing at Mark, 'is an accountant. And that one,' she said, her voice rising in pitch as she pointed at Glen, 'is a security guard at Waitrose!'

She ignored Pierre. As usual.

'What, no judges?' Mrs Rosenberg asked sarcastically, trying to shrug out of Laura's grip.

'What are you implying, as if I didn't know?' Laura demanded.

A loud grunt of pain from Hugh stopped them. 'Get... this... fucker... off... me,' he urged through gritted teeth.

Laura took command. 'Let him go, Steven,' she said, releasing her own grip on Mrs Rosenberg.

'If he'll behave himself...'

'Me!?' Hugh shouted. 'What about you...?'

Steve tightened his grip on Hugh's arm. Hugh shut up immediately.

'Now, are you going to behave yourself?' Steve hissed into Hugh's right ear. Patrick couldn't bear to watch or listen any more. He covered his ears and ran from the room. Steve grinned as he taunted Hugh. 'See, you've made your boyfriend cry now...'

'That's enough, Steven,' Laura barked. 'Now, let him go.'

Steve threw her a vicious look. 'Good idea, then he can have another go at me. No, I think we'll just wait for the police to arrive and then they can arrest him...'

Mark stepped forward. 'No Steve, that's unfair. Let him go.'

Steve glared at Mark. 'Excuse me,' he said, 'but he's just assaulted a police officer...'

'You're not in uniform and you deserved it!' Mark turned to Glen. 'Glen, you're big enough – you get between them, ok?'

Glen nodded and took up position. Steve suddenly let go of Hugh with a push that sent him reeling across the sofa. Glen just managed to prevent him from bouncing off onto the coffee table. Steve stalked from the room, grabbing his jacket on the way. Hugh tried to go after him but Glen's grip was too strong.

Mark was unsure what to do next. His bold words seemed to have upset Steve, which was presumably why he had stormed out. He turned to Hugh who regarded him solemnly. Hugh's hair was all messed up and his shirt torn at the neck. Blood was trickling from his nose and he was breathing heavily.

'You'd better go after him, Mark,' Hugh said, taking deep breaths. 'But be careful, ok? I think he's a dangerous man to know.'

Glen nodded his head knowingly as he relaxed his grip on Hugh. 'That's sound advice. And, believe me, I should know.'

'You're bleeding,' said Mark lamely. He took out his clean handkerchief and went to Hugh, dabbing at his nose, then grabbed him by the shoulders and hugged him. On his way past Laura, he hugged her briefly, gathered up his jacket and hurried up the stairs after Steve.

Mrs Rosenberg, who had backed surreptitiously into the kitchen, stopped and watched him go and missed her chance to escape.

'Mrs Rosenberg,' Laura said menacingly, advancing towards the kitchen. 'Don't run off just yet. You have some explaining to do to the police.'

ᔥᔍ

Outside Netherhall, the air was cool and Mark pulled his jacket around him. He could see a pulsating blue light as it bathed the darkened houses that lined the cul-de-sac culminating in Netherhall itself. Only the steep steps leading down to the Finchley Road remained untinged.

He could see Steve standing in the headlights of the summoned police patrol car, talking to a short, stocky policeman in uniform. He stood in the shadows and watched.

The blue light was suddenly extinguished and he heard men's laughter and a slap on the back, followed by the slamming of doors. The patrol car disappeared slowly back up Netherhall Gardens.

Mark walked the length of the front garden path and reached the gate where Steve was waiting for him.

'Took your time, didn't you?' Steve said.

'I might have known that would be your attitude,' Mark replied. He took a deep breath. 'It's over between us,' he said. 'I'll be around sometime tomorrow to pick up my things.'

Steve was stunned. 'Just like that?'

'You didn't have to let the cat out of the bag about Hugh, but you just couldn't help yourself, could you?'

'Cats don't stay in bags very long; their claws are too sharp.'

'And so are yours.'

'Oh come on! And anyway, where will you stay tonight? With Hugh, I suppose.'

Mark shrugged. 'I'll just go home to my place, probably, or stay here with Laura. Whatever. I don't really care right now.'

Steve moved closer and went to put his arm around Mark, but Mark shrugged it off. Steve turned away angrily and stomped off towards the Finchley Road. He didn't stop or look back once. Mark watched him go with mixed feelings. It sure had been fun whilst it lasted.

☙◊❧

Slumped low in the bucket seat of his sleek black Toyota Celica, Patrick was mesmerised momentarily by the pulsating blue light of the police patrol car as it passed by him, heading for Netherhall. He had been about to gun the engine and leave behind the madness that was Laura's party, but decided to wait and watch for a while.

The police car completed a three-point turn and then came to a halt outside the front gate of Netherhall, facing the way it had come. The headlights were bright and Patrick slumped further in his seat. The two policemen sat in the car for a couple of minutes, then the doors opened simultaneously and they met in front, silhouetted in the bright lights. They stood talking and looking up at Netherhall itself. They didn't appear to be in any particular hurry.

Another figure appeared through the front gate and Patrick could hear raised voices. They stood talking for a while and then the taller of the two policemen returned to the car and the blue light abruptly disappeared. Patrick heard laughter and saw the other figure slap the stocky policeman on the back before he climbed back into the car. As the police car drove off, he realised that the lone figure watching them depart was Steve. That made sense. Obviously he must have known the policemen and sent them away.

Patrick watched as Mark appeared through the gate and approached Steve. Moments later, Steve was striding off towards the steps with Mark watching him go. Had they just split up or was it a silly argument that would blow over tomorrow? Patrick had to admit that they seemed well suited. He watched as Mark turned and retraced his steps to Netherhall's front door. He decided to continue his surveillance a while longer.

ଞଠେ

Netherhall's front door was closed. Damn. Mark didn't want to ring the doorbell this late and he better not ring Stella's own doorbell, and he certainly wasn't going to fight his way through the brambles in the dark. What could he do? What should he do? He couldn't go home to his bed-sit in Bayswater because he'd left his keys at Steve's and he certainly didn't want to go home with Steve. Besides, something was keeping him here. Maybe it was the house, or someone inside it…

He was musing thus as the porch light came on together with the hallway light and Iris opened the door. She looked at him in surprise. 'Locked out of the madhouse are we?'

Mark grinned sheepishly. 'How's Stella?'

'Och, about as well as can be expected for a woman whose boyfriend's been exposed as an arsehole-bandit shagging men behind her back, giving her crabs and god knows what else when he's supposedly been making love to her. Yeah, she's great. And, as for you, Mark, well, Stella thought you were her best friend. She doesn't half pick them, doesn't she eh?' Just then, they heard the unmistakable sound of a diesel engine. 'That'll be our cab. Now, if you'll excuse me, I'm going to get Stella and my mother, so make yourself scarce…'

'If it's worth anything at all, please tell Stella that I haven't slept with Hugh.'

'Yet,' Iris added. She turned and headed back upstairs.

Mark sighed inwardly. Then he nipped inside and down the stairs to Laura's.

ഇരു

Patrick was pleased to see the cab draw up. It gave him something else to think about other than the image of Hugh being forced into submission by Steve. He watched as Iris and her mother helped Stella out through the front gate and into the back of the cab. Iris was carrying a small suitcase and he could hear Stella sobbing and wailing loudly. He felt truly sorry for her.

The cab driver made a three-point turn and roared past him. Patrick didn't try to hide. He looked in the back of the cab and saw Stella sitting between her mother and sister, their arms tightly wrapped around her.

ഇരു

The door to Laura's kitchen was still open. Mark could hear voices.

'I don't think the police will be coming now. How long's it been? Maybe you should just go home?'

Mark tapped on the door and entered the kitchen.

Laura came rushing through from the lounge. 'Oh, hi. We thought you were the police.'

'They've been and gone,' Mark explained. 'Steve sent them away.'

Laura smiled in relief. 'Thank God for that. I think I'll make some more coffee. Would you like some?'

'That'd be lovely. Thank you.' Mark closed the door behind him, took off his jacket and dumped it on the nearest chair.

'So, where is Steve? Should I make him some coffee too?' Laura asked, busying herself with the kettle.

'Er, no,' he said. 'We just broke up.'

Laura put her head through the door into the lounge. 'Yet

another casualty of Laura's fabulous dinner party,' she announced to her remaining guests. Pierre, Hugh and Glen looked up anxiously. 'Mark has split up with Steve,' she continued. Then she looked back at Mark. 'You may as well go in and join them.'

Mark walked into the lounge to the surprise and delight of both Hugh and Glen, but it was Hugh who jumped up first. 'Where's Steve?' he asked.

Mark held up his hands. 'Calm down,' he said, 'he's gone.'

Hugh could scarcely contain his joy. 'And you've split up?' he prompted.

Mark nodded. 'I saw a side of him I didn't like. It put me off him.'

'I found the same thing,' Glen agreed. 'Took me a while longer though.'

Mark sat down beside Glen on the sofa; Hugh settled in the easy chair; Pierre at the table.

'So, are the cops coming or what?' Pierre asked.

'Apparently Steve sent them away,' Laura explained as she returned with a full tray.

'That's another thing he was good at,' said Glen. 'Dealing with the law. Say Mark, did he ever dress up in his uniform for you?'

Laura gave Glen a stern look. 'That's quite enough,' she said, looking anxiously across the room at her elderly neighbour.

Fanny Rosenberg stood up, her lemon chiffon nightgown wafting as usual on an unseen warm air current, small flakes of white face pack fluttering to the ground. 'I think I'll be going now, my dears,' she said. 'It's been quite an evening. I can see I made a dreadful mistake. Please accept my apologies.'

'Think nothing of it,' Laura said generously, following her through into the kitchen. 'And I'm sorry about the noise... things got a little out of hand.'

Mrs Rosenberg gave her an old fashioned stare. 'You must pop in for a nice cup of tea soon and tell me all about it,' she smiled as a few larger flakes of face pack detached themselves and fell to the floor, reminding Laura of something out of Michael Jackson's *Thriller* video. Laura closed the door this time and returned to the lounge where Pierre was rolling another joint. She glanced at the clock above the piano.

'My goodness. It's only just gone eleven,' she said to her remaining guests. 'Right then, who wants that coffee?'

ഇറ

Patrick threw his cigarette butt out of the window and glanced at his dashboard clock. Nearly midnight. What on earth were they still doing in there? As he watched, the porch light came on but he couldn't see any more until two figures appeared through the front gate. He felt a pang of jealous rage as he saw the object of his most recent desires put his arm around the object of his previous one. Hugh and Mark disappeared out of sight down the steps to the Finchley Road.

Patrick's inner rage calmed as he admitted to himself that he didn't really want either Hugh or Mark. He liked them both, sure, but they were far too intense for him, and they came with far too much baggage. No, if the truth were known, he just wanted a good shag.

No sooner had this realisation hit him than the porch light went on again and the tall, muscular figure of Glen appeared through the gate. Instead of turning right towards the Finchley Road, Glen turned left and headed up Netherhall Gardens towards the sodium glare of Hampstead. Of course, Glen lived locally. Patrick smiled to himself as he gunned the engine, crabs or no crabs.

ഇറ

Hugh was sleeping restfully for the first time in a few weeks when the shrill persistent ringing of the telephone roused him suddenly to his senses. He reached out and fumbled the receiver to his ear.

'Mm, yes?'

'Hugh, it's Stella.'

Hugh sat up immediately, switching on the bedside lamp. 'Hi, Hon, look, I'm sorry...'

'Save it for someone who cares. Put Mark on will you?'

Hugh was suddenly terrified. 'Um, who... what...?'

'I said, Put Mark on!'

Silence

'I said, Put Mark on the bloody phone will you!!?'

Hugh handed the phone to Mark who was by now sitting up in bed too. 'It's Stella,' he whispered.

Mark took the phone and put it to his ear. 'Stella, it's me.'

'Iris told me what you said,' she began. She sounded drunk. 'Presumably, you have been to bed with him now. That would make it just so perfect, don't you think? A fairytale ending for you, with the emphasis on *fairy.*'

'You're drunk, Stella.'

'Am I indeed?' she said. 'Do you blame me?'

Mark couldn't say that he did, so he remained silent.

'Well?' she demanded.

'No,' he said quietly. He looked over at Hugh who was watching him intently.

What's she saying? Hugh mouthed silently.

Mark just widened his eyes and shrugged.

Stella continued. 'You'll know then, what a good fuck he is. So, all I can say is... you're welcome to him...'

The line went dead.

Mark handed the receiver back to Hugh who replaced it carefully next to the clock. It was 3.30 am.

'So, what did she say?'

'She said that you were a good fuck and that I was welcome to you.'

Hugh grinned sheepishly, lowering his lashes over his seductive green eyes. 'And am I?' he asked, his thick black moustache, recently trimmed, quivering ever so slightly.

'Mmm. Perhaps you could do with just a tad more practice...'

Hugh pounced on him.